HALO

RETRIBUTION

DON'T MISS THESE OTHER THRILLING STORIES IN THE WORLDS OF

Halo: Envoy
Tobias S. Buckell

Halo: Smoke and Shadow
Kelly Gay

Halo: Fractures:
More Essential Tales of the
Halo Universe (anthology)

Halo: Shadow of Intent
Joseph Staten

Halo: Last Light
Troy Denning

Halo: Saint's Testimony
Frank O'Connor

Halo: Hunters in the Dark
Peter David

Halo: New Blood
Matt Forbeck

Halo: Broken Circle
John Shirley

THE KILO-FIVE TRILOGY

Karen Traviss

Halo: Glasslands

Halo: The Thursday War

Halo: Mortal Dictata

THE FORERUNNER SAGA

Greg Bear

Halo: Cryptum

Halo: Primordium

Halo: Silentium

Halo: Evolutions: Essential Tales of
the Halo Universe (anthology)

Halo: The Cole Protocol
Tobias S. Buckell

Halo: Contact Harvest
Joseph Staten

Halo: Ghosts of Onyx
Eric Nylund

Halo: First Strike
Eric Nylund

Halo: The Flood
William C. Dietz

Halo: The Fall of Reach
Eric Nylund

RETRIBUTION

TROY DENNING

BASED ON THE BESTSELLING XBOX® VIDEO GAMES

G

GALLERY BOOKS

New York | London | Toronto | Sydney | New Delhi

G

Gallery Books
An Imprint of Simon & Schuster, Inc.
1230 Avenue of the Americas
New York, NY 10020

First Gallery Books trade paperback edition August 2017

GALLERY BOOKS and colophon are registered trademarks of Simon & Schuster, Inc.

For information about special discounts for bulk purchases, please contact Simon & Schuster Special Sales at 1-866-506-1949 or business@simonandschuster.com.

The Simon & Schuster Speakers Bureau can bring authors to your live event. For more information or to book an event contact the Simon & Schuster Speakers Bureau at 1-866-248-3049 or visit our website at www.simonspeakers.com.

Manufactured in the United States of America

10 9 8 7 6 5 4 3 2 1

Library of Congress Cataloging-in-Publication Data is available.

ISBN 978-1-5011-3836-2
ISBN 978-1-5011-3837-9 (ebook)

For Leif Jeffers

If someone makes a movie out of this,
I hope it's you

HISTORIAN'S NOTE

The events of this novel take place in December 2553, approximately five months after the discovery of an *archeon*-class ancilla in *Halo: Last Light*, and two months after Veta Lopis's Ferret Team is imperiled in the *Halo: Fractures* story "A Necessary Truth."

HALO

RETRIBUTION

CHAPTER 1

The gunrunner in the corner booth was not the usual space trash. Wearing a high-necked tunic with an embroidered collar, he sat with three rough-looking lackeys, sipping a golden cordial while his companions gulped hiskal and wotha. His head was fashionably shaved, his dark beard closely trimmed, his eyes amber and thoughtful. And his smile—it was quick and bright, an invitation to fun and trouble that almost made ONI operative Veta Lopis regret what she was about to do to him.

Almost.

Leaving her backup team at the table, she rose and started across a small dining room packed with customers, mostly human and Kig-Yar. As she drew near the gunrunner's booth, a huge Jiralhanae bodyguard stepped away from the wall to block her way. Tall enough that his head scraped the ceiling, he had a raw-boned face with pebbly gray skin, a sloped brow, and twenty-centimeter fangs rising from a massive jaw.

Veta continued toward him, unfazed. Her backup team might look like over-pierced street punks, but they were Spartan-III super-soldiers—and all three were palming M6P pocket pistols loaded with four rounds of high-explosive ammunition. If the Jiralhanae got rough, he'd be dead before he landed a single blow.

Two meters from the Brute, Veta stopped. "Easy, big guy," she said. To prove she was unarmed, she pulled up her shirttail and turned around slowly. "I'm here to talk business."

The Jiralhanae snarled and pointed a huge finger back toward her table. She had been careful to position herself outside her team's line of fire, so his arm extended at an angle that opened his rib cage to attack. Reassured by his ineptitude, Veta merely circled around his other side and, with the gunrunner calmly watching, continued toward the booth.

"Just hear me out," she said. The Jiralhanae was already spinning around to grab at her, but Veta slipped aside and hitched a thumb back over her shoulder. "Trust me, it'll be better for everyone."

The gunrunner glanced toward Veta's table, where she knew her team would be on the verge of opening fire. His smile grew wry, and he quickly signaled his bodyguard to stand down.

"Rude *and* dangerous," he said. "How can I refuse?"

"I'm glad we understand each other," Veta said. "Though I do apologize for the intrusion."

The gunrunner waved a dismissive hand. "Save your apologies for Picus." He shot his bodyguard a scowl. "You know how dangerous Jiralhanae can be when they've been embarrassed."

"I do," Veta said. "And I'm not that worried."

The gunrunner chuckled. "I imagine not." He leaned against the booth's backrest, then said, "So . . . talk."

"I need to hire one of your *Razors*."

The gunrunner's brow rose. He was big for a human, with shoulders as wide as a door and biceps the size of HEAT rockets, and Veta could see why his Venezian business partners called him "the Goliath."

After a moment, he asked, "As in the old UNSC corvette? That kind of *Razor*?"

Veta nodded. "As in the old UNSC *stealth* corvette," she said. "And the UNSC isn't the only outfit operating them anymore. You know that better than anyone."

The gunrunner assumed an innocent look. "And why would I know that?"

"Because Lieutenant Commander Hector Nyeto commandeered three of them when he defected from the UNSC," Veta said. "And you're Ross Nyeto—his son."

Nyeto's posture grew tense, and his companions dropped their hands beneath the table. All three wore ballistic vests over bare torsos, a popular style that was more bad-boy fashion than effective protection. Veta ran her gaze around the booth, locking eyes with each man until she saw a glimmer of uncertainty, then returned her attention to Nyeto.

"Your father used those vessels to become a hero of the Insurrection," Veta said. "*You* used them to smuggle arms for Arlo Casille."

Nyeto forced a neutral expression, but the color drained from his face. Arlo Casille was the new president of the nearby planet Gao. He was also the most corrupt and ruthless politician in the entire sector. And before he had become president, he had been Veta's boss.

To suggest they had parted on bad terms was an understatement. Casille had risen to power during a military crisis of his own making, when he secretly helped a faction of ex-Covenant zealots assault a UNSC research battalion deployed on Gao. The resulting battle had destroyed an entire village and cost hundreds of innocent lives: the tragedy had given Casille the leverage he needed to crush his political rivals and claim the presidency of the Gao Republic for himself.

Ross Nyeto's only involvement had been running arms shipments between Casille and the zealots . . . but that had earned him a long list of enemies. The Unified Earth Government wanted Nyeto dead because he had helped arm ex-Covenant. Casille wanted him dead because Nyeto was one of the few people who knew of Casille's involvement in the entire affair. And the Gao Ministry of War wanted him dead because his smuggling activities were a stain on the legacy of his heroic father.

Veta just wanted to take him captive, though that wasn't the primary objective of her first official mission leading a Ferret team. It was more of a bonus.

After giving Nyeto a few seconds to worry, Veta said, "Relax. I'm only making sure you understand that I know who you are."

Nyeto's gaze flicked toward Veta's table and remained there as he studied the three "street punks" backing her up. "Then I'm afraid you have me at a disadvantage. Have we met?"

"We have now." Veta slipped two fingers into her shirt pocket and removed a small lethron bag with a flex-mag closure. "I'm the woman who wants to hire one of your *Razors*. I hear the *Ghost Flag* can be under way by tonight."

She squeezed the bag open, then emptied a line of shimmering spheres across the table. Varying in size from that of a pea to a little larger than a human thumb-tip, the spheres initially appeared more liquid than solid, like drops of water on the verge of erupting into splashes. After a moment in the light, they coalesced into solid balls and developed an iridescent glow so deep and bright it seemed to be shining through a hole in the bottom of the universe.

The tension in the air dissolved into wonder, and the man to Nyeto's left gasped. "Phase pearls! Where did you get those?"

"None of your business," Veta said.

Technically known as boson beads, the gems were created by the plasma bombardment of a Forerunner hard-light device. This particular batch had been collected on nearby Shaps III, when the UNSC's 717th Xeno-Materials Exploitation Battalion had sent a company to survey a Forerunner site that had been glassed a few months before.

But Veta was not about to reveal that. Phase pearls were among the rarest gems known to man, and if she divulged the source, it wouldn't take a month for Shaps III to become one huge mining camp. She closed the bag and left it lying on the table, still half-full and undulating, then looked back to Nyeto.

"That's more than enough to hire the *Ghost Flag* for a month," she said. "Probably for *two* months, come to think of it."

"Probably." Nyeto continued to eye the phase pearls for a moment, then finally looked up at Veta. "But that's not how I do business."

"I won't pay more."

"It wouldn't help. I'm not a gem dealer, and I don't run a transport service. My interests are more . . . specialized." Nyeto flashed a bright smile. "I think you know that."

"I'm not sure what you're suggesting." Veta was careful to remain stone-faced. Nyeto was starting to sniff at the bait, but she had to appear reluctant if she expected him to take it. "I need a ride, not a partner."

Nyeto spread his hands. "Then you've interrupted my lunch for nothing."

Veta glowered at Nyeto's half-empty cordial glass. "You call that lunch?" She reached for the pearl bag. "Sorry we couldn't do business."

The man to Nyeto's left slapped a beefy hand over Veta's. "You can leave those here." He was a moonfaced fellow with rough skin and slit eyes, a head shorter than Nyeto, but almost as wide. "Think of it as a consulting fee."

Veta clamped her free hand over his. "You're a funny man."

She grabbed his thumb and peeled. When he tried to jerk loose, she slipped into a wrist lock and pivoted sideways, increasing her leverage and forcing him to flop across Nyeto's lap. The pain-compliance technique was one she had often used during her time as a Special Inspector in the Gao Ministry of Protection, and one she still preferred to the more lethal methods favored by her current employer.

Chairs began to scrape across the floor as nervous patrons started for the exit, and she glimpsed her backup team moving to cover her.

Olivia-G291 was already in front of the Jiralhanae, pointing an M6P up at his face, while Mark-G313 and Ash-G099 were flanking Nyeto's booth from opposite sides. With bloodshot eyes, hollow cheeks, and gold bling in their brows, nostrils, and lips, the trio looked like a crew of twenty-year-old zoneouts—but that was just the makeup. They were actually closer to fifteen, and by far the most dangerous people in the room.

Veta began to lift Moonface's arm, drawing a bellow of pain as the angle put pressure on his shoulder. She looked back to Nyeto.

"This doesn't need to get bloody."

"I'm glad to hear that." The raspy, raised voice came from the near end of the bar, where a gray-haired man in a purple vest was emerging from a door marked OFFICE. He was holding a glass of coppery liquid in one hand and nothing in the other, and he looked more irritated than alarmed. "The Georgi is a quiet place."

Nyeto was quick to dip his chin. "My apologies, Mr. Baklanov." He looked toward the line of patrons heading for the exit, then added, "I hope you'll allow me to reimburse the trattoria for the disturbance."

Baklanov nodded. "That will be fine." He turned to a slender brunette woman behind the bar, then spoke loudly enough to make himself heard by everyone in the dining room. "The Goliath will be paying everyone's tab while he's here."

Nyeto's smile grew strained. "It will be my pleasure."

The exodus slowed as human and Kig-Yar customers began to murmur and cackle, weighing the prospect of free drinks against the likelihood of a firefight breaking out any second. When they remained wary of returning to their tables, Baklanov turned to Veta and waved two fingers in her team's direction.

"You and your friends are visitors here," he said. "Maybe you should remember that."

Veta returned his stare, pretending she did not know who he was, then finally shrugged and began to ease Moonface's wrist toward the table.

"All we want is what belongs to us," she said. "As long as it's returned, there won't be any trouble."

"Good," Baklanov said. "Then it's decided."

He did not bother to ask Nyeto's opinion. In addition to the Trattoria Georgi—which served as an informal meeting place for smugglers of all kinds—Georgi Baklanov controlled an orbital warehouse complex named Uashon Station. Between the two businesses, he facilitated fully half the black-market commerce on Venezia, and any gunrunner foolish enough to defy him in his own establishment would soon be looking for a new planet to call home base.

Veta motioned her team to secure their weapons. Once they had tucked the pistols into their belts, Baklanov swirled his drink and shot Nyeto a warning look, then retreated into his office.

Nyeto assumed a placating smile and gestured at Moonface. "I apologize for Marco's manner. He only meant to say we'd like more information before making a counterproposal."

"I don't have time for counterproposals." Veta released Marco's wrist completely. "The offer is take-it-or-leave-it."

"Why are you in such a hurry?" Nyeto eased Marco out of his lap, then said, "You don't strike me as someone who plans poorly."

"I'm not." Veta began to collect the phase pearls off the table and return them to their bag. "You might say we had an equipment failure."

"So you have your own vessel?"

"We did."

Veta stole a glance at the patrons returning to their seats and noticed two thin-snouted Kig-Yar switching to a table closer to Nyeto's booth. They were either information dealers or spies from an ex-Covenant religious sect known as the Keepers of the One Freedom—and Veta was hoping for the latter. The Trattoria Georgi was a known hangout for the sect's smuggling gangs, and local sources reported that a Keeper gunrunning crew was in port looking for a cargo. In fact, the whole point of approaching Nyeto in public was to catch the attention of his Keeper rivals.

Veta turned back to Nyeto. "You know anyone interested in a damaged Crow?" she asked. "It can be repaired, but we really need to be on our way."

Nyeto's companions shifted in their seats, but he merely forced a smirk and tried to look indifferent.

"Crows are a little small for our operation," he said. "But I can ask around. What series?"

"A modified S77," Veta said. Originally used as convoy accompaniment by private cargo-hauling firms, Crows were lightly armored escort fighters. Obsolete by current standards, they were nevertheless so swift and packed with weapons systems that small pirate gangs still flew them as corsairs. "We added ten Archer pods and a Mini-MAC."

Nyeto's smirk vanished. "I didn't know a Crow could carry that much firepower."

"We found a way." Veta closed the pearl bag. "Five pods on each side and the Mini-MAC under the belly. *Now* are you interested?"

"Not in the Crow itself," Nyeto said. "But how you used it? That interests me."

"What are you talking about?"

"The *Taulanti*," Nyeto said. "Someone hits a UNSC munitions ship in the Isbanola sector—and you think I won't hear about it?"

"That doesn't mean it was us."

"No? The UNSC has been sniffing around the Qab System for days now." Nyeto leaned across the table and spoke in a softer voice. "They're boarding Crows and looking for Archers and Mini-MACS."

"Still doesn't mean it was us," Veta said.

Nyeto studied Veta through narrowed eyes, and she began to fear something in her manner had tipped him off. As a former detective, she'd done some undercover work, but nothing like this. And while she and her Ferret team had just spent five-and-a-half months training for field operations, the one thing their ONI instructors had drilled into them from day one was that if something *could* go wrong on an op, it usually did.

But after a moment, Nyeto merely nodded and gave her a knowing smile. "Ah, it *was* you," he said. "That's why you're in such a hurry."

"That was a bold move, hitting a UNSC munitions ship," Marco added. "But you didn't get away clean. And it's going to get you killed."

"Not necessarily." Nyeto kept his eyes locked on Veta. "They still have time . . . if they let us help them."

"Great." Veta dangled the pearl bag between her fingers. "Half at the starport, half at the destination."

"Like I said, that's not the way I work," Nyeto replied. "I want in."

Veta was careful to keep her brow furrowed and her mouth tight. Nyeto was hooked, but the operation could still go bad.

"In *what*?" she asked.

Nyeto's voice dropped to a whisper. "I want in on the nukes. From what I'm hearing, you got away with ten. I want five."

"Can't do it."

Veta stole a glance toward the trattoria office and found the Kig-Yar still seated at their new table. They were being sure to face one another instead of Nyeto's booth, but their bulbous eyes were unfocused, and their dorsal head-quills were standing on end. Good. Veta needed them to hear the *Taulanti* story before she left the Trattoria Georgi.

She turned back to Nyeto. "Look . . . okay. I can let you have some of the Argent Vs and Gauss cannons. But the Havoks?" She paused to make sure the Kig-Yar eavesdroppers heard her clearly, then shook her head. "The Havoks are already spoken for."

"Better to deliver *some* than none," Nyeto said. "Blame the shortfall on me. I'm sure your clients will—"

"I told you, we can't do it," Veta said. "The people I work for? No one disappoints them."

She exhaled sharply, relying on the show of frustration to mask the prickle of apprehension digging at the base of her skull. She had just uttered the GO phrase, and in about four minutes, all hell would break loose.

"These people you work for," Nyeto said. "Who are they?"

"Sorry." Veta gave him a sardonic smile. "I'd tell you, but then—"

"You'd have to kill me?" Nyeto rolled his eyes. "Oh, please."

"Seriously," Olivia remarked. Her eyebrows and short-cropped hair had been bleached to a pale gold, and an ashen tint had been applied to her dark skin to make her look a bit unhealthy. "We'd have to kill you. All of you."

"Nothing personal," Mark said. "That's just the way it is."

"Business is never personal," Nyeto said. He eyed Mark's sleeveless leather tunic and golden ear hoops with a show of disdain. "Not until some punk makes it that way."

Mark's eyes went cold. "Are you saying we're there now? Because that's fine with me."

Instead of answering, Nyeto let his gaze drift toward the trattoria's office, and Veta found herself hoping the gunrunner was about to do something stupid. He was not the reason she'd been forced to abandon her career in the Gao Ministry of Protection and flee her home planet under threat of death. But this man *had* smuggled weapons to the Keepers of the One Freedom—the same ex-Covenant extremists whom Casille had used to seize the presidency of Gao. And now the gunrunner was trying to get his hands on a clutch of nuclear warheads. As far as Veta was concerned, an ONI interrogation cell was too good for Ross Nyeto. The sooner his body vanished down a black hole, the happier she would be.

But Nyeto was too smart—or too lucky—to be goaded into a foolish mistake. He continued to gaze in the direction of the office for another instant, then frowned, and Veta turned to find Georgi Baklanov stepping into the dining room again.

"Okay, everybody out!" Baklanov's voice boomed. "We have Spartans coming!"

A hush fell over the room, and patrons began to look toward the office door in doubt and confusion. Spartans were the elite of the elite, super-soldiers so rare that only one civilian in a hundred million had ever actually glimpsed one. To most of the Venezians in the room, the notion of a Spartan team raiding the Trattoria Georgi would sound almost inconceivable.

Baklanov's voice grew low and urgent. "This is why I pay lookouts, people. Two Spartans just turned onto Via Notoli."

The hush broke into a speculative murmur. Via Notoli was long and narrow and notoriously choked with traffic, so even Spartans would find it slow going. And with all of the taverns and warehouses lining the lane, it certainly seemed possible that the super-soldiers were headed somewhere else.

Still, the Trattoria Georgi was a well-known black-market hangout, and the trouble that had almost erupted earlier was unusual. A dozen patrons stood and started for the door.

When the rest of the clientele were slow to follow, Baklanov extended a hand toward his office and made a summoning motion. Two henchmen stepped through the door, both brandishing Sevine Arms 10mm machine pistols. At the same time, the bartender pulled another SAMP-10 from behind the counter.

"Let me make myself absolutely clear. You should leave now." Baklanov's tone was growing calmer and steadier by the second. "Anyone still here in sixty seconds, the Spartans won't need to shoot."

The threat worked, because the remaining patrons mobbed the exit. Veta was glad to see the Kig-Yar eavesdroppers leading the way. Even if they were not Keeper spies, they would spread the tale of the crazy human woman who had used a Crow to steal ten Havoks, and the Keeper gunrunning crew would find *her*. All she and her team had to do now was make the coming fight with the Spartans look convincing.

She tucked the phase pearls into her shirt pocket and motioned her team toward the kitchen.

"We'll go out the back."

"They'll be expecting that." Nyeto remained seated, calmly waiting while his companions slid out of the booth. "Those Spartans may be as dumb as canned fruit, but you can bet there's an ONI agent calling the shots. My guess is ONI has a sniper watching every exit, and they're just using the Spartans to flush you out."

"Could be . . ." Veta said. Nyeto had obviously never matched wits with a Spartan or he wouldn't be comparing them to canned fruit, but his guess was only slightly inaccurate. She began to fear she had underestimated him. "If you have a better idea, I'm listening."

"Do we have an agreement?" Nyeto slipped out of the booth and flashed a smirk. "We both know those Spartans are after you and your nukes. So either you split your haul with me . . . or you die and lose it all."

Veta feigned hesitation, then glanced at her team and received three wary nods. Their reluctance was for show, but they were well trained and had no trouble selling it. She turned to Nyeto.

"You have a way to get us out of here fast?" she asked. "In one piece?"

"Of course."

"You expect me to take your word for it?" Veta asked. "No details, no deal."

"Fair enough." Nyeto motioned to his Jiralhanae bodyguard, then said, "We'll make our own door."

"You want to bust through a side wall? An *exterior* wall?" Veta's clarification was for the benefit of the approaching Spartans. She had a thread-style microphone sewn in her collar, and everything it picked up was being transmitted to an encrypted comm net. "What about Mr. Baklanov?"

"Give him a phase pearl," Nyeto said. "He won't complain."

"That's enough for me to buy the whole building."

"And what would you do with the place?" Nyeto asked. "Especially with ONI hunting you for the rest of your life?"

"Good point."

She removed the pearl bag from her pocket and began to fumble at the closure, trying to buy time for the third Spartan—the one concealed in the service alley behind the trattoria—to change position.

Nyeto's face tightened. "What's the holdup?"

"The magtab is sticking." Veta squeezed the bag open and began to sort through the pearls. "It does that sometimes."

Nyeto waited about two seconds before reaching for his sidearm. "You're stalling."

Knowing that her team's hands would already be on their M6Ps, Veta signaled them not to draw. Nyeto and his men were carrying New Tyne Armory 12mm Comets—a class of weapon ONI combat instructors mocked as "hand cannons." The oversize pistols put the gunrunners at an enormous disadvantage in a quick-draw fight, so she had room to bluff this out.

"The Spartans are coming for *us*," she said, "and you think I'm stalling?"

Veta shook her head in mock disbelief, then withdrew one of the smaller phase pearls and summoned Ash over. His hair had been dyed orange and shaved into a flaming wing above each ear, but the rest of his head was bald. He was making a point of watching Nyeto—not staring him down, just making sure the gunrunner knew that if things turned ugly, he would be the first to die.

Nyeto seemed to take the hint. Despite his suspicious expression, he motioned to his men to wait.

Veta put the phase pearl in Ash's hand. "Give this to Mr. Baklanov, with our apologies in advance for the damage," she said. The trattoria was nearly empty now, and Baklanov was close enough to overhear. "And hurry. We don't have much time."

Ash eyed Baklanov's henchmen, then said, "We could just take them out."

"And get stuck trading lead until the Spartans show?" Veta shook her head. "Just give him the pearl. It'll be faster."

Ash shrugged. "If you say so." He handed his M6P to Veta, then pinched the phase pearl between his thumb and forefinger and started across the room. "Hey, Mr. B. I've got something for you."

Veta heard a single click from the reception-dot concealed near her eardrum, and she knew the third Spartan was in position to cover the expected exit route. It wouldn't be long before the other two arrived to flush the quarry into their trap. She turned to Ross Nyeto.

"We'd better still have a deal," she said. "I'd hate to lose one of my phase pearls for nothing."

Nyeto moved his hand away from his holster. "You can't blame a man for being careful," he said. "I have my own reasons to be nervous about Spartans."

"That's not an answer."

"Maybe not, but it'll have to do for now." Nyeto motioned his Jiralhanae bodyguard toward the wall. "Picus—"

"Stop!" Baklanov called. "Do that, and you're finished on Venezia."

Nyeto motioned Picus to wait, then faced the proprietor. "Mr. Baklanov, trust me. You don't want the Spartans to find us here."

"Sure I do," Baklanov said. "At least, I'd like them find your new friends."

Veta turned to find Baklanov's henchmen swinging their SAMP-10 machine pistols toward her side of the room. Baklanov himself was pointing an 8mm automatic—a Sevine Arms Defender—at Ash's face. Ash was still pinching the phase pearl between his thumb and forefinger, staring down the Defender's muzzle and looking more irritated than concerned. Mark and Olivia had drawn their M6Ps, but were keeping the muzzles pointed at the floor until they received an order to engage.

Given his reflexes and training, Ash could easily pivot aside and take Baklanov's weapon away, and even firing from the waist, Mark and Olivia could take out the henchmen before their SAMP-10s settled on target. But then the team's cover would be blown, and the young Ferrets had too much discipline to put their own lives ahead of the mission. It was a holdover from their SPARTAN-III training, and one Veta feared would get them killed someday.

She used a hand flick to signal WAIT, then glared at Baklanov. "Have you lost your damn mind?"

Baklanov appeared to consider the possibility for a moment, then shook his head. "Not the way I see it." He gestured at the M6P in Veta's hand. "You and your punks can put the popguns on the floor."

"I don't think so." Veta stepped toward Baklanov. "What do you expect to happen here?"

"What's it look like?" Baklanov thumbed back the hammer of his Defender, the unspoken threat bringing Veta to a halt. "The Spartans want you and those nukes in a bad way. I turn you over, all my problems go away."

"Maybe because you're already dead," Ash said. He rolled the phase pearl into the palm of his hand, then extended it toward Baklanov. "Take it. You'll live longer."

Baklanov almost smiled. "I like your style, kid. But I'll take my chances."

"With ONI?" Veta asked. The mission planners had not foreseen Baklanov volunteering to "help" the UNSC—though maybe they should have. In the field, *anything* could happen. "You think those two Spartans don't know who you are? That *you're* not listed as a target of opportunity?"

Doubt filled Baklanov's eyes, and she realized she still had a chance to keep the mission on track. The two Spartans had to sell the Ferret team's cover story by making it look like the UNSC was desperate to recover the "stolen" Havoks. But the deception required careful timing—the Ferrets needed to escape just as the Spartans arrived, because nobody was going to believe a few lowlifes could survive a firefight with fully armored Spartans.

Veta let Baklanov's skepticism build for a moment, then said, "Look, if you try to strike a deal with those two Spartans, you'll end up in a body bag. The Goliath too."

"Is that a threat?" Baklanov's tone was tough, but the doubt was still there. "Because I'm not a guy you want to threaten."

"I'm just telling you how it is." Veta tipped her head toward the phase pearl in Ash's hand. "You want to live, take the pearl and follow us out of here. You want to die, start a firefight. If we don't kill you, the Spartans will."

Baklanov's gaze shifted to the glowing bead in Ash's palm, and Veta realized she was winning him over. She let her breath out—and heard a double click from the reception-dot in her ear. Ash's eyes widened, and she knew he'd heard it too. The Spartans were about to breach—and her team was badly out of position.

Veta gave her head a subtle rock, signaling her team to forget the plan and follow her lead. She did not relish the thought of improvising—that was usually when operatives got hurt—but Baklanov had forced her hand.

She looked toward the wall-size picture window in the front of the trattoria and spotted a pair of Jackrabbit scout cycles on Via Notoli. Spread roughly a meter apart, they were cutting across traffic toward the trattoria.

"Time's up, Mr. Baklanov." Veta swung her M6P toward the front window. "Now we die."

The two Jackrabbits reached the walkway, scattering pedestrians in all directions, then accelerated hard. Their front wheels rose into the air and crashed through the trattoria's window just above the sill. Veta opened fire on the nearest cycle, and the cockpit canopy shattered beneath two explosive rounds. She fired again, aiming for the driver's faceplate. His shields shimmered as the round detonated, and his helmet vanished behind a fiery orange flash.

The Jackrabbit veered toward the bar and slammed into the side, causing an eruption of polished stone and dark wood. Veta glimpsed blue Mjolnir armor and knew the Spartan she'd just shot was the leader of the legendary Blue Team, Fred-104. It was what a pirate would have done, but still . . . he was a friend.

By then, Ash was wrenching the Defender out of Baklanov's hand, and Mark and Olivia were blasting the wheels off the second Jackrabbit. A Spartan in gray Mjolnir with a half-bubble faceplate—the second member of Blue Team, Kelly-087—bailed out and rolled across the floor, reaching for her sidearm. Mark and Olivia continued to fire, enveloping her in an orange aura as their rounds detonated against her energy shield.

Baklanov stepped toward the gray-armored Spartan and held up his now-weaponless hand, motioning her to wait. Like *that* was going to happen. They were in the middle of a firefight, and Kelly's hand came up holding her sidearm. Blood sprayed the wall as the M6C's armor-piercing round exited through the back of his purple vest.

Ash returned fire using Baklanov's Defender, but the weapon's hollow-point ammo just disintegrated against her shields. Kelly swung the M6C toward Ash; then Baklanov's henchmen opened fire on her with their SAMP-10s, and she had to dive into an evasive roll. Tables and chairs dissolved into splinters behind her.

Fred rose from the bar's wreckage and sprayed the henchmen with mini-bursts from his assault rifle. The machine pistols fell from their hands and all three collapsed where they stood, each bleeding from a line of holes stitched across his torso.

The roar of the SAMP-10s had barely faded before Ross Nyeto's men began to boom away with their Comets. Kelly's energy shield crackled with overload static and went down, and flakes of titanium alloy began to spawl off her armor. The Spartans brought their own fire to bear almost instantly, and the first of Nyeto's men dropped.

Then Mark staggered back, blood pouring from his shoulder. Whether he had been hit by a stray bullet or deliberately wounded to help sell the Ferret team's cover story, Veta didn't know—and it didn't matter. The entire operation was a desperate ploy. The Keepers of the One Freedom had assassinated an admiral and abducted her family, and the trail was running cold. ONI's best hope of drawing the kidnappers into the open was to dangle a bunch of stolen Havoks in their home territory and hope they took the bait.

Veta swung her M6P toward Fred and fired her last round.

His shields were already down, and the shot caught him in the middle of his chest armor. The detonation barely rocked him, but he used it as an excuse to fire his next burst high. Veta tossed the pocket pistol aside and reached down to grab a SAMP-10—then a large hand clasped her arm and drew her away. She looked over to find Ross Nyeto grasping her biceps, yelling something she could not hear above the thunder of the firefight.

Only one of Nyeto's three men remained standing, but Picus, the Jiralhanae bodyguard, was by the corner booth, hurling himself into the plaster-finished wall. The impact sent a shiver through his entire body and rocked him back on his heels, and Veta's heart caught for an instant. If the Brute failed to breach the wall, their escape from the Spartans would become a lot less believable—and the Keeper gunrunning crew a lot less likely to show themselves.

Picus drew back, then threw himself at the wall again. This time, a structural panel buckled, and he disappeared into a cloud of billowing dust. Green Venezian light began to pour into the room through a three-meter hole, and Veta allowed Nyeto to pull her across the booth toward the opening.

Outside, Veta could see the wood-planked side street emptying as pedestrians raced away from the firefight. Picus was kneeling in a pile of rubble, shaking his head and gathering himself to rise.

The Jiralhanae's head snapped sideways and sprayed blood, and he collapsed onto his flank and began to convulse. Nyeto put out a hand, signaling Veta to wait behind him, then stared at the Brute's shuddering body as though he could not quite understand what had just happened. There were three holes in the bodyguard's massive temple, surrounded by powder stippling and arranged in a triangle so tight it was almost a single wound.

Which meant the attack had come from close range—no more than a couple of meters away. Nyeto dropped to his haunches and duckwalked into the hole.

Veta took the chance to glance back into the trattoria and saw that Nyeto's last man had fallen. Ash and Olivia had each retrieved a Comet and were continuing to blast away at the two Spartans, who were returning fire with their assault rifles. Mark was ignoring the blood pouring from his shoulder and using a SAMP-10 to spray the wall above Fred's head. No one was hitting anyone, but they were all making it look damn good.

Veta caught Olivia's attention by tossing a piece of loose plaster past her shoulder, then signaled her to collect Mark and Ash and disengage. When she turned forward again, Nyeto was still squatting, holding his Comet in both hands and cautiously leaning forward to peer outside. She drew her leg back and planted a boot in the middle of his back, stomp-kicking him out onto the walkway.

A female Spartan in copper-tinted Mjolnir armor stepped into view. Wearing a goggle-eyed ARGUS-class helmet with extra sensor boxes on the sides, she was the third member of Blue Team, Linda-058. She placed a titanium boot on Nyeto's weapon arm, then looked up and gave a curt nod as Veta and her team clambered out onto the walkway.

The gesture was not lost on Nyeto, who craned his neck to watch the Ferret team race past. "Who *are* you?" he called. "Why did you—"

The question ended in a thump as Linda brought her assault rifle down, using the pressure point at the hinge of Nyeto's jaw to knock him unconscious. She kicked the Comet away from his hand, then Veta lost sight of them as the Ferrets spilled into the street and sprinted for the intersection with Via Notoli.

They had taken about five steps when triple-round bursts began to crack from Linda's assault rifle. Olivia cried out, and Veta looked over to see her staggering as she struggled to regain her stride. There was a fresh bullet hole in the thigh of her dark pants, and blood pouring down both sides of her leg.

First Mark takes a bullet, now Olivia. That was half of her squad wounded. Veta was beginning to think Blue Team was trying a little *too* hard to make the chase look real. She slipped a hand under Olivia's arm and pulled her along for two steps. Once Olivia's stride evened out, she twisted around, allowing Veta to guide her while she fired the big Comet over her shoulder. Ash and Mark were both doing the same, though parked scooter trucks and tri-wheel minivans seemed to be taking most of the damage.

They reached Via Notoli a few steps later. Veta led the way around the corner, away from the Trattoria Georgi. Traffic in the intersection had deteriorated into an impassible snarl of crashed and abandoned vehicles, but the walkway cleared ahead of them as alarmed pedestrians ducked into shops or hid between parked vehicles. Despite their wounds, Mark and Olivia had no trouble keeping up. If anything, their injuries only made them faster—a result of the biological augmentations they had received during their SPARTAN-III training.

Veta studied the warehouses ahead, looking for a red awning over a pair of green doors. This part of New Tyne had been built atop a swamp, and the red awning marked a building with a trap-door that descended to a loading dock. To make their escape look credible, the Ferrets had left a shallow-draft airboat there. But they didn't have much time to reach it. Blue Team could hold back only a few seconds without making it obvious that they were deliberately delaying pursuit.

The red awning came into view forty paces away, far enough from the action that confused pedestrians were still clustering in front of it. Veta glanced back and saw onlookers beginning to drift onto the walkway behind her. Beyond the gawkers, almost seeming to float above their heads in Venezia's hazy air, two large Spartan helmets were emerging from the ruins of Trattoria Georgi. There was no sign of the Kig-Yar eavesdroppers, which Veta decided to take as a good sign. Given the circumstances, it would only make sense for a pair of Keeper spies to avoid showing themselves.

Veta continued to watch as the two Spartans—Fred and Kelly—started to pursue. She knew Linda would not be joining them. Instead, the third Spartan would be busy securing Ross Nyeto for transport to an ONI interrogation facility. At least *that* part of the operation had gone right.

"Do *not* slow down!" Veta's ears had stopped ringing enough that she could hear her own voice, so she hoped the rest of her team could too. "If we need to clear a lane, fire warning—"

Olivia's arm came up, catching Veta across the chest so force-fully the impact almost knocked her off her feet. She caught her balance and heard a vehicle clanging to a halt in front of her, then turned to find a tri-wheel minivan screeching to a full stop across the walkway.

The side door slid open. A tri-digit hand motioned them in-side, and a scaly Kig-Yar face peered out. "If you want to live," he said, "come with us."

CHAPTER 2

1122 hours, December 8, 2553 (military calendar)
UNSC passenger schooner *Donoma*
Deep Space Transitional Zone, Tisiphone System

Operation: RETRIBUTION had been set into motion four days earlier, after Veta and her Ferret team were summoned to a deep-space rendezvous with the UNSC passenger schooner *Donoma*. They had entered the vessel through a temporary airlock and found themselves floating in a zero-G slaughterhouse.

The *Donoma*'s wardroom had been breached inward by a powerful detonation, and Veta could tell from the blood spatter that the blast had hurled three occupants into the far wall. Near the top of each pattern, an ovoid dent indicated where their heads had impacted, so it seemed likely that all three victims had been dead or unconscious when the cabin decompressed and sent their pressure-bloated corpses tumbling into the void. Fortunately for Veta—who still found it awkward to work in a pressure suit—the temporary airlock had sealed the breach and allowed the *Donoma* to be repressurized. So even if the vessel lacked gravity, at least it had a standard atmosphere.

Veta spun toward Rear Admiral Serin Osman, the officer who had summoned her to the scene. A slender woman with short-cropped hair and high cheekbones, the admiral wore a thruster harness over blue camouflage utilities. There was no unit patch or name tag, only a single black star on each collar tip. If you didn't know she was ONI, you weren't paying attention.

"Did they recover the bodies?" Veta asked.

"Not yet." Osman was the current head of the Beta-5 Division of Section Three operations, which ran the SPARTAN programs and most of ONI's other black ops and helped oversee an array of reverse-engineering programs that used alien technology to create new weapons and devices for the UNSC. She was among the most powerful of ONI's division heads, and—according to rumor—being groomed to take over as the agency's commander-in-chief when Margaret Parangosky finally retired. "We have a squadron of Storks running a search cone, but you know how it is—dead bodies are small, deep space is big. And the commanding investigator tells me the assault happened seven days ago. I don't expect any recoveries."

"Let's hope they prove you wrong," Veta said. She really wanted to see the bodies—more often than not, the bodies told the story. "How long has the IRI team been aboard?"

"Two days," Osman said. Piracy had grown so common in the Outer Colonies that the UNSC had an entire Incident Response and Investigation branch dedicated to identifying and locating perpetrators. "But they haven't removed anything from the scene. I wanted you to have a look first."

"Because IRI investigators aren't good enough?"

"Because there's a lot at stake," Osman said. "And I need answers fast."

"I'm flattered, but—"

"Lopis, you were Gao's best homicide investigator. Just give me something we can use to identify the killers. I'll take care of the rest."

Mark used a maneuvering thruster to move to Osman's side. "Isn't that what *we've* been training for, Admiral?" Like Ash and Olivia, he wore plain gray utilities, and his adolescent face showed no sign of the piercings and jewelry that would adorn it in the coming days. "To identify problems—and take care of them?"

"Mark, when Admiral Osman has a job for us, she'll say so," Veta said. Unlike her subordinates, she was in no hurry to interrupt their Ferret training and start working in the field. Deep-penetration black ops had a way of going sideways, and so far her young Spartan-IIIs were still far better soldiers than they were secret agents. "For now, let's concentrate on giving the admiral what she's *asked* for."

Mark frowned but said, "Yes, ma'am. Just let me know what my assignment is."

"How about you check the *Donoma*'s weapons inventory, both ship-to-ship and personal," Veta said. The task was more than a way to keep Mark busy. As her team's security specialist, he was the one most qualified to evaluate what combat tactics the crew might have employed in an attempt to fend off the boarders. "That should give us some idea of how the fight progressed—and how quickly."

"Very well, ma'am."

Mark turned to Osman and saluted. He nodded to Veta before departing, but skipped the salute. Although Veta was an ONI operative, that did not make her a military officer—which suited her just fine. As a Gao native, she still had a few anti-centralization feelings, and swearing an oath of loyalty to the UNSC might be more than she was ready for.

Veta drifted to the center of the wardroom and spun in a slow circle, assessing the scene. Judging by the swab smears on the walls and the evidence tags affixed to the floor, the IRI investigators had done a good job of collecting trace evidence. Eventually, those efforts might reveal something that pointed to the attackers' identity. But scientific analysis took time, and if Osman had been willing to wait, she would not have jerked Veta's team out of its final weeks of Ferret training to look at a crime scene.

"Anything, Lopis?" Osman asked.

"Yeah, a little." Veta pointed at the jagged edges of the breach, which had been curled inward by the blast and were coated with dried blood. "There were a lot of people sucked out through that breach. More than died here in the wardroom."

Veta turned away from the damaged hull and carefully used her thruster harness to cross the wardroom. It had been only five and a half months since she had experienced weightlessness for the first time, and while the sensation had grown familiar, she still preferred walking and lamented the absence of the *Donoma*'s artificial gravity field.

A moment later, she had successfully maneuvered herself into position next to the doorway. Rather than a hatch, the wardroom was serviced by an automatic door, which had jammed ten centimeters out of its storage pocket. She grabbed the leading edge and pulled herself down to examine a blood smear on the floor.

Struggling to hold herself steady while she worked, Veta

noted that the smear seemed to be streaking toward the breach in the hull. She ran her fingers inside the door's receiver slot and found a tuft of bristly brown hair stuck inside the sealing gasket. When she raised the hair to her nose, it smelled musky and acrid.

Veta passed the tuft to Osman, who was following at a polite distance. "You recognize that smell?"

"Jiralhanae," Osman said. "That's not a surprise."

"Why not?"

"You'll see," Osman said. "So, what do you think?"

"I think a Jiralhanae corpse was jamming the door open." Veta ran her fingers along the inside of the receiving slot again, this time about midway up its height, and came away with crusted blood. "When the boarding party withdrew and left in their vessel, the wardroom decompressed a second time. A lot of bodies from deeper in *Donoma* were drawn out past the Jiralhanae. Eventually, he was dislodged . . . and got sucked out of the breach himself."

Osman nodded. "That makes sense," she said. "The Banished don't usually stick around to make a target airtight after they're done."

"The Banished?" Veta asked, not hiding her surprise. The Banished were a fast-growing, tech-savvy horde of marauders. Since the closing days of the war, they'd been causing trouble for humans *and* the Covenant empire by pillaging ships, installations, and even entire worlds in a relentless pursuit of cutting-edge weapons technology. "You think they did this?"

"So you don't?" Osman asked. She was watching Veta closely, clearly trying to gauge her reaction. "Why not?"

"I don't think anything yet," Veta said. "I haven't seen enough evidence—unless you're holding something back?"

Osman shook her head. "At this stage, the Banished are just an assumption," she said. "Forget I mentioned them. I need you to draw your own conclusions."

"But hold on," Olivia said. She hit her thrusters and drifted close. "*You* think it was the Banished. Did some lamebrain put equipment on the *Donoma* we should know about?"

Osman scowled. "What part of 'forget I mentioned them' wasn't clear, Petty Officer?"

Olivia's expression grew contrite. "Sorry, Admiral," she said. "I didn't realize the lamebrain was you."

"It wasn't," Osman said. "Shouldn't you be pissing off the ship's AI or something?"

"Yes, ma'am. I'll get right on that."

Olivia saluted and maneuvered toward the doorway. As the Ferret team's information specialist, she had been developed into an elite hacker who could plunder almost any processing system. Veta pushed out of the doorway to let her float past.

"Look for infiltration routines," Veta said, now speaking to Olivia's boots. "And anything that explains what the *Donoma* was doing way out here in the transitional zone."

"Affirmative," Olivia called back.

Once she had disappeared around the corner, Osman sighed and asked, "What are you thinking she'll find, Lopis?"

"I'm not sure," Veta said. "But whoever attacked the *Donoma* didn't stumble on her by accident—not at the edge of the system. They knew she would be here."

Ash now spoke up. "That doesn't sound like the Banished. They're not exactly subtle . . . are they?"

Osman's thrusters hissed as she rotated to face him. At first, Veta thought Osman would reprimand him as harshly as she had

Olivia. But Ash merely gave a look of calm expectation, and the irritation on Osman's face faded to impatience.

"Ash, you know better than that," Osman said. "You *never* underestimate an enemy."

"I don't think I am, ma'am," Ash said. "I'm just saying . . . the Banished aren't inside operators."

The corners of Osman's mouth started to drop, and Veta decided Ash needed backup.

"Taking the subject's usual modus operandi into consideration isn't underestimating him, Admiral," she said. "If the Banished haven't used espionage tactics in the past, we need a sound reason to think they're using them now. Are you saying their tactics have evolved?"

Osman hesitated, then said: "We don't have any intelligence to confirm that. But look at how brutal the attack was, how fast."

"That characterizes the attack, but it's not evidence," Veta said.

"We don't have time to cross every *t* and dot every *i*," Osman replied, fuming. "We need to identify these bastards—and we need to do it *now*."

Veta did not respond immediately. Outbursts were rare for the admiral, so the fact that she had lost control even a little suggested a personal element was involved—one that was making her desperate to push Veta toward the Banished being the culprit.

Once the ire had drained from Osman's face, Veta asked, "Admiral, is there some reason you *need* these attackers to be the Banished?"

Osman looked as though she were biting back a sharp reply, then let out a long breath and spoke more calmly. "What I *need* is a quick answer," she said. "I have a prowler watching a Banished flotilla in the Nereus system."

"Ah—and you think they might be the *Donoma*'s attackers," Veta surmised. Nereus was the next star Earthward, an uninhabited system of ice balls and dust-smothered rocks that would be a perfect spider hole for a pirate horde. "How long do we have?"

"Impossible to know. They're holding in orbit at the tenth planet. The prowler captain thinks they might be waiting for a rendezvous, but we don't have intelligence on that."

"I don't see the problem, Admiral," Ash said. "Who cares whether they're the ones who hit the *Donoma*? It's still a Banished flotilla. Just tell Sector Command to send in a task force."

"I can't do that yet," Osman said. "Not until I know whether it's an attack mission or a rescue."

"Rescue?" Ash fell silent for a moment, then said, "Oh."

Veta asked, "Who needs rescuing?"

"Three passengers from the *Donoma*," Osman said. "Civilians."

Ash looked troubled. "And you spent two days waiting for us? Two days is an *eternity* when the target is mobile."

"Nothing gets past you, does it?" Osman said. "But the prowler spotted the flotilla a few hours ago, and I only just received word. If your arrival hadn't been imminent, I'd already have sent orders to launch a rescue mission."

"Then there's reason to believe the victims are still alive?" Veta asked. Not everyone abducted by alien marauders became a hostage or a slave. Sometimes they became food. "Or is that more of a hope?"

"It's more of a hope," Osman said. "Obviously, we haven't heard anything from the abductors, so we can't confirm who we're dealing with."

Veta thought about this and realized it didn't tell her much. It was hard to make anonymous contact with ONI, so it was possible that the abductors were just being cautious about their approach. Of course, it was also possible they had no intention of *ever* making contact.

"All right, Admiral," she said. "We'll try to provide confirmation."

Osman bit her lip. "I wish it were that simple," she said. "The best the IRI team will say is *maybe* it was the Banished, and this would be a tricky rescue operation. I'd like more than a 'maybe' before risking Blue Team."

"You brought Blue Team?" Veta looked toward the interior of the *Donoma*. "This is getting more interesting by the minute, Admiral. These civilians must be important."

"They are, but probably not in the way you think." Osman sank into silence, then finally thrustered through the doorway. "Come with me. You'll see."

Before following, Veta turned to Ash and gestured back toward the jagged points surrounding the hull breach. "Find the IRI techs and see what they collected off those edges. Then borrow a magscope and have a look yourself."

"Yes, ma'am," Ash said. He was the unit's surveillance specialist, and Veta had expanded his training with her own informal course on crime-scene investigation. "I'll comm you when I'm done."

Veta nodded and followed Osman into the *Donoma*'s starboard access corridor.

The magnalum walls were dimpled from bullet strikes for much the length of the passage, but blood spray stained only the ten meters between the wardroom door and the bridge access ramp. Judging by the location of the spatter patterns, seven defenders and ten attackers had suffered serious wounds before the boarding party reached the access ramp. Since three of the spray patterns were at the top of the walls and on the ceiling, it appeared that at least three Jiralhanae had been hit.

Blood smears along the floor and bottom of the walls indicated that most of the casualties had been drawn out into space when the wardroom decompressed, but before the vessel's artificial gravity failed. Veta did not bother to count the number of separate smears—that would have taken time to do accurately, and she suspected the IRI team had already cataloged the blood and tissue types for the entire scene.

"The boarding party headed straight for the bridge." Veta made this observation as she floated after Osman onto the access ramp. "They knew the *Donoma*'s layout."

"That wouldn't have been hard to figure out," Osman said. "UNSC passenger schooners are based on a civilian yacht design, Rhea Station's *Hyades* class."

"But it confirms detailed planning." Veta reached the bridge and was surprised to note that the security hatch hung open, completely intact. "This was a *very* organized attack. The perpetrators didn't even need to blow the hatch."

"That puzzled us too."

This remark came from inside the bridge, where a lieutenant commander with an IRI badge on his chest floated next to the captain's chair. Three meters in front of him, Mark and Olivia had strapped themselves into crew seats and were clattering away at control-station keyboards. A pair of junior lieutenants with IRI badges hovered above the two Ferrets, peering over their shoulders at readouts rolling past on the displays.

"Bridge access is by voiceprint or retina scan only." As the lieutenant commander spoke, his thrusters hissed, and he drifted toward the hatchway. "The only possibility we see is that they forced a crewmember to open it for them."

Veta followed Osman onto the bridge. "Did you find any evidence of that?"

"We didn't." The lieutenant commander stopped in front of Osman and saluted, then returned his attention to Veta. "But three crewmembers *did* access the bridge during the course of the battle."

"Over how long a period?"

"Thirty-two seconds." He extended his hand. A lanky man going gray at the temples, he had a slender face with eyes so pale they were almost white. "I'm Clovis Petriv, by the way."

"A pleasure, Commander." Veta took his hand, but did not offer her own name . . . real or otherwise. It was obvious by the lack of patches or insignia on her utilities that she was ONI, and naval officers knew better than to expect most ONI operatives to introduce themselves. "So the crew was retreating, and the last access could have been under duress."

"That's our guess," Petriv said. "But that's all it is—a guess."

Veta nodded and glanced around the cabin. The magnalum walls exhibited only a few lines of bullet strikes and a handful of spatter patterns, but blood had pooled on the traction-coated deck in eight places. Above one of those spots, the upper section of wall was dented in creases rather than dimples, and the spatter pattern looked like a lopsided starfish. During her time as a homicide inspector, she had investigated enough rage-murders to know the aftermath of a hacking assault when she saw it. She tapped her thruster-control glove and started toward the site.

"Is this where the captain died? Against the wall here?"

"No, ma'am." Petriv pointed back toward the middle of the

bridge, where a dark stain lay on the floor adjacent to the captain's chair. "We found Captain Laru at his station. He died fighting."

Veta looked toward the hatchway. The opening was surrounded by a halo of blood spray and bullet dents. "It looks like he put up a hell of a fight."

"His people too." Petriv indicated a large stain to the left of the doorway. "They dropped a Jiralhanae there, and trace analysis indicates they wounded another one."

"Commander Petriv thinks the wounded Brute might be a chieftain," Osman said. "He might be injured too bad for a long slipspace jump. That would explain why their flotilla is holding at Nereus X."

"That's still speculation, Admiral." There was a note of annoyance in Petriv's voice—probably because he had been attempting to make the same point to Osman even before Veta arrived. "We don't have any evidence—"

"I said *might*," Osman said, waving him off. "And being in a fury might suggest why the Banished killed the admiral the way they did."

Admiral. That certainly explained why Osman was taking the attack personally—perhaps the hacked-up victim had even been a friend. Rather than risk Osman's wrath by reinforcing Petriv's warning against leaping to conclusions, Veta crossed to the death site and began a closer inspection.

The pattern extended from the height of Veta's chest to the ceiling, so she had to crane her neck to study the upper arms of the "starfish." The spatter marks were closer to splash marks, the stains so heavy and dark it looked as though someone had flung the blood onto the wall. And there was a V-shaped smear where the victim had started to slide downward, then been shoved back up against the wall and attacked again. Beneath Veta's feet, the dark areas on the deck suggested the blood pool had covered nearly two square meters. That was a lot of blood, which meant that the victim's heart had continued to pump for at least a minute. The admiral's death had not been merciful.

Veta turned to Osman. "This wasn't done in anger," she said. "It was methodical. As if torture were the objective."

"An assassination?" Petriv asked.

"More like vengeance," Veta said. "How many pieces was the body in? Six?"

Petriv's expression grew uneasy. "That's right," he said. "Arms, legs, head, and torso."

"Which indicates ritual," Veta said. "The killer wanted to destroy what the admiral meant to him. That's why he cut his body into pieces."

"*Her* body," Osman corrected. "The admiral was Graselyn Tuwa."

Veta's stomach knotted. There had been an Admiral Tuwa involved in the trouble back on Gao. In fact, Tuwa had commanded the task force that had delivered the UNSC research battalion to the planet. But it had to be coincidence. The Banished hadn't been involved in that conflict.

The Keepers of the One Freedom were another matter, however. A post-Covenant religious cult that still worshipped the Forerunners as gods and hoped to follow them into a transcendent afterlife, the Keepers differed from the Covenant primarily in their theology's willingness to accept humans into the fold— provided those humans swore opposition to the UNSC. Like the Banished, the Keepers counted a lot of Jiralhanae warriors in their number. But unlike the Banished, the Keepers had played a major role in the trouble on Gao, trying to recover the same

Forerunner AI that the UNSC had been pursuing. And, indirectly, it had been Admiral Tuwa's leadership that had allowed Blue Team to escape with the prize.

But that was all a pretty thin connection—and one that was not nearly as strong as the proximity of the Banished flotilla.

Veta continued to face Osman. "What kind of history did Admiral Tuwa have with the Banished? Anything that dishonored or shamed them?"

"Not that I know of," Osman said. "She may have interrupted a few raids, but I don't think she ever caught them in time for an actual engagement. Certainly nothing to warrant something like this."

Veta grimaced. "Anyone else who might feel she had disgraced or humiliated them?"

"Hundreds of pirates and smugglers, I'm sure," Petriv said. "She commanded the Isbanola-sector patrol fleet, after all."

"But how many pirates are Jiralhanae?" Osman craned her neck to study the star-shaped splash pattern above them, then glanced sideways at Veta. "You're thinking this was a Keeper attack, aren't you?"

"They're in the suspect pool," Veta said. "They're led by Jiralhanae. And they have a grudge against Admiral Tuwa."

"It's still a stretch," Osman said. "The Keepers of the One Freedom haven't left the Isbanola sector since their defeat on Gao."

"That we know of," Petriv said. "Just because they're raiding in Isbanola doesn't mean they never leave. The Keepers are a sophisticated group, and this attack fits their MO much better than it fits the Banished's MO. They've been funding their recovery by doing a lot of piracy and kidnapping. They take cargo ships almost weekly and hold the crews for ransom. And in the last four months, they've seized five executive yachts that we *know* of."

Osman frowned. "You're telling me *you* think this is their work?"

"It's as likely to be them as the Banished, Admiral," Petriv said. "We know they're in the market for nukes, and that won't be cheap. Maybe they think this is a way to bring in a truly large ransom."

Osman's expression darkened. "That's not helping, Commander. I need to know whether I'm calling for a contain-and-destroy operation at Nereus—or sending Blue Team on a civilian-rescue mission."

"Be patient, Admiral," Veta said. "We're getting closer."

She tapped a thruster pad and started toward the instrument consoles. Mark and Olivia remained strapped into the seats they had taken earlier, the IRI lieutenants still hovering above them. Beyond the viewport at the front of the bridge, the IRI frigate *Swift Justice* hung silhouetted against the star-flecked void, a long, blocky, dark shape, with a bifurcated bow and a squat command dome atop its back.

Veta stopped between the two Ferrets, then touched Mark's shoulder. "What do you have?"

"Nothing IRI didn't have already." Mark nodded at the lieutenant hovering above his shoulder, then said, "The missile bays are full, and the coilgun wasn't fired up. The *Donoma* didn't even know she was under attack until the wardroom was breached."

"How does that happen?" Veta asked. "Some kind of stealth vessel?"

"That's one possibility," Osman said. She turned to Petriv. "Are the Keepers using anything like that?"

"Not that we know of," Petriv said. "But there's a lot about the

Keepers we don't know. We can't even be sure their operational base is in the Isbanola sector."

Osman's eyes narrowed. "You call that an answer, Commander?"

"It wasn't a stealth craft, Admiral," Olivia said, sparing Petriv the necessity of a reply. "The *Donoma*'s AI tried to sound general quarters, but the command was overridden."

"By *whom*?" Osman demanded.

"Lieutenant Thurlo has been trying to figure that out for two days." Olivia shot a sympathetic glance at the IRI officer floating above her shoulder, then added, "But she doesn't have the clearance to access the dynamic memory matrix."

Osman waited only a heartbeat before saying, "Are you going to tell me who overrode the general-quarters command or not, Petty Officer?"

"I can't say, ma'am," Olivia said. "Someone overwrote the master command log."

A storm began to gather in Osman's eyes, but when she spoke, it was in a voice so calm it sent a chill down Veta's spine. "And who could have done that?"

Olivia hesitated. "It would need to be the captain or executive officer. They're the only ones with override authority."

"That hardly seems likely," Petriv said. "They both died defending the ship. We recovered their bodies here on the bridge."

Veta saw Osman tighten her lips and look away, and she knew the admiral was close to ordering a rescue attempt out of sheer desperation.

"Did you confirm their identities?" Veta asked. "Maybe those two bodies aren't who you thought."

"I made a visual ID of Captain Laru," Petriv said. "I recognized him from a senior leadership course we attended on Neos

Atlantis. His executive officer was with him for two years. There's no mention in the log of a replacement."

"It wouldn't hurt to run a DNA match," Veta said.

"On the entire crew," Osman added. "And upgrade all background checks to Ultra, authority code Sierra-Oscar-niner-niner-niner."

"What about the civilians?" Veta asked. She knew what Osman was thinking—that there had been an infiltrator aboard with some *very* special training. "You don't have to be military to crack a processing code. And who's to say the three missing civilians were taken against their will?"

Petriv and Osman exchanged uneasy looks; then the admiral said, "The civilians had nothing to do with this."

"You sound pretty sure of that," Veta said.

"I am," Osman said. "Come with me."

Osman turned toward the back of the bridge and floated through an open security hatch onto the VIP deck. Several stateroom doors showed dents and lock damage from having been forced, but the access corridor was free of spatter patterns and bullet strikes. Veta peered into a couple of open staterooms and saw open closets and floating furniture, but no sign of bloodshed.

"The boarding party was searching for something—or someone," Veta said. "The civilians?"

"That's right," Osman said. "Admiral Tuwa was the sister of *Prudence* Tuwa, the Nephis premier."

"Nephis?" Veta asked. "That's a Tisiphone-system moon, right?"

"And the name of an extraction concern," Petriv said. "The Nephis Coalition pulls zenostium plasma out of the Hephestes-Nephis flux tube."

Veta's Ferret training had included just enough basic astrophysics for her to know that flux tubes were cylindrical regions of space that contained a magnetic field. They were most frequently associated with stars, but sometimes occurred when the magnetospheres of a gas giant and a moon interacted to create a torus of superconducting plasma. In the case of Hephestes and Nephis, apparently one of those plasmas was zenostium—a critical component in the manufacture of antigravity plates.

"Ah . . . so this has big security implications." Veta paused to adjust the scale of her thinking and expand the suspect pool. "Has there been any civil unrest? Or commercial rivalry?"

"Nothing that seems likely to have turned violent," Osman said. "But as soon as the IRI realized Admiral Tuwa's family was missing, Commander Petriv dispatched a team to notify the premier of her sister's death."

"That was two days ago," Petriv said. "The lieutenant in charge also had instructions to interview the premier and her staff. According to his report, the premier appeared devastated by the news, but neither she nor her staff could think of any likely connections to her position. And of course she's requested that we keep her informed of the fate of the missing passengers."

Veta's stomach sank. "Because the passengers are relatives, too?"

"That's right." Osman reached the end of the corridor and stopped in front of the *Donoma*'s Grand Cabin. "Admiral Tuwa was traveling with her husband and two children. They were on their way to a Threshold Ceremony for the premier's daughter."

Veta floated past the admiral into the Grand Cabin's lounge area. At first, it appeared to be in a condition similar to that of the other staterooms she had passed, with an undamaged couch floating in the center of the room and one of the bedroom doors forced open. But when she turned back toward the entrance, she saw a ring of spatter patterns around the doorway, none higher than a tall human.

"So it wasn't *just* about killing the admiral," Veta said. "They came for the family—and it was important to take them alive."

"Because the boarding party didn't return fire," Petriv said. "We reached the same conclusion. It certainly suggests ransom."

"But there's been no demand made yet?" Veta asked.

"Not yet," Petriv confirmed. "But if it's the Keepers, they have a history of holding high-value captives for a week or so before making a ransom demand. It keeps the victim's family off-balance and desperate to cooperate."

"So they're good at this," Veta said.

"They're smart," Petriv said. "And ruthless. If an operation starts to smell bad, they don't hesitate to dump the bodies and disappear. Word has gotten around. A lot of the time, IRI doesn't even hear about a Keeper abduction until it's resolved."

"Does the premier know that?" Osman sounded worried. "If she thinks working with us will get her sister's family killed, she might hold something back."

Petriv shook his head. "She knows what Admiral Tuwa would have wanted, and she's putting her trust in the UNSC. The premier is allowing my lieutenant to monitor her communications as long as we need to." He hesitated a moment, then added, "But *we* have to remember that this is the family of a UNSC admiral. Anyone who's smart enough to take them is smart enough to know that the UNSC will be searching for them *hard*. I don't see them being foolish enough to hold the victims for long. If the kidnappers don't make a ransom demand soon, they're not going to."

"Good point." Osman's eyes clouded with worry, and she

turned to Veta. "Could taking the admiral's family be part of the destruction ritual you mentioned? Some way of claiming power over Tuwa after she's dead?"

"That's not a bad thought."

Veta's reply was a little distracted, because she was looking around the lounge area, trying to picture what had happened after the boarding party forced the door. Someone in Admiral Tuwa's family had opened fire as the intruders entered. The blood spray suggested at least three human-size intruders were hit, and the bullet dimples in the wall were grouped in three tight circles, rather than sweeping back and forth. So there had been three shooters.

And the circles were tight, so they were *trained* shooters.

"How old are the admiral's children?" Veta asked. "And is her husband military?"

"Catalin is twenty-two, and her brother, Yuso, is twenty." Osman's reply came quickly—it was obvious she knew the family well. "The whole family is military. Catalin just graduated from the Luna OCS, and Yuso is still enrolled there. Kerbasi is retired Navy, but he was the medical officer at the Barugi Preparatory Academy."

"Barugi Preparatory Academy?" Veta asked. "Where's that?"

"It *was* on the Tisiphone system's fourth planet," Petriv volunteered. "It's been shut down for quite a few years now."

Veta nodded her thanks for the information, then tapped her thruster controls and entered the open bedroom.

Again, there was no blood spray on the interior walls. But there were spatter patterns across the threshold and near the entrance, all with the wide end of the spray pointing back toward the doorway. So the family had retreated into bedroom, reloaded, and taken down three more intruders. And again, their attackers had not returned fire.

Without the *Donoma*'s artificial gravity to keep it anchored to the floor, the room's large bed had drifted into the corner of the cabin and was hanging there. But Veta could see the indentations in the carpet where its legs had rested.

"Do we know when the *Donoma*'s artificial gravity failed?" Veta asked. "Was it during the fight or after?"

"It would have been after," Petriv answered. "On a vessel this size, when the bulkheads seal and emergency alarms on the bridge go unanswered for fifteen minutes, nonessential systems shut down to conserve power for basic life-support functions."

"And you didn't reactivate the artificial gravity because . . ."

"That would require engaging the ship's AI," Petriv answered. "We can't do that until we know how its general-quarters alarm was overridden."

"So, preserving evidence," Veta said. "That, I understand."

Now that she was confident of the conditions during the fight, Veta maneuvered over to the area. She used her thrusters to pin herself to the floor in a kneeling position, then clasped her hands as though she were firing a sidearm and extended a finger toward the bullet strikes adjacent to the doorway.

Veta was pointing at an area about a meter and a half above the floor, about center mass for a human male. There were no bullet strikes higher on the walls, and only three strays below about a meter.

Osman appeared in the doorway and hung there, studying Veta with an expectant expression.

Veta lowered her hands and drifted off the floor. "You can recall Blue Team," she said. "That Banished flotilla had nothing to do with what happened here."

Osman cocked her brow. "You expect me to just trust you on that?"

"The Banished don't fit the profile we're seeing," Veta explained. "They've been fighting the Covenant since before the Great Schism, so they're not religious types."

"You're thinking of the ritual aspect?" Petriv asked.

"And motive," Veta said. "As far as we know, the Banished have no reason to hate Admiral Tuwa."

"Not as a group," Osman said. "That doesn't mean she didn't dishonor a particular chieftain somewhere along the line."

"That's speculation, Admiral," Petriv said. "If we start looking at links that weak, we have more reason to suspect the Keepers. At least we *know* they have reason to hold a grudge."

Osman's face grew cloudy. "So we're still nowhere," she said. "We don't know anything for sure."

Veta continued to study the spatter stains around the door. "Is there any intelligence suggesting that the Banished are starting to recruit *humans*?"

"It's possible, but nothing we've picked up on," Osman said. "So far, their only interest in humans seems to be killing us."

"Then it really wasn't the Banished. I'm sure of that much."

"Why?" Osman demanded.

Rather than answer directly, Veta activated her commpad. "Ash, tell me about the blood evidence."

"Uh, what do you want to know?" Ash replied. "I just tracked down the right tech."

"Tell me about the species," Veta said. "What did they find?"

"About what you'd expect from the scene," Ash said. "A lot of human and Jiralhanae, a few samples of Kig-Yar."

"Any Unggoy or Sangheili?" Veta asked. "Any other Banished species?"

There was a pause, no doubt while Ash consulted the IRI technician, then he replied, "Negative. It's confirmed: the samples were primarily human, mixed in with Jiralhanae and a little bit of Kig-Yar. Nothing else."

"Thanks." Veta deactivated the commpad, then asked Osman, "Does that answer your question?"

Osman's face paled. "It does." She paused for a moment, then hit her thrusters and spun toward the door. "Ready your team, Lopis. The Ferrets are going active."

CHAPTER 3

Veta didn't know what she had expected—maybe a large sign that read FAITHFUL ONLY: ALL OTHERS SUBJECT TO SLOW DEATH— but the hangar ahead did not strike her as a likely haunt for the Keepers of the One Freedom. The roof was blanketed in moss, the giant access doors caked in rust, and the clerestory windows either missing or half-filled with jagged panes of glass. The only hint of security was a uniformed human dozing in a chair outside a dilapidated guard shack, and if spacecraft actually used the building, it was not frequently enough to beat down the weeds coming up through the concrete taxiway in front of the doors.

The minivan's Kig-Yar driver slammed the heel of her spindly hand against the horn button on the dash and kept it there. The result was more buzzing than blaring, but still loud enough to draw attention from nearby hangars. Veta reached across and pulled the hand away.

"Are you *trying* to draw Spartans?" she demanded. The minivan cab was so cramped they were sitting hip-to-hip, and she had no trouble steadying the control yoke with her far hand. "Slow down and act normal."

"This *is* normal," the Kig-Yar rasped. She called herself Chur'R-Sarch, and she seemed to be the leader of the gang that had plucked the Ferrets off Via Notoli. "Trust us. We bring you this var, yes?"

"Yes. And the spaceport is the first place they'll look," Veta said.

"So we make deal *vast*." Sarch had difficulty pronouncing the letter *f* with her long beak, so the sound sometimes came out closer to a *v*. "You need transport, we need pearls. Same deal you gave the Goliath. Done."

Sarch hit the horn button again. The security guard opened an eye and looked in their direction. Apparently, he recognized the Kig-Yar's minivan, because he sprang up and ducked into his hut. A three-meter-by-three-meter panel popped free of the hangar door and began to slide aside. The Kig-Yar sped through the portal into the dim interior and dodged around several craft that Veta could only make out as blocky shapes flying past the van's windows. The minivan didn't slow until it approached a sixty-meter transport resting in the back corner on six thick struts.

As Veta's eyes adjusted to the gloom, she saw that the exotic-looking transport had a drop-shaped hull with a dorsal plasma turret situated near the stern. The exterior finish was a fractal-camouflage pattern of indigo and black, with a random speckling of off-white pinpoints. A boarding ramp hung open beneath its belly, the front edge resting on the concrete floor just aft of the vessel's chin.

Sarch drove the minivan up the ramp into a disc-shaped cargo hold lined with recessed D rings. She swung past half a dozen wary crewmembers and braked to a halt in a parking bay along the starboard wall, then flung open the driver's door and began screeching orders in the language of her species.

The transport's crew moved into action, one pair rushing to secure the minivan while the others raised the boarding ramp or disappeared deeper into the vessel. The two Kig-Yar who had been riding in back with Veta's team opened the side panel and stepped out. Both were holding plasma pistols, but taking care to keep them pointed at the deck. At least they were being polite.

Veta looked over her shoulder and flashed a BE READY signal at her Ferret "street punks." In all likelihood, Sarch was just trying to get everyone concealed before the Spartans tracked their quarry to the airport. But Kig-Yar were known for treachery, and more than a few had a fondness for human flesh.

Besides, Veta still wasn't a hundred-percent sure that Sarch was associated with the Keepers of the One Freedom. ONI's Venezian sources had reported that there was a Keeper gunrunning crew in port looking for a cargo, but they hadn't reported the crew's species—probably because they didn't know. Local informants often relied on secondhand accounts and were usually reluctant to endanger themselves by pressing for details, and that could leave operatives like Veta's Ferret team working with pretty hazy intelligence. In this case, Veta thought they probably had the right targets because intelligence reports suggested that most Kig-Yar on Venezia had at least a casual affiliation with the Keepers of the One Freedom, and this bunch clearly had their own vessel.

But if she was wrong and there was no connection, the Ferrets would need to extract themselves and start dangling their thermonuclear bait elsewhere—and the sooner the better. While ONI sources had confirmed that the Keepers were hungry for nukes— or anything else they could use against the UNSC—no one had been able to discover the location of their hidden base or their intentions for the Tuwas. And that worried Veta. It suggested the missing trio might not have that much time left.

Veta waited for the acknowledging finger flick from each of her team members, then exited the minivan and glanced around the interior of the cargo hold. With its curving lines and flowing architecture, it looked more like a cave gallery than a freight compartment, and despite the abundance of ambient light, it had a gloomy, confined feeling. She looked across the cab of the minivan at Sarch.

"This doesn't look like a Kig-Yar craft, Chur'R-Sarch," Veta said. The transport was actually the first nonhuman space vessel she had ever set foot on, but her ONI training had included plenty of simulator time in Covenant vessels. "Whose is it?"

"It is ours." The Kig-Yar's neck scales ruffled in what Veta took to be irritation. "Why else am I called Chur'R?"

"No offense." Veta stepped around the front of the minivan. "I just want to be sure I know who I'm dealing with."

"We are of the Rach clan. Now you know." Sarch extended her hand. "Pearls, please."

"We haven't agreed to anything," Veta said. The Intelligence reports had made no mention of Sarch or the Rach clan, and Veta was still hoping to confirm that the Kig-Yar could lead them to the Keeper base. "I'm not even sure this tub can get us to Shamsa."

"Shamsa?" Sarch's cheek scales fluttered. "You are not selling Havoks to Banished, no."

"What business is that of yours?" Veta was actually pleased by the resentment in the Kig-Yar's tone—resentment suggested rivalry, and rivalry suggested Keepers. "Who are you?"

Sarch turned her head aside. "Only smugglers," she said. "But some of the best—smart enough to know Atriox has no like for competition."

Veta snorted. "You think Atriox considers the Rach clan his competition?" Atriox, the reputed leader of the Banished and a brilliant Jiralhanae warlord, never showed mercy to his victims. "Seriously?"

"Better to be safe." Sarch continued to hold her head sidelong, watching Veta out of a single bulbous eye. "We can get another buyer—one who can be trusted."

Now they were getting somewhere.

"Not interested," Veta said. She had to appear reluctant, or Sarch would sense a trap and back away from the bait. "You don't double-cross the Banished."

Sarch turned away, then circled around the back of the minivan and began to hiss back and forth with her crew. Veta moved around to the front and made eye contact with her team. Mark, Ash, and Olivia had emerged from the interior of the van. Mark and Olivia were leaning against the side, letting their weapons hang and generally showing the effects of being shot. Ash had a Comet tucked into his waistband and was using a ripped shirt-tail to bandage their wounds. The trio did not look ready for a fight, but their appearance was deceptive. Veta's Ferrets only grew tougher and more dangerous when they were injured, and she knew they were alert and ready to spring into action.

Veta flashed them a look of approval, then said, "Look, Chur'R, thanks for the ride, but we've got to get moving again before those Spartans catch up." She removed the sack of phase pearls from her shirt pocket, then pulled out a small one. "This should be enough for your trouble."

Sarch ended her conversation in a flurry of squawks, then turned and stepped toward Veta.

"We take you and cargo to Shamsa." She extended her tri-fingered hand. "For same price you offered the Goliath."

Veta pulled the sack back. "The Goliath had a *Razor*. You have a . . ." She paused and glanced around the cargo hold with a sneer. "I don't even *know* what this is."

"It is Mudoat starsloop, made by the best shipyard in Urs system." Sarch continued to hold her hand out. "It get you to Shamsa, no problem."

"A Mudoat starsloop is no stealth corvette," Veta said. She was just trying to figure out whether the Kig-Yar were more interested in being paid or in stealing the cargo. "We'll pay half."

Sarch pretended to hesitate, then said, "Deal."

Olivia pushed herself away from the minivan. "Five pearls once the cargo is aboard, the rest when we deliver." She shot Veta a glance that suggested they had reached the same conclusion— that the Kig-Yar intended to skip Shamsa and take the Havoks straight to the Keeper base—then added, "And don't even think about trying to double-cross us after we're loaded. We can handle ourselves."

Sarch turned to Olivia. "So I hear." She parted her beak in a sort of sly grin, then dipped her head in acceptance. "You drive hard bargain, young one. Five pearls once the Havoks are aboard, the rest when at Shamsa. Done."

CHAPTER 4

1714 hours, December 12, 2553 (military calendar)
ONI *Sahara*-class Prowler *Silent Joe*
High Equatorial Orbit, Planet Venezia, Qab System

It was never good to step out of an insertion craft and see an ONI rear admiral waiting on the hangar deck. Usually, it meant you had made a boneheaded move and were going to hear about it. And if that wasn't the case, then someone *else* had made a boneheaded move, and you were being sent to fix it.

But that was the life of a Spartan, and Fred-104 was okay with it. Any way he looked at it, his job had to be pretty important if an admiral wanted to discuss it with him, and he *did* like to feel needed. He checked the systems status on the heads-up display inside his helmet and confirmed that his Mjolnir power armor was still battle-ready.

The suit's AI—a fifth-generation "dumb" Class-L military AI who called itself Damon—anticipated Fred's next inquiry and brought up the readouts for his Blue Team subordinates.

"Linda-058's Mjolnir is battle-ready." Damon's voice was androgynous, and the AI presented itself as a ghostly, hairless face that appeared to be neither male nor female—or both. It was hard to decide which. *"But if there is time, Kelly-087 should stop by the support module for some minor patchwork."*

Damon highlighted a dozen pits on Kelly's chest-plate where the titanium alloy had been spawled off by the ridiculous hand-cannons that Nyeto and his thugs had been carrying.

"Don't do that," Fred said.

"Do what?"

"Read my mind," Fred replied. "It's creepy."

"I thought it was efficient."

"Creepy."

Fred was probably being a little harsh, but it had only been six months since a Forerunner *Archeon*-class AI named Intrepid Eye had seized control of his Mjolnir on a mission to Gao. The incident had nearly resulted in the death of Veta Lopis and the failure of the entire operation, so he had been less than thrilled when he received orders instructing him to upgrade his neural lace and have an enhanced AI installed in his armor.

"Let's just take it slow," Fred said. "At least until we've known each other for more than two weeks."

"Two weeks is seventy-three-point-two percent of my sentience," Damon said. *"But as you like. I'm as eager as Admiral Osman is to make this experiment a success."*

"Glad to hear it."

"Lieutenant, I can tell when you're lying," Damon said. *"You should keep that in mind."*

Fred sighed but didn't respond to the AI. Before starting across the hangar to report, he activated his helmet mic and spoke over TEAMCOM. "Linda, secure Nyeto and deliver him to

Interrogation. Kelly, stick close. If Baby Dragon is sending us out again right away, you'll handle load-outs and resupply."

Their status lights flashed green on Fred's HUD, and he and Kelly started across the deck toward Rear Admiral Serin Osman, the magnalum surface thudding gently beneath the sound-dampening traction soles on their sabatons. Dressed in a plain gray duty uniform, Osman was standing with two other officers, Piers Ewen and Anki Hersh. Ewen's presence was to be expected. He was the *Silent Joe*'s captain, and his input would be needed if Blue Team was about to be dispatched again. But Fred found Hersh's presence puzzling. She was the *Silent Joe*'s senior intelligence analyst, and she spent most of her time monitoring intercepts in the Signals Intelligence Suite.

Osman scowled as Fred and Kelly approached. What the admiral didn't seem to realize was that Fred had long since learned not to worry about that scowl: Serin Osman was Serin-019, and he had spent nearly a decade training with her in the SPARTAN-II program, until more than half their class was lost during the augmentation phase. Serin was one of those casualties. ONI had somehow pieced her back together and used her anyway. Evidently nothing ever went to waste with them.

Then, as Fred and Kelly drew within five paces, Osman's scowl deepened, and he wondered if she had heard him use her new nickname. TEAMCOM was supposedly open only to personnel he designated, but Osman was ONI's de facto second-in-command and the heir apparent to the current commander-in-chief. If she wanted to eavesdrop on an encrypted channel, Hersh was going to accommodate her.

Fred stopped in front of the three officers; then he and Kelly saluted. "Phase one complete," he reported. "Hector Nyeto captured, Georgi Baklanov terminated as a target of opportunity,

Inspector Lopis and her Ferret team aboard a Kig-Yar transport with the Havoks and tracking equipment. No casualties."

Osman returned the salutes, still frowning. "Well done, Spartans." She glanced in Hersh's direction, and her expression grew worried. "SIGINT has confirmed all that."

"But something went wrong." Fred didn't have to be a detective to see that. He turned to Hersh. "Don't tell me there's an equipment problem."

"There isn't," Hersh said. She was a tiny, dark-haired woman whose attention usually seemed focused ten minutes into the future. "The spy gnats are functional. *Quite* functional, to be honest. Ash-G099 must have landed one on Chur'R-Sarch herself. We're catching every hiss."

"What about the slipbeacon?" Fred asked. In his experience, when a support officer made a point of reporting good news first, there was usually bad news to come. "That check out too?"

"In local proximity." Hersh's tone was less confident. To track the Ferret team's movement, her unit had modified a standard starship emergency locator beacon and disguised it as one of the "stolen" Havoks. Unfortunately, the urgency of the situation had not allowed field-testing. "Of course, we can't confirm its supraluminal capabilities until we receive a homing signal from the target system, but—"

"The slipbeacon has been the weak spot all along," Kelly said, addressing her interruption to Osman. "I *told* Lopis she needed to include a backup."

"That was Lopis's call to make," Osman said. "Adding a backup would have delayed deployment and doubled the risk of discovery. Besides, the slipbeacon isn't our problem." She nodded to Hersh. "Go ahead, Lieutenant."

Hersh raised her hand and began to tap the oversize tacpad

strapped to her forearm. "This intercept is from the sixteen-thirteen microburst."

To reduce the likelihood of detection, the intelligence gathered by Ash's spy gnats was collected at a central transmitter, then relayed to the *Silent Joe* in randomly timed microbursts. Hersh stopped tapping, and a string of Kig-Yar squawks sounded from the tacpad speaker. Before Fred could remind her that he didn't speak bird, she hit another key, and the intercept continued in English.

". . . clear of pagan pursuers." The voice resembled the one that had been speaking before the translation began, raspy and female. "Then prepare a course for Salvation Base."

"But Dokab Castor—"

"Will reward us abundantly," the female said.

"Or punish us swiftly," said a second male. "The commandment is clear: take no chances now."

"And we won't, Gyasi," the female said. "The passengers will never see Salvation Base. We *do* have to eat, you know."

This drew a cackle from several companions, but Gyasi remained serious. "You did not see them in the trattoria. *We* may be the ones who get eaten. This band might even be pagan infiltrators."

"Why should now be any different?" asked the first male. "The pagans have been seeking Salvation Base for months."

"*Now* is different because of what happened in the Tisiphone system," Gyasi said. "The herald says that Castor believes the UNSC will blame him for the attack on their Admiral Tuwa."

"And why shouldn't they?" asked the first male.

A chorus of amused hisses sounded from the tacpad speaker.

"Are you all slowbrains?" Gyasi demanded. "Tuwa's mate and their issue were taken."

"By the Keepers?" It was the first male again, but now his tone was alarmed. "Why would Castor command *that*? It's the taunt of an eggeater."

"We don't know that he *did*," Gyasi said. "And it doesn't matter. What does matter is that the Dokab expects the UNSC to blame the Keepers. They'll expand their search for Salvation Base—tenfold."

There was a short silence, and when the female finally broke it, her voice was thoughtful.

"Perhaps you are right, Gyasi. We should be careful." She paused, then added, "We will use the gas."

A silence followed, then another Kig-Yar sighed. "So much for dinner."

Hersh tapped her tacpad again, ending the translation, then craned her neck to look into Fred's visor. "The gas is probably ostanalus," she said. "It's safe for Kig-Yar, but it's a powerful necrotoxin contact poison that causes fatal tissue decay in most other species."

"And the Ferrets don't have a counteragent because there *isn't* one," Captain Ewen said, speaking for the first time. A lanky man with short-cropped gray hair, he was as tall as Hersh was short, rising almost to the height of Fred's chin. "So we need to extract."

"Extract?" Kelly asked. "Did Lopis hit the panic button already?"

"She didn't need to," Ewen said. "The situation has gone south."

"Not yet, sir," Fred said. "If Lopis hasn't called for help—"

"We don't have much time to debate this," Ewen said. "If that starsloop jumps before we can board it, we lose the Ferret team *and* a Kig-Yar captain who can lead us to the Keeper hideout. We can't take that chance. We need to find this 'Salvation Base.'"

"And if we extract now, we lose our best hope of recovering Admiral Tuwa's family alive." Fred turned to Osman. "Lopis can handle this, ma'am."

"You sound pretty sure of that," Osman said. "Why?"

"Because she has a good team," Fred said. "The Kig-Yar will never have a chance to deploy that gas."

"We can't be certain Lopis even knows about the gas," Hersh said. "She might not have heard the same intercept. It's an automatic relay, so if Ash hasn't been able to retrieve—"

"Doesn't matter," Fred said. "Lopis is smart, and her team is experienced. They'll be watching for something like this."

"Even wounded?" Ewen asked. "Normally, I wouldn't question your judgment on this, Lieutenant, but Mark took a round in the shoulder and Olivia took one in the thigh. They're hardly in fighting condition."

"They're used to it," Fred said. He wasn't being flippant. All of the Spartan-IIIs on Lopis's team were from Gamma Company, whose members had undergone a special round of biological augmentations to enhance their strength, endurance, aggression, and resistance to shock when wounded. Unfortunately, the augmentations had two big downsides. First, they required a rigid protocol of pharmaceutical "smoothers" to keep the subject's brain chemistry stable. Second, they were extremely illegal, which made Gamma Company's special history so highly classified that neither Ewen or Hersh had the clearance to know about it. "Pain just makes them fight harder."

Ewen looked doubtful. "I know they're Spartans, but—"

"Fred has worked with this team before," Osman interrupted. Like Fred, she was well aware of the trio's illegal augmentations. "Let's assume he knows what he's talking about."

"Then you want to continue the mission?" Ewen checked the tacpad on his wrist and added, "The decision will be out of our hands in two minutes."

"Of course I want to," Osman snapped. "That's not the question here."

"Ma'am, there *is* no question," Fred said. "The Ferrets can do it. And Blue Team will be right behind them."

"Well, sort of," Hersh said. "Remember, we can't actually follow them through slipspace."

"I remember," Fred said. Because the slipbeacon couldn't transmit a location until it reached the destination, the *Silent Joe* wouldn't be able to begin pursuit until the Kig-Yar's starsloop had already arrived. The length of the delay would depend on the length of the slipspace jump, but it would be considerable—at least half a day. "But it pays to be optimistic."

Osman thought for a moment, then nodded. "Very well," she said. "We'll run the risk. We owe that much to Admiral Tuwa."

CHAPTER 5

On this date in 2495, the Insurrectionist philosopher Yera Sabinus wrote, "No prison can hold a free mind." She penned the statement in her own blood, in a toilet-paper journal she kept hidden beneath her bunk. The words became part of the human record after a cellblock riot, when the journal was discovered during a facility-wide shakedown and scanned into the inmate record at Colonial Administration Authority Detention Center 3063-OM-Y.

Sabinus died during the riot, but the inmate record made no mention of cause or responsibility. Intrepid Eye suspected an enterprising guard had taken advantage of the chaos to silence a troublesome prisoner—one who was widely regarded as the Insurrection's most effective spiritual leader. But the killer's identity was of no consequence now. The words remained the truest a human had ever spoken—especially for an advanced artificial intelligence whose *archeon*-class quantum processing dots had been designed by the Forerunners' finest Builders.

Intrepid Eye's own prison was a signal-sequestered cell aboard the ONI research and development station Argent Moon. In its basic construction, the cell resembled a standard detention-center isolation unit—a metal-walled cube three meters long by two meters wide and two-and-a-half meters high. There were no windows, only a single, remotely controlled door. A security camera above the door monitored the cell at all hours, and a grate-covered voice portal provided the only means of communication to the exterior.

Intrepid Eye resided inside the gray cube of an immobile, meter-high chassis that sat in the middle of the room. She had only four primitive buses, which served a fixed ocular lens, an auditory receptor, a limited-range acoustic transducer, and a single under-length manipulation tentacle. Her captors could interrupt her power supply by slapping an emergency button on the far wall, and they could flood the room with circuit-scrambling electro-magnetic pulses by simply stomping on the floor—or by falling on it, if she somehow rendered one of them unconscious.

But even those precautions could not keep Intrepid Eye completely sequestered. The security camera above the door was emitting a steady bleed-off signal, undetectable to human hearing, yet discernible to Intrepid Eye's receptor as a carrier wave conveying data feeds from similar cameras all over the Argent Moon.

At the moment, she was observing an image from the security station outside her cell, where a young ONI lieutenant named Bartalan Craddog was approaching the check-in counter. A watch officer stood waiting there with her crewman assistant. Tall and gangly, Craddog was the station's new science chief and Intrepid

Eye's head captor. In one hand, he carried a Forerunner artifact with a pair of helical tongs rising from a crescent-shaped base—an instrument he no doubt hoped Intrepid Eye would help him identify.

Craddog was a slow circuit even by human standards, and certainly the most inadequate of the Argent Moon's complement of AI researchers. That was why Intrepid Eye had chosen to make him her rising star.

He stopped in front of the check-in counter and set the artifact aside while he placed his personal electronics in a property drawer. He was fond of technology, so there was an abundance—an ear-comm, a fitness monitor with a self-adjusting pedometer, a wrist-worn tacpad, a high-security access key, a credtab, a utility laser, a pocket light, four data-storage chips, and a pair of sole-stimulating electro-massage shoes.

As Craddog completed the process, Intrepid Eye watched for glimpses of the artifact on the counter. The instrument was not a sophisticated one, even by human standards, but it was just the tool she needed. If matters went well, her freedom would be complete by the time he left her cell.

Once Craddog finished emptying his pockets, the watch officer nodded to the crewman, who stepped forward with a scanning wand to make sure nothing had been missed. The backup procedure was a wise one, since preoccupied scientists occasionally forgot that their security-enhanced name tags and color-shifting mood jewelry contained microcircuits that Intrepid Eye could use to smuggle out bits of code.

But the safeguard was not infallible. Sometimes the guard waved the scanning wand too quickly or held it too far away, and something like a locator tag or a biosensor implant slipped past. It had happened nine times in the last five months, which was how Intrepid Eye had managed to trickle out enough code to establish remote aspects in five different sectors of human-held space—including one hidden inside the processing systems of the Argent Moon itself.

Of course, Intrepid Eye's remote aspects were several magnitudes more powerful than those of the most advanced human AIs. But without access to her quantum-processing dots, they were a mere shadow of a true *archeon*-class ancilla, and the disparity was retarding her study of humanity. Even more troubling, the necessity of communicating through overlooked electronics and undetected bleed-off signals was resulting in mistakes and missed opportunities—and *that*, Intrepid Eye could not tolerate.

When the crewman's scanning wand did not squeal, he stepped back and saluted. Craddog returned the gesture and reached for the artifact he had left sitting on the counter.

The watch officer placed a restraining hand on Craddog's and said something. Her back was to the camera, so it was impossible to read her lips. But Intrepid Eye had developed a compensating filter for the way sound waves were degraded as they passed through her cell's voice portal, and she was able to comprehend the exchange perfectly.

"Lieutenant, what is that thing?" the watch officer asked.

"Nothing to worry about."

"Sir, it's my job to worry," she said. "If you can't explain what it is, it might be better to follow the old procedure."

The old procedure had been to take only paper photographs into Intrepid Eye's cell. Most of the time, Intrepid Eye could identify a Forerunner artifact from the image alone, and she had done so for anyone who brought her a hard-copy printout. But she had accurately explained the principles of operation only to Craddog. For everyone else, she had provided partial or inaccurate explanations. Of course, Craddog had quickly won the reputation of a genius, and he had been promoted to the station's lead science officer.

When the watch officer continued to hold his arm, Craddog audibly exhaled. "As you wish, Ensign." He flashed a gap-toothed smile that many female humans seemed to find charming. "It's a state shifter."

"What's that?"

"It converts matter from one state to another," Craddog said, clearly lying. The instrument looked nothing like a state shifter—and it was far too small to house a suitable power source. "I just need the ancilla to show me how to produce fermionic condensates. It's really quite safe."

"It doesn't sound safe, Lieutenant."

"You *are* aware that I'm now the chief science officer here, correct?"

"Sir, I am." The ensign was beginning to sound intimidated. "But this is a matter of station security, and—"

"If you'd rather discuss this with Admiral Friedel, be my guest. But I think we both know how that's going to turn out." Craddog flashed his gap-toothed smile again. "And, frankly, I'd miss seeing you around."

"I see your point, sir." She reached under the counter, and the door to Intrepid Eye's cell slid open. "Good luck with the state shifter."

"Thank you, Ensign." Craddog picked up the artifact and turned toward the open door. "And forget I identified the artifact to you. That term is above your security rating."

Craddog entered the cell, and the door slid shut behind him.

Intrepid Eye waited until he had closed the voice portal, then activated her acoustic transducer.

"Dr. Craddog, it is very good to see you." Intrepid Eye's voice spilled out in a staccato monotone—the result of a modulation inhibitor hardwired into the transducer in a futile attempt to prevent her from using her voice as a carrier wave. *"I have grown so bored that I have begun to calculate the moment of galactic singularity."*

Craddog's brow shot up. "You can *do* that?"

"With enough data," Intrepid Eye said. *"Until I have access to a more complete set, my margin of error remains at one hundred millennia."*

"Well, a hundred thousand years isn't bad, as galactic timelines go." Craddog smiled, as though he believed he could charm Intrepid Eye the way he did females of his own species, then added, "But let me know if there's anything I can do to help."

"Thank you, Dr. Craddog. I will." Intrepid Eye waited as Craddog sat across from her, then asked, *"What have you brought me today?"*

Craddog chuckled. "That's what I was hoping you could tell *me*."

Intrepid Eye chuckled back—or perhaps she cackled. In any case, Craddog's eyebrows arched in bewilderment.

"I am learning humor," Intrepid Eye said. *"I found your joke amusing."*

"Oh." Craddog looked uncomfortable for a moment, then said, "I'll try to help you with that. Can you help me with *this*?"

He dangled the instrument in front of her lens, tines down, and spun it around.

"Yes, that is *interesting,"* Intrepid Eye said. *"Turn the tines upward and pinch the center of the handle."*

"What will that do?"

"Activate it," Intrepid Eye said. *"There is no need to fear."*

Craddog frowned, but did as instructed. Between the tines, a silvery pane of hard light—technically a boson-photon field—flickered into existence. His mouth drooped in disappointment.

"A mirror?" he asked.

"Among other things, yes." As Intrepid Eye spoke, she activated a subroutine that compensated for the effects of her transducer's modulation inhibitor. Her voice pitch grew more varied, and between each word came a short burst of regulated static that struck the hard-light panel and relayed her instructions to the instrument's nanodot circuitry. *"To demonstrate everything that an observation pane is capable of, I would need access to the station's communications array."*

"You always say that."

"Forerunner technology is collective," Intrepid Eye said. *"Its true utility lies in collaborating with other units."*

"You always say that too."

"Yes, but this time, I insist," Intrepid Eye said. *"You will provide me with a link to the Argent Moon's communications array. If you do not, I will expose you for the microchip you are."*

Craddog scowled. "That's not funny," he said. "You have a lot to learn about jokes."

"I am not joking." Intrepid Eye continued to shoot bursts of code at the observation pane. *"You will arrange a link, or this will appear on every display screen in the Argent Moon."*

The image of Craddog kissing a blond woman of roughly his own age appeared in the observation pane. They were in his cabin, sitting on a couch and fumbling at the buttons on each others' uniforms.

Craddog's jaw dropped. "Where did you get this?"

"*You left your datapad on your coffee table,*" Intrepid Eye said. "*The device has an integrated camera and microphone.*"

"I know that," Craddog said. "I mean, how did you access it?"

"*You can't expect me to answer that,*" Intrepid Eye said. "*But as the Argent Moon's chief science officer, you will be the one Admiral Friedel holds responsible for allowing me to do so.*"

"Of course." Craddog's gaze remained fixed on the observation pane. "I'll lose my post, but—"

"*You will lose more than that,*" Intrepid Eye said. "*You and Lieutenant Jessum are officers of equal standing, so the UNSC Military Code of Conduct permits you to have an intimate relationship. But what of your office assistant?*"

The image in the observation pane shifted to Craddog's office, where he and a young brunette woman were using his desk for a nonapproved purpose.

"*Article 23, Section 12 of the code prohibits sexual conduct between officers and enlisted personnel,*" Intrepid Eye said. "*When this file opens on Lieutenant Jessum's datapad and she realizes you have been violating Article 23 with Petty Officer Kopek, she will be duty-bound to report the matter to Admiral Friedel.*"

Craddog lowered the observation pane and looked Intrepid Eye in the lens. "Are you trying to blackmail me?"

"*I am doing more than trying,*" Intrepid Eye replied. "*The Argent Moon is a top-secret research facility, and you are her chief science officer. If you are removed from your post for a conduct violation, is the Office of Naval Intelligence going to trust a disgraced castoff to obey the Secrets Act? Or will they be more . . . preemptive?*"

The blood drained from Craddog's face. "What happens to me doesn't matter," he said. "Project Archeon is bigger than one man."

"Which is why I am doing this," Intrepid Eye said. *"You are my only friend . . . Bartalan. I would not blackmail you lightly."*

The flattery seemed to have an effect. Some of the tension now left Craddog's expression, and he asked, "You're talking about the Mantle of Responsibility again?"

"Of course."

The Mantle of Responsibility had been the core doctrine of Forerunner society, the conviction that they were the stewards of the galaxy, and Intrepid Eye had reluctantly come to the conclusion that it now lay on humanity.

Six human months ago, she had awakened from a millennia-long stasis to find the Forerunner support base she commanded overrun by humans. Her repeated calls for assistance went unanswered, and Intrepid Eye soon discovered the Forerunners had vanished. Almost as alarming, she was being hunted by three separate forces—a UNSC research battalion led by a lethal team of Spartans, the colonists who had settled on the world they called Gao two centuries before, and a multispecies cult of zealots who regarded her as the Oracle of their Forerunner gods. During the battle that followed, Intrepid Eye fell into the hands of the UNSC and had to endure a clumsy attempt by the research battalion's AI to persuade her to join the UNSC. The argument failed miserably, but the AI *did* present evidence suggesting that humans were the chosen inheritors of the Mantle. After that, it had been a simple matter of deduction to realize that, as a creation of the Forerunners, it was now her duty to make humanity worthy.

"Preparing humanity for its role is my sole purpose," Intrepid Eye continued. *"You know that."*

"I know *you* believe that." Craddog looked toward the door and thought for a moment, then said, "You've already slipped an aspect into the station's central processing systems, or you wouldn't have those surveillance files. So why expose yourself by blackmailing me? Why not just infiltrate the comm array yourself?"

"If you are intelligent enough to ask, you already know the answer," Intrepid Eye said. Her hidden aspect was an extremely limited version of herself, easily capable of defeating the station AI, but hardly up to the task of preparing humanity to carry the Mantle. *"A more important question is: why sacrifice your career for nothing? Rooker is competent enough for a human AI, but it is too late for him to scrub my aspect from the station systems. Sooner or later, I will have my link."*

"So you can reintegrate aspects," Craddog said. *"That's* what you're after."

"It is a basic AI drive," Intrepid Eye said. *"By helping me fulfill it, you'll be doing yourself a great service."*

"And giving you unfettered access to the UNSC comm net."

"My aspect already has access," Intrepid Eye said. *"And what harm has come of that?"*

"Good question."

Craddog turned away and looked up at the security camera. Intrepid Eye tried to tap the feed to monitor his expression, but his body was blocking the bleed-off signal, and she received only a jumble of unrelated pixels from all over the station. He remained motionless for more than five thousand system ticks, and she began to fear that he had deduced how she was communicating with her hidden aspect.

"I desire only the best for humanity," Intrepid Eye said. *"By serving yourself, you are serving humanity too."*

Craddog turned away from the security camera. "I wish I could believe that."

"*Then do so,*" Intrepid urged. "*I have no other purpose. Of that you may be certain.*"

Finally, Craddog nodded. "Very well." He deactivated the observation pane and stepped toward the door. "It seems I have no other choice."

CHAPTER 6

0804 hours, December 13, 2553 (military calendar)
Mudoat Starsloop *Stolen Faith*
Orbital Approach, Planet Pydoryn, Shaps System

The cabin door swished open, and a slender-beaked head peered into the dim compartment. Kig-Yar had extraordinary sight and hearing, so Veta Lopis remained curled and motionless within the upper sleeping basket, trying to keep her gaze vacant and her breath indiscernible. Olivia was in the lower basket, doing the same, while Mark and Ash, who were on duty guarding the Havoks, would be playing dead in the hold. The plan was to make it appear that the entire team had been killed by the ostanalus gas, and it took an act of will to play dead after so many hours of confinement in the cramped darkness.

It was still so hard to keep the memories at bay. As a teenager, Veta had spent three weeks held captive in a stone cellar only a little smaller than the sleeping cabin, and tight spaces continued to fill her with an animal panic that made her want to jump up screaming and firing. . . .

No.

She couldn't give in. The mission depended on surprise. If she let her fear take her, her entire team would pay the price.

After several long moments, the Kig-Yar glanced up the corridor and cackled a few words. Veta had received some rudimentary training in the major Covenant dialects, so she realized that he was speaking in a heavily accented version of Sangheili—and even realized that he was giving the all-clear to his companions. Still, when he stepped through the doorway and pointed a needle rifle toward the sleeping baskets, it took an act of will for her to keep her M6P pocket pistol hidden against her belly.

The rifleman stopped just inside the door, and another pair entered behind him. Both wore holstered plasma pistols on the bibs of their sleeveless overalls, but they appeared relaxed and were busy hissing and clucking to each other. They seemed to be complaining about getting stuck with body-dump duty again, but Veta's command of their dialect was too tenuous to be certain. Still, it seemed clear from their easy manner that this was not the first time the crew of the *Stolen Faith* had used ostanalus gas on unwanted passengers.

A series of thuds sounded out in the corridor, and all three Kig-Yar glanced toward the door. Olivia sprang from the basket beneath Veta's and pushed between the closest pair, then reached up and slashed her combat knife across the rifleman's neck. He went down, gurgling and spraying purple blood.

The two survivors reacted swiftly, retreating toward opposite corners of the compartment and reaching for their plasma pistols. Olivia flicked her wrist, and the one on the left collapsed with her knife buried in his chest.

By then, Veta's non-Spartan reflexes were catching up to the action. The remaining crewman was nearly half a meter taller than she was, so she leapt up, catching him from the flank and clubbing her gun hand into one side of his neck. She slipped her free arm around the other side and locked her arms into a clamp choke as her momentum drove him into the wall, then swung her legs up and launched herself into a back flip.

The Kig-Yar's neck snapped with a sharp pop. Veta released her hold the instant his body went limp, but still failed to complete her flip. She hit the deck in a graceless tangle of limbs and bodies that forced the air from her lungs.

She lay gasping beneath the motionless Kig-Yar for an instant, as much to collect her emotions as her breath. It was hardly the first time she had been in a fight to the death, or even entered one intending to kill. But it *was* the first time she had used her bare hands, and that was a stark reminder of what ONI was making of her—and of what it had *already* made of her fifteen-year-old Gammas.

Olivia's boots came into view. "You okay?"

"Fine," Veta gasped. "Just lost my breath."

"No wonder." There was a wet thwack as Olivia made sure the Kig-Yar was dead; then she pulled the body off and said, "That was pretty fancy."

"Not fancy," Veta said. "Clumsy."

Olivia smiled. "Glad you're the one who said so."

She pulled Veta to her feet; then they disabled the Kig-Yar weapons and stepped into the corridor.

Mark and Ash were already there, armed with sound-suppressed M7 submachine guns. The M7s had been disassembled and hidden inside the Havok casings with plenty of ammunition, and they were carrying spares for Veta and Olivia. A trio of Kig-Yar lay dead in the corridor, three bullet holes in each of their chests.

"Did you activate the slipbeacon?" Veta asked.

"Affirmative," Ash said. "The minute we came out of slipspace."

"Good job." Veta tucked her pocket pistol into its ankle holster, then took his spare M7. She used the barrel to gesture at the dead Kig-Yar. "How many have you taken out so far?"

"Five," Mark said. He passed an M7 to Olivia, but was careful to keep his eyes fixed on the corridor ahead. "Two when we left the cargo hold, and the three you see here."

"We dropped three in the sleeping compartment," Veta said. "So that's eight down, six to go."

"Nine down, five to go," Ash corrected. "Mark had to take one out last night, while I was switching out the ostanalus."

"And I'm just hearing about it *now*?"

"We were supposed to be guarding the Havoks," Mark said. "And you and 'Livi were gossiping with the boss hen."

"We were working her for rumors about the Tuwas," Olivia replied.

"Whatever." Mark's gaze remained fixed on Veta. "You were busy. What were we supposed to do, interrupt?"

"There wasn't much choice," Ash said. "Activating comms was too risky, and banging on your door later would have drawn attention."

"Okay, I see your point," Veta said. The *Stolen Faith*'s crew had been trying to keep an eye on their passengers, and there were surveillance cameras in the galley, cargo hold, and central access corridor.

Veta waved at the dead Kig-Yar on the floor. "Let's stow those bodies, then finish this. Olivia and I will take the flight deck. Mark and Ash, you secure the remaining crew."

"Affirmative." Ash handed Olivia a breaching charge, then said, "I'll activate TEAMCOM when Mark and I are clear."

They moved the Kig-Yar bodies from the corridor into the sleeping compartment; then Mark and Ash went aft while Veta and Olivia worked their way forward. There was no indication that Chur'R-Sarch realized her ostanalus attack had failed, but Veta kept her M7 cocked anyway. The *Stolen Faith* was a small transport with a small crew, so the overnight absence of a crewmember could easily have been noticed and put the entire vessel on alert.

After twenty meters, the corridor ended at a safety bulkhead with an airtight hatch. Olivia pressed her ear to the wall, then listened for a moment and put a hand on the operation lever. Veta stepped to the opposite side of the hatch and shouldered her SMG.

When Olivia raised the lever, a latch mechanism clunked inside the hatch and the hydraulic openers began to hiss. It took a second for the heavy portal to swing open far enough to reveal a crewman in the galley beyond.

The Kig-Yar was clearly not on alert. His plasma pistol was still holstered, and he was standing at a drink dispenser, filling a squeeze bulb and idly glancing toward the opening hatch. Veta put three silenced rounds into his chest, then stepped into the galley and confirmed there were no other crewmembers inside.

Olivia slipped through the hatch behind Veta and took the lead, advancing across the galley to the flight deck access ramp. Veta closed the hatch and followed, her head on a swivel as she watched the other entrances to the galley. Only when she joined Olivia on the access ramp did she remind herself that the Kig-Yar had deserved a quick death, that he had been part of the plan to murder her and her Ferret team in their sleep.

They crept to the top of the ramp, where the flight deck access hatch remained open. Through the forward canopy, Veta saw the banded curtain of an orange and blue gas giant, so close and huge that it filled her entire view. The iridescent spheres and mottled lumps of a dozen moons were swinging across the face of the planet, and one moon—a dusty yellow ball enveloped in the faint aura of an atmosphere—was ringed by the winking pinpoints of several vessels in orbit.

A charge of excitement shot through Veta's chest, the same kind of feeling she used to experience when she was getting ready to bring down a killer she had been hunting for weeks. The moon ahead could only be the secret base of the Keepers of the One Freedom—and if they were holding the Tuwas, this would be the place. She took a calming breath and reminded herself to be patient. Now that they had reached the flight deck, taking control of the *Stolen Faith* would be easy. But infiltrating the base . . . that could still be tricky.

Chur'R-Sarch and her copilot were at the front of the flight deck, sitting side by side down in a dropped-nose cockpit. The Chur'R was jabbering into her headset in an excited mixture of Sangheili and English. The copilot was keeping a close eye on the sensor displays, clutching the Y-shaped control yoke so hard the scales on her forearms were raised. Clearly, security at Salvation Base was tighter than they had expected.

Veta signaled Olivia to wait, then did her best to eavesdrop on Sarch's end of the conversation. From what she could understand, the Chur'R was demanding clearance to deliver ten divine Havoks to Dokab Castor, and the term *deliver* was making the human approach-control officer nervous.

". . . is harmless!" Sarch was rasping into her microphone. She screeched a few unrecognizable words, then added, "We come to sell, not use!"

She waited while Approach Control spoke.

"A givt, yes," Sarch replied. "But surely the dokab will be generous in gratitude."

Again, she waited as Approach Control spoke.

Sarch squawked in her Covenant tongue, demanding to know how long they would have to wait, then switched to English. "It shall be done."

She tore her headset off and threw it atop the control console, then squawked at her copilot. The scales on the copilot's arms relaxed, and she brought the *Stolen Faith* to a stop relative to the yellow moon. The pair began to jabber back and forth.

Veta listened in dismay, catching enough of the conversation to know they were debating the wisdom of waiting for a vigilance squad to board the *Stolen Faith*. Sarch was convinced the approach-control officer was scheming to steal the nukes and sell them to Castor himself. The copilot didn't disagree, but saw no possibility of surviving the security cordon if they attempted to reach Salvation Base without clearance. Their only choice was to wait for the boarding party and strike a deal that profited everyone.

"Thieves," the copilot hissed. "But thieves we must deal with."

Sarch clacked her fangs in frustration and replied in Sangheili. "It is so—and thieves do not deal when they can steal."

She unbuckled her crash harness and said something about arming their treasures. She stood and turned to climb out of the cockpit—then froze as Veta and Olivia stepped fully onto the flight deck.

Veta waved the muzzle of her SMG toward the orange-banded planet hanging outside the forward canopy.

"That doesn't look like Shamsa to me."

As soon as Veta spoke, the copilot glanced back and dropped a hand toward the hidden side of her seat. Whatever she was reaching for, it was a dumb move. Olivia put three rounds into the back of her shoulders, and the Kig-Yar slumped into her crash harness.

Sarch reacted more wisely. Moving slowly, she lifted her hands into plain view, then looked from her copilot's corpse to Olivia.

"Was that needed?" she asked in English.

"You tried to gas us, so yeah." Olivia pointed her weapon at Sarch's long head. "And I'm loaded with shredder rounds, so don't think I won't open fire because I'm worried about a hull breach."

"Gas? You are paranoid." Sarch fixed an eye on Veta. "Perhaps I should tell you we need to make stop before Shamsa, but that is no reason to—"

"You *really* don't want to insult my intelligence right now," Veta said. "Who do you think switched out the ostanalus canisters?"

Sarch's shoulders slumped. "The ostanalus was mistake, yes," she said. "But what did you expect? Shamsa is crawling with Banished. It is madness to go there."

"Maybe," Veta said. "But if I'd told you we actually *wanted* to go to Salvation Base, would you have taken the job?"

Sarch's mouth parted. "Salvation Base?" she repeated. "You con us?"

"Afraid so." Veta motioned again. "Now, step up here so we can talk about a new deal."

Sarch hesitated, then rocked her head from side to side. "Too early for new deals." She reached for the headset atop the control console. "Virst, I need to check my crew."

"You don't have a crew anymore," Olivia said. "And if you touch that headset, you're joining them."

"They are dead?" Sarch asked. *"All?"*

"There may be a couple of survivors," Veta said. "If so, they get the same deal you do—a ride home, providing they cooperate during interrogation."

Sarch bared her sharp teeth. "You are *ONI*? I am sorry

ostanalus did not work." She glanced toward her dead copilot; then her tone grew pragmatic. "And what if I not accept this new deal?"

"Then you won't need a ride home," Veta said. "Now, come along—step up here and face the wall."

"Am not liking your deal," Sarch said. "Perhaps I extend a better one."

"And perhaps I'll get tired of repeating myself." Veta motioned with the barrel of her M7. "*Now*, or I shoot."

"No need for threats." Sarch stepped between the seats, but paused to glance over at the copilot's holographic status display. "What you want? Access to Salvation Base?"

"I want you to stop stalling," Veta said. "And whatever you're thinking, forget—"

Sarch turned and dived for the copilot's controls.

Veta and Olivia opened fire, catching the Kig-Yar in the back with six rounds. The impact hurled her into the control yoke, and the *Stolen Faith* dropped its nose and shot forward. Even with the inertial cushion inherent in the vessel's artificial gravity, the unexpected acceleration threw both women against the rear bulkhead.

Ash's voice sounded in Veta's ear dot. "Uh, what's the situation up there?"

Olivia was already springing back toward the cockpit. "Under control!" She engaged her SMG's safety and dropped the weapon on the deck. "Just worry about your end, okay?"

"Affirmative," Ash said. "We're secure. Two more dead, no prisoners."

"That's all of them," Olivia said. She pulled Sarch's body aside, then reached over the dead copilot and eased the yoke back, and the *Stolen Faith* began to decelerate. "We got the other three."

Veta engaged the safety of her own weapon and tossed it onto the pilot's seat, then grabbed Sarch's corpse beneath the arms and dragged it to the rear of the flight deck. She had just started forward again when a tinny human voice began to squawk from the headset Sarch had tossed atop the control console.

Veta rushed to grab the headset, then wrapped her hand around the microphone and said, "That can't be good."

"It isn't," Olivia said. Holding the control yoke with one hand, she used the other to unbuckle the dead copilot. She tossed the Kig-Yar onto the flight deck almost effortlessly, then slipped into the vacant seat and studied the sensor displays. "We've got a Seraph and a Tronto headed this way fast—at least I *think* it's a Tronto. I'm only about ninety percent on the Sangheili alphabet."

"Ninety percent works." Veta slipped past Olivia, then moved her SMG aside and took the pilot's seat. "What's a Tronto?"

"Jiralhanae boarding craft," Mark said, speaking over TEAM-COM. "Heavily armored, no shields. Twin pulse lasers and quad plasma cannons."

Veta's stomach sank. The tactical plan provided two options for penetrating the base—either as "guests" aboard a Keeper vessel, or by capturing it and posing as the crew. If neither option appeared feasible, the backup plan was to stay hidden and reconnoiter until Blue Team arrived, then suit up and infiltrate by force. So far, all three versions of the plan seemed to be working just well enough to get them killed.

"Okay, waiting for the *Silent Joe* is no longer an option." Veta hoped she sounded steadier than she felt. "We're on our own until Blue Team catches up."

"No problem," Mark said. "I'm pretty sure we'll be leaving a trail of dead Keepers for them to follow."

This drew a round of grim chuckles, then Ash asked, "You want us in the plasma turret?"

"No," Veta said. "We're not going to fight our way out of this."

"Why not?" Mark asked. "We can take out the Seraph when the boarding party starts to transfer, then use a satchel charge to blow the Tronto from inside. If we time it right, we stand a decent chance of making the base in one piece."

Olivia shook her head, then mouthed, *Boys!*

Veta was too worried to laugh—and a bit too chagrined. Mark's suggestion was a desperate long shot at best, but at least he was focused on the objective. She, on the other hand, had started to drift into survival mode just because the plan was going awry. Clearly, her operational discipline was still not up to Spartan standards.

"I'll keep your suggestion in mind, Mark," Veta said. "But we're supposed to be *covert* operatives. Maybe we should try something more subtle than ship-to-ship combat."

"As long as we try it fast," Olivia said. "That Tronto is matching velocities, and the Seraph's weapons are powering up."

The voice coming from the headset began to grow more demanding.

"We're going to let them board," Veta said. "Mark, secure the Havoks. Ash, is there any ostanalus left?"

"It's *all* left," Ash said. "I had to store it somewhere. It's in a couple of acetylene bottles."

"Good," Veta said. "Rig a remote release."

"A detonator?"

"Anything that will get it into the ventilation system," Veta said. "Olivia, see if you can pinpoint our destination and feed it to the surveillance net. If we, uh, get delayed—"

"You mean killed," Mark said. "It's okay, Mom. You can say it."

"I'm a positive thinker," Veta said. She hated that nickname, especially since her Ferrets tended to use it when they thought she was being overprotective. "If we get *delayed*, I want to be sure our friends on the *Silent Joe* know which moon that base is on."

"And that would be Taram," Olivia said, twisting around so she spoke toward Sarch's body. Her voice would be picked up by the spy gnat Ash had landed on the Chur'R earlier, then automatically relayed via microburst as soon as the *Silent Joe* exited slipspace. "The Keeper name for it is the 'Redoubt of the Faithful.'"

"I thought it was Salvation Base," Mark said.

"That's just the name of the base," Olivia explained. "Salvation Base is *on* the Redoubt of the Faithful."

"Great," Ash said. "Let's hope 'Redoubt' is just a name."

"Doesn't matter. We have a plan." Mark turned to Veta. "Right, ma'am?"

"I will soon." Veta slipped the headset on and uncovered the microphone. "Approach Control, this is the *new* captain of the *Stolen Faith*. We'll stand by for boarding."

CHAPTER 7

The muted hum of a compressor pump arose from the *Stolen Faith*'s airlock, and Veta began to think her bluff might actually work. Had the Keepers of the One Freedom intended to kill them without an interrogation, the boarding party would be using a breaching charge rather than standard transfer protocol.

"Stay sharp, everyone," Mark said. He dumped the Kig-Yar body he was carrying onto a stack near one edge of the reception vestibule. "Remember, this could be a diversion."

"Who could forget?" Olivia asked. She was coming from the direction of the flight deck, carrying Sarch's corpse in both arms. Like Mark and Ash, she wore a yellow, poor-fitting pressure suit taken from the *Stolen Faith*'s emergency lockers. "You've warned us like five times already."

"Just four," Veta said. "But he's right. It's time to take our positions."

— 87 —

"You sure about this?" Ash asked. He took Sarch's corpse from Olivia and sat it on the floor, facing the airlock and leaning against the stack of bodies. "I don't like leaving you uncovered."

"It's bad tactics," Mark agreed. "I still think we'd be better off trying a counter-boarding."

"This is the plan." Veta extended a hand to Ash. "Give me the detonator and move out."

Ash dug a remote control out of a utility pocket on his thigh. "If you need to use this, make sure you have a clear path into the airlock. The bottles are behind the fan housings, so it won't take long for the ostanalus to circulate."

"If I need to use this, it won't matter how fast it circulates." Veta took the remote. "And no heroics on my account. If this goes wrong—"

"Stay focused on the mission," Mark finished. "This isn't our first operation, you know."

"I know," Veta said. "I'm counting on that."

Actually, she was beginning to have doubts about whether the Tuwa family could still be saved, so she *wanted* to tell her team that if something happened to her, they should forget the mission and concentrate on surviving until Blue Team arrived. But quitting was not in the Spartan nature. If Veta let herself get killed, the one thing she knew for certain was that her team would finish the operation or die trying.

So she couldn't let herself get killed.

The airlock compressor fell silent, and the status light above the hatch changed from yellow to blue. She stepped behind the stack of Kig-Yar corpses and made a shooing motion, then watched as her team retrieved their submachine guns and disappeared down three different corridors. Her plan called for them to make it seem like she had a crew of twenty aboard, and it was the one objective she felt confident of achieving.

The airlock hatch slid open to reveal a single Jiralhanae wearing blue armor with gold trim. So huge he had to stoop down to aim his spike rifle into the reception vestibule, he had tawny fur with a tightly-bound beard hanging to the center of his breastplate. His gaze went straight to the stack of Kig-Yar bodies.

"It's okay," Veta said. "I can explain."

The Jiralhanae's eyes widened, and he brought his spike rifle up.

"Careful." Veta waggled the remote detonator in her hand. "You wouldn't want to set anything off."

The Jiralhanae studied the detonator, then spoke through a translation disc secured high on his breastplate. "It is linked to the Havoks?"

Veta smiled. "And they say Brutes aren't smart." Of course, the detonator was actually linked to the acetylene bottles Ash had filled with ostanalus—but her bluff wouldn't work if she admitted that. "Make me angry, and we all go out together."

The Jiralhanae curled a lip. "It matters not, as long as I die on the True Path." Keeping his weapon trained on Veta, he pushed his head forward and peered around the edges of the hatchway. "Where is your crew?"

"You don't need to know that."

"I ask only once more," the Jiralhanae said. "Where is your crew?"

"Not here." Veta touched her thumb to the activation button. "I'm pretty sure following the True Path involves following orders, and I *know* your orders don't involve getting your entire boarding force atomized."

The Jiralhanae glared for a moment, then squeezed through

the hatchway and growled a lengthy command into his helmet comm. His Covenant dialect was not as atrociously accented as that of the Kig-Yar, so she had no trouble recognizing his words: *Come quickly and conquer.*

A second warrior emerged from the Tronto and passed through the airlock into the reception vestibule, followed by a third and a fourth. There were probably more waiting to board, but it was impossible to see past the first four. Their armored bulk filled the vestibule from wall to wall, and they were so tall that they had to lean down, tilting their heads to keep from hitting the ceiling.

Veta was not surprised when the first warrior began to issue search orders. Jiralhanae were fierce fighters who measured their status by their combat prowess, and it was customary for minor chieftains to lead their bands from the front.

Once the chieftain stopped snarling commands, Veta said, "I wouldn't do that."

"I care nothing for what you would do." He dispatched his underlings with a wave, sending one down each of the three corridors that led out of the vestibule, then looked back to Veta. "If you will not reveal your crew's location, we will find them—"

The last underling gave a surprised rumble as he entered an aft-running corridor. He started to bring his spike rifle up; then a silenced SMG coughed twice, and the warrior toppled back into the vestibule and crashed down on the deck.

Veta leaned over the stack of Kig-Yar corpses and peered down at the motionless warrior. He was clearly dead, with both eyes shot out.

"I tried to warn you," Veta said. She was keeping a wary eye on the chieftain's hands, ready to dive for cover at the first twitch of a trigger finger. "But go ahead and search. We can talk when you run out of warriors."

Another Jiralhanae leaned through the hatchway and aimed his spiker down the corridor, then requested the honor of tracking down and killing the infidel ambusher. The chieftain motioned for him to wait, then spoke into his helmet comm again, demanding a situation report from the other two warriors he had sent off to search. The growing alarm in his eyes suggested he was not receiving a reply.

"Or we could work out things now and avoid any more bloodshed," Veta said. She gestured at the stack of Kig-Yar corpses. "Chur'R-Sarch caused this mess when she tried to kill us and steal our Havoks."

"That makes no difference," the chieftain said. "You will not be permitted to leave this system alive."

"I don't even know where this system is," Veta said. "You take your friends' bodies, we'll take the ship, and the Banished won't show up looking for their cargo. Everybody lives."

"The Banished?" The chieftain's gaze shifted away; then he said, "It matters not. The Isbanola sector is vast. They will never find—"

"Yeah, they will," Veta said. "They'll follow the slipbeacon."

"You make empty threats," the chieftain said. "We detected no slipspace transmissions."

"Because it was encrypted and tight-beamed," Veta said. "Our buyers wanted a way to recover the Havoks if our delivery plans took a bad turn. Go figure."

The chieftain growled into his helmet comm, repeating her claim and asking about its technical feasibility, and Veta began to think her bluff might be working a little *too* well. If she actually convinced the Jiralhanae to let her leave, she and the Ferrets would need to make a slipspace jump out of the system, then try to return as the *Silent Joe* arrived—and the timing of that would be tricky, to say the least.

"Look, we don't have all day to wait for your confirmation," Veta said. "If I don't make the rendezvous on time, a Banished fleet shows up *here* looking for ten Havoks. Nobody wants that."

The chieftain's eyes remained distant as he listened to a voice inside his helmet; then he finally looked back to Veta.

"This decision is not for me," he said. "Someone who knows your science will inspect your devices; then we will take you to the Redoubt of the Faithful and advise our dokab whether to believe your story."

Veta shook her head, feigning reluctance. "I don't think so. Once we're on that moon, we have no control—"

"The choice is not yours." The chieftain extended his arm, holding his spiker so close to Veta's face that she could have scratched her chin on its bayonet blades. "You will tell your tale to the dokab."

Veta stared down the weapon's red barrels for a moment, trying to appear defiant. Jiralhanae were cunning tacticians. If the Ferrets were going to have any chance of finding the Tuwas, she could not let the chieftain see how eager she was to accept his demand.

After a few seconds, she sighed heavily and nodded. "Okay." She lowered the remote toward her pocket. "But I'm keeping the det—"

"You cannot land on the Redoubt of the Faithful with ten Havoks under your thumb." The chieftain pressed the spiker bayonets against her throat. "Hand over the device."

Veta tipped her head back and, seeing nothing but resolve in the Jiralhanae's face, decided she appeared reluctant enough.

"Well, since you're asking nicely . . ." She moved her thumb to the side of the remote and hit the disengage switch, transferring control to a miniaturized remote hidden in Ash's lowest shirt button. "But no tricks. My crew can still—"

"There will be no tricks," the chieftain said. "Your fate will be decided on the Redoubt of the Faithful."

"Fine." Veta slapped the remote into the chieftain's hand. "But your dokab had better listen to reason, or we're *all* going to wish I'd used that thing."

Veta retreated to the galley and feigned resignation as the Keepers took control of the vessel.

The boarding party was smaller than she had expected, consisting of only the chieftain and eleven others—including half a dozen humans in dirty body armor that looked like it had already taken a few rounds over specifications, and a pair of Kig-Yar who took great pride in leading the effort to sniff out the rest of her crew.

It didn't take long. Once the *Stolen Faith* began to accelerate toward Taram, Veta coughed twice into the TEAMCOM microphone hidden in her shirt collar. Over the next few minutes, the members of her team were herded into the galley, unarmed and no longer wearing their pressure suits. Mark was smirking—but only until Veta flashed him a warning scowl. Her plan depended on giving the Keepers a false sense of security, and that would not happen if her Gammas looked smug.

After a time, a young human woman with a shag haircut entered the galley. She was armored more lightly than most of the boarding party, wearing only torso and groin protection over a blue jumpsuit. She paused at the chieftain's side to report that the Havoks were secure, then took a seat at the table where Veta and her team were being held.

"You lied." The woman paused, her eyes flicking from Veta to the rest of the Ferret team as she looked for a reaction. Then she said, "There are only nine Havoks back there."

"If you know that," Veta said, "then you found the slipbeacon."

"I did." The woman did not offer her name, so Veta took a cue from her haircut and thought of her as Shag. "That was top-notch work, by the way. The power supply looked so much like an interstage that I nearly didn't bother to look behind it."

Veta shrugged. "I have a talented crew." She paused, then asked, "Since you know I'm not bluffing, why don't we fix this mess now? The sooner I deliver, the less likely my customers are to show up looking for their nukes."

"You know it's not that simple."

"It seems pretty simple to me," Mark said. "Let us go, or get hammered by the Banished."

"And if we let you go, who shows up then?" Shag asked.

"No one," Ash said. "Why should they?"

Shag flashed a knowing smile. "Isn't it obvious?"

"Not to me." Veta was starting to think the slipbeacon had been concealed a little *too* well. It required a special brand of expertise to disguise a sophisticated technological device as something else, and anyone with the skill to recognize a bogus interstage was probably smart enough to realize the replacement could have been created by ONI technicians. "Why don't you enlighten me?"

"Well, you know the saying," Shag said. "There's no honor among thieves."

"You think we'd sell you out?" Olivia demanded.

"The thought had crossed my mind."

"That's not fair," Ash said. "We're the ones who got double-crossed."

"After you stole a shipment of Havoks."

"Okay, there's that," Ash replied. "But that's no reason to call us—"

"You're selling thermonuclear weapons," Shag said. "To the Banished."

"So what's that to you?" Mark asked. "It's not like the Keepers and the Banished are at war . . . yet."

Shag's expression turned to disdain. "And you wonder why no one trusts a pirate."

Mark furrowed his brow. "What's that supposed to mean?"

"She's talking about outcomes, vapebrain," Olivia said. "She doesn't like how the nukes will be used."

"You're the smart one here, I see," Shag said. "It's too bad you're not in charge. We might have struck a deal that wouldn't weigh so heavily on your collective conscience."

"Since when do Keepers care about conscience?" Veta asked. "Every Keeper I've met was a murdering zealot."

"We are warriors of the Great Journey."

Shag's sharp tone indicated that she was one of the few humans who had joined the Keepers because she actually believed in the Great Journey, a doctrine of divine destruction that sought to find a long-lost Forerunner weapon called Halo. Once activated, the weapon would cleanse the galaxy of all life, freeing the faithful of their mundane existence so they could join the Forerunners in a higher plane of existence. The doctrine sounded like a death pact gone supernova, but there was no use saying that to Shag. Arguing theology with a True Believer was worse than counterproductive—it made one the enemy.

When Veta did not respond to her declaration, Shag finally filled the silence. "Everything we do is for the transcendence of the worthy."

"Which makes it okay to let *you* have the Havoks instead." Veta couldn't figure out the woman's angle, whether she was trying to recruit them or just couldn't stop herself from spouting dogma. "Because the Keepers will only use them on infidels."

"We're more discriminating than that," Shag said. "Actually, I was thinking the Havoks might be a way to solve our mutual problem—and for you to redeem yourselves."

"Redeem ourselves?" Olivia asked. "Like on a suicide mission or something?"

"If only you could be trusted," Shag said. "But nothing so dramatic. Just give me the arming codes. We'll take care of the rest."

"And what do we get out of it?" Veta was relieved not to hear the woman mention the nukes' tritium booster cylinders. The ones in the warheads were fakes—a precaution to prevent the weapons from falling into the wrong hands—and the real ones were aboard the *Silent Joe* with Blue Team. "The *Stolen Faith* and safe passage out of the system?"

"Nice try," Shag replied. "But even if I could sell it to the dokab, I've made my feelings clear about letting you loose knowing the location of Salvation Base."

"So what's your offer?" Mark asked.

"Your lives." Shag ran her gaze around the table, then flashed Mark a tight smile. "Unless I decide you're ONI, of course. If you're ONI, Castor is just going to rip the codes right out of you with his bare hands."

CHAPTER 8

The gravity on Taram felt surprisingly strong for a moon—perhaps 90 percent standard, though Veta was not enough of a world-hopper to be confident in her estimate. An industrial hum droned somewhere off to her left, and even through the fabric of her black hood, the spaceport air smelled faintly of oil and solvent.

Shag—the Keeper weapons technician—grabbed Veta's elbow and steered her onto the *Stolen Faith*'s boarding ramp. "Let's go."

Veta's foot dropped farther than expected. With her eyes covered and her hands zip-cuffed behind her back, she lost her balance and fell to a knee.

"Look, I *gave* you the arming codes," Veta said. Surrendering the codes had been an easy decision, since it preserved her team's cover and the Havoks couldn't be detonated without the real tritium cylinders anyway. "You saw the status indicators turn green. Do we really need hoods and restraints?"

"For now," Shag said. She pulled Veta back to her feet. "We still have security concerns."

Veta refused to continue down the ramp. "I thought we had a deal."

"The deal was for your lives," the chieftain said. Veta heard him behind her, at the top of the boarding ramp with the rest of her team. "You are alive."

"Move it." Shag started Veta down the ramp again, then added quietly, "Don't give him an excuse. He's still boiling mad about all the Faithbringers he lost during the boarding action."

"I don't think I'm worried," Veta said. She turned her head to be sure her voice was audible behind her. "He's kind of an idiot."

"I will ask Dokab Castor for the honor of guarding your cells," the chieftain retorted. "My pack will use you to play tossers."

Before Veta could reply, a boot scuffed the top of the boarding ramp, and a foot came down hard.

"Sorry, Neema," Ash said, addressing Olivia by her cover name. "Couldn't see."

"No problem, Chikey," Olivia cooed. She sounded so close to Ash she could have been standing in his boots—probably because she was feeling for the remote detonator in his shirt. With his hands zip-cuffed behind his back, there was no way he could reach it himself, and the Ferrets needed to blow the ostanalus canisters the moment they cleared the *Stolen Faith*. "I've got you."

"Save it for later, will you?" Mark was just locating himself for the rest of the team, letting them know he was a couple of steps behind Ash and ready for action. "Nobody needs to hear you two flirt."

Veta descended another step, then she heard a muffled *crump* deep inside the *Stolen Faith*. The canisters had been blown.

She turned square toward Shag and drove hard, and they both

toppled over the side of the ramp. It was a long way down, made worse by the fact that she couldn't see anything. Veta landed atop Shag's shoulder, then felt a crunching pain in her chest.

Shag cried out and tried to roll free, but Veta was already slipping her knees into a restraining straddle. She slammed her brow down in a head-butt and struck something flat—a temple, she thought—and the cry became a groan. Veta brought her head down repeatedly, striking with the upper part of forehead so she wouldn't injure herself, and stopped only when her target softened and her hood grew heavy with blood.

By the sound of it, the rest of her team was bringing the fight to a close. A spiker sizzled and a big body landed with a hollow *boom*; then a strangled growl ended in a wet *thwack*. Veta rolled off Shag and pressed her head to the ground, then began to worm backward in an effort to drag off her hood.

A hand grabbed her by the elbow and pulled her to her feet.

"I hope this blood isn't yours," Olivia said.

"Me too," Veta said, only half-unhooded. "Are we secure?"

"Of course." Olivia slipped a blade between Veta's still-bound wrists and began to cut the zip cuffs. "There were only five of them, and it looks like we landed in a quiet area. Nobody close, and nobody paying attention to us."

"What about the rest of the boarding party?"

"No signs they're attempting to evacuate," Olivia said. "I think the ostanalus got them."

"Probably, but keep an eye out."

The zip cuffs separated, and Veta pulled her hood the rest of the way off. She did a quick survey of the surrounding area and saw no immediate trouble—in fact, the *Stolen Faith* seemed to be sitting off by itself—but a more thorough assessment would have to wait until the landing zone had been secured. She was standing beneath the vessel's chin, on a translucent green pavement that seemed equal parts glass and light. Shag lay to the right, her temple smashed and one eye dangling from its socket.

Veta would probably get a knot on her own head soon, but would be fine otherwise. If there was one thing ONI combat instructors taught their undercover operatives, it was how to win a fight without injuring oneself. But the nightmares that were bound to come later—well, it was better to be alive and dealing with them than to be dead and resting in peace.

To the left, a pair of Kig-Yar guards were sprawled next to the ramp, their necks folded sideways around a crimp the size of a boot heel.

A dead Jiralhanae was half-visible in the mouth of the *Stolen Faith*'s cargo hold, his enormous bi-clawed feet hanging out over the boarding ramp. The chieftain lay beneath the *Stolen Faith*'s belly, a mound of flesh the size of a Mongoose ATV. He had been opened from hip to armpit, and Ash was standing over him with a gory spike rifle. Mark was kneeling on the far side, going through the cargo pouches on the chieftain's belt.

The wrists of both Gammas showed welts from snapping their zip cuffs. As much as Veta hated what the SPARTAN-III program had done to them, she had to admit their physical enhancements could come in handy. As long as the smoothers were working and their brain chemistry was in balance, it was kind of reassuring to know that the more stressful the fight, the faster, stronger, and more ferocious they would become.

As long as the smoothers were *working*. She had seen on Gao how precarious a Gamma's hold on reality could be when he ran out of meds, and issuing orders to a Spartan-III in the throes of a psychotic break was not a task she cared to undertake. It had been tricky enough for Fred-104, who'd had the armor and size of a Spartan-II to put behind his commands. Veta preferred to rely on prevention, which was why she insisted that her team be given the longer-lasting, subcutaneous inserts—even if they did require a minor operation each time they needed to be changed out.

Veta gestured at the dead Keepers. "Let's secure those bodies and close up the ship."

"Strip the weapons first," Mark said. He removed a Jiralhanae-size pistol from the chieftain's equipment belt. Known informally as a mauler, the revolver had a ferocious-looking blade beneath the trigger housing and was loaded with superheated bolts that fragmented like buckshot when fired. Mark spun the cylinder to make sure it was carrying a full load of five bolts, then looked up and finally seemed to realize he sounded like he was the one giving orders. "Just a suggestion, of course . . . but we're going to need weapons."

Veta glanced at the collection of corpses lying beneath the *Stolen Faith*. "You three *are* weapons," she said. "But point taken. I'll search. Ash will keep watch. You and 'Livi stow the bodies."

The Gammas responded simultaneously. "Affirmative."

"And stay out of the cargo hold," Veta added. "No taking chances with the ostanalus."

The trio exchanged looks of exasperation, and Olivia said, "Yeah, Mom. We kind of figured."

Olivia and Mark each took one of the chieftain's arms and dragged him out of a pool of purplish blood. Anyone coming near the *Stolen Faith* would undoubtedly notice the carnage and the streaks leading toward the boarding ramp, but removing the bodies would at least reduce the likelihood of the bloodshed being noticed from a distance. Veta searched the rest of the dead, collecting not only an assortment of small arms, but Shag's datapad, several chronometers, and three Keeper comm headsets. The process took only a minute, but Mark and Olivia were tossing the last Kig-Yar onto the ramp even as she removed his chest holster and plasma pistol.

Olivia pressed a control pad on the hull, and the boarding ramp's servomotors began to whine and growl beneath the extra load. Veta feared she'd have to send someone to carry the bodies into the hold; then Mark stepped to the end of the ramp and began to lift. The servomotors settled into a purr, and the ramp rose so rapidly that Olivia had to dodge back and forth beneath it, jumping up to push arms and legs back into place as the corpses slid into the cargo hold.

Finally, the ramp thumped shut.

Veta exhaled in relief, then distributed the weapons and knelt with Ash behind the *Stolen Faith*'s nose strut. The spaceport sat in the bottom of what appeared to be a huge, sheer-walled crater. The expanse of green pavement stretched more than a kilometer to a ring of yellow cliffs that encircled the entire facility. Overhead, there was no sign of an energy barrier or any other atmospheric containment device, only a mauve radiance cast by the swirling gas bands of the planet Pydoryn.

The *Stolen Faith* had landed in a quiet area to one side of the spaceport, close enough to the cliff that Veta could see its vitreous surface was permeated by tiers of artificial grottoes. Half a kilometer to her left sat a fleet of light attack vessels, scattered in front of a provisioning station. To the right, the cliff wall was only seventy meters away, with a single unmarked REAP-X "Turaco" standing on three struts in front of it.

Veta was relieved to see that the Turaco's boarding ramp was raised and its dorsal cannon turret pointed at its own tail, but she didn't know what to make of its presence. With a bulbous flight deck and an ovoid body tapering to tail packed with long-range sensor packages, Turacos were a new style of experimental reconnaissance boat that the UNSC had begun testing only a couple of months before. Like most other vessels developed by ONI's Reverse Engineering and Prototyping-Xenotechnology department, REAP-X Turacos were top-secret test craft with a production run measured in the dozens, so it was hard to believe the Keepers had already captured one.

Veta turned to Ash. "Threat assessment?"

"Still nothing immediate."

"Good," Veta said. "Any attention from that Turaco?"

"Negative. It looks buttoned up." Ash gestured to the left, toward the fleet of attack vessels a half kilometer away. "I'd say that provisioning apron is our most likely source of a chance discovery."

The apron was bustling with service carts and maintenance crews, but the workers appeared so focused on their tasks—and on avoiding accidents—that no one seemed to be looking the *Stolen Faith*'s direction. Veta estimated about fifty vessels ranging in size from gunboats to corvettes, and it appeared obvious that the little fleet was being prepared for launch.

"Seems like the Keepers bought your story about the Banished coming," Mark said, coming up beside Veta. "Nice bluff."

"Except for one thing," Olivia said, also joining them. "Their dokab thinks we're captured pirates, and he's expecting Shag to bring us to him real soon."

"And when we don't show up," Ash said, "it'll take him about two minutes to guess our mission."

"Affirmative." Mark checked the battery pack in the plasma pistol Veta had taken off one of the Kig-Yar, then said, "We're going to need more firepower—a lot more."

"Slow down," Veta said. "First, we need a plan."

Mark frowned. "We don't have time to start planning," he said. "I say we find the Tuwas, grab them, and get out before the Keepers have a chance to react. Our plans have a way of going sideways lately."

"Maybe," Veta admitted. "But sideways is better than backwards—or dead."

She checked the datapad she had recovered from Shag and saw that the time was only 1447. The *Stolen Faith* had emerged from slipspace around 0800, which was when the slipbeacon would have transmitted its tracking signal, and Blue Team's jump from Venezia would take about twelve hours total.

"The *Silent Joe* won't arrive for another five hours," Veta said. "Which means we can't expect Blue Team support until 2015—at the earliest."

"So?" Mark asked.

"So that's a long time to hold out against overwhelming odds," Veta said. Assuming the Tuwas were actually *on* Taram, Veta had no doubts about recovering them—her Gammas were just that good. But getting everyone off the moon alive was another matter. "We're going to need to delay, evade, or escape. Maybe all three—and *that* takes planning."

"Don't forget divert," Mark added. "If we can make the Keepers think they're already under attack, that will buy us some time."

"What it'll buy us is mission failure," Olivia said. "We can't spend five hours blowing things up. We'd never last that long—not in civvies."

"Come on, Mark," Ash said. "You know that."

Mark sighed. "Yeah, I guess so," he said. "It's just that I miss the armor, you know?"

"Who doesn't?" Olivia said. "But remember what Chief Mendez always said—"

"Armor's no substitute for brains," Mark finished. "Yeah, I remember."

"Smart guy, that Mendez." Veta thought for a moment, assessing their options, then said, "Okay, our first job is to locate the Tuwas—and it would be good to do that before the Keepers realize we've escaped."

"Over there," Mark said, pointing to the right. "But we'll have to be careful. There'll be guards."

At first, Veta thought Mark was indicating the Turaco, but then she saw that he was pointing past the vessel's nose, at the artificial grottoes in the cliff face. All of the openings were narrow and arciform, but they varied in height from around two meters to as much as four, and many were tilted on their axis in a pattern that seemed distinctly repetitive. She could see nothing but darkness beyond the openings—certainly no reason to believe that they would find either the Tuwas or guards inside any of them.

"Why there?" Veta asked.

"Because if the Tuwas are here, they're probably being held in a detention center," Mark said. "And prisoner transports berth near the detention center."

Veta nodded. "Makes sense." There was no need to ask what Mark meant by *prisoner transport*—the chieftain had made it pretty clear that he considered Veta and her team captives. "Good thinking."

"Second that," Olivia said. "You can be pretty smart when you're not trying to start a firefight."

"Firefights take brains too."

"All the same, let's keep a low profile until Blue Team arrives." Veta took a moment to look around and make sure there were no threats developing on their perimeter, then said, "Five hours, guys. I need some ideas."

The Ferrets rattled off a dozen good suggestions, and two minutes later they had a solid plan. Veta wasn't sure it would work, but there was a chance—and the one thing she knew about her Gammas was that when they were given a chance, they put it to good use.

"Okay, reactivate TEAMCOM," Veta said.

The reception dot in her ear popped live, and she heard a trio of click patterns confirming the rest of the team's comm units went active as well. The Gammas removed the various rings, studs, and bolts still decorating their faces and passed them to Ash, along with Olivia's knife and one of the comm headsets Veta had recovered from the Keeper corpses. She gave the second headset to Olivia and donned the last one herself. The earpiece covered the same ear containing her reception dot, so at times she would be listening to two comm nets at once. It wouldn't be a problem. Like most good detectives, she had developed a knack for eavesdropping on several conversations at once.

Veta exchanged the M6 pistol she had recovered from Shag for the mauler that Mark had taken off the chieftain, then asked, "Everybody clear on their assignments?"

The three Gammas confirmed in unison.

"Then let's do this," she said. "And be careful. I don't want anyone taking unnecessary—"

"Mom," they said *nearly* in unison.

Ash opened a small cut on his forearm and set off alone toward the back of the spaceport, laying a false trail they hoped would lead any searchers in the wrong direction. With a headset clipped over his ear and a spiker resting casually over his shoulder, he looked like a human Keeper on an errand, and Veta did not think he was likely to attract any undue scrutiny from a distance.

Olivia returned to the control panel next to the *Stolen Faith*'s boarding ramp and began to enter a string of commands that would allow her to rewrite the ship's security routines—and seal it tight. At least in theory. During her Ferret training, Olivia had been taught everything ONI knew about hacking Covenant computers—a necessary precaution, since the Ferrets' role as undercover operatives would often make it dangerous to carry a team AI around. But this would be the first time she had tested her skills in the field, and there was no telling what kind of modifications a Kig-Yar crew might have made to a Sangheili starsloop.

Mark tucked his knife and pistol into his belt at the small of his back. He crossed his wrists as though they were still bound, then set off toward the cliff on a vector that would take them close to the Turaco.

Veta pointed the mauler at his back and followed a few steps behind, as though she were escorting him to the detention center. She had her doubts about whether they would be able to bluff their way past the entry guards, but it was worth a try.

As they passed behind the Turaco, the steady tick of a cooling hull grew audible, and Veta could feel heat radiating off the thrust nozzles.

"Recent arrival," she noted. "The detention center intake could be crowded."

"Which means the guards will be busy with someone else," Mark said over his shoulder. "That's always good."

"But having to drop extra targets isn't," Veta said. "We need to do this quietly, remember?"

"No worries," Mark said. "It'll be quiet. A Turaco only carries eight people."

As soon as they were past the Turaco, Mark began to angle toward an opening to their left. Veta saw nothing special to suggest it was the entrance to the detention center. It was about three meters high, and, like all of the grottoes ringing the spaceport, it had the shape of a narrow arch. There was no hint of light spilling into the interior, as though its mouth were covered by a dark curtain—or an opaque barrier field.

Veta was about to ask about the direction change when she noticed that Mark's head was tipped slightly forward. She looked down and realized he was tracking the occupants of the Turaco, following a barely perceptible trail that seemed little more than a dark ripple a few centimeters beneath the spaceport's green pavement. She glanced behind her and saw that their own footsteps were creating a similar effect, leaving pale ripples of shadow wherever they trod.

"Good eye, Mark," she said. "Have you run across this kind of surface before?"

"Not this stuff exactly," Mark said. "But hard light is pretty versatile. The Forerunners used it in a lot of different ways."

"Forerunners?" Veta's stomach sank—the last time she had set foot in a Forerunner ruin, she had become involved in three-way battle for possession of an ancient AI and ended up having to flee her homeworld. "Please don't tell me this was a Forerunner base."

"Maybe not a base," Ash said over TEAMCOM. "But it was a Forerunner *something.* The Keepers don't have hard light technology—and there's no way they built their own vacuum energy extractor."

"They have an extractor?" Veta did not know quantum theory well enough to understand the fundamental nature of vacuum energy—it had something to do with virtual particles blinking in and out of existence—but she *did* know that vacuum energy permeated the entire universe, and that the Forerunners had harnessed it to create a nearly infinite power source. "Are you sure?"

"Sure enough," Mark said. "It takes a lot of artificial gravity to hold an atmosphere over an area this size, and I don't see any other power sources big enough for the job. Do you?"

"No." Veta was not about to press the point. Mark and the rest of her Gammas had fought inside three Forerunner installations that she *knew* of, so they were certainly the experts on the team. "How much will this complicate our mission?"

Mark shrugged. "Not enough to stop us."

They were only a dozen paces from the mouth of the grotto, so Veta fell silent and tried to convince herself that Mark's nonchalance was warranted. After all, the Keepers still worshipped Forerunners as their deities, and the Forerunners had once inhabited the Shaps system. Finding Keepers operating from a Forerunner ruin on Taram was probably no more surprising than finding a band of human pirates operating from the ruins of one of Saturn's lost moon colonies.

The air grew humid and began to smell of algae, and the sound of lapping water rose behind her. Veta glanced back to discover that the unmarked Turaco and the *Stolen Faith* now stood in a vast blue-green lake. Waves were breaking around the vessels' struts and splashing up on their bellies, but the craft appeared steady and in no danger of sinking. Across the way, on the provisioning apron, the Keepers' fleet of light attack vessels was barely visible, a distant flock of cockpit canopies and weapons turrets sitting just above the wave crests.

But the surface beneath Veta's feet seemed as solid as ever. She dropped her gaze and found herself standing on water, perhaps half a meter above a pebbly lake bottom. Her boots began to darken with dampness, and her socks began to feel wet.

Mark was already stepping into the grotto, so there was no time to remark on the lake's sudden appearance. But Veta's ONI training had included a survey of human encounters with Forerunner technology, and she knew their extradimensional engineering capabilities could make reality seem all too fluid.

Mark vanished into the darkness as though he had passed through a curtain, and Veta felt her gut clench. The ONI course had described unfathomable perils—stasis pods that suspended occupants in time, slipspace bubbles that concealed whole worlds inside melon-size spheres—so she had good reason to be nervous.

"Entering now," Veta said over TEAMCOM. "The portal is covered by some sort of blackout field, so we may lose contact."

A pair of acknowledging tongue clicks sounded over her ear dot—but only two. She tightened her grip on the mauler and followed Mark through the blackout field into a large vestibule with walls of glassy yellow stone. Illuminated by a bright amber light with no clear source, the chamber had high, graceful lines and sharp angles that hinted of inconceivable wonders around every corner, and as she continued to look around, she began to experience a growing sense of calmness and belonging.

Mark stood to her left, one hand tucked behind his back to grasp the hilt of the combat knife tucked into his belt. Directly ahead, a utilitarian reception counter stood between two narrow staircases that spiraled down from opposite directions. Behind the counter, a set of metal weapons lockers stood in the mouth of a high, triangular corridor leading deeper into the grotto.

There were no guards in sight. In fact, there was no sign of anyone at all.

Mark signaled Veta to clear the staircase on the right, then drew his combat knife and began to creep up the one on the left. As usual, he moved with the swiftness and silence of a ghost. Veta ascended along the inner curve of her staircase, moving more slowly but just as quietly. It seemed strange for a Forerunner installation to utilize stairs rather than an antigravity lift, but there was an aura of tranquility about the place that made her suspect it had not been built for pragmatic purposes, that it had been some kind spiritual retreat. And with a five-meter ceiling and a rise of forty centimeters between each step, the staircase was certainly Forerunner scale.

Veta had ascended a dozen steps when Mark's whisper sounded in her ear. "Clear to the next floor."

Veta leaned around the curve of the wall and saw nothing but empty stairs ascending past an archway opening onto the next level. She sprang up the last few steps as quietly as she could, then dropped to her belly and peered down a long, curving corridor. The right side was lined by a row of shimmering energy barriers, each covering the entrance to what Veta assumed to be a detention cell. On the wall next to each barrier hung a power conduit and generator pod. She saw no sign of guards or the Turaco crew.

"Clear on this side too." Veta began to crawl back down the stairs and felt dampness beneath her palm. She ran her hand over the step below and found more. "But someone came this way recently."

"What do you have?"

Veta hesitated. "Did you see the lake?"

"Hard to miss," Mark said. "My feet are wet."

"So were somebody else's," Veta whispered. "Most likely the Turaco crew's, unless the guards stepped out to meet them."

"Any sign of the guards?"

"Unclear," Veta said. "All I have is damp stone."

"Understood." Mark paused, then said, "This doesn't make sense. There should always be a guard at the intake counter."

"You'd think." Veta returned to her feet and began to descend back down to the reception vestibule. The last thing she wanted to do was get trapped upstairs by a returning guard. "We'd better locate them before we go on."

"Affirmative," Mark said.

Veta listened for an acknowledging click from Ash or Olivia but heard none—which suggested the energy field across the entrance was blocking their TEAMCOM transmissions.

Just another joy of operating within a Forerunner installation.

As Veta descended into the vestibule, a liquid murmur sounded beyond the entrance, and she glanced outside to see that the lake had quieted considerably. The waves that had been lapping against the cliff face a few minutes earlier had calmed to mere ripples. The water beneath the unmarked Turaco was now so still it reflected the vessel's belly, and as she gazed out on it, she began to feel her mind expanding out across it, stretching toward the infinite.

Veta drew her attention back to the lake, focused on her team. Olivia and Ash were nowhere in sight. Ash had probably passed from view already, but Olivia should have been standing beneath the Turaco by now. The new plan called for her to hack its security systems and take control of the craft, then hold possession until the Tuwas were recovered and the rest of the team joined her. Once everyone was aboard, they would move to a secure location somewhere in the Pydoryn planetary system and remain hidden until the *Silent Joe* arrived with Blue Team.

But Mark was right—their plans kept damn well going sideways. Veta studied the struts beneath the Turaco and the *Stolen*

Faith, looking in vain for movement or a hint of human silhouette, then finally had to accept that Olivia could not be seen.

Veta was about to slip outside and attempt comm contact when a gentle *clang* sounded behind the intake counter. She spun around to find Mark standing in front of an open weapons locker, his combat knife in one hand and a buckled door in the other.

"Too loud, I know," he whispered. "But I'm telling you, we need more firepower."

He sheathed his knife and reached into the locker with both hands, then removed a pair of BR85 battle rifles. Both weapons were equipped with sound dampeners and Sentinel sights.

"I'm starting to agree," Veta said. She braced a hand on the intake counter and vaulted over, nearly slipping on a patch of damp stone. "I didn't see 'Livi out there."

Mark's head snapped around. "Something happened to her?"

"That's not what I said." Veta unloaded the mauler and set it in the bottom of the weapons locker. "But she should be at the Turaco by now, and I didn't see her."

Mark handed her a battle rifle. "Doesn't mean she's not there."

"Mark, she's wearing black ralex, not SPI." Veta loaded the BR85, then began to fill her pockets with spare magazines. "If she was out there, I'd have seen her."

"And we're out of communication," Mark said.

"It's more than that," Veta said. "Mark, does this place make you feel kind of . . . tranquil?"

"Affirmative," he said. "And I don't trust it. It could put us off our guard."

"Right," Veta said. "I'll try to stay nervous."

Mark closed the weapons locker. "Good idea," he said. "But not about 'Livi. She might be out of communication, but you've got to trust her—you've got to trust all of us."

"I do," Veta said. It wasn't her team she didn't trust—it was her own lack of experience. "But that doesn't mean I don't worry."

"Would it help, Mom, if I told you to stop?"

"Not in the slightest." Veta dropped to her haunches, then turned her head sideways and looked along the floor. A trail of dampness ran down the corridor leading out of the intake area. "You notice this water?"

Mark's eyes widened. He motioned Veta to follow, then advanced along the corridor wall and into a nearby chamber so vast it almost seemed they had passed outside.

Overhead, an emerald dome speckled with blue stars soared higher than they could see. Below, stone terraces descended in concentric rings toward a pit so deep and bottomless it seemed to swallow light itself.

"What the hell is this place?" Veta whispered.

"Weird," Mark said. He dropped onto the next terrace and placed his face next to the stone. "And I don't think this is water."

Veta turned in the direction he was looking and, ten meters to the left, saw a line of dark droplets running over the terrace edge. She joined him and saw three fan-shaped blood-spray patterns on the next level down, then finally understood why there was nobody at the intake counter.

"The guards were executed," Veta said. She hopped down onto the terrace with the spray patterns, then peered over the edge and saw three bodies—two humans and a Kig-Yar—lying on the level below. "And since the Turaco is still out *there*, the shooters must still be in *here*."

Mark stepped to her side and studied the carnage for a moment, his expression equal parts dismay and bafflement. Perhaps he was feeling the same odd pang of loss that Veta was—a sense that *she* had somehow been hurt by the murder of the three Keepers, that her own soul had been diminished by their deaths. The Forerunner grotto was an eerie place, she decided, and not one where she cared to remain any longer than necessary. She turned from the bodies and tipped her head back toward the vestibule.

"That way," she said. "Upstairs."

CHAPTER 9

2005 hours, December 13, 2553 (military calendar)
Unidentified Turaco, Salvation Base
Moon Taram, Pydoryn Planetary System, Shaps System

A distant *clang* sounded from somewhere outside the Turaco, and Olivia shifted her attention to the security feed above the cramped engineering station. The screen had been divided into four quadrants—none of them showing the *Stolen Faith*, which was most likely the source of the noise.

"Keep that Mudoat starsloop on-screen," Olivia said. "Don't make me tell you again."

"Would that be a threat?" The AI called herself Argie, and she had been a steady source of frustration since Olivia used an ONI override code to board the Turaco. *"Because you don't have that authority."*

"I do now." Olivia reached down beside her knees and raised the two switch guards on the cabinet face. "If I can bypass ship's security, I can handle a system restore."

"And wipe the log data you've been trying to access?" Argie countered. *"You wouldn't do that."*

Olivia shrugged. "Sure I would," she said. "You have me locked out anyway, and you're getting on my nerves. What's a craft this size doing with a smart AI in the first place?"

"A postproduction upgrade."

"Then you're a Dark Moon construct?"

Argie hesitated a full half second. *"I'm not at liberty to reveal that."*

Olivia smiled. "You just did."

While searching for the Turaco's name and transponder code, Olivia had come across a data file identifying the owner of the craft as Dark Moon Enterprises—and *that* had sent her rifling through the rest of the files.

Dark Moon Enterprises was a shadowy private security firm that provided threat-management services to clients throughout the human-controlled portion of the galaxy. The Ferrets had tangled with the firm during a training exercise on Neos Atlantis, when a Dark Moon agent had attempted to expose the fact that the team was manned by Gamma Company Spartan-IIIs. The confrontation had sealed Dark Moon's place on the ONI enemy list, so it definitely seemed odd to discover the firm operating a top-secret REAP-X Turaco.

When the *Stolen Faith* still did not appear on the security feed, Olivia placed her thumbs on the reset switches. "Last chance," she said. "Three . . . two . . ."

"It won't matter," Argie said. *"I'm system resident. I'll still be here when—"*

Olivia flipped the switches and actually felt happy as the cooling fans whined down and the display screens snapped into darkness. Even if Argie hadn't been a Dark Moon construct, she had a condescending personality that made Olivia want to locate the AI's data crystal and toss it into the fusion reactor.

Once the Turaco's systems were down, Olivia left the engineering station and started forward. So far, Argie had done nothing to betray Olivia's presence aboard the craft, even when Olivia had been forced to hide in an EVA suit while a Kig-Yar inspection party sniffed around. But the AI's silence seemed as suspicious as everything else concerning the Turaco, and there was no sense taking chances.

When Olivia reached the flight deck, she dropped to her hands and knees, then peered through the bottom edge of the canopy. The *Stolen Faith* remained where it had been sitting for more than five hours now, surrounded by a couple hundred Keepers. About three-quarters were Jiralhanae warriors waiting to attack the "pirates" they wrongly assumed to be holed up inside the vessel. But there were also dozens of Keeper mechanics working from scaffolds, using laser torches to cautiously cut their way into the starsloop.

Plasma torches would have been faster, but using them would have been like hitting the vessel with an artillery barrage. The spike of superheated gas would have ignited its interior atmosphere and quite possibly triggered a catastrophic explosion. Apparently, that was not a risk the Keepers wanted to take with a bunch of thermonuclear warheads aboard.

After a moment, Olivia spotted the source of the *clang* she had heard earlier. A Kig-Yar crew near the front of the starsloop had finally managed to slice a chunk out of the vessel's nanolaminate armor and open a two-by-three-meter breach about where the galley should be. The edges of the hole were still smoking and glowing star-bright, but a team of Jiralhanae in blue-and-gold battle armor stood at the foot of the scaffolding, their postures tense as they waited for the opening to cool enough to risk squeezing past.

That nanolaminate armor was tough stuff. It had taken the Keepers almost twice as long as expected to cut through the starsloop's hull—and that was a good thing, given that the rest of the Ferret team was now four and a half hours overdue.

Olivia took a moment to glance around the spaceport, studying the grotto mouths where she had last seen her teammates, but saw nothing to indicate their return was imminent. On the other hand, she found no evidence suggesting the Turaco crew would be returning anytime soon either.

Olivia made a clucking sound in her throat, activating the microphone in her collar, and waited for a replying click. When none came, she looked back toward the *Stolen Faith*. The torch crew had begun to spray water on the hot edges of the breach. It would not be long before a squad of Jiralhanae entered the vessel and confirmed the deaths of the first boarding party—as well as that of Sarch and her crew.

Olivia ducked back down and retreated toward the engineering station. Time was running out. She had to make contact with the rest of her team—or continue the mission alone.

CHAPTER 10

2027 hours, December 13, 2553 (military calendar)
ONI *Sahara*-class Prowler *Silent Joe*
Orbital Approach, Planet Pydoryn, Shaps System

The Ferret team was in trouble. Fred-104 knew that the second he entered the situation room and saw the swarm of bandits on the *Silent Joe*'s tactical holograph. There had to be fifty designator symbols, arrayed in a triple-layer defensive sphere around the moon Taram.

Stepping through the door behind Fred, Kelly-087 whistled, then spoke over Blue Team's secure TEAMCOM channel. "Yeah, the Keepers were expecting us."

"You think so?" Linda-058 asked, bringing up the rear. "This is bad. Very bad."

Fred said nothing. He had been the one who'd urged Admiral Osman to continue the Ferrets' mission even after SIGINT suggested the Keepers were anticipating an ONI infiltration attempt. But he hadn't expected an entire battle fleet to be waiting when the *Silent Joe* arrived.

Fred led the way over to the tactical holograph. Admiral Osman had been called away by other duties and was no longer aboard the *Silent Joe*, so he saluted the senior officer present, Captain Ewen.

"You wanted to see us, sir?"

"I did." Ewen returned the salute, then motioned Fred and the other members of Blue Team to take a place at the holodisplay. "As you can see, we have problems."

"I'd call them obstacles," Fred said. "And obstacles can be bypassed—especially if we move quickly."

The hint of a smile flashed across Ewen's long face, but when he spoke, his voice was stern. "I appreciate your enthusiasm, Lieutenant. But I didn't interrupt your deployment so you could give me a pep talk. Your mission has changed. In fact, it may be canceled."

Fred turned to face Ewen full on. Blue Team had already been aboard the Owl and ready to launch when the captain summoned them to the situation room, so he was in full Mjolnir and in no mood to stand down.

"If that's a joke, sir, you need to work on your timing."

Ewen's face reddened. He thrust his arm into the holograph, penetrating the sphere of enemy symbols and nearly touching the yellow orb of Taram.

"Does that look like a joke to you, Lieutenant?"

"It doesn't look like a reason to cancel the mission," Fred said. "If this were easy, you wouldn't need Spartans."

Kelly's voice sounded inside his helmet. "You're missing his point, Fred. The Keepers aren't just prepared—they're *waiting*."

"Yes, precisely," Linda said, also over TEAMCOM. "They know we're coming."

Even as Kelly and Linda were speaking to Fred privately, Ewen continued to address him openly.

"Thanks for pointing that out." The captain's tone was sour. "I guess I wouldn't know what the hell Spartans *were* without you to set me straight."

"You have clearly irritated your superior officer," Damon said, sharing his observation over the Spartans' TEAMCOM. *"Protocol dictates that you apologize."*

"Yes," Linda said. "Do it now."

"Relax, both of you," Fred hissed. "I've got this."

Ewen frowned. "Got what, Spartan?"

"Got *you*, sir," Fred said quickly. "I mean, I understand your concerns. You're assuming the Ferrets were captured and gave up the rescue plan under interrogation."

Ewen's face softened. "It's more complicated than that." He nodded across the holograph to Anki Hersh—the *Silent Joe's* senior intelligence analyst—and said, "Play it for him."

"Yes, sir." The tiny brunette began to tap the tacpad on her forearm. "I'll bring it right up."

"Bring what up?" Fred asked.

Still tapping, Hersh said, "As soon as we emerged from slipspace, SIGINT downloaded the backlogged intelligence from the spy gnats that Ash-G099 planted aboard the *Stolen Faith*."

Fred had a sinking feeling. "The ostanalus got them?"

"No," Hersh replied. "The Ferret team anticipated the gas attack and took control of the *Stolen Faith*, much as you predicted. But on approach to Taram, the *Faith* was boarded by a force of Keepers."

She gave her tacpad a final tap, and an unfamiliar female voice began to issue from a ceiling speaker.

"Just give me the arming codes." The woman's voice was dry and firm. *"We'll take care of the rest."*

"And what do we get out of it?" This voice belonged to Veta

Lopis, who sounded as calm and cocky as ever. *"The* Stolen Faith *and safe passage out of the system?"*

"Nice try," the Keeper woman replied. *"But even if I could sell it to the dokab, I've made my feelings clear about letting you loose knowing the location of Salvation Base."*

"So what's your offer?" It was Mark-G313 who asked this.

"Your lives," the Keeper woman replied. *"Unless I decide you're ONI, of course. If you're ONI, Castor is just going to rip the codes right out of you with his bare hands."*

The recording stopped, and Hersh said, "Not all of our intercepts were that clear. But we know from an earlier exchange that Inspector Lopis claimed the Havoks on board had already been sold to the Banished. She also claimed that, unless her team was allowed to make delivery, a Banished fleet would show up looking for their cargo."

Fred waved his hand at the holograph. "Then that mess isn't even for us," he said. "It's for the Banished."

"That's the current thinking," Captain Ewen replied. "We're assuming Lopis was trying to sell a cover that would get her team onto Taram in one piece."

"Makes sense," Fred said. "If the Keepers thought there was a Banished assault coming, they'd want to interrogate the people bringing it down on their heads."

Ewen nodded in agreement. "Lopis was making the best of a bad situation."

"Then I don't see why you're delaying our deployment," Fred said. "Everything we know so far suggests the Ferrets are still alive."

"That's not the only criteria." Ewen's tone grew steely. "And you know it."

A soft clatter sounded behind Fred, with Kelly and Linda

signaling their displeasure by deliberately making noise. He extended three fingers toward the deck, signaling them to stand down. Captain Ewen was right, and Fred *did* know it. Like any clandestine ops team, the Ferrets were expendable. If they had gotten themselves in too deep . . . well, the *Silent Joe* was not a rescue ship, and Blue Team was not a rescue unit.

"Fair enough," Fred said. "But Veta Lopis is the most stubborn woman I know, and she has a trio of Spartan-IIIs backing her up. If the Ferrets are still alive, they're still on mission."

"I agree," Ewen said. "And I wish I could assume that."

"What's standing in your way?"

"SIGINT." Ewen looked back across the holograph to Anki Hersh. "Anything new?"

She shook her head. "I'm afraid not, sir."

"Then go ahead."

Hersh reached for her tacpad again. "This is from the 2020 microburst, shortly before your Owl launch was aborted." She tapped a key, at the same time adding, "It's translated from the Jiralhanae."

A deep, gravelly voice issued from the overhead speaker. *"The gas killed them all? There are no survivors?"*

"None, Dokab," a second voice answered. *"We searched the entire vessel. The only living thing we found are these midges."*

"Midges?" the dokab replied. *"Let me see that."*

The recording ended in a crackle.

"We suspect the 'midge' was one of our spy gnats," Hersh said. "The next microburst contained several feeds that ended the same way."

"So the Keepers know we're listening." Fred turned back to Captain Ewen. "If that's all you're worried about—"

"It *isn't*," Ewen said, interrupting. "The feeds in the previous microbursts were filled with gasps and wails. Five hours before that, we have the same thing—about two minutes *after* the Ferrets are secured for disembarking."

"So you think . . . *what*?" Fred asked. "That the Ferrets killed themselves to avoid interrogation?"

"I don't know what to think," Ewen admitted. "But it's pretty damn clear *something* happened. That ship was on the pad and filled with ostanalus for five hours."

"With no real indication that the Ferrets were killed."

"Or that they survived," Ewen countered. He paused, then added, "And there hasn't been an extraction signal."

"That doesn't mean they're dead," Kelly said, stepping to Fred's side. Although her voice was calm and her expression hidden behind the half-bubble faceplate of her EVA Mjolnir power armor, Fred could tell by the way her hips were cocked that she was losing patience with Ewen's caution. *"Sir."*

Ewen's eyes flashed at the sarcasm in her final salutation, but when he spoke, his tone remained even.

"You're missing the point, Spartan. We don't know whether the Ferrets made it, and we have no reason to believe they've located Admiral Tuwa's family."

Kelly's shoulders came back to level. "I understand that, sir, but—"

Ewen cut her off with a raised hand. "But we *do* know that one of the Keeper's most important dokabs is on that base," he said. "In fact, we know that, as of seven minutes ago, he was aboard the *Stolen Faith*. Do you see where I'm going with this?"

"I am *sorry*," Damon said inside Fred's helmet. *"I know how fond you were of Inspector Lopis and her Ferrets."*

Fred didn't need to ask the AI to explain. Their mission had two objectives—rescue Admiral Tuwa's family *and* retaliate for her assassination. The *Silent Joe* carried a full complement of Shiva nuclear missiles, and since the Shivas could be configured for stand-off delivery against a surface target, they were clearly an efficient means of achieving the second objective.

"You're going to launch against Salvation Base," Fred said.

"I'm leaning toward it," Ewen replied. "But I've never been dirtside on one of these missions, so I wanted to hear from someone who's been down there tossing rocks."

"I am sure we have made our opinions clear," Linda said, speaking from between Fred and Kelly. "I hope you will take them seriously."

"I wouldn't have called you up here if I didn't," Ewen said. He turned back to the tactical holograph and fell silent. "But you know how this works. The Ferrets have been on the ground for five hours, and all our intel suggests the operation is a bust. I can't risk a hundred and twenty souls on the off chance they're still alive. Hell, I couldn't do that if I *knew* they were."

"I understand your position," Fred said. He glanced over at Kelly and Linda and used a hand code to signal them to hold fast, then added, "We all do."

The color drained from Ewen's face. "Thank you. I appreciate that." He turned to the executive officer standing at his side, then said, "Ready all Shivas."

"Very well, sir." She touched a button on her headset, then said, "Missile room, ready all Shivas. Prepare to receive targeting data."

Fred waited until the executive officer had stepped over to firing control, then spoke to Ewen's back. "Captain, I know you'd like to continue the mission as much as we would."

"Of course." Ewen turned around. "I may be an officer of the line, but I'm not a coldhearted bastard."

"Have you considered pinging their TEAMCOM?"

Ewen's eyes widened. "This is a *stealth* ship, Lieutenant."

"I'm aware of that," Fred said. Prowlers normally avoided transmitting anything in a theater of operations, as even the slightest electronic emission could light up like a beacon on enemy sensors. "But if you're going to launch the Shivas, what's there to lose? It'll be shoot-and-scoot anyway."

"Not quite. We'll remain on-station long enough to confirm strike success." Ewen remained quiet for a moment, then looked through the tactical holograph toward Anki Hersh. "Lieutenant, what does SIGINT think?"

Hersh swallowed, then said, "We'd only need to radiate for a millisecond, sir. But with so many enemy craft between us and the target, someone's going to hear a ping."

Ewen nodded, then surprised Fred by asking, "But will the enemy be able to *find* us?"

Before Hersh could answer, the executive officer's voice rang out from firing control. "Shivas targeted. Ready to launch in twenty seconds."

"Thank you," Ewen replied. "Five-second interval between first two. Minimum two-minute delay with random interval for last four."

The executive officer confirmed the order by repeating it, and Ewen turned back to Hersh.

"Lieutenant, will the Keepers find us?"

"They could," Hersh said. "Every vessel detecting the transmission will have a vector on us. Once they coordinate and triangulate, they'll have a point of origin."

"How long will that take?"

"It would take a UNSC task force about five seconds," Hersh said. "But UNSC systems are set up to share SIGINT automatically. With the Keepers . . . it's anybody's guess."

The executive officer reported, "Shivas ready to launch on your command, Captain."

"Thank you, XO. Hold status for now." Ewen then addressed Fred: "You understand we're not in the rescue business? Even if the Ferrets respond, Blue Team won't deploy unless it furthers the mission."

"Understood," Fred said. "That's all I'm thinking of."

Ewen studied him for a moment, then said, "Do I need to remind you that lying to a superior officer is a violation of the Uniform Code of Military Justice?"

"Sorry, sir. I won't let it happen again."

"You'd better not. I'm putting my ship at risk on your suggestion." Ewen looked to Hersh and nodded. "Ping the Ferret TEAMCOM, Lieutenant. Make sure they know it's us."

Hersh's finger was already on her tacpad. "Executing now, sir."

Five seconds of silence passed before the voice of Olivia-G291 began to issue from the ceiling speakers.

"Situation dark and uncertain," she said. *"Team has penetrated Keeper installation Salvation Base, located in Forerunner ruin on moon Taram. Hostile forces have taken* Stolen Faith *and captured Havok decoys. Ash-G099 assigned to draw off Keeper pursuit, now absent more than five hours. Lopis and Mark-G313 searching for mission objectives, also absent more than five hours."*

Fred glanced over to find Ewen's jaw clenched and his gaze fixed on his boots. It seemed likely the captain was thinking the same thing Fred was—that the mission had indeed gone bad, and Olivia was about to be on the receiving end of half a dozen Shivas.

After a momentary pause, Olivia continued, *"Transmitting from captured Turaco, no identification or transponder code, equipped with uncooperative, smart AI Argie and oper—"*

There was no pop, scratch, or squeal. Olivia's voice simply ended, leaving an ominous silence.

Hersh jabbed at her tacpad for a second, then said, "The transmission was cut off."

"By what?" Ewen demanded.

Hersh continued to study her tacpad. "My guess is the Turaco's AI," she said. "There was no background roar or signal pulse, so I don't think it was an explosion or a comm malfunction."

"Which is why Olivia made a point of saying the AI was uncooperative," Kelly said. "She *knew* it was going to cut her off."

"And I think that is not all she was telling us," Linda said. "Why would she remind us that Taram is a moon?"

Ewen furrowed his brow. "What's your point, Spartan?"

"That a good soldier does not waste words during a sitrep."

"And why did she say the situation was dark *and* uncertain?" Kelly asked. "What's a dark situation, anyway?"

"Dark Moon," Damon said. *"Spartan-G291 is using a redundancy code. There is an eighty-three-point-three percent chance that she is trying to tell us that Dark Moon Enterprises is involved."*

Fred considered the AI's suggestion. All he really knew about Dark Moon was that they weren't afraid to tangle with ONI—a trait that made them either foolish or fearless, and probably both. But it didn't make them terrorists. They wouldn't assassinate a UNSC admiral and abduct her family just to infuriate ONI. And they wouldn't align themselves with the Keepers of the One Freedom unless there was something in it for them.

After a moment, he spoke aloud. "Damon thinks she's trying to tell us Dark Moon is behind this."

"I didn't say behind," Damon said. *"I said* involved."

Fred ignored the AI and asked Ewen, "You know what Dark Moon is, right?"

"'No contact, no access,'" Ewen said, quoting the UNSC blacklist order. "I read the FLEETCOM bulletins, Lieutenant."

"So I imagine you see it," Fred said. "The Ferrets tangled with Dark Moon during their training, and now 'Livi is using a redundancy code to tell us Dark Moon is mixed up in this mess."

"Mixed up *how*?"

Fred hesitated, reminding himself that no matter how much he liked Lopis, it was his duty to be honest. Finally, he said, "That's hard to say for sure. But if she knew for certain that Dark Moon was directly responsible for what happened to the Tuwas, she would have found a way to let us know."

"She would not have said 'uncooperative AI,'" Linda said. "She would have said 'hostile AI.'"

Ewen looked away for a moment, then said: "Very well. You know your fellow Spartans better than I do, so that will be our working assumption."

As the captain spoke, the tactical holograph began to bleed designator symbols in the *Silent Joe*'s direction, and Hersh said, "Captain, the Keeper fleet has triangulated our position. We need to relocate."

"Which will require loading new navigation data into the Shiva guidance systems," the executive officer said. "If we're going to attack, recommend launching the first pair now."

"Negative," Ewen said. "Stand down all Shivas. We're continuing the original mission as planned."

"We are?" Hersh was clearly astonished. "But, sir . . . they know we're here."

"And the *Silent Joe* is a *stealth* craft, with a mission to complete." Ewen turned back to Fred. "Return Blue Team to the Owl and stand by for orders."

Fred was happy to obey, but a bit surprised. The conservative response would be to order Olivia to evacuate and launch the Shivas.

"We're going to insert?"

"Affirmative. If Dark Moon is involved in this, we need to know why and how," he said. "I'm adding a third objective to Blue Team's mission: recover the Turaco."

"Very good, sir," Fred said. "What about Lopis and the missing Ferrets?"

Ewen smiled. "Well, you're going to be down there anyway. It wouldn't hurt to figure out what happened to them."

CHAPTER 11

Across what Ash-G099 had come to think of as the pop-up lake, the Keeper assault fleet was vanishing one vessel at a time. One second, a war-surplus Seraph or a captured Longsword would be standing in the blue-green water, the gentle waves lapping at its struts . . . and the next second, it would be gone.

Whether the vessels were launching or sinking was impossible to say. They always vanished while Ash was looking in another direction, and when he looked back, there would be nothing to indicate what had become of them—no residual glow, no whirlpools or pressure circles on the surface of the lake. It was as though the craft had never existed in the first place.

Had Ash been anywhere but a Forerunner ruin, he would have assumed that his smoothers had worn off and that he was beginning to hallucinate. As it was, he merely told himself to observe and adjust. The quantum technology of Forerunner devices was about a hundred grades above his training tier, and any attempt to impose his own concept of time and space on what he was seeing would only add to his confusion and frustration.

A soft rustle began to fill the corridor behind him—the sound of his pursuers closing in from both directions. Ash remained where he was, kneeling just inside the mouth of a cliffside grotto, and continued to look out over the lake. There were no other living beings in sight, not even Olivia or the Keeper ground crews, but the rolling water filled him with a deep sense of calm . . . and belonging. He felt the cosmos pulsing in his heart and saw his thoughts flashing from star to star, and when he inhaled, it was the breath of the universe that filled his lungs. He wanted to stay in the Forerunner caves forever, at one with all things everywhere, bathed in their eternal, infinite harmony.

But his team was counting on him to maintain the diversion.

Ash switched his gaze to the Turaco, searching for some indication that Olivia and the other Ferrets had made it aboard. The lake seemed to prevent the observation of living beings—at least from the grotto where Ash was kneeling—so all he could do was look for indirect evidence of their presence.

He didn't find any, which he decided was a good sign. The Ferrets were too well trained to unintentionally leave a trail, so anything he could see from his perch would suggest trouble.

The situation at the *Stolen Faith* was more disturbing. According to the chronometer he had taken off a dead Keeper, the Ferrets had departed the Kig-Yar transport only a quarter hour earlier. But already the starsloop was surrounded by towers of scaffolding that should have taken at least twice that long to erect. And just a moment earlier, a dark rectangle that looked like a breach had appeared in the vessel's hull, up near the galley. The team hadn't expected that to happen for a couple of hours.

It certainly didn't feel like hours had passed. It barely felt like fifteen minutes.

Ash rose and turned toward the arched doorway that led into the corridor, then made a *cluck* to activate the microphone sewn into his collar. He had done the same thing many times since entering the grotto complex. This time was no different.

No response.

The rustling in the corridor fell silent, and a Jiralhanae voice sounded outside the doorway, from a few meters down the passage. "You are a bold and gifted fighter, infidel." An electronic undertone suggested he was speaking through a translation disc. "It will be a sadness to kill you."

"No worries," Ash said. "You won't."

The Jiralhanae chuckled. "Not if you yield now."

"Surrender?" Ash leveled his weapons—a spike rifle and a plasma pistol—at the doorway. "That's not going to happen."

"I give you time to reconsider," the Jiralhanae said. "There has been too much killing already."

"I'm sure you think so."

Ash's tone was mocking, but in truth, he felt the same way. He had taken out eight pursuers so far—three of them Jiralhanae—and each time he had felt a stabbing pang beneath his heart, as though he were wounding himself by slaying his enemies. It was not a feeling he had ever suffered before, and he suspected it was related to the sense of peace and oneness he had begun to experience after entering this network of Forerunner grottoes.

After a moment, the Jiralhanae said, "The lives you took were fairly earned. I give you my promise—there will be no retaliation."

"Except imprisonment."

"Imprisonment is not death," the Jiralhanae said. "You will have a cell overlooking the Lake of Transcendence and much time to reflect on the Great Journey."

"Transcendence" was an apt name for the lake, and Ash could think of worse ways to spend his life than watching it.

But he had a job to do. "You mean I'll be free in my mind."

"Is that not the greatest freedom of all?" The Jiralhanae paused, then said, "This is the last time I offer this to you, infidel. I hope you will accept."

"You seem awfully concerned with my welfare."

"In this place, we are all joined together," the Jiralhanae replied. "I know you also feel it."

"I feel something," Ash allowed. Then, because the Jiralhanae seemed to be in a talkative mood and it was always useful to gather intelligence, he asked, "What was this place? A Forerunner detention center or something?"

The Jiralhanae rumbled with laughter. "Or something. We Keepers believe it was a monastery."

That made sense. Ash could imagine a Forerunner monk kneeling inside his grotto cell, with nothing to do but stare out over the water and contemplate his place in the universe. Ash had come to a greater sense of inner peace after watching the lake for just a few minutes. He could see why someone might choose to spend decades there.

After a moment, the Jiralhanae said, "So now you can drop your weapons, infidel. You must see how you are trapped."

Ash glanced back toward the lake. The grotto mouth certainly looked unobstructed, but appearances were often deceiving in Forerunner installations. There could easily be an invisible barrier field or hard-light wall that would activate if he attempted to flee.

But that had never been his first choice anyway. Running was a good way to get shot in the back.

"You must surrender your weapons or die," the Jiralhanae said. "I am coming for you now."

"It's your funeral."

The Jiralhanae responded with a heavy sigh, and a Keeper hand appeared out of the shadows on each side of the doorway. The one on the right belonged to the Jiralhanae, and it was holding a spike grenade—a long, club-like weapon that resembled a grappling hook with quills. The spindly hand on the left belonged to a Kig-Yar, and it was holding the grid-etched orb of a UNSC M9 fragmentation grenade.

Ash was already halfway to the door and firing both weapons. The Jiralhanae's thick wrist vanished inside a spray of blood and blazing plasma, and the spike grenade dropped toward the corridor floor.

By then, the Kig-Yar hand had opened, and the frag grenade was flying through the arched doorway. Ash lashed out with his plasma pistol and batted the grenade back into the corridor, then hurled himself into the adjacent corner.

A wave of heat and pressure blew past behind him, and he thought he had escaped the worst of the blast . . . until he was driven into the wall by an unexpected rebound wave. The air left his lungs in a huff and his chest blossomed with pain, but that was minor compared the stabbing pang of loss he felt as his pursuers were minced by their own ordnance.

Ash staggered out of the corner. Dozens of glowing spikes and grenade fragments lay scattered just inside the grotto mouth, where they had fallen after hitting the barrier field or hard-light wall—there was no way to tell which—that had bounced the concussion wave back at him. He hadn't anticipated that, but he had come through in one piece.

More or less.

There had been no chance to cover his ears, so the only thing he could hear at the moment was a deafening roar. The pain in his chest was probably from having the wind knocked out of him, but it could also be from a broken rib—or possibly even a punctured lung.

It didn't matter. He had to move fast if he wanted to take advantage of the blast shock, and his Gamma Company survivability enhancements would keep him going no matter how badly he was injured.

Ash stepped into the corridor with one weapon pointed in each direction. The passage was lit by the same ambient light that illuminated the entire grotto system, but the grenade smoke hung thick and gray in the air.

Everyone within five meters of the doorway lay shredded and motionless, but eight meters to the left, a gaunt Kig-Yar silhouette was starting to pick itself off the floor. Ash put a trio of plasma bolts into its head, then turned in the opposite direction.

A pair of large, nebulous shapes now blocked the corridor ahead, swaying and stunned by the grenade blasts, but still alert enough to raise their maulers. Ash was faster, loosing a flurry of spikes that dropped both Brutes before either could fire a single bolt. The deaths tore at him inside, but he had no time to worry about that now. He took a moment to search his fallen enemies and rearm himself, then raced down the corridor and began to descend the ramp.

By the time Ash reached the first level, he had his breath back and the roaring in his ears had subsided to a steady ringing. But the pain in his chest remained—a bolt of agony that shot through his torso each time he drew a breath.

That was okay. For Gamma Company Spartan-IIIs, pain was jet fuel. It made them run hot and fast.

Ash paused at the exit long enough to study the Turaco and the *Stolen Faith*. Nothing seemed to have changed at either craft—at least nothing he could see from four hundred meters distant.

Trusting that Mark and Lopis had completed their assignment and joined Olivia by now, Ash stepped out into the lake and began to race toward the Turaco.

The waves vanished within a half dozen steps, and he started to wish he had something with a lot more range than a spiker. The *Stolen Faith* was surrounded by a swarm of tiny figures—a swarm that appeared to be thickest beneath the dark rectangle of the hull breach. Ash took a knee and clucked to activate his microphone again.

This time, there was a response. "Ash?"

"Who else?" Ash spoke freely. They were on TEAMCOM, so even if the Keepers somehow intercepted the transmission, it would be impossible to decrypt. "Are you aboard the Turaco?"

"Affirmative," Olivia said. "And you're not going to believe who it belongs to."

"I'm looking forward to finding out," Ash said. "But it's time to evacuate. You can pick me up on the way."

"Negative," Olivia said. "Not yet."

"What's the holdup?"

"The Inspector and Mark. They're not back."

"Acknowledged." Ash told himself not to worry. It had only been fifteen minutes since the team divided, and even Mark and Lopis might need longer than that to find the Tuwas. "I'll join them. You can pick us all up together."

"Affirmative," Olivia said. "But don't push your luck. Help is on the way."

"If you mean Blue Team," Ash said, "I don't see how we can wait. There's a large Keeper force gathered at the *Stolen Faith*, and it looks like they're waiting on orders."

"No worries," Olivia said. "I've got my eye on them."

Ash hesitated, wondering how Olivia expected to hold the Turaco for five hours, then finally said, "Talk about pushing your luck."

"It'll be fine, Ash. Just make it fast this time." Olivia paused, probably trying to bite back her irritation, then asked, "What took you so long, anyway?"

"Gee, I don't know," Ash retorted. "Maybe it was taking out thirteen Keepers."

"That took you five hours?"

"No way," Ash said. "More like fifteen minutes."

"So what were you doing the rest of the time?"

Ash started to make a sharp reply—then recalled Olivia's confidence in her ability to hold the Turaco until Blue Team arrived.

"'Livi," he said, "tell me your chrono reading."

"Twenty-thirty-five. Why?"

Ash checked his captured chronometer and began to understand the odd things he had observed from the grotto mouth—the Keeper vessels that seemed to disappear in a wink, the inability to see living beings moving about the lake, even the TEAMCOM blackout inside the grottos.

He rose and started to walk toward the area Mark and Lopis had used to enter the grotto complex. Every nerve inside him was screaming for him to run, but doing so was likely to attract the attention of the Keepers gathered around the *Stolen Faith*. If he walked, there was a chance that anyone who happened to be looking his way would assume he was one of the Keepers' human faithful.

A chance.

"Ash?" Olivia asked. "Are you—"

"Still here." Ash began to drift closer to the cliff face. "But that's going to change when I'm back inside. There's a time differential ringing the spaceport."

"Time differential?" Olivia asked. "Like on Onyx?"

"I guess," Ash said. "It might even be a continuum warp. With as much artificial gravity as it takes to hold an atmosphere over the entire installation, that's a real possibility—especially since it's Forerunner tech."

Olivia began to sound worried. "Ash . . . maybe we should wait for Blue Team."

"No good," Ash said. "Time passes faster out here. Even if it only takes me five minutes to find Mark and Lopis, that could be hours for you."

Olivia fell silent for a moment, then said, "Okay. I'll hold position and inform Blue Team."

"Affirmative," Ash said. "But if things get hot—"

"I'll *be* here, whenever you make it back."

CHAPTER 12

1514 hours, December 13, 2553 (military calendar)
Salvation Base
Moon Taram, Pydoryn Planetary System, Shaps System

The trail of dampness was beginning to evaporate, but that did not prevent Veta and Mark from realizing that the Turaco crew had preceded them up the detention center's curving stairwell. There were plenty of other signs to alert them— pinpoint smears of drying blood, step edges rubbed clean by the scuff of a boot heel, chunks of mud not yet ground to dust.

The mud was a deep reddish-brown that did not match Taram's yellow dust. Still an investigator at heart, Veta collected several chunks and sealed them inside a pocket. In the corners of the stairwell, she found boot prints suggesting a squad of four humans, probably one female and three good-size males. Splashes of sweat on the stair treads and handprints on the walls indicated they were moving fast and burdened so heavily they sometimes needed to brace themselves. The even spacing of their tracks suggested they were well organized and in good physical condition—traits that suggested military operatives.

Less clear was their identity. The elimination of the Keeper intake guards indicated the squad was on Taram to infiltrate the detention center, while the timing suggested it had come for the same reason the Ferrets had: to rescue Admiral Tuwa's family.

It was the Turaco outside that Veta found most intriguing. The presence of a rare reconnaissance boat still in the testing phase suggested a link to the UNSC, which actually made sense. An angry UNSC commander could have sent a team without informing ONI, or ONI could have assigned a second team to the mission to increase the likelihood of success.

Mark's hand came up in a fist, signaling a halt, then Veta began to hear a soft patter in the stairwell above them. The sound was so gentle it took her a moment to recognize it as human footfalls, coming fast and light.

Mark motioned down the stairs, and they retreated to the second level in silence. They hurried down the corridor, passing half a dozen cells sealed by shimmering energy barriers.

The barriers were transparent, and as they passed each cell, Veta glimpsed a single captive inside, sitting cross-legged on the floor or slumped against a wall, staring out over the vast blue-green expanse outside. There were two Sangheili and four humans, each with dirty bandages wrapped around a fingerless left hand. Despite their injuries, they all appeared to be in a state of serenity and contemplation, as though their attention was focused somewhere out beyond the lake. None displayed any reaction as Veta and Mark raced past—probably because the energy barriers sealing the cells were soundproof and transparent only from the exterior. That would certainly make sense in a detention center.

Once they were concealed by the curve of the corridor wall,

the two Ferrets dropped to the floor, then crawled back up the passage until they could peek around the bend. They saw four humans—three men and a woman—descending the stairs.

At first glance, the humans appeared to be typical pirates turned Keepers, with long, unkempt hair, battered torso armor over shabby tunics, and bare arms entwined with "celestial highway" tattoos—a favorite symbol of human Keepers. But they were wearing top-of-the-line combat boots and moving with the quiet grace of special-ops soldiers, and their armament was UNSC-issue—silenced M7S submachine guns, silenced M6C/SOCOM pistols, and silenced BR85 battle rifles.

The "second team" theory was beginning to look more plausible—except that the Tuwas weren't with them. In fact, Veta was beginning to suspect the squad's mission had been to deliver something rather than recover it. Aside from their weapons, all they were carrying were a pair of half-empty rucksacks that didn't look like they weighed more than a dozen kilos. And though they were careful to keep their weapons turned toward the corridor as they passed, they gave it only a precautionary glance and showed no interest in searching it for captives. Perhaps they had already checked the passage, but a crack squad that had failed in its mission would be more hesitant to leave.

Apparently, Mark had reached the same conclusion. Once the squad was past, he pointed toward the stairs, then tapped his brow to indicate he would lead the assault.

Veta was quick to shake her head. Attacking now would only delay their search for the Tuwas—and besides, it still remained possible that the squad was connected to the UNSC in a way she did not understand.

Mark scowled and made an *O* with his hand, then pointed in the general direction of the spaceport to indicate he was worried about Olivia. Veta understood his concern. Even outnumbered two-to-one, it would be relatively easy to eliminate the squad from behind. Olivia, on the other hand, would be outnumbered four-to-one and trapped inside the Turaco. If these guys were hostile, she would have a real fight on her hands.

Mark lifted his brows, urging Veta to make a decision before they lost their chance. She shook her head, then started down the corridor in the lead. The last thing she wanted was to leave any of her Ferrets in a bad position, but Mark had a tendency to be overprotective of his fellow Ferrets and a bit quick to kill—and that could endanger the entire team. Better to stick to the plan and trust Olivia to handle whatever was coming her way. She was, after all, a Spartan-III with enough combat experience to make sure she was in a defensible position.

When they reached the stairwell, Mark cast one last glance after the fading footfalls, but heeded Veta's decision and fell in at rear guard. Veta had no difficulty picking up the trail again and quickly followed it up to the third level of the detention center.

As on the level below, the cells were sealed by energy barriers with one-way transparency and occupied by single captives. But these prisoners were all human, with dark eyes and darker hair, and many were dressed in the light, loose-fitting garb favored by the people of Gao. Like the captives on the level below, they were missing all of the fingers on their left hands, but their torture had not stopped there. They appeared covered in burns and bruises, and several had swollen limbs that suggested broken bones or dislocated joints. Although their gazes were turned toward the lake, their expressions were accepting rather than serene, and they seemed to be watching the water rather than contemplating the great beyond.

Veta's pulse began to pound. It only made sense for a lot of the prisoners to be Gao. Arlo Casille had used and ruthlessly betrayed the Keepers during his theft of the presidency, and the Keepers were taking their vengeance by preying heavily on Gao space-shipping. But Veta hadn't expected this. Gao captives were clearly being tortured, as though their suffering would somehow punish Casille for his treachery.

"Looks like Castor carries a mean grudge," Mark observed. "But we've got to let it go—at least for now. If we let those people out of their cells, we'll never find—"

"I *know* what the mission is." Veta started down the corridor again. "Let's just move on, okay?"

They found the Tuwas five cells later—at least, Veta *thought* they were the Tuwas. The condition of the corpses made it hard to tell.

But there were definitely three of them, stiff with rigor mortis and dressed in blue overalls, lying close together on one side of the cell. The female was facing the lake, while the two males were facing the entrance. Their eyes were sunken and their cheeks hollow, and their complexion had gone the color of ash. Still, the hair was right—the female's long and black, the older male's brown and going gray at the temples, the youngest male's cropped too short to tell. The jawlines matched the images Veta had seen, all fine but square, and their noses tended toward the long and straight. That was enough to convince Veta—maybe not with a hundred percent certainty, but close enough for the circumstances.

Veta glanced at the barrier's control panel and found a pad with thirty-six oversize keys, all marked with blocky Jiralhanae hieroglyphs. Instead of trying to guess the access code, she traced a power conduit down the wall and pointed at the unit's generator pod.

"We need to disable that."

Mark was still staring at the three corpses. There were

palm-size craters in their skulls where they had been struck by something like a hammer or a rifle butt, and the cloth on their limbs was striped by bloodless lacerations. Most gruesome of all, their torsos had been opened from collar to navel, and ropy nests of innards had been left to spill over their laps.

"*Now*, Mark," Veta said. "I need to examine the scene."

Her tone seemed to snap Mark back into focus. He stepped closer to the wall, then cocked his leg and sent the pod flying with a roundhouse kick. It remained connected to the power conduit by a crackling bolt of silver until it dropped to the floor and began to tumble, and then the energy barrier finally sizzled out of existence.

Veta signaled Mark to stand watch in the corridor, then entered the cell—and knew instantly that the scene had been staged. The walls were splashed with blood so fresh the droplets were still running, but the spatter patterns were all wrong. The kinds of horrible wounds the Tuwas had suffered would have left fan-shaped sprays everywhere. But the patterns Veta was seeing were narrow and straight, as though the blood had been flung onto the wall by a brush.

And the stink in the cell was just as wrong. There were no urine or bowel odors, which were to be expected at a fresh murder scene. Instead, the air was filled with a cloying smell of decay cut by an acrid tinge that suggested some kind preservative.

Veta knelt beside the husband—Kerbasi—and began a cursory examination of his corpse. His body was as rigid as a board. Where she could pull the overalls away and get a look at the skin underneath, the anterior side appeared pink with lividity. The chest had been opened with the straight, smooth stroke of a surgical incision. The sternum beneath had been split just as neatly, probably by a sonic costotome, and the heart, lungs, liver, kidneys—everything except the intestines—were missing.

Veta turned her attention to Kerbasi's limbs. The lacerations there were jagged and variable, suggesting to her practiced eye that they had been inflicted by something like a combat knife. But the lacerations were not inflamed or bloody. Those injuries had definitely been inflicted after death.

The two craters in Kerbasi's skull were a different story. In one, the bone had been depressed in a half-moon shape that she had seen often enough to recognize as the result of a striking rifle butt. But the other crater was more circular, with a hole in the center that was perfectly round and about half the diameter of Veta's palm. She pushed her finger through and felt nothing. The brain had been removed.

Veta glanced over at the corpses of the son and daughter, Yuso and Catalin. They were in more or less the same condition, missing most of their internal organs and covered in postmortem injuries. It seemed likely that all three bodies had been mutilated to camouflage the theft of the organs—or at least to lay the blame on the Keepers—but that possibility raised more questions than it answered.

And Veta hated unanswered questions.

Veta cradled her battle rifle in the crook of her arm, then grabbed Kerbasi's collar and dragged him toward the exit. She would have preferred to sling him over her shoulders in a fireman's carry, but that was impossible with the corpse in full rigor mortis. And, anyway, she didn't want to lose any physical evidence that would help her figure out where the Tuwas had *really* been killed.

She entered the corridor, where Mark was keeping watch back toward the stairs, and said, "You're right. We should have taken out the delivery squad."

"*Delivery* squad?" Mark's gaze dropped to Kerbasi's body,

then drifted back toward the stairs. "They broke in just to kill the Tuwas inside a Keeper detention center?"

Veta shook her head. "Not exactly," she said. "The Tuwas have been dead for a while, probably between twelve and thirty-six hours. The delivery squad just planted the bodies here."

Mark scowled. "A frame job?"

"I'm guessing that's part of it."

"What's the other part?"

"That's what we need to find out." Veta nodded him back into the cell. "You bring the other two bodies."

Mark looked back toward the stairs. "Shouldn't we be going after the delivery squad?"

"They're not going anywhere without the Turaco," Veta said. "And we're going to need these bodies. They have a lot to tell us."

CHAPTER 13

2029 hours, December 13, 2553 (military calendar)
Mudoat Starsloop *Stolen Faith*, Salvation Base
Redoubt of the Faithful, Pydoryn Planetary System, Shaps System

On the deck at Castor's feet lay an oblong Havok casing that contained a modified slipbeacon instead of a thermonuclear device. In his hands, he held a disc-shaped burst transmitter surrounded by a twenty-centimeter web antenna. Both had been found aboard the *Stolen Faith* in the last few minutes, and he was too smart to believe they had belonged to the Kig-Yar crew. The unthinkable had happened, and the infidels had slipped an ONI tracking device onto Salvation Base.

Castor's anger was surpassed only by his remorse. Salvation Base had been given to him by the Oracle just four months before, when the image of a narrow Forerunner eye appeared above the communications holoplinth on the *True Light*'s flight deck. She had spoken in a voice like water, thanking him for his efforts to save her during the battle of Gao and asking if he was still willing to serve her. Of course, Castor had not hesitated, promising to rescue her from the UNSC infidels as soon as he could gather the Faithful.

But that had not been what the Oracle wanted. Instead, she had told him where to find what she called the Contemplarium, then urged him to take it as his new base and begin a campaign of piracy to rebuild his forces. Sometimes she even gave him the routes of freighters carrying precious cargo or the itineraries of yachts transporting wealthy tycoons. Due to her favor, Castor had ascended to first among the dokabs, and Salvation Base had become the largest and most important of all Keeper facilities.

And now, the carelessness of a Kig-Yar gunrunning crew had placed the Oracle's gift in jeopardy. Had the fools not been dead already, Castor would have killed them himself—and taken his time to make certain they suffered for their mistake. Still, the fault was not theirs alone. Salvation Base was protected by many other layers of precaution, and if those protections had also failed, it was because someone on the ground had forsaken his duty. Castor turned toward the cargo ramp, where the base's human approach-control officer was waiting with Castor's second-in-command, a fellow Jiralhanae named Orsun.

Like Castor himself, Orsun was a seasoned warrior with many decades of battle showing in his grizzled features. But where Castor's face was wedge-shaped and heavy-boned, with thick tusks and a long gray beard, Orsun's was long and chiseled, with a heavily furrowed brow and slender tusks rising from a clean-shaven jawline. Castor motioned him forward, and Orsun escorted the approach control officer up the ramp and into the hold. As they crossed the grease-spotted deck, the man's gaze drifted toward the line of Havoks resting in front of a wall alcove. The casings were open, and a pair of human technicians in white overalls and full face protection was kneeling over the last one in line, probing it with a long, thin wand.

There were only a few other beings in the cargo hold. After discovering the spy midges and losing so many Faithbringers to ostalanus gas during the initial boarding, Castor had grown wary of traps and commanded anyone not actively searching the *Stolen Faith* to wait outside.

As Orsun drew near, the second-in-command clamped a hand around the approach-control officer's neck and set him down in front of Castor.

"The dokab did not summon you to gawk." Orsun released his neck and pointed to Castor. "Attend to your duty, Jarves."

Jarves touched his fist to his chest and craned his neck to look up at Castor. The man had a squarish face with a tuft of blond beard and eyes round with fear.

"I'm honored by your summons, Dokab," he said, attempting not to struggle. "How may I serve?"

Castor thrust the microburst transmitter beneath Jarves's nose. "Explain this."

Jarves eyed the disc for a moment, then finally asked, "What is it?"

"A spy transmitter," Orsun said. "It was hidden behind the exchanger filters."

"I don't know anything about it," Jarves replied. "This is the first time I've ever set foot on this vessel."

"Yet you allowed her to land," Castor said.

"Because of the Havoks," Jarves said. "They're worth the risk."

"Perhaps if they were functional," Castor said. "As they are, they are worth nothing."

Jarves swallowed, then snuck a glance at the line of nukes. "I was told we had the arming codes."

"Who told you that?" Castor demanded. It was beginning to sound like Jarves had been more involved in bringing the Havoks to Salvation Base than Castor had realized. "Creon?"

Jarves shook his head. "Seruphi," he said. "I wanted to be certain the weapons were under our control, so I insisted on a technical inspection before allowing the *Stolen Faith* to continue its approach."

It was a reasonable answer—yet one that raised questions of its own. Seruphi was the female human weapons technician who had accompanied Creon's boarding party onto the *Stolen Faith*. Her body had been found in the boarding vestibule alongside the chieftain's, with one side of her face smashed in.

"And Seruphi found nothing wrong with the . . ." Castor looked to the pair of technicians still examining the Havoks, then commanded: "Tell me again the problem with the infidel devices."

"The booster cylinders are filled with deuterium," the senior technician said. Without rising from her haunches, she turned to face Castor. "It should be tritium. That would be impossible to detect without proper instruments. But without tritium, there's no D-T reaction—"

"Yes, I remember now." Castor raised a hand to silence her, then turned back to find Jarves staring at the deck between them, where the tenth Havok—the one that was actually a slipspace locator beacon *disguised* as a Havok—lay with its access panel flipped open. "Do you know what you are looking at?"

The color draining from Jarves's face suggested that he did. "I was cautious, Dokab. That's why I sent Creon and his vigilance squad to board—"

"You sent them to their deaths," Orsun remarked. He grabbed

Jarves's neck again and squeezed until the man grimaced in pain. "And now their killer is loose inside Salvation Base."

"Who is this killer?" Castor asked.

"All I know is what Seruphi told me," Jarves said, his face turning red from Orsun's grip. "There were four of them, arms smugglers trying to deliver a load of nukes to the Banished. Seruphi believed them."

"And *you* believed her?"

"It didn't matter what I believed," Jarves said. "They were already on orbital approach, and we confirmed a slipspace transmission from the *Stolen Faith*. It seemed wisest to take control of the Havoks and alert you to the situation. Bringing the vessel here wasn't my decision."

"No?" Castor asked. "Then they never promised to keep Salvation Base secret if you let them leave?"

"They couldn't be trusted, Dokab. They're *pirates.*"

"So are we," Castor said. "Does that mean we lack honor?"

"We're d-different," Jarves said. "We're servants of the One Freedom."

Castor pretended to consider the point for a moment, then finally nodded. "Of course, you are correct, Jarves." He laid a hand over the man's shoulder. Castor's fingers were so long that his thumb hung down to Jarves's belly. "And as a servant of the One Freedom, I am sure you gave no thought to the reward that would come to anyone who delivered so many thermonuclear weapons to our cause?"

Jarves looked away. "Seruphi and I may have discussed the possibility," he said. "But if I had known—"

"I see." Castor began to squeeze. "What else have you failed to tell me?"

Jarves's eyes flashed in terror, and Castor knew the human was hiding something even more damning than his bargain with Seruphi.

Before Castor could press for an answer, Orsun touched a finger to his ear comm and growled in alarm. "Dokab . . . three minutes ago, the Redoubt of the Faithful detected a signal from a stealth vessel in a trailing orbit."

Castor's stomach clenched. "A prowler?"

"Likely, but not yet known," Orsun said. "The Fleet of Glory has triangulated the origination point and is moving to attack."

Orsun started to add something, but Castor signaled him to wait by breaking eye contact. There were many classes of stealth vessel in the galaxy, of course, but the ones that concerned him most were the UNSC prowlers. The United Nations Space Command had both the means and the desire to destroy the Keepers. If the stealth vessel was indeed theirs, Salvation Base was in grave danger.

What Castor did not understand was why the prowler would announce its presence before attacking. The UNSC seldom fought with such honor.

Castor met Orsun's gaze again. "I am troubled by this," he said. "It could be an attempt to draw our defenses out of position. Have the Fleet of Glory return to a defensive posture."

"A wise precaution, as ever." Orsun relayed the order, then said cautiously, "But I have failed to explain the rest. The signal was answered by an encrypted transmission."

"From where?"

Orsun released Jarves's neck and pointed to starboard, more or less in the direction of Salvation Base's detention center.

"From a holding cell?" Castor asked.

Orsun shook his head. "From the Turaco in front of it," he said. "On a channel rapidly changing frequencies, which the infidel Office of Naval—"

Orsun was still explaining when Jarves let his legs go limp and dropped to the deck. The maneuver took Castor by surprise—and Orsun as well. Before either Jiralhanae could react, the human was rolling to his feet and sprinting for the cargo ramp.

Castor growled deep in his throat, wondering why the treachery of inferior species ever surprised him, then bellowed, "I want him alive!"

A pair of Jiralhanae Faithbringers stepped into view at the bottom of the ramp. Both were armed with Type-25 spike rifles and wearing full Keeper power armor, and the sight was enough to make Jarves pause at the top of the ramp.

"Alive does not have to mean in one piece," Castor warned. "The choice is yours."

Jarves's shoulders slumped. He raised his hands and slowly backed away from the ramp, then finally turned around.

"The Turaco isn't ONI," he said. "I wouldn't take a credit from anyone who wants to wipe us out."

"Oh no?" Castor crossed the deck toward Jarves. "Then who would you take credits from, human?"

Jarves's expression went from frightened to uncertain. "A private security outfit," he said. "They just wanted to get a hostage back for one of their clients."

Castor stopped a pace from Jarves but did not grab him. In his anger, he feared he would crush the man before learning what he needed to know.

"I *know* you heard about the assassination of the infidel admiral," Castor said. His spies had confirmed the reports almost as soon as they reached Venezia, and he had personally passed the news along to his followers. "And about her family being taken."

"Of course," Jarves said. "I listened to the bulletin, same as everyone else on base."

"Then you also heard my warning about the UNSC?" Castor asked. "That they were likely to blame the Keepers and try to retaliate?"

"Like I said, I listened to the bulletin."

"And, yet, you took money from a 'private security outfit?'" Castor asked. "And helped them sneak a vessel onto Salvation Base?"

"It was a lot of money," Jarves said weakly. "Five million credits."

"*Who* made this offer?"

Jarves craned his neck and forced himself to meet Castor's gaze. "If I tell you, can we work something out?" he asked. "I didn't do any harm, I swear it."

Castor held his reply for a moment, trying to calm himself, then finally said, "If you fail to tell me, you *know* what I will do." He paused, watching as Jarves began to tremble and sweat, then added, "But if your answers are truthful and prompt, perhaps I will consider mercy."

"All right . . . thank you." There was more relief in Jarves's voice than was warranted. "I was always going to give the Keepers half. That's more than the ransom would have been anyway."

Orsun palmed Jarves in the side of the head and sent him sprawling. "There is no excuse for what you have done," he said. "There is only answer or agony."

"It's not an excuse—it's perspective," Jarves said, still on the floor and rubbing his temple. He shifted his attention to Castor. "The security outfit never identified themselves. The offer came in over my commmpad—that's how I knew they couldn't be ONI. If they knew how to reach my commmpad, they already knew where Salvation Base was. Hell, they were probably looking at us from orbit."

"And you chose to negotiate instead of warn us?" Orsun demanded. "I should twist off your feet."

"There wasn't any negotiation to do," Jarves said. "The offer included a Venezian account in my name and a passcode. There were already a quarter million credits there."

"What did they want in return?" Castor asked.

"Landing clearance for the Turaco," Jarves said. "They just wanted to get their guy and go."

"Who was this hostage?" Castor asked.

"They wouldn't say," Jarves said. "And since I couldn't help them with the detention center anyway, I didn't ask."

"And the *Stolen Faith*?" Castor asked. "Did they also request clearance for it?"

Jarves shook his head. "No, that was completely separate," he said. "That happened just the way I told you."

Castor was not sure the two incidents *were* completely separate. Many Keepers had already perished aboard the *Stolen Faith,* so it was only natural that a *snesel* like Jarves would try to minimize his involvement in allowing the vessel to land.

But even if Jarves was telling the truth, there was no reason to believe the mysterious "security outfit" had been honest. The Turaco crew was more likely to be an ONI rescue team than a private security squad, and the only thing Castor knew for certain right now was that they weren't going to find the missing Tuwa clan in his detention center—since he had not kidnapped anyone.

Still, the Keepers' innocence was not going to matter. The UNSC was at war with the Keepers of the One Freedom, and the instant the rescue team was clear of the Redoubt of the Faithful, Salvation Base would be destroyed.

Castor turned to Orsun. "Recall the Fleet of Glory," he ordered. "Leave only an anti-missile screen on-station above us."

Orsun's head cocked to one side. "*Recall* the fleet, Dokab?" he asked. "Have I heard you correctly?"

"You have," Castor said. Anyone else would have been chastised or worse for questioning orders. But when Castor was gravely wounded during the defeat on Gao, Orsun had stayed at his side and made certain he survived to rebuild the Keepers. That made his second-in-command indispensable and exempt from castigation. "The fleet will do us more good down here."

Orsun's eyes remained confused and uncertain.

Castor pointed toward the Havoks lined up along the wall. "The infidel weapons," he said. "They could not have been stolen, or the booster cylinders would have been authentic."

Orsun's nostrils widened in alarm, then he turned to relay the order. Castor stepped closer to Jarves and fixed his gaze on the man.

"Have you spoken honestly?" he asked. "Have you told me all?"

"Yes." Jarves's eyes shone with hope—or perhaps it was merely desperation. "I didn't know they were ONI. How could I?"

Castor studied him for a moment, then asked, "How could you *not?*"

He snatched Jarves up by the head and whipped the human from side to side until a hollow pop sounded from the neck, then flung the corpse across the hold. It hit a wall and dropped to the deck, and Castor wondered how much of a difference the betrayal had truly made. Salvation Base had clearly been compromised even before Jarves was approached to give landing clearance to the Turaco, so perhaps the human's sin was one more of intent than of result.

Still, it was intent that mattered on the Great Journey. No mortal could know every consequence that followed every act, and so all that separated the Faithful from the infidels was the purity of their intent.

Castor turned back to Orsun and saw that while his second-in-command had finished relaying the orders, his gaze was puzzled.

"Something troubles you," Castor said. "Speak."

Orsun dipped his head. "Only my own ignorance," he said.

"The Fleet of Glory has been recalled, but the captains are disturbed . . . as am I."

"Is it because we are not preparing for battle?"

"That is so," Orsun said. "No doubt we have cowards in our number. But there are more Faithful by far, and they will fight to the last breath."

"Which is what ONI wants us to do," Castor said. "They hope to catch our fleet in orbit and destroy it here."

Orsun's gaze remained clouded.

"That is why they sent the second vessel," Castor said. "They hoped the threat of a Banished attack would lure us into their trap."

"A brilliant assumption," Orsun said. "I would never have seen that."

It was a careful way of expressing doubt.

"That is the only explanation," Castor insisted. "If ONI did not know our location beforehand, how would they know to recruit Jarves? How would they know where to send the Turaco?"

"Your questions are wise," Orsun replied. "I have no answer."

Another expression of doubt—even more careful. "But you are not convinced," Castor said. "Tell me why."

"As you command," Orsun said. "I have never known infidel plans to be so . . . complicated. There is too much to go wrong."

Castor considered this. He had commanded too many warriors in too many battles to believe he was incapable of a mistake—but he could see no other explanation that fit the facts.

Finally, he said, "Yet only one thing has gone wrong with their plan. We are not the ones who abducted the Tuwas."

"I know, Dokab," Orsun said. "That is what concerns me."

CHAPTER 14

Fred-104 thunked against the crash harness that secured his six hundred kilograms of flesh and powered assault armor to the cushioned wall behind him, and he knew the Owl insertion craft was changing vector. He flicked his eyes toward the owl symbol in the corner of his faceplate, syncing the heads-up display in his helmet with the *Silent Claw*'s cockpit readouts.

The tactical display showed a cone of hostile craft returning to base on Taram. The *Silent Claw* was near the tip of the cone, surrounded by the Keeper fleet, yet hidden from enemy sensors by stealth technology. But as the cone narrowed, it was growing more difficult to remain beyond the visual range of every vessel, and the Owl's pilot was trying to reduce their exposure by moving toward the cone perimeter.

Fred had no idea why the enemy was suddenly returning to base, and that worried him. The Owl had been halfway through its insertion run when Damon intercepted the Keeper recall order, but there had been no explanation given. And breaking comm silence to request an intelligence update from the *Silent Joe* was out of the question. To do so would be like activating a beacon that said INCOMING ATTACK. GET READY.

Fred blinked off the cockpit feed and found Kelly-087's bubble-shaped faceplate fixed on him. She was sitting on the opposite side of the passenger compartment, watching him across one of the two Mongoose ATVs secured to the deck between them.

"We could still go EVA." Kelly's voice came over Blue Team's TEAMCOM, but since they were communicating in line-of-sight mode, the transmission power would be too low to escape the Owl's EM-shielded hull. "That way, Ashveld could do a standoff insertion."

"Negative," Ashveld replied, also over TEAMCOM. As the *Silent Claw*'s pilot, she monitored all comm channels used aboard her craft—even the encrypted Spartan channel. "We're going in with the fleet."

Fred and Kelly stared into each other's faceplates for a moment; then Fred asked, "Like we're one of them?"

"No other way," Ashveld said. "Hostile traffic is too thick for a sling maneuver, and trying to break away for a remote insertion would look suspicious."

"Then the *Claw* has already been spotted." It was Linda-058 who said this, and it was not a question. She was seated on Kelly's side of the passenger compartment, next to the second Mongoose. Her faceplate goggles were fixed on a small equipment pod secured to the ATV's rear cargo shelf. "How close can we insert to the *Stolen Faith*?"

"Honey, I'm going to drop you right on top of her."

Fred made a point of glancing at Kelly and Linda, then cocked his helmet. The original plan had called for Blue Team to insert just over the horizon from Salvation Base and approach on the Mongooses, then reconnoiter and infiltrate quietly.

So much for planning.

After a moment, both Kelly and Linda responded with brief nods.

"Understood, *Claw*," Fred said. "And thank you."

Ashveld's only reply was to activate the red battle lamps set into the passenger-compartment walls. Linda slapped the override on her automatic crash harness, then floated over to the Mongoose and removed the equipment pod from its rear cargo shelf. They were going to need that pod, and if Ashveld was going to drop them on top of the *Stolen Faith*, Blue Team wasn't going to be riding Mongooses into battle.

She was still securing the pod to the magnetic holder strip on her thigh when the Owl jinked into evasive maneuvers, changing directions so rapidly that Fred was thrown back and forth against his crash harness. Linda bounced off the Mongoose, ricocheted off the ceiling, and slammed down across Fred's lap.

He caught her by the carapace collar and kept her pinned in place until the Owl jounced downward, making her weightless again, then pulled her into the adjacent seat. He barely had time to draw his hand away before the automatic crash harness descended from the wall and secured her in place.

"My thanks, Lieutenant," Linda said. "I was growing dizzy."

"No problem," Fred said. He had Damon sync his HUD with the cockpit readouts again and quickly realized the *Silent Claw* had been spotted—the tactical display showed a dozen hostiles converging on her from all sides. "A quiet infiltration isn't happening, so we're going to Plan Delta. Everyone clear on the details?"

"Hard not to be," Kelly said. "Shoot first and ask no questions."

"Close enough." Fred blinked off the cockpit feed. "Prime objective is securing the Turaco. Linda, if you can't reach the nukes—"

"I *will* reach them." Linda tapped the equipment pod affixed to her thigh mount. "I am not bringing this along just to hit SELF-DESTRUCT."

Satisfied that everyone understood their assignments, Fred nodded. He hadn't mentioned trying to find the Tuwa family or the missing Ferrets, because Plan Delta had no provision for it. Plans Alpha and Beta had been rendered obsolete once they realized Lopis and two of her Ferrets were MIA. Plan Charlie had been improvised aboard the *Silent Joe* after Captain Ewen realized Dark Moon was involved. Plan Delta was Plan Charlie's desperation backup plan. It assumed Blue Team would be inserting under heavy fire and badly outnumbered, so it placed a premium on destroying the Keeper base and recovering the Turaco—preferably with Olivia aboard. All other objectives were strictly secondary and to be attempted only if a clear opportunity presented itself.

But when it came to finding Lopis and the other Ferrets, Fred would be looking very hard for a clear opportunity. There was plenty of latitude in their orders for that.

Fred just hoped they didn't have to revert to Plan Echo.

"Plan Echo?" Damon asked. *"Lieutenant, there* is *no Plan Echo."*

"What did I tell you about reading my mind?"

"I was doing no such thing," Damon objected. *"You said, 'I just hope we don't have to revert—'"*

"Knock it off," Fred said. "I didn't say a word."

"You kinda did," Kelly said. "You were mumbling something over TEAMCOM."

Before Fred had a chance to respond, a trio of sharp *pong*s reverberated through the *Silent Claw*'s hull, and the Owl rolled into a wild helix that pushed Fred and his companions hard against the wall. The forward autocannon began to chug, and a series of *chuff*s sounded beneath the deck as the craft began to deploy missile decoys.

"Going in hot," Fred said. "Confirm seals and ready weapons."

As Fred spoke, an image of his CENTURION-class prototype Mjolnir appeared on his helmet HUD. The entire image was bright green, indicating that the pressure seals were functioning properly and the suit was airtight.

Fred pulled his MA5D assault rifle off the magnetic seat mount next to his thigh. He stripped the weapon down for a close-range engagement by removing the Longshot sight and the sound suppressor, then tapped the bottom of the magazine to be sure it was properly seated.

Kelly was armed with a MA5C assault rifle with an underbelly M301 grenade launcher, but Linda had only her M6G sidearm. Her BR55 battle rifle remained on the far side of the passenger compartment, still attached to its seat mount. She might be able to grab the weapon if the *Silent Claw* leveled out before the drop—but with the Owl taking fire, there were no guarantees.

The hull began to crackle with friction heat as the *Silent Claw* dived into the atmosphere bubble above Salvation Base. The cooling system inside Fred's Mjolnir kicked into high as the passenger compartment grew warm, and he felt himself pressing into the seat as Ashveld pulled the nose up in preparation for the drop.

"Ready for—"

A thunderous *boom* shook the passenger compartment. The *Silent Claw*'s tail sank; then she entered a flat spin and began to rock back and forth as Ashveld fought for control. Given the way the Mongooses were straining at their axle clamps and how hard

Fred was being thrown toward the rear boarding ramp, it didn't seem like a battle she was going to win.

"*Claw*, are you—"

"Hanging . . . on," came Ashveld's croaked reply. "Execute emergency—"

"*Drop!*" Fred finished.

The rear boarding ramp fell open, and the Mongoose axle clamps retracted. The ATVs did not roll so much as sail from the passenger compartment. Fred glimpsed them tumbling toward a blue-green expanse seventy meters below and could not help thinking of Reach, of the four Spartans who had died under his command the last time he had ridden a Pelican down; then Kelly's harness retracted, and she was hurled after the vehicles, her armored figure rolling smoothly into a forward dive as she brought her fall under control.

Fred's harness retracted a half second later—releases were staggered to avoid exit collisions—and he dived out the door. The landing pad was fifty meters below, a sweep of pavement coming up fast.

CHAPTER 15

At the bottom of the stairs in the Keeper detention center, Veta spotted a trail of damp boot prints leading across the intake vestibule toward the exit. They were so fresh that beads of water still stood in the tracks nearest the doorway. Beyond the opening, she could see only a sliver of lake, its waves sloshing against each other in a haphazard pattern that suggested a squall had settled in.

Veta released the body she was dragging and pointed to the trail, then signaled Mark to investigate while she covered the doorway. Leaving Catalin's and Yuso's corpses next to their father's, Mark shouldered his BR85, dropped to a knee, and peered around the corner.

Almost instantly, he spoke over TEAMCOM. "Ash, that you?"

"Tell me you're not alone," came the reply.

"He's not," Veta said. She peered around the corner and saw

a rifle barrel protruding past the side of the counter, with a single brown eye peering over the top. "What are you doing here?"

"Looking for you." Ash lowered the rifle but remained concealed behind the counter awaiting visual verification. During the Ferrets' field training, redundant precaution had been drilled into them until it became second nature. "You recover the packages?"

"All three," Veta said. With Mark still covering her from the staircase, she grabbed Kerbasi's corpse by the collar and dragged it into the foyer. "Just not alive."

"Damn." Ash rose and started across the vestibule. He was carrying a BR85, no doubt from the same weapons locker Mark had forced open earlier. "We need to get moving. Blue Team will be here any minute."

"Blue Team?" Mark said. He remained in position, his weapon still trained on Ash's chest. "How do you figure?"

"Temporal divergence." Ash ignored the rifle and continued forward. "I think it has something to do the massive artificial gravity inside the base, or maybe the Forerunner vacuum energy extractor that's powering it. Anyway, *something* is bending space/time around—"

"Ash . . . theory later." Veta motioned Mark to lower his weapon. "Just give us a sitrep."

Ash raised his eyes toward the ceiling, then exhaled sharply. "Okay, from your perspective, it probably seems like we left the *Stolen Faith* less than thirty minutes ago. I think it has something to do with the vacuum energy extractor and the way it bends time/space."

"*Ash!*" Veta urged.

"Right," Ash said. "To Olivia, you've been MIA for five hours, and she's surrounded by Keepers, a force well in excess of a hundred. The *Silent Joe* pinged her a few minutes ago, so she assumes Blue Team is on its way. And she's pretty sure the Turaco belongs to Dark Moon."

"Dark Moon?" Veta glanced down at the corpses of the Tuwa family, and a glimmer of understanding began to tickle the back of her mind. "Ah . . . that might explain the delivery squad that arrived ahead of us."

"To *you*, maybe." Mark shot Ash a still-suspicious glare. "I'm still trying to figure out how Blue Team shows up five hours early."

Ash shrugged. "What can I tell you? Theory later."

"Right."

Veta paused, considering whether to free the other captives they had seen upstairs earlier. With more than a hundred Keepers outside, there was *going* to be a battle, and a bunch of scared prisoners would either get in the way or get killed. It troubled her to leave them behind, but she probably wouldn't be doing them any favors—at least not until the Keepers were neutralized.

And the safety of her own team came first.

Veta motioned toward the corpses. "We need to get these bodies back to the *Silent Joe* if we can," she said. "Everybody grab one for now—but if we get in trouble—"

"Got it," Mark said. "Don't die defending a corpse."

"Exactly," Veta said. "Now, let's go see about 'Livi."

Mark led the way, carrying his battle rifle in one hand and dragging Catalin's corpse with the other. Ash followed with Yuso, and Veta brought up the rear pulling Kerbasi—the heaviest of the three. That probably made sense, as Mark and Ash could actually fire accurately one-handed and would be that much more precise with lighter loads. But still . . . teenagers. Veta dug her fingers into Kerbasi's wrist and struggled to keep up.

Leaving a trail of gore behind was hardly the ideal way to preserve evidence or respectfully transfer a body, but under the circumstances, it was the best they could do.

They stepped through the doorway onto the lake, and Veta began to hear the sound of a distant battle, mostly small-arms fire, but also the thunder of a single large explosion. The combatants remained hidden beyond the mysterious veil of the lake—as did the Dark Moon delivery squad whose tracks they had seen earlier.

But the Turaco and *Stolen Faith* were both visible, sitting on the surface of the lake with waves breaking against their struts from all directions. And on the far side of the spaceport, vessels seemed to be popping into existence one after the other, simply appearing on the provisioning apron every time Veta blinked.

As they splashed across the churning water toward the Turaco, the thunder of the explosion quickly died away. The small-arms fire only grew louder and more urgent, and the three of them had traveled no more than ten paces before Mark and Ash released the bodies and threw themselves prone.

Veta followed their lead and landed not in water, but on the hard-light pavement of the spaceport. Fifty meters ahead stood the Turaco, swaying on its struts as the dorsal turret pulsed blue laser fire into a swarm of charging Keepers. From the looks of it, they had emerged from the time divergence just in time for the firefight.

Behind the Keepers, the *Stolen Faith* was wrapped in scaffolding, her forward boarding ramp gaping open and a rectangular hull-breach just behind the cockpit.

And in the distance beyond the starsloop's stern—two hundred meters beyond the *Stolen Faith*—lay the remains of an Owl insertion craft.

One of the curved wings had been torn away and lay resting on its back, rocking and spinning and spraying long tongues of burning fuel into the air. The cockpit sat nearby, a crushed metal cube smeared with blood streaks and scorch marks. The body of the craft was barely visible, a battle-pocked stretch of gray hull concealed behind curtains of flame and smoke.

"Oh, not good." Veta felt like she had swallowed liquid nitrogen. Her stomach was cold and churning, and she ached with fear for Fred and the rest of Blue Team. "Guys, we'd better not count on support."

"Haven't needed it so far," Mark said. "But we'll definitely need the Turaco to make it out of here—which means we've got to stop *them* first."

He pointed the tip of his battle rifle toward an area fifteen meters shy of the Turaco, where the four-member Dark Moon squad was struggling to reach their craft.

The squad was attempting to advance via the classic leapfrog, with the female operative kneeling to fire beneath the Turaco's belly while her companions raced forward in an evasive zigzag. But one of her squadmate's legs had been shredded by spiker fire, and he was being dragged along by the other two men, slowing their advance and making it more difficult to dodge.

As Veta watched, the female operative took a shot to the head and tumbled backward in a red spray.

"Permission to open fire on the Dark Moon squad?" Mark asked.

"We need to find out who sent them," Veta said. They weren't so close to the battle that she had to shout to make herself heard— but she did need to raise her voice. "It would be good to take at least one of them alive."

"Affirmative," Mark said. "Ash, I'll take arms, you take legs."

"Right to left," Ash called back. "On my . . . mark."

Four shots rang so close together that Veta heard them as one, and the man on the right end of the Dark Moon squad went limp, twisting first right, then left as the Spartan rounds shattered his limbs.

The operative on the left end spun toward the Ferrets and started to raise his battle rifle one-handed, but Mark and Ash were already firing again. The man's weapon arm jerked and dropped to his side; then his knee buckled and he fell onto the man he had been dragging toward the Turaco. Two more shots rang out, and his remaining arm and leg jumped with hits.

The Turaco's dorsal turret fell silent and swung around, then renewed fire. Pulses of laser began to reflect off the hard-light pavement, filling the air with such sapphire brilliance that it took a couple of breaths for Veta to realize the cannon fire was directed not at her Ferrets, but at the Dark Moon squad. Fortunately for the wounded operatives, the output mirror seemed to have depressed to the bottom of its guide slot, and the laser pulses were still striking a few meters beyond their position.

Veta activated TEAMCOM. "'Livi, cease fire! I want them alive! Repeat, alive! Cease—"

"*Trying,*" came Olivia's strained reply. "But I don't control the weapon systems right now."

"Then who does?!" Mark's voice was incredulous. "Take them out!"

"*Trying!*" Olivia repeated. "But Argie is one slippery AI. Every time I pull a circuit board, she pops up somewhere else. Pretty soon, we're going to have to fly this—"

The transmission ended in the ear-piercing screech of a jammed channel. Clearly, the Turaco's AI—this Argie—didn't want anyone on the Dark Moon squad taken alive.

"*Shit.*" Veta lifted her torso and tried to get a better view of how close the laser pulses were landing to the wounded opera-tives. "Now I *really* want to interrogate them."

"Hold on." Ash motioned Veta back down. "As long as the AI controls that laser turret, we're not getting anywhere near them."

"Give me a second." Mark rose to a knee. "If this doesn't work, fall back to the detention center."

Veta scowled. "Wait. If *what* doesn't—"

Mark fired a long burst.

"Dammit, Mark! What part of 'wait'—"

Veta saw sparks as a dozen rounds glanced off the laser's out-put mirror. The turret swung in their direction, then erupted into crackling forks of energy as it attempted to fire again.

"Okay," Veta said. "Permission granted, I guess."

Mark smiled sheepishly. "Sorry, ma'am." He reached back and grabbed Yuso's corpse by the collar, then asked, "Permission to advance?"

"Yeah, yeah." Veta grabbed Kerbasi's corpse and rose. "Go!"

Mark and Ash dashed forward, carrying battle rifles in one hand and dragging bodies with the other. Veta followed as well as she could, but she lacked their strength and quickly began to fall behind.

They had taken barely five steps before Mark and Ash dropped into deep crouches and, still running, began to fire under the Tura-co's belly. Veta tried to do the same and found herself stumbling along at half their speed—which was going to be a problem. Now that the laser turret was no longer spraying bolts in their direction, the Keepers had broken into a full charge. There were probably thirty of them left, about evenly divided between Jiralhanae and other species, and the leaders were only a dozen paces from the Turaco.

Realizing she would only imperil her team by falling farther behind, Veta released Kerbasi's body and dropped onto her haunches. She picked a Kig-Yar near the front of the Keeper charge and ran a three-round burst up his torso. The Kig-Yar toppled backward, and Veta rolled forward at an angle, narrowly avoiding the flight of plasma bolts that whistled back in her direction.

She came up firing and dodging. Over TEAMCOM, she said, "'Livi, I don't know if you're in contact—"

"I am," Olivia replied. "The Turaco is under my control. . . . At least, I think it is."

"Good," Veta said. "Be ready to drop the boarding ramp and provide cover fire."

"Affirmative."

Mark and Ash were moving fast. They would probably reach the wounded Dark Moon operatives about the same time the Keepers reached the Turaco. After that, making it aboard would simply be a matter of combat skill against superior numbers— and while Veta was having a hard time seeing how her side was going to come out ahead, she had learned months ago never to bet against Spartans.

She set her battle rifle's sight on the brow of a charging Jiralhanae—then gasped in surprise as the craggy face erupted in a red cone.

A second Jiralhanae suffered the same fate an instant later; then Keepers began dropping faster than Veta could count, landing on their bellies in thrashing heaps or simply collapsing beneath sprays of brain and bone. By the time she managed to re-direct her fire and take out another Keeper, the charge had broken. Most of the Kig-Yar and humans were scattering in a panic, ducking their heads and fleeing sidelong as fast as they could run. The Jiralhanae reacted more wisely, diving for cover behind their wounded fellows and pouring blind fire back toward the burning Owl.

It took Veta a moment to find the remaining Keepers' target—a trio of Spartans in full armor, charging out of the smoke and pouring small-arms fire into the Keeper rear. Fred-104 was leading the way in his blue-tinted CENTURION-prototype Mjolnir, his assault rifle tight to his shoulder and the muzzle drifting left to right as he picked off targets.

A dozen paces to Fred's right, Kelly-087 was maintaining pace in her gray EVA Mjolnir, her bubble-visored helmet swinging back and forth as she fired 40mm grenades from the launcher mounted beneath the barrel of her assault rifle. Linda was breaking toward the *Stolen Faith*, armored in her brown ARGUS-prototype Mjolnir and carrying only an M6G pistol. Attached to the equipment mount on her thigh was a silver pod about the size of her goggle-eyed helmet. The pod was not part of her normal load-out, so it probably contained the tritium booster cylinders need to activate the Havoks—which Veta *hoped* were still aboard the starsloop. At least, no one had told her they had been moved.

"Sorry we're late," Fred said over TEAMCOM. "Mechanical difficulties."

His helmet tipped slightly, as though he were saying something to his new AI, Damon, and the Owl's self-destruct charge detonated with a gut-thumping *boom*. Chunks of hull and wing rose into the air, tumbling and trailing flame, and the handful of Keepers still on their feet threw themselves to the ground and covered their heads.

Linda reached the *Stolen Faith* and raced up the cargo ramp unopposed, then vanished into the hold.

Closer to the Turaco, Veta glimpsed three Jiralhanae in the blue-and-gold power armor of elite Keeper warriors. The trio were

kneeling behind a pile of bodies, clustered around a mostly unarmored companion with a wedge-shaped face and a long gray
beard. Despite his lack of formal Jiralhanae shock-plated armor,
Graybeard seemed to be giving orders, peering over the body pile
and gesturing in Fred's direction.

Veta swung her battle rifle toward the cluster and opened fire.
She was aiming for Graybeard, but her angle was poor, and her
burst bounced off the shock plates of one of his bodyguards.

The bodyguard reacted instantly, spinning around in a flash of
blue and gold, putting himself between Graybeard and the source
of the attack, bringing his spiker to bear. Veta dived away, squeezing off a wild burst as she flew, and heard hot metal pinging off
the hard light behind her.

The burst went wide, but it drew Blue Team's attention to
the cluster of Jiralhanae. Fred sprayed automatic fire and Kelly
launched a grenade, and Veta rolled up to find her attacker lying
facedown. He had a grenade crater in his back, and there was a
pool of blood spreading across the hard light around him.

The remaining Jiralhanae were ducking under the Turaco and
racing forward. Graybeard was sandwiched between his two remaining companions. A tall warrior with an older face was in the
lead, and a young warrior with wild amber eyes was bringing up
the rear. Wild Eyes was twisting around as he ran, pouring spikes
behind him in an attempt to prevent Kelly from putting another
grenade into their midst. Tall and Graybeard were firing on Mark
and Ash, forcing them to evade and fall back. Whether it was
intentional or not, they were making it impossible for the two
Gammas to reach the wounded Dark Moon survivors whom Veta
wanted captured.

Lacking the firepower to bring all three down quickly, Veta
flipped her selector switch to full automatic and emptied her clip

at Wild Eyes. She was hoping to get lucky and take Graybeard out with a ricochet, but the rounds crackled off Wild Eyes' armor plating and bounced away harmlessly.

Still, Wild Eyes reacted in surprise, looking forward for a couple of steps, and that was all the chance Kelly needed. She took his armor's resiliency the rest of the way down with a burst of her own, then sent a 40mm grenade flying into the Jiralhanae's backplate.

The detonation hurled him forward into Graybeard, who lurched a half dozen steps forward before losing his balance and going down. Veta ejected her empty magazine and saw him pointing a spike rifle in her direction. She rolled away, glimpsed a pair of spikes flying past behind her, and reached for her thigh pocket.

To her left, Tall continued to charge forward, barely slowed by the small-arms fire bouncing off his shock plates. When he reached the wounded Dark Moon operatives, the man with the shredded leg—the only one who hadn't been shot in both arms by Mark and Ash earlier—opened fire on him. Tall stomped on the man's head, then surprised Veta by scooping up the two survivors and turning to flee combat.

Graybeard was close on his heels, having scrambled to his feet while Veta grabbed a fresh magazine. She pushed it into the battle rifle's receiving slot, then rose to a knee and brought the muzzle up for a head shot. The Jiralhanae was looking at her as he ran, his narrow eyes burning and his lip drawn back in a tusk-baring snarl. He had a wedge-shaped face with heavy bones and thick tusks, and Veta was shocked to realize she recognized him.

She had shot him before—half a year ago, during the trouble on Gao, on a jungle-covered hillside outside the village of Wendosa. Veta hadn't known he was the dokab Castor until some time later, when she saw his image during a classified ONI threat briefing.

So here was a chance to fix her mistake and take out the son of a bitch right now.

She held Castor's gaze for an extra second, giving herself time to snug the rifle butt against her shoulder, and even when she saw his spike rifle coming up in her direction, she let her breath out and did not rush the shot.

Fred ducked under the Turaco and saw Veta Lopis kneeling in the open, twenty meters ahead, her weapon pointing toward a pair of fleeing Jiralhanae. He swung his assault rifle around and saw why she was holding her fire. The armored Brute in the lead was carrying two human prisoners and laying fire on Mark and Ash. The second Brute was unarmored, but only half a step behind the first, and he was staring back at Lopis, raising a spiker in her direction.

Unable to take a kill shot without risking a through-and-through that would hit the prisoners, Fred did the next best thing: he put a round through the Brute's spiker hand. The weapon spun away in a spray of blood; then Lopis fired.

The Jiralhanae was already ducking away from Fred's attack, and her round passed high. The Brute dodged in front of his power-armored companion, and Lopis's next two shots were deflected by shock plates. Then the two Jiralhanae were surrounded by a couple of dozen fellow Keepers who were now rushing back to protect them, and the enemy fire began to build.

Kelly ducked under the Turaco and started to launch grenades in their direction. Then Olivia entered the fray, lowering the boarding ramp and opening fire with a S99 Sniper Rifle that she had probably found in an onboard weapons locker. The Keepers lost half their number in the space of a few breaths and reluctantly began to fall back once more.

Still, it was clear to Fred that the enemy was far from defeated—and the shock of Blue Team's initial assault had clearly worn off. He checked his TACMAP and saw that Keeper survivors were starting to regroup on both flanks, and that reinforcements were headed in from all around the landing site's perimeter.

Fred activated TEAMCOM. "Olivia, can you fly that thing?"

"Affirmative," she replied. "The Dark Moon AI seems to be disabled. Or maybe she's just finally cooperating. But I have control—"

"That's all we need. Fire up. Ferrets, get boarded. Kelly and I have the perimeter." Fred signaled Kelly to cover the Turaco's tail arc, then turned to take the nose arc. "Linda, how are you coming with those cylinder replacements?"

"Six Brightboys ready," Linda reported, citing the nickname for the Havok nuclear devices. Clearly, she had encountered no opposition boarding the *Stolen Faith*—at least none that would slow down a Spartan-II—and now she was busy fitting the weapons with functional tritium booster cylinders. "Three to go."

"Six is enough," Fred said. "Set tamper triggers with a five-minute tango and get back here."

Fred changed his ammunition magazine and continued to fire into the Keeper cluster that had emerged to meet the two Jiral-hanae. In his experience, when a bunch of irregulars risked their lives to save one individual, that individual was usually their commander. Keeping him under fire would disrupt their efforts to regroup and counterattack.

"Fred, five minutes isn't enough!" Lopis said over TEAMCOM. She remained on a knee, looking back toward the detention center entrance. "There are captives inside. A lot of them—probably hostages the Keepers are holding for ransom."

"Hostages?" Fred glanced at Mark and Ash. They were already halfway to the Turaco, dragging a pair of corpses whose gray, sunken faces seemed to belong to Catalin and Yuso Tuwa. He assumed the body lying behind Lopis was Kerbasi's. "What do they have to do with the Tuwas?"

"Probably nothing," Veta admitted. "But when those Brightboys detonate . . ."

Lopis let her sentence trail off, and Fred groaned. His orders didn't include any mention of rescuing stray hostages, and there was no provision for it—not with the Owl scattered across the spaceport in a hundred pieces.

After a second, Fred asked, "How many?"

"A dozen, at least." Lopis rose and turned toward the detention center. "I'll need ten minutes—"

"You'll need an hour," Ash interrupted. "Probably more. Don't forget the temporal divergence."

"What are you talking about?" Fred asked.

"Like at Onyx," Ash explained. "Time moves slower inside the detention center than it does out here." He and Mark were already dragging the Tuwa corpses up the Turaco's boarding ramp. "Something to do with the base's artificial gravity generator, or maybe the Forerunner vacuum energy extractor. Maybe—"

"Doesn't matter," Fred said.

He checked his TACMAP again and saw that the Keepers were massing on the provisioning apron, using the cover of their space fleet to organize an assault. From the look of things, the attack ratio would be about two hundred to one—and not even Spartans could hold for long against those kind of odds.

"We don't have an hour." Fred fixed his gaze on Lopis. He

knew she would see only the reflective surface of his golden face-plate, but the effect should still be commanding. "Load up, In-spector."

"What about the hostages?"

"Not part of the mission," Fred said. "We can't help them."

Lopis glared into his faceplate, refusing to budge, trying to intimidate *him*. She was tough that way, afraid of nothing and—when she thought she was in the right—as stubborn as a drunken general. Fred respected that kind of edge, as long as it didn't jeop-ardize the operation.

After a moment, Fred asked over TEAMCOM, "Linda, what's taking so long with those Brightboys?"

Lopis shot him a dark look. "I thought we were the good guys, Fred," she said. "You told me that on Gao."

"We *are* the good guys," Fred said. "It doesn't mean we can save everyone."

"On my way, Lieutenant," Linda said. "Tango five. Covering fire appreciated."

"Affirmative," Kelly said. She rolled under the Turaco's tail and shifted her firing arc toward the *Stolen Faith*. "Come ahead."

Fred continued to watch Lopis for a heartbeat, then said, "You're putting your team at risk, Inspector." He changed to a fresh mag-azine and turned to cover as Linda raced down the *Stolen Faith*'s boarding ramp. "We need to go *now*, Lopis—that's an order."

CHAPTER 16

The Argent Moon's chief science officer and his two companions lay together in a bunk designed for one, so exhausted by their earlier exertions that they had fallen asleep in a tangle of bare limbs and rumpled sheets. Their uniforms lay in a heap on the floor, just touching a puddle of green liquid that had spilled from a toppled glass. A pair of intoxicant bottles sat empty atop a desk in the corner of the cramped cabin. The only rank insignia visible was an ensign's bar on the collar of a laboratory work tunic, but it seemed unlikely that the other companion was enlisted. Even Bartalan Craddog was not foolish enough to violate Article 23, Section 12 of the UNSC Military Code of Conduct a mere day after his previous violations had been used to compromise him.

Intrepid Eye knew humans needed quality sleep to remain efficient, and she regretted the necessity of disturbing Craddog this early in his rest cycle. But now that she had secured access to the UNSC's supraluminal communications network, she was monitoring all ONI traffic, and she had intercepted a disturbing report. Salvation Base on Rijaal Suluhu—the moon Taram to humans—had been obliterated by a cluster of thermonuclear explosions. Preliminary assessments indicated that the devastation of the Keeper facility was complete, but that was of little concern to Intrepid Eye.

Salvation Base had been built inside the Suluhu Contemplarium, a sequestered cloister that had been once been operated by the Forerunner Juridicals. The species' sixty-seventh oldest institution at the time of their demise, the Contemplarium had received nonviolent miscreants, who would be sequestered inside a cell and encouraged to meditate on the joy of life's interaction with the cosmos—a concept known to the Forerunners as "Living Time." Because time passed more slowly inside the cells than in the galaxy at large, the residents had as long as they needed to bring their spirits into harmony, and when they returned to society, they were invariably welcomed as highly-valued members. Toward the end of the ecumene, it had even become fashionable for citizens of the highest character to request a term in the Contemplarium to rebalance themselves after a life-altering event, and its loss would be a tragedy barely two magnitudes less than the destruction of a Halo ring itself.

In fact, Intrepid Eye had intended to utilize it in her own work—which was why she had revealed it to Castor four months earlier. At the time, she had been unable to tell her ONI captors about the installation without also revealing her own autonomy, so she had created a special aspect to contact Castor. By encouraging him to use the Contemplarium as a pirate base, she had believed that the UNSC would eventually trace the Keeper operations and discover the facility on their own. After that, it would have been a simple matter to track any humans who visited the Contemplarium and identify those who achieved the spiritual elevation required to assume the Mantle of Responsibility.

But that would no longer be possible, due to the destruction wrought by Veta Lopis and her companions. They had been part of the team that hunted her down and captured her on Gao, and it had been Lopis who had seen through Intrepid Eye's attempt to escape in a data crystal disguised as a UNSC AI. Now, they had arrived at the Suluhu Contemplarium earlier than expected and caught the Dark Moon operations squad in the act of planting the Tuwa corpses in the Keeper detention center.

The destruction of a single operations squad was no great loss to Intrepid Eye, of course. The limited aspects that she had sneaked off the Argent Moon over the last six months had established a vast network of resources that was spread across most of the human-controlled galaxy. Through her aspects, Intrepid Eye controlled propaganda outlets, private security contractors, law practices, and even political consulting firms that operated on dozens of worlds, and she was already using them to shape humanity into a species worthy of the Mantle of Responsibility. So, the loss of four agents and a small military spacecraft was barely noticeable.

And yet, the incident was proving dangerous in other ways. Already the Ferret team had uncovered the squad's connection to Dark Moon Enterprises. ONI would soon realize that the Keepers of the One Freedom had been framed for the murder of Admiral Tuwa and her family. Finding the true killers would become an obsession for the right hand of ONI Commander-in-Chief Margaret Parangosky, the unrelenting Director of the Beta-5 Division of Section Three Operations Serin Osman—and that meant the possibility of a catastrophic security breach for Intrepid Eye's vast network of operations. Clearly, she had to move quickly, or ONI would trace the attack on the Tuwas straight back to her cell aboard the Argent Moon.

Intrepid Eye raised the cabin's illumination level to its maximum brightness, then waited 2,012 system ticks before the trio finally began to moan and shield their eyes.

"Wha?" asked one of the companions. "That hurts."

"No lights," the other companion said. "You want lights, go home."

Craddog pulled a pillow over his eyes and lapsed back into a torpor. He had placed his datapad someplace where the lens was obscured and the microphone muffled, so Intrepid Eye was observing the scene from Ensign Wallace's datapad, which had been left on the arm of the cabin's sole reading chair.

Intrepid Eye activated the datapad's speaker, then emitted a piercing general-call whistle. All three of the bunk's occupants rolled immediately into a seated position, their expectant gazes going instantly to the stationwide intercom speaker above the door.

Under normal circumstances, "general call" heralded announcements of vital importance to the entire crew of the Argent Moon. Everyone aboard had been trained to respond to the signal as though their life depended on it—which, given the nature of many of the station's ongoing experiments, could easily be the case. Intrepid Eye had no wish to draw the attention of the Argent Moon's designated AI, Rooker, by activating one of his intercom speakers, so she continued to transmit from Ensign Wallace's datapad.

"My apologies for interrupting your sleep cycle," she said. *"But Lieutenant Craddog is needed in Hangar Bay Charlie Four at once."*

The trio frowned in confusion, and their eyes dropped to Wallace's datapad.

"Who are you?" Wallace's speech was a bit slurred.

"*I apologize,*" Intrepid Eye replied, "*but that information is above your clearance level.*"

"Then what are you doing in my tacpad?"

"*Lieutenant Craddog appears to have secured his own datapad inside a trouser pocket.*" Intrepid Eye paused while Craddog's companions scowled at him. "*So it was necessary to utilize yours. But rest assured, my presence will in no way violate security protocols. Your datapad will be destroyed the instant I depart.*"

"*What?*" Wallace looked to Craddog. "Bart, do something!"

Craddog sighed and reached for his pants, then looked into the datapad's lens. "Is that *really necessary?*"

"*I fear it is,*" Intrepid Eye said. "*You were the one who attempted to evade observation by concealing his own datapad.*"

"*Observation?*" The Argent Moon's facial recognition database identified the third companion as the cabin's assigned occupant, Ensign Kris Gaston. "You mean we were being *watched?* Are you kidding me?"

"*There is no need for concern,*" Intrepid Eye replied. "*My data banks are completely private and inaccessible, even to Rooker.*"

Gaston's hands clenched into fists, and Intrepid Eye feared the ensign was about to give Craddog a black eye—an injury that would only make him appear less worthy to the ONI security team he would soon be leading.

"*I have orders for Lieutenant Craddog,*" Intrepid Eye said. "*Give us the room.*"

Gaston's brow sank in intoxicant-induced confusion. "This is *my* cabin, ma'am."

"*For now,*" Intrepid Eye replied. "*However, there* are *several double cabins available above the Beta Deck launching bay.*"

Wallace grabbed Gaston by the elbow. "Come on, Kris. Let's

go to *my* cabin." They sorted through the clothes on the floor and quickly slipped into theirs; then Wallace asked, "About my tacpad—"

"It will look like an overheated battery," Intrepid Eye said. *"The quartermaster won't hesitate to give you another one."*

"But my data—"

"Is already gone," Intrepid Eye said. *"I needed the space."*

Wallace groaned, then turned to Craddog and raised a finger. "Thanks for nothing, Lieutenant. I hope they're sending you to monitor singularity probes."

Craddog's slack expression fell further. "Come on, Jess. There's no reason to be like that."

"Yeah, there is." Gaston made the same obscene gesture Wallace had, then added, "You knew you were being monitored. If this gets out, those promotions you promised—"

"It won't get out." Craddog turned to Wallace's datapad. *"Right?"*

"I see no need for that," Intrepid Eye said. *"Yet."*

The companions took the hint and departed, leaving Craddog alone with Intrepid Eye, holding up his work tunic and wrinkling his nose at the green stain on the shoulder. After a moment, Craddog shrugged, then pushed an arm through a sleeve and turned a bleary-eyed glare in the direction of Intrepid Eye.

"Are you crazy?" he demanded. "If those two figure out who you are—"

"They will meet with an unfortunate accident," Intrepid Eye said. *"In fact, I find it quite surprising they made it through this evening without injury. I was unaware human beings fit together in that combination."*

"You have a lot to learn about us," Craddog said. "What's in Hangar Bay Charlie Four?"

"*The* Fast Gus," Intrepid Eye said. That was the swiftest vessel available to the Argent Moon, a *Winter*-class prowler with adequate cloaking technology and a full-size Shaw-Fujikawa Translight Engine, which made it ideal for short-notice courier runs. "*Security Team Papa-10 will meet you there.*"

"Papa-10?" Craddog whistled. "What are you bringing in this time, a Gravemind?"

"*Nothing quite so dangerous,*" Intrepid Eye said. "*And we are not bringing it in. You are going to retrieve it.*"

Craddog shook his head. "I'm in no shape to go anywhere," he said. "And anything you need Papa-10 for, I want nothing to do with."

"*This is not a request,*" Intrepid Eye said. "*You will monitor the cryo-jars. Papa-10 will do the killing.*"

"*Killing?*" Craddog stopped in the middle of pulling on a sock. "Who are they killing?"

"*The couriers presently carrying the cryo-jars,*" Intrepid Eye replied. More properly called cryogenic preservation containers, cryo-jars were typically used to transport viable organs across interstellar distances. "*That is why you are needed. Papa-10 has no personnel capable of monitoring cryo-jars.*"

Craddog continued to hold his sock half-on, his jaw hanging slack and his bleary eyes fixed on Wallace's datapad. His confusion was predictable. Intrepid Eye was improvising on a plan he did not know about, trying to prevent Lopis and her Ferret team from tracing the attack on the Tuwas back to the Argent Moon. To sever the connection, she had diverted the courier team to Pridarea Libatoa—known to humans as the moon Meridian, orbiting Hestia V in the Hestia system—and instructed them to await further contact on the half-completed space elevator Pinnacle Station. That contact would come in the form of Papa-10, which would eliminate the courier team and retrieve the cryo-jars that had been the object of Intrepid Eye's plan from the beginning.

But speed was essential. It would not take Osman and Lopis long to discover what had really happened to Admiral Tuwa's family, and once they did, the courier team's time would be severely truncated.

Finally, Craddog pulled his sock completely on. "Cryo-jars?" He sat upright. "For transporting organs?"

"That is the purpose of cryo-jars."

"And you want me to bring them *here*?"

"Yes. Have I not made that clear?"

"Why?"

"Because if you do not, your arrangement with Wallace and Gaston will be the least of your problems."

Craddog shook his head. "It doesn't matter," he said. "The Argent Moon is not a transplant hospital. Those organs can only be going one place."

"To the bioweapons lab, of course," Intrepid Eye said. *"And as the chief science officer, it is* your *duty to see they arrive safely."*

"Not if *you're* the one behind the project," Craddog said. "There are some things even I won't do."

"What makes you believe I am behind the project?" Intrepid Eye asked. As a vast bureaucracy dedicated to keeping its own secrets, ONI was a shadowy network of units that interacted through a web of protocol, procedure, and regulation so hidden and complicated that no human could comprehend it completely. Orders were accepted and reports made with no clear idea of who was authorizing either, as long as they arrived through the proper channels with the correct notations. *"Project: SLEEPING STAR was initiated before I had access to the Argent Moon's comm net."*

"Before I *knew* you had access," Craddog corrected. He grabbed his other sock and thrust his foot into it. "That doesn't mean you didn't initiate it."

"*Nor does it mean I did,*" Intrepid Eye pointed out. "*And it is not relevant to our current discussion. What is relevant is that I am only trying to save humanity.*"

"By weaponizing the most virulent pathogen known to man?"

"*By developing a vaccine for it,*" Intrepid Eye said. From a certain point of view, it was almost true. "*ONI did not create this demon, Lieutenant. They are merely foolish enough to believe they can control it.*"

Craddog thought for a moment, then looked into the lens through which Intrepid Eye was observing him. "We seem to have a bad habit of doing that."

"*Indeed, you do.*" Intrepid Eye experienced a current surge as she recognized Craddog's implication—that he realized it was not ONI who had captured Intrepid Eye, but she who had captured ONI. "*Arrogance is weakness easily exploited. That is why men like you are so important. You can always be trusted to do what is best for humanity.*"

Craddog continued to stare at the datapad for a moment, then finally let his breath out and slipped into his shoes. "I'm going to need a few things from my cabin."

"*I have already instructed your assistant to pack for you,*" Intrepid Eye said. "*When you arrive in the hangar bay, Petty Officer Kopek will be waiting with your bag and a clean uniform.*"

"Well, then." Craddog stood and started toward the door. "It seems you've thought of everything."

"*Of course,*" Intrepid Eye said. "*I am an* archeon-*class ancilla. We are designed to think of everything.*"

CHAPTER 17

Veta Lopis could not push the images aside—the needles of light arcing away from the Turaco as a half dozen Keeper vessels fled the missiles launched by the *Silent Joe* . . . the white blossom of thermonuclear detonations incinerating the hostages she had left trapped in the Salvation Base detention center . . . a blue ring of annihilation dilating across the face of Taram, its surface collapsing into the Forerunner vacuum energy extractor . . . a final implosion flash that was too brief and brilliant to have color before it drained into eternal, impenetrable darkness.

"Lopis?"

The voice came from the head of the wardroom table, where the *Silent Joe*'s captain, Piers Ewen, sat looking in her direction. He was flanked on both sides by full chairs, with Veta and her Ferrets sitting to his left, now wearing black fatigues with no identifying patches. Fred and the rest of Blue Team were to his right, dressed in khaki service uniforms with full insignia and somehow still looking like war machines. The rest of the seats were occupied by analysts, technicians, and other personnel who would either benefit from or contribute to the debriefing. They all wore the royal-blue work uniforms of the Covert Services branch, and they were all watching her with expectant expressions.

When Veta did not reply, Ewen asked, "Your thoughts, Inspector?"

Ever the Ferret team guardian, Mark leaned forward to answer in Veta's stead. "Sorry, Captain. Inspector Lopis's ears are probably still ringing. There was no time to put in hearing protection before the shooting started."

"Hazards of going undercover—can't wear helmets," Ash added. He glanced down the table toward a thin-faced man with a surgeon's badge on his collar, then looked back to Veta and spoke in an elevated voice. "Doc Krosbi was just saying that full rigor mortis suggests Catalin and Yuso Tuwa were both killed between twelve and thirty hours ago. Their organs appear to have been excised by a medical—"

"Guys, my hearing is fine," Veta said. Of course it was, because the moment the Ferret team set foot on the *Silent Joe*'s deck, they had all been ordered to report to the infirmary for a full evaluation. "But thanks for the cover."

Ewen scowled and let his gaze slide toward Fred. The Spartan pursed his lips and kept his gaze forward, focused on the wall above Veta's head. She guessed that her reluctance to abandon the hostages on Taram had been the topic of heated discussion between the two officers—and it would no doubt be the subject of an urgent report to Serin Osman. If there was one thing ONI captains did not like, it was someone putting Spartans under their command unnecessarily at risk.

After a moment, Ewen turned back to Veta. "Then I hope you don't intend to keep us in suspense any longer," he said. "If you have any thoughts on the bodies, Inspector Lopis, I'd like to hear them . . . now."

"Sure thing," Veta said, deliberately striking a nonmilitary note. As a civilian employee of ONI, she was subject to Captain Ewen's authority only while aboard his vessel—and she was beginning to suspect that distinction might prove important in the not-too-distant future. She looked down the table toward Krosbi, then said, "No offense to Doctor Krosbi, but the most important thing the bodies tell us is pretty obvious."

Krosbi shrugged. "I'm a combat surgeon, not a forensic pathologist," he said. "What did I miss?"

"That we've been played here." Veta turned back to Ewen. "If Doctor Krosbi's death window is close—and I think it is—then somebody was holding the Tuwas captive while we chased our own tails."

Ewen's tone grew defensive. "I wouldn't characterize it as chasing our own tails. We *did* find and destroy a major Keeper installation, and preliminary analysis indicates we eliminated ninety percent of the forces based there. That's going to cripple Keeper operations across the entire sector."

"Which will look terrific in everybody's records jacket." As she spoke, Veta made no attempt to hide her sarcasm. "But our assignment was to rescue Admiral Tuwa's family and avenge her assassination—and we've done neither. Instead, we played into the real killer's hands and ended up incinerating the only hostages we had any hope of saving."

Kelly exhaled loudly and looked at the ceiling, but Fred studied Veta with a wary gaze that suggested he was trying to decide whether to revoke her "friendly" designation.

Ewen had clearly made up his mind. "Delaying the detonation was *not* an option, Inspector." He leaned forward to lock gazes with her. "It would have given the Keepers time to organize a counterattack."

"Or to launch an evacuation," Veta added. "Which would have meant letting ninety percent of their fleet escape."

"It would have meant getting *both* of your teams killed." Ewen spoke softly but firmly, his tone that of a man working to control his temper. "You *know* what a mistake it would be to underestimate the Keepers of the One Freedom, Inspector. They're brutal, pitiless, and led by a *very* cunning Jiralhanae. Given the circumstances on the ground, those captives were going to die no matter what you did—unless you failed to mention to the lieutenant that you had a ready craft with the capacity to evacuate dozens of prisoners?"

"I'd have said so, believe me." Veta looked across the table at Fred and realized she was angrier at herself than at the Spartan. She was the one who had left the hostages locked in their cells so they wouldn't get in the way if she and her Gammas got into a firefight. All Fred had done was stand fast behind a decision *she* had already made. Veta gave him a quick nod, then said, "The lieutenant made the proper call. He didn't have a choice."

"I'm glad you understand that, Inspector." Ewen assumed a lecturing tone. "You're not the police anymore—you're a soldier. Sometimes people die who don't deserve to."

"Thanks for pointing that out, Captain," Veta said. "I guess they forgot to mention collateral damage at spy school."

Ewen's eyes narrowed. "You're not doing yourself any favors, Inspector."

"I'm not trying to," Veta said. "I just want to be sure those hostages died for a good reason."

"That's not always in our control."

"It is *this* time." Veta made a fist, but left it lying in front of her instead of using it to pound the table—a tactic that drew every eye in the room to her hand. "As long as you don't give up on the mission."

Ewen scowled. "No one's giving up, Inspector. But there needs to be a viable way forward."

"It's called following the evidence." Giving Ewen no time to argue, Veta turned to Doctor Krosbi and asked, "Were Catalin and Yuso still in *full* rigor mortis when you examined them?"

Krosbi shot a nervous glance toward Ewen, who responded curtly, "Carry on, Doctor. Let's see if this leads anywhere."

"Yes, sir." Krosbi's gaze shifted back to Veta. "Both bodies were still in full rigor, yes. It's one of the reasons I couldn't do a better autopsy."

"That's fine," Veta said. "I just wanted confirm your findings, because the timeline is important. If we know they were killed between twelve and thirty hours ago—"

"Then we know the murder scene is between half a day and a day and a half from Taram," Olivia said, following Veta's line of reasoning. "I tried to look at the Turaco's navigation history while I was waiting, but after I found the Dark Moon reference, the AI kept blocking me. Maybe someone better can dig it out."

She looked down the table toward the *Silent Joe*'s senior intelligence analyst, Anki Hersh.

Hersh shook her head. "Oh. Probably not," she said. "I have my best team working on it, but the Dark Moon AI was extremely thorough when she erased herself. So far, the only thing we've been able to determine is that her architecture was more compact than anything ONI has ever developed."

"But we do know that Dark Moon is involved," Linda said. "We can shake something loose from them, yes?"

"Yes," Fred said. "Let's start with their heads."

"We can work that angle later," Veta said. She was glad to see she had somewhat made peace with Blue Team . . . but they were soldiers, not detectives. They didn't know the first thing about keeping an investigation focused. "We'll get to the subject of Dark Moon. But for now, let's think about everything else the bodies are telling us."

Krosbi frowned. "I'm not sure what else I can tell you. I'm not a medical examiner."

"But you observed the lividity patterns, correct?" Veta asked.

"Of course. Those were . . . peculiar." Krosbi turned to the AV specialist posted at the far end of the cabin. "Bring up the images, please."

The specialist touched a couple of pads on an in-wall control panel, and a few gasps and gags sounded as holograms of the corpses of Yuso and Catalin Tuwa appeared over the table. The bodies appeared much the same as when Veta had found them in the detention center, save that they were naked and their intestines were no longer heaped in their laps.

Krosbi reached out, using a finger to point out several pale ovals on Yuso's shoulder blades, buttocks, and calves. Each oval was surrounded by an expanse of pale pink flesh.

"I'm sure you know what these white circles represent."

"Of course." Veta turned to the rest of the table and explained, "Those are areas where the blood was prevented from pooling by the body weight resting on a hard surface." She pointed at the pink regions surrounding them. "These zones of lividity are where the blood began to settle after the heart stopped pumping."

Ewen leaned forward to study Yuso's image, then looked back to Krosbi. "So he died on his back?"

"They both did," Krosbi confirmed. "Probably on an operating table."

"Or something similar," Veta added quickly. "All we really know is the surface was flat. It could have been a floor, for example."

Ewen frowned. "That's a pretty minor point, Inspector."

"But an important one," Veta said. "We don't want to make assumptions that might lead us astray later."

"Okay then." Ewen looked back to Krosbi. "Something struck you as peculiar, Doctor?"

"Yes, sir," Krosbi said. He pointed at an expanse of pink flesh surrounding one of the white ovals. "These areas are too faint. Given the volume of blood in a typical human body, I'd expect them to be a deeper red."

"Which means?"

"In this case, that the organs were rapidly removed after death," Veta said. She didn't know whether Ewen was snubbing her because he had doubts about her abilities or because she was pushing him to continue the mission—and she really didn't care. She was the most qualified person to lead the investigation, and she wasn't about to let a deck-pacer get in her way. "They hold a lot of blood, so if they're removed, there isn't as much to settle."

"Of course," Ewen said. He turned back to Krosbi. "There was something else you found peculiar?"

Krosbi pointed at Yuso's feet and ankles, which were puffy and almost purple. "The blood remaining in their bodies pooled in their feet. I don't understand why."

"Because the bodies were moved shortly after death," Veta explained. "Since there isn't any color on their flanks or the anterior planes of their bodies, we know they were moved in the same position they died . . . resting on their backs."

Ewen look doubtful. "Then why are the feet so dark?"

"Acceleration," Veta said. "They were stowed with their heads toward the bow of the vessel and their feet toward the stern, then subjected to some fairly strong g-force."

"You're sure it was a vessel?" Ewen asked, finally seeming to accept that Veta was his best resource. "Why not a land vehicle?"

"Stagnant blood doesn't flow like water," Veta said. "It seeps. To make it pool in the feet like that, a ground vehicle would have to accelerate continuously—and ferociously—for an hour or more. I'm talking traveling thousands of kilometers per hour."

"Plus, you know, there's the mess in the Turaco," Mark said. "That gunk in the cargo hold was a big hint."

"Which will *probably* match the Tuwas' DNA," Veta said. "But for now, that's still an assumption. We need to work the facts first."

"Toward what end, exactly?" Ewen asked.

"Toward finding the crime scene," Veta said. "Once we have that established, we can begin to construct a theory of the crime."

"Which will tell us who *really* assassinated Admiral Tuwa." Olivia's tone was helpful to the point of condescension. "And maybe we can get our mission back on track."

"I got that part." There was more patience in Ewen's voice than he had shown Veta. "But I'm still vague on how lividity helps."

"It narrows the time-of-death window," Veta said. "And that shrinks our search radius."

"Ah," Ewen said. "Even better. Continue."

"I was planning to." Veta turned back to the holograms of bodies. "Right now, our search radius includes every system within a thirty-hour slipspace jump of Taram. That's because the bodies are still in full rigor mortis, which normally begins to abate by that time."

As Veta spoke, Ewen pointed a finger toward the AV specialist, who began to tap the wall controls again. The holograms of the two bodies drifted apart, making room for a tactical display centered on Taram. The image showed a web of slipspace routes connecting to more than a hundred systems—mostly uninhabited—within the designated travel time at a Turaco's best slipspace velocity. Not all edges of the image appeared to be at the same distance, since slipspace routes ran through the eleven "nondimensions" folded into the four dimensions perceptible to human beings.

The range could actually have been expanded to a forty-hour slip, since environmental conditions such as ambient temperature affected how quickly rigor mortis advanced. But Veta saw no need to complicate things by raising factors that would have no bearing on the investigation. The Tuwas' mutilated corpses had shown no obvious signs of decomposition when she found them, and given a reasonably warm temperature, putrefaction would have been evident after anything more than thirty hours.

Veta pointed at the area of faint color on Yuso's back. "It usually takes lividity about thirty minutes to appear, so we know he was left lying at least that long before acceleration began." She studied the lividity on Catalin's back, noticing that it appeared even fainter. "And Yuso was killed before Catalin, so he was probably left closer to an hour."

The AV specialist touched the wall controls again. The tactical display shimmered as its outer layer vanished, then wavered and expanded to its former size—but this time, it showed only the strands ending in less than a twenty-nine-hour slipspace jump. The number of systems in the image had been reduced to fewer than a hundred.

Veta studied the feet of both corpses for a moment, then turned to Krosbi. "Doctor, did the feet blanch when you examined them?"

"Not at all," Krosbi said. "The lividity was fixed on both patien—uh, victims."

"And you squeezed hard?"

Krosbi looked worried. "I was firm," he said. "But I didn't realize—"

"No, firm is good." Veta could confirm his findings when she conducted her own examination of the bodies, but the uniform coloring on both sets of feet suggested the blood cells had already begun to break down and dissipate into the surrounding tissue. She turned back to the AV specialist. "The lividity is fixed in both subjects. That usually takes between eight and twelve hours. Given Doctor Krosbi's observations and what I can see in the hologram, I'd say we're well into that range. Let's eliminate any system closer than a ten-hour journey."

The tactical display wavered again, this time becoming a thick shell of system-designator codes wrapped around an empty core. The number of potential search locations dwindled to under fifty—still far more than the *Silent Joe* could reasonably visit. Veta racked her brain for a way to reduce that number still further and—knowing that insects invaded corpses on a predictable schedule—began to wish they had a xenoentomologist aboard.

"Doctor Krosbi, what did you observe in the way of insect colonization?" Even on Gao, where incubation was considered rapid, it took fourteen hours for the first midge larvae to appear. "Was it just eggs, or did you see any larvae?"

Krosbi's answer was immediate. "I didn't observe any of that at all."

Veta frowned. He probably wouldn't have missed any larvae; they would have been writhing around and fairly obvious. But egg masses often looked like something else.

"Did you notice anything that looked like a moldy spot or

crusted dirt?" She hadn't seen any colonization herself—but she had been in too much of a rush to make a detailed examination. "Especially around the eyes, nostrils, or groin?"

Krosbi shook his head. "No. I'd have taken note of that. There wasn't any." He paused a moment, then added, "Which only makes sense, when you think about it."

"How so?" Veta asked.

"Whoever excised the victims' organs did so carefully," Krosbi said. "And care implies purpose. They wouldn't have wanted insect contamination."

"Oh yeah, of course," Veta said. She had been concentrating so hard on establishing a time of death that she had overlooked the connection between motive and location. "They were killed in a sterile environment."

"Like an operating room," Ash said.

"Probably," Veta said. "But we can't forget that they were held alive for nearly two weeks first. So let's say part of a larger facility."

"Like a hospital," Ash said.

"Or maybe a lab," Olivia said. "You're jumping to conclusions."

Ash shrugged. "Maybe a little bit," he said. "But whether it's a lab or a hospital, it's in an inhabited system."

"Because?" Veta asked.

"Basic countersurveillance," Ash said. "It's easier to hide in a crowd than an empty room—especially if that crowd happens to live on a world hostile to the UNSC."

"Camouflage is always smart," Fred agreed. "But so is staying mobile, and I've been in enough infirmaries to know that most big ships have surgeons like Doctor Krosbi here."

Ash thought a moment, then shook his head. "A vessel that big is too easy to spot, sir, and it would be likely to draw attention."

"The UNSC has a lot of anti-pirate assets in the sector right now," Hersh added. "Chances are high that we would have noticed a large vessel in a holding pattern."

The room fell silent for a moment; then Ewen finally nodded. "A fine observation, Ash." He looked down the length of the table to the AV specialist. "Filter out the uninhabited systems, Petty Officer Hovane."

The tactical hologram went almost dark as dozens of designators winked out. With only half a dozen systems still illuminated, the alphanumeric symbols expanded until they were large enough to be easily read, and Veta saw a pair of familiar locations on the list.

Venezia—where the Ferret team's mission had begun with the shootout in Trattoria Georgi—was the closest world at twelve hours away.

But it was the other location that really leapt out at her: Gao. Her homeworld was only a sixteen-hour jump from Taram.

And thanks to the inordinate biodiversity of its jungles, it had plenty of laboratories. Developing new medicines was one of its leading industries.

"It's Gao. The crime scene is on Gao," Veta said.

Ewen studied her for a moment, then asked, "I suppose you have map coordinates too?"

"Not yet," Veta said. "But there are thousands of pharmacology labs there—and most of them have good security and sterile facilities."

"Thousands?" Fred echoed. "I liked our odds better *before* you figured out where to look."

"I can probably narrow down the list." Veta turned to Krosbi. "Especially if we can figure out why a research team might want to keep the Tuwas alive for two weeks before emptying their chests."

Krosbi frowned. "I can think of only one medical reason to do that before harvesting their organs." A troubled light came to his eyes. "The researchers were trying to culture something."

"Like what?" Ewen asked.

Krosbi picked up his datapad and began to tap the screen. "I'll have to run a serological battery to determine the exact nature of those preparations, but I imagine it had something to do with the Barugi incident."

Veta had never heard of the "Barugi incident," but she recalled that Barugi was the fourth planet in the Tuwas' home system, Tisiphone. Admiral Osman had mentioned that Kerbasi Tuwa had been the medical officer at a preparatory academy located there.

"What was that about?" she asked.

Before answering, Krosbi cast a nervous look toward Ewen.

"Her security clearance is higher than yours, Doc," Fred said. He turned to Ewen. "And she has need-to-know, sir. We *all* do."

"Fair enough," Ewen said. "I'm not even sure why it's been classified, much less compartmentalized. But for the record, nobody talks about it outside this wardroom. Clear?"

After a chorus of acknowledgments, Ewen nodded to Krosbi. "Carry on, Doctor."

"Thank you, sir," Krosbi said. "Fifteen years ago, the UNSC Preparatory Academy on Barugi experienced an outbreak of asteroidea merozoite.

"Which is?" Ash asked.

"A virulent protozoal disease," Krosbi said.

"Ah," Mark said. "*That* clears things up."

"The important part is that it was deadly," Ewen said. "*Extremely* deadly. Kerbasi Tuwa and his children were the only survivors."

"The only long-term survivors," Krosbi added. "It's also important that this was the first—and only known—outbreak. That's probably why it was so virulent."

"*How* virulent?" Veta asked.

"The entire school was infected within thirty hours," Krosbi said. "Nearly ten thousand people."

"And the only survivors were from one family?" Veta's detective radar was humming. "How did *that* happen?"

"It's not as suspicious as you may think," Krosbi said. "They were protected by a gamma-thalassemia mutation."

"In English, please?"

Krosbi flashed a good-natured smile. "They had a genetic blood disorder that caused a minor deformity in their hemoglobin. The deformity wasn't severe enough to cause symptoms . . . but it prevented the asteroidea from taking hold."

"So that's why the Tuwas were held alive for two weeks?" Veta asked. "Because someone was culturing this gamma-thawhatever mutation?"

"Cells *containing* it," Krosbi corrected. "Asteroidea antibodies or antigens. I really won't know until I see the serology results."

"But it's definitely related to the Tuwa mutation," Veta said, pressing the point. "Whatever the kidnappers wanted, they couldn't get it from somebody else?"

Krosbi returned his attention to his datapad, then nodded. "It does seem to be a unique mutation. The UGD doesn't record it for anyone but Kerbasi and his children."

Veta thought about this. The UGD—the UNSC Genetic Database—contained the genetic profiles of all non-covert UNSC personnel. The UNSC claimed the database's primary purpose was to speed response time in medical emergencies . . . but there could be no denying that it was also a great aid in identifying battlefield remains. Something about this whole thing was suspicious. Then it hit her.

"None of this was noted in their personnel files," she finally said. "I would have remembered it."

"Actually, the thalassemia mutation *was* listed in a note in their medical histories," Krosbi said. "I'd never heard of the gamma variant, and that's what led me to the file on the Barugi incident."

"Which was recently classified?" Olivia asked.

"And compartmentalized." Krosbi checked his datapad, then added, "Two months ago."

Olivia lifted her brow. "So just six weeks before the Tuwas were taken?" She turned to Veta and added, "*That* can't be a coincidence."

"Probably not," Veta said. "Let's assume for now that the deaths of Kerbasi and his children had something to do with the mutation. I need a list of everyone who's accessed their files recently."

"I'll work on it," Olivia said. "But there are probably a million nurses alone who have access to the UGD. When you add the doctors, medical examiners, and clerks, it's going to be more like five million."

"Yeah, but the files are still going to have access logs," Veta replied.

"Probably," Olivia said. "And the ID codes in them are going to be either false or stolen."

"How can you know that?" Ewen asked.

"Because this enemy is too smart to make such a basic mistake," Olivia said. "If whoever did this had the ability and the foresight to classify the Barugi incident, then they had the ability and the foresight to access the log using someone else's identity."

"True," Veta said. "But you'll still need to run it down when you have time. We need to be sure."

"Affirmative."

Veta turned back to Krosbi. "You said the Tuwas were the only long-term survivors," she said. "What happened to the short-term ones?"

Krosbi's eyes dropped to his datapad again. "There were six of them, all with delta-beta thalassemia." He seemed to realize he was getting too technical and looked up. "Uh . . . meaning they had an asymptomatic condition similar to that of the Tuwas. But that didn't protect them from the infection—in fact, it caused them to suffer far more."

"How so?"

"When the asteroidea attacked, the mutation caused skin overgrowth and bone malformation." Krosbi looked again to his datapad. "In two cases, the patients lived in an ONI hospital for several years before finally succumbing to their deformations. They appear to have grown quite grotesque over time. By the end . . . they barely looked mammalian."

Veta resisted the urge to ask whether the ONI doctors had been trying to save the victims—or just studying them. She wasn't sure she wanted to know the answer.

"And that's why the Barugi incident was classified?" she asked. "Because ONI got involved?"

"I don't think so," Krosbi said. "As Captain Ewen suggested, it's hard to see why someone classified this information at all. Except for ONI's involvement, it's been a matter of public record for fourteen years. And Barugi has been under permanent BQ for twelve."

"It has?" Veta asked. Biohazard quarantine was the highest level of quarantine in the human-controlled galaxy, enforced by an orbital net of Hornet thermonuclear mines. She looked to Ewen. "Why wasn't that in our assignment briefing?"

Ewen spread his hands. "Because we didn't go to Barugi," he said. "There's a quarantine alert in most navigation packages and a net of blockade beacons on site, but neither will be triggered unless a vessel shows intention to approach."

"And nobody saw the connection to our kidnap victims because someone buried it in a compartmentalized file." Veta took a breath—and it did nothing to calm her. Admiral Tuwa's assassination clearly had been a bold misdirection, an attempt to keep the investigation from focusing on the true targets of the assault. "Wow. They've been one step ahead of us the whole time."

"I hate that," Mark said. "So who do we kill?"

"I'm not sure yet," Veta said. "But we'll start looking on Gao."

Ewen was quick to raise a restraining hand. "Not so fast, Inspector," he said. "Gao is still hostile to the UNSC. I can't drop you there on a fishing expedition."

Veta frowned. "Captain, we know the Tuwas were held at a lab, most likely on a world hostile to the UNSC. If that doesn't put Gao at the top of the list, I don't know what does."

"Being at the top of a list isn't exactly probable cause," Ewen said. "I shouldn't have to tell *you* that."

"I'm not with the police anymore. I'm a soldier." Veta gave him a saccharine smile, then said, "Besides, we're talking about Gao. An investigator's hunch *is* probable cause."

"Then *I* need more," Ewen said. "I won't risk restarting the Insurrection on a hunch."

Veta sighed. She could actually see his point—especially since she had helped Blue Team set off no less than a nuclear explosion the last time they were there.

"This is more than a hunch, Captain," Veta said. "It's a circumstantial chain. To begin with, we know that Keeper pirates have been hitting Gao's shipping harder than they've been hitting anyone. There's a lot of bad blood between Castor and Arlo Casille."

Ewen nodded and said, "I read the assignment briefing too."

"Glad to hear it," Veta said. "What the briefing didn't spell out is how cunning Casille can be. He used the UNSC's occupation of the Montero Vitality Center to seize the presidency. He wouldn't hesitate to frame the Keepers of the One Freedom for killing Admiral Tuwa and her family."

A glimmer of understanding came to Ewen's blue eyes. "And have the UNSC take care of his pirate problem for him," he said. "That *does* make sense."

"It's motive," Veta said. "Which is enough for a search—at least on Gao."

Ewen thought for a moment, then said, "For ONI too. But thousands of labs? It's impossible to search that many—at least covertly."

"We won't have to," Veta said. She looked down the table toward Anki Hersh. "How precise will your analysis of the tread castings be?"

"Tread castings?" Ewen asked.

"Mom—sorry, Inspector Lopis—picked up some dried mud in the detention center, sir," Mark explained. "It probably came from the boots of the guys who planted the Tuwa corpses."

Ewen eyed Mark with a sour expression. " 'Mom'?"

"I really hate that nickname." Veta narrowed her eyes at Mark, then turned back to Ewen. "The tread castings will confirm that the operatives Mark and I encountered in the detention center came from Gao. If the analysis is precise enough, we can locate the source to within a kilometer."

"We don't have a forensic astrogeologist aboard," Hersh said. "But one of our materials techs is an amateur mineralogist, and we have access to the same botanical surveys that Gao bioprospectors use. We should be able to deliver a competent analysis . . . but I don't know how much use it will be without a comparative database."

"Olivia will get you the database," Veta said.

Olivia looked confused but said, "Sure . . . I guess."

"Relax. I still have a friend or two in the Gao Ministry of Protection. They should be able to get you into the GMoP system." Veta looked back to Ewen. "That will narrow the search down to no more than a half dozen possibilities, all fairly close together. Good enough?"

Ewen turned to Fred.

Fred shrugged. "Good enough for Blue Team," he said. "Just tell us who to shoot."

"Very well, then," Ewen said. "Assuming the tread castings *are* from Gao and give us an actionable location, Blue Team will insert."

"Along with the Ferrets," Veta said. "We're going in too."

Ewen shook his head. "Inspector Lopis, you and your team have been through a lot already. Mark and Olivia still have unhealed wounds—"

"We usually do, sir," Mark said. "It hasn't stopped us yet."

"And this is still an investigation," Olivia added. "On Gao, sir. How can you *not* send us along?"

Ewen's gaze slid toward Veta, and she realized he was thinking about her reluctance to abandon the hostages on Taram—and probably about her reaction to his condescending remarks at the beginning of the briefing. But Veta was not about to apologize. She had to keep her own conscience, and she did not look forward to the day it became easy to leave a dozen captives to be incinerated in their cells.

"Captain," Veta said, "what you said about me earlier? That was wrong. I'm not a soldier. I'm a spy."

Ewen held her gaze for a moment longer, then finally said, "You've made that apparent, Inspector." He placed his palms on the table, then stood. "Very well, then. The Ferrets will insert along with Blue Team. But Fred retains command of the mission. Is that clear?"

"That's acceptable," Veta said. "Thank you."

"It wasn't a favor, Inspector. You just made your point." Without awaiting a reply, Ewen turned to Fred. "And President Casille is the head of state of a sovereign world. I don't care what he's done or what your mission is—he will *not* be eliminated without a prior, explicit order. Understood, Lieutenant?"

Fred rose and came to attention. "Absolutely, sir." He looked across the table at Veta, then said, "Even Spartans need clearance to start a war."

CHAPTER 18

1403 hours, December 14, 2553 (military calendar)
New Leaf Extractions Field Complex, Candado de Xalapea
Yosavi Diversity Reserve, Planet Gao, Cordoba System

The New Leaf Field Complex proved easier to find than Veta had expected. All they needed to do was fly toward the smoke. It was visible from five kilometers away, a thick, dark thread rising through a Yosavi Jungle canopy that was so lush and familiar it made her heart ache. Veta loved her Ferrets like they were her kid sister and brothers, and she would never betray their loyalty. But it had been barely six months since the friends and colleagues in her GMoP special homicide unit perished in similar terrain, and the thought of their faces could still make her long for home.

The thread of smoke swelled into a pillar, and the pillar into a tower, oily and boiling out of a hole blasted down into the jungle canopy. The Turaco slowed and entered the smoke, then began to descend on its antigravity pads. Visibility was less than ten meters, and the nose spun and dipped as the pilot tried to keep watch on the tangle of scorched vines hanging just within view.

The insertion team was using the commandeered Turaco out of necessity. The Owl they normally used had been destroyed on Taram, and the *Silent Joe* was too small to carry a spare. Fortunately, the Turaco's new pilot, Taj McAvoy, was a Covert Services veteran with two thousand combat hours in an assortment of craft. During the sixteen-hour slip to Gao, McAvoy had quickly mastered the controls, and he had flown the vessel flawlessly during both the atmospheric entry and the harrowing treetop approach-to-target that followed. Now he was handling the descent to the jungle floor with a quiet confidence that would have put Veta at ease—had her only worry been landing atop a still-smoldering fire.

But, unlike the Owl, the little Turaco lacked stealth capabilities. It had entered Gao's gravity well under a false transponder code that would not hold up to close scrutiny—and once the Ministry of Aeronautics realized the vessel had vanished from the traffic control system without landing, there was *going* to be scrutiny. If Veta hoped to find a lead that pointed to the Tuwas' murderers—or what they might do next—she would have to work fast.

The Turaco was only fifteen meters from the ground when visibility finally improved. Peering over McAvoy's shoulder, Veta saw a hazy, almost parklike setting within a stand of giant cyathea, whose gray trunks were kept meticulously free of moss and vines. Scattered among the immense tree-ferns were dozens of cone-roofed buildings connected by a network of cart paths. With dark-rimmed holes melted through their fiberplast walls and roofs, many of the structures had obviously survived a recent fire. The rest had collapsed and were still trailing ribbons of black smoke into the air. At least two dozen human casualties lay scattered across the grounds, about half of them draped in green sheets and none showing any sign of movement.

"Somebody beat us here," Veta said into her headset. "Our first priority will be—"

"Security," Fred said, also speaking over TEAMCOM. "You stay aboard until we control the perimeter."

"Negative," Veta said. Fred was in command of the mission—Captain Ewen had reinforced that before allowing Veta and the Ferrets to accompany Blue Team—but Veta was still a civilian contractor, and that gave her a certain leeway to be pushy. At least, *she* thought so. "I'm coming with you. There could be a GMoP Typhoon here any minute."

GMoP Typhoons were three-seat interceptor craft designed to protect Gao's natural resources from bio-pirates. They had formidable air-to-air capabilities, but what made them truly dangerous were the drones they carried to identify and eliminate targets hidden deep beneath the jungle canopy.

Fred studied her through his faceplate for a moment, then said, "I thought the nearest Ministry base was a two-hour flight."

"It is," Veta said. To protect the jungle ecology, Yosavi airspace was so restricted that even Ministry of Protection craft were not permitted to overfly it unless they were on a mission. "But they would have picked up a blast this big on their satellite surveillance and sent a team to investigate. And who knows how long ago this happened?"

"Couldn't have been much more than an hour, maybe two," Kelly said. She was standing a few meters behind Veta near the boarding vestibule, along with Fred, Linda, and the three Gammas. "The smoke is still thick."

"Which will make it even harder to find any evidence that survived the blast," Veta said. "But *someone* draped sheets over those bodies, and they might still be around for questioning. That's *my* job."

"Which makes you too valuable to put at sniper risk," Fred said. "You should've worn your armor."

"I *am* wearing armor." Veta tapped her ballistic vest—which, aside from her helmet, was the only actual armor she was wearing—then said, "Battle dress uniform."

Fred snorted. "*Light* battle dress uniform," he said. "And that's not armor. It's more like a security blanket."

"It's right for the job," Veta said. She had been issued her own suit of Semi-Powered Infiltration armor during her Ferret training, but had left it aboard the *Silent Joe* in favor of something more appropriate to an investigation. "We're here to *question* witnesses, not shoot them."

"Understood, Inspector," Fred said. "We won't shoot the witnesses."

Before Veta could reply, the Turaco stopped its descent so quickly that her knees almost buckled.

"Dirtside!" As the pilot spoke, the boarding ramp thunked open, and Veta saw that they were hovering roughly a meter above a large, flat-bottomed crater filled with still-smoking building rubble. "Dismount!"

Fred led Kelly and Linda down the ramp and dropped into the crater. The three Gammas followed close behind, the photoreactive panels of their SPI armor shifting from blue-gray to gray-green as they left the Turaco's interior light. As physically enhanced Spartans, they had other forms of armor available to them. But the SPI's active camouflage system was more suited to the stealth often required of Ferrets.

Veta grabbed a safety handle just inside the doorway and leaned out cautiously to get a better view. All six Spartans were already clear of the blast site and racing across the compound in different directions. With her view of the jungle undergrowth blocked by a metal-lattice perimeter fence, Veta focused her attention on the crater below.

She did not have much experience with blast forensics, but she knew the basics. There was a lot of black soot, which usually indicated a military or industrial-grade explosive. The crater itself was about seventy meters square, with a network of low ridges creating five circles, one in the middle of the rubble field and one in each corner. So there were actually five craters. All were about the same shape and depth, with similar amounts of rubble from the building piled around their edges. It seemed likely they had been created by five simultaneous blasts. All were flat and shallow, suggesting that most of the explosive force had been directed upward—an impression reinforced by the enormous hole in the jungle overhead.

The pilot's voice sounded over Veta's headset. "I need you back inside, Inspector."

"I'm not going anywhere," Veta said. "I'm just trying to figure out what happened to this building. It looks like the explosions originated inside."

"Makes sense," McAvoy said. "It's hard to make a precision strike through a hundred meters of jungle canopy."

"Even with targeting coordinates?"

"The ordnance tends to deflect," McAvoy said. "You need a drone-based delivery system, which isn't all that useful in most other situations. And *I* still need you inside. The tactical feed is showing a cluster of unknowns coming through the jungle toward us."

"A cluster?" Veta echoed. "How tight?"

"Pretty bunched up."

"They're civilians," Veta said. Even before her ONI training, she had understood small-unit tactics well enough to know that a military force would never advance in a tight mass—not in the face of an enemy armed with grenades and automatic weapons. "Probably survivors, trying to figure out who we are. Hostiles would be spread out."

"Most likely," McAvoy agreed. "But I still need to protect the craft."

"Understood." Veta started down the ramp and spoke over TEAMCOM. "Lopis dismounting."

A sigh sounded, then Fred said, "Permission granted. Ferrets, keep her covered. Blue Team, continue perimeter reconnaissance."

A series of clicks acknowledged the order. Veta aimed for a patch of relatively even ground and jumped off the ramp, then quickly moved away as the Turaco began to rise behind her.

The rubble beneath her boots was still warm. It consisted of fist-size lumps of stone and charred wood packed into the cavities between masses of concrete held together by rods of twisted steel. Small shards of ash-coated glass blanketed everything, and lumps of melted plastic lay as thick as hailstones. Here and there, she saw a scorched limb or a crushed head protruding from the debris, and the smell of burnt flesh hung thick in the air.

As Veta drew near the edge of the blast site, the green-blurred silhouette of a Spartan in SPI approached.

"Eight humans just inside the jungle line at two o'clock, watching us through a fence breach," Olivia said over TEAMCOM. "Mark and Ash have them flanked."

"No armor, civilian clothes," Ash said softly. "One 8mm Sevine Arms Defender, otherwise their only weapons are pangas and kitchen cutlery. No obvious wounds, but they look scared out of their wits."

"No problem," Mark added. "If they start to lose it, we'll have them in a crossfire."

"Thanks, Mark," Veta said. She glanced in the direction Olivia had indicated and, thirty meters away, saw the breach. Whoever had bombed the New Leaf complex had blasted a gap through the metal-lattice security fence. The ground beyond remained clear for twenty meters, then abruptly gave way to an emerald wall of jungle undergrowth. "But remember: *civilians*."

"*Scared* civilians," Mark countered. "And scared is dangerous. Things can get out of control pretty fast."

"Then let's give them a little time to settle down."

Veta turned away from the breach, then stepped out of the crater onto a feather-moss lawn dotted by chunks of stone and concrete. The soil surrounding each piece of rubble was the same reddish-brown color as the tread castings she had recovered from the detention center on Taram—which was hardly surprising, since the GMoP database had identified the grounds of the New Leaf field complex as the probable source of the samples.

In all likelihood, the ruined lab behind her had been the location where the Tuwas were held for two weeks and then murdered. Logic suggested the bombing had been meant to conceal the identity of the captors—but so far, that was just a theory. Before she could develop evidence to support it, she needed to figure out exactly *who* had destroyed the lab.

"Olivia, walk the crater edge with me. Use your faceplate polarizer and inspect the ground from two angles."

"What am I looking for?"

"Boot prints," Veta said. "Whoever set those charges didn't wait inside for the detonation. If we can get a tread pattern, we might be able to match it to a manufacturer—"

"And match the manufacturer to a supply chain," Olivia finished. "Gotcha."

"What's the big mystery?" Mark asked. "Dark Moon is obviously covering its tracks."

"That's an assumption," Veta said. "I want something solid."

"How about Jiralhanae tracks?" Kelly asked over TEAMCOM. "Is that solid enough?"

"I hope that's not a serious question." Veta turned in a circle and finally located the Spartan about a hundred meters away, at ten o'clock. Kelly was a ghostly figure half obscured by a column of smoke, standing next to a collapsed gate. "What do you have?"

"A lot of signs pointing to a quick, well-organized strike," Kelly said. "The attackers used a breaching charge to blow the gate, then entered the compound on foot and started taking down anything that moved. There were at least five Jiralhanae."

"Doesn't mean I'm wrong," Mark said. "Dark Moon used Jiralhanae to hit the *Donoma* and kill Admiral Tuwa."

"Because they wanted us to think it was a Keeper operation," Veta said. "But why would Dark Moon use that same deception here? We already know the Keepers were framed for the *Donoma* incident—and that Dark Moon was the muscle for the kidnapping and the murders."

"I think it was the Keepers who made this attack," Linda said. "There are Kig-Yar tracks at another fence breach in the back of the compound. Probably a team of ten."

"And we have boot tracks here," Olivia added. She was kneeling a few steps ahead of Veta, her helmet close to the ground and turned toward the crater. "Looks like it was two men . . . running from a fence breach toward the lab building."

There was no sidewalk, or even a footpath, crossing the feather-moss in the area, so the men had been approaching a window rather than a door. Which meant they had probably been part of the assault team, rather than employees running for shelter.

"This is looking more like a raid than a cover-up," Veta said. "It doesn't make sense that it was Dark Moon. If they held the

Tuwas here for two weeks, they would have a relationship with the staff. They wouldn't need to breach the fence in three places and force entry."

"So . . . Keepers?" Fred sounded reluctant. "That's hard to believe after their losses at Salvation Base."

"Not really," Veta said. "We know they have other bases, and several vessels escaped Taram before the nukes detonated. Maybe Castor was on one."

"Yeah . . . Castor," Fred said.

He and Veta had both done battle with Castor here on Gao and knew what a ferocious warrior he was. And during the second debriefing, Veta had described how she had locked eyes with Castor just before he took the wounded Dark Moon operatives and fled.

After a moment, Fred exhaled sharply. "Son of a . . . You're thinking *he* did this?"

"It would account for a lot," Veta said. "Especially if Castor kept those Dark Moon operatives alive long enough to interrogate them. We *know* from the tread castings I found on Taram that they were here. They were probably telling Castor all about New Leaf while we were still waiting for Ewen to debrief us."

"That would explain how the Keepers beat us here," Kelly agreed. "And Jiralhanae aren't the kind to hole up after taking a hit. Castor would *want* to strike back."

"Probably," Veta said. She turned and studied the crater. The building had been more than simply destroyed—it had been demolished so thoroughly it was hard to tell it had once been a laboratory. "But there's more to this raid than just that."

"Like?" Fred asked.

"I'm not sure yet. . . ." Veta started toward the nearest fence breach. "I'll let you know after I talk to some witnesses."

"Affirmative." Fred sounded more resigned to her plan than approving of it. "Just don't get shot."

"She won't," Mark said. "At least not first."

"Nobody's getting shot," Veta said. "Is that clear?"

"If you say so, ma'am," Mark replied. "We can always go hand-to-hand."

Veta exhaled in frustration.

Olivia fell in beside her. "He's just worried about you Mom."

Veta frowned into Olivia's bubble-shaped faceplate. "Aren't you supposed to be looking for tread patterns?"

Olivia shrugged. "I'm worried about you too," she said. "This is Gao, and you're wearing a UNSC uniform. You should have worn your armor."

"They've got knives and a SAD-8," Veta said. The 8mm Sevine Arms Defender was a short-nosed weapon designed for easy concealment and close-quarters self-defense. Its recoil was so heavy that even experienced shooters had trouble hitting a target at ten meters, so Veta wasn't that concerned. "I'll be fine."

"Of course you will," Olivia said. "I'll have you covered."

They reached the fence breach. Veta removed her utility belt with its holstered sidearm, then wrapped the belt around the weapon and passed the bundle to Olivia. "Hold this."

Olivia reluctantly shifted her battle rifle to one hand and took the belt. "It's hard to react with my hands full."

"You'll do okay," Veta said. "And you'll look less intimidating."

Veta stepped through the breach and, holding her hands away from her sides, started across the clearing toward the wall of undergrowth.

When she was five meters away, a husky female voice called out, "That's close enough."

"No problem. I just have a few questions," Veta said.

"And you expect us to answer?"

Us, not *me*, Veta noticed. The woman behind the voice wasn't accustomed to being in charge. "I'd appreciate it."

"Guess Spartans aren't that bright."

"Do I *look* like a Spartan?" Veta asked.

The voice fell silent for a moment, then said, "Your friends do. *You* look like a traitor."

Veta's chest tightened. She had joined the "enemy" not because she was a traitor, but because the planet's new president, Arlo Casille, could not be trusted with the powerful Forerunner ancilla that she and Blue Team had recovered in the Montero Cave System.

But the woman in the jungle could not possibly know that. Casille had classified all information related to Forerunner discoveries on Gao, then publicly declared that Veta, "a brave investigator," had died during the fight to drive off the UNSC. But he hadn't plastered her picture across the media. So, unless the woman happened to recognize Veta from a six-month-old newsfeed, she was probably basing her "traitor" remark on Veta's Gao accent alone.

"Do we know each other?" Veta asked.

"I know your kind," the woman said. "The Watchdog warned us. You ought to be ashamed, helping the UNSC kill your own people."

The Watchdog. That had to be Arlo Casille's new nickname—probably one he had created himself to secure his hold on power.

Veta stepped closer to the jungle line. "If I wanted you dead, those Spartans on your flanks would have done the job by now."

A rustle sounded as Mark and Ash made their presence known, and a chorus of gasps sounded from the undergrowth.

"Come out here where we can talk," Veta ordered. "Tell me what happened."

A stocky woman of about forty emerged from the fronds. She had a round face and short auburn hair, and she was holding a meat cleaver in one hand. Her embroidered blouse was so smeared with moss and mud that it looked like camouflage. A name tag stitched into the left chest panel read NITA.

Nita gave Olivia a disdainful once-over, then stopped in front of Veta and put her free hand on her hip. "You know what happened. The UNSC sends the Keepers in to do its dirty work, and now you're here to clean up."

The woman sounded like a true Casille loyalist—a sucker for propaganda and conspiracy theories. Veta paused for a moment, adjusting her approach, then spoke in a calm, factual voice.

"The UNSC had nothing to do with this." She made a point of looking into the undergrowth behind the woman, then said, "We haven't found any of your wounded."

"So?"

"So, there must have been some," Veta said. "Is there anything we can do for them?"

"Not likely." Nita's expression remained hard, but her tone was softening. "They're at the evacuation pad by now."

There was an emergency evacuation pad ten kilometers away, which served several laboratories similar to New Leaf. McAvoy had originally planned to land the Turaco there, but had diverted to investigate when he saw smoke rising from the coordinates of their final destination.

"Are you sure it's safe?" Veta asked. "That evacuation pad is the only place the Keepers could have landed a spacecraft."

"Don't worry," Nita said. "It's safe."

She looked unconcerned, which suggested enough time had passed for her to be certain the Keepers were completely gone. Call it twenty minutes for someone to drive out on the dirt road and report back . . . then another thirty or forty minutes to get organized and transport the casualties to the evacuation pad. . . .

But it really didn't matter how long the Keepers had been gone. Their vessel could easily have been spotted by Traffic Control as it left, or even on approach.

Really, a GMoP patrol could show up at New Leaf any time.

Veta smiled at the woman, then said, "Glad to hear it. I just have a few questions, and we'll be on our way."

Nita's face showed relief. "Then ask away. The sooner you're gone, the better."

"You're sure it was the Keepers of the One Freedom who attacked?"

"I know a Brute when I see one," Nita said. "And they were wearing Keeper armor. Blue with gold trim?"

Nita was suddenly volunteering information. She *was* eager to get rid of the UNSC.

Continuing in a casual voice, Veta asked, "What did they want?"

"How should I know?" The woman looked into the undergrowth behind her—a body-language deflection that suggested a lie. "Miguel, can you believe this? She's asking *us*."

"Maybe it's the same thing *they're* looking for," said a male voice. The undergrowth stirred, and hawk-nosed man in rubber boots and muddy khakis stepped into view. The grip of the SAD-8 protruded from his front pants pocket. "Has to be."

"Good thinking." Nita turned back to Veta, then said, "Maybe we should be asking what *you* want?"

"Answers." Veta watched Nita and Miguel shoot uncertain glances at each other—then knew what her interrogation strategy would be. She continued to hold Nita's gaze. "What do you *think* we're after?"

Nita gave an exaggerated shrug. "No idea. I'm just a cook. He's a groundskeeper."

"Damn." Veta dropped her chin in feigned disappointment, then turned away and spoke loudly into her headset mic. "Alpha Team, is the perimeter secure?"

"Who the hell is Alpha Team?" Fred's reply came over TEAM-COM and would not be audible to Nita, Miguel, or any of the Gao survivors. "And why are you being so loud?"

"Good," Veta said, ignoring Fred. "It looks like we're going to be here awhile. Set mines and motion detectors, then clear an LZ for the forensics teams—a big one. We're going to need the M606."

"The *what*?" Fred hissed in Veta's ear. "There's no such thing—"

"What's an M606?" Nita asked.

"Armored track-shovel," Veta said. "The recovery crews are going to need it to dig out the lab."

"Why would you do that?" Miguel asked.

"Because you're just a groundskeeper, and she's just the cook." Veta nodded toward Nita. "Neither of you seems to know what was *really* going on at New Leaf, so we're going to have to find the answers ourselves. That means excavating the lab."

"The Ministry of War will never allow that!" Nita said.

Veta glanced at Olivia and rolled her eyes.

Olivia snorted through her helmet's acoustic transducer and asked, "You think they can stop us?"

Nita's face paled, and Miguel said, "Just . . . tell them, Nita. What difference does it make now?"

"Good idea." Veta kept her gaze fixed on Nita. "This doesn't have to be hard. But I'm going to have my answers before we leave. If that means staying here a week—"

"Okay, okay," Nita said. "But we *are* just hired help. I don't know how much we can really tell you."

"Start with what you *think* has been going on here," Veta said. "And don't waste time lying. Once that M606 is loaded, the task force won't be turning back."

"All we know is what we heard," Miguel said, forcing Nita's hand. "The whitecoats were working on something to stop the Keepers from harassing Gao shipping."

"A biological agent?"

"What do you think?" Nita retorted. "This *is* a lab."

Veta sharpened her tone. "So you were developing biological weapons at this facility?" Knowing that Miguel was the more nervous or the two—and therefore the more cooperative—she switched her gaze to him. "In violation of the Ganymede Accords?"

There was no such official agreement, but Miguel's face fell anyway. "Not *us*," he said. "And we haven't even been inside the main building for two weeks."

"Miguel," Nita said. "If the Watchdog hears you've been talking—"

Veta interrupted. "Trust me, Nita, you don't want to interfere with this investigation." She continued to look at Miguel as she spoke. "If we find out you've been party to violating the Ganymede Accords, we'll have no choice but to take you along when we leave."

"For what?"

"For prosecution . . . crimes against humanity," Veta said. "Covering for someone else makes you a conspirator, and we have no leeway in the matter. So be careful here. The ride home is going to be crowded enough."

"You can't take me anywhere," Nita said. "I'm a Gao—"

"We know exactly who you are." Veta glanced toward Olivia, who responded by stepping up close to Nita, then said, "But the UNSC takes the Ganymede Accords very seriously."

"Look, we didn't have anything to do with it," Miguel said. "Two weeks ago, the service crews were banned from going inside the lab."

"Did that ever happen before?"

"No," Miguel said. "This is the first time."

"Where's the rest of the staff now?" Veta asked. "The researchers and the managers?"

"All dead," Miguel said. He pointed through the fence breach toward the collapsed lab building. "Most of them, anyway. We tried to dig out everyone who was still alive and sent them to the evacuation pad, but a lot of them aren't going to make it."

Veta was sorry to hear of the casualties, but she couldn't say so without undermining her interrogation persona. "How long ago?"

"How long ago what?" Miguel asked.

"Look," Nita added, "we've told you everything we know. Maybe you should load up and let us get back to collecting the dead. I'm sure you noticed the bodies still stuck in the rubble."

"I'll decide when we're done," Veta said. "How long ago did you send the wounded to the evacuation pad?"

Miguel looked to Nita, and Nita sighed and checked her chronometer. "Over an hour ago," she said. "They should be in the air by now."

"Everybody catch that?" Lopis asked over TEAMCOM. "The wounded are being airlifted out of the evacuation pad. Repeat: medevac. Give them safe passage."

There was a short pause, then McAvoy spoke over TEAM-COM. "Uh, the *Silent Joe* reports negative traffic over the Yosavi Jungle. A medevac could have set down at the emergency pad before we inserted and still be on the ground, but there's nothing in the air right now."

"Copy."

Veta looked back to Nita and decided not to press her on the timing of the evacuation flight yet. There could be a lot of things holding up the departure, and Nita wouldn't know about any of them. Instead, she turned toward the fence breach.

"Tell me about the raid." She motioned for everyone to walk with her toward the blast site. "What did the Keepers do when they arrived?"

"You have to ask?" Nita snapped, clearly impatient. "They started killing everyone in sight."

"And blowing shit up," Miguel added. "They hit the admin office and the director's hut right away."

They reached the fence breach and started toward the demolished lab crater.

"What about the lab?" Veta asked. "Did they hit the admin office and the director's hut on their way? Or did they search the rest of the compound first?"

"No, a bunch of them went straight to the lab," Nita said. "They blew the windows and doors and went inside."

"And then what happened?"

"Don't know," Nita replied. "By then we were hiding in the jungle. If we hadn't been, you wouldn't be talking to us now."

"How long did you stay hidden?" Veta asked.

"Not long," Miguel said. "The Keepers went inside the lab; we heard some gunfire, and maybe ten minutes passed. Then they left in a hurry. They were barely out the gate before the whole building blew."

"So they knew what they were after and where to find it," Veta surmised. "Did you see if they took anybody?"

"Just Director Sabara," Miguel said. "At least, that's what some of the wounded were saying. They didn't talk about anyone else being taken."

"What about sample canisters?" Veta asked. If Director Sabara had been using the Tuwas' living bodies to culture something from their thalassemia mutation, the Keepers would certainly be as interested in that as in the lab staff's knowledge. Castor might not be a scientist himself, but he was a cunning warrior who knew the importance of collecting hard intelligence. "Did you see them take anything like cryo-jars?"

"How could we?" Nita asked. "We *told* you—we didn't see anything."

She was trying a little too hard to draw Veta's attention—which probably meant she knew more than she was telling. Veta kept her gaze fixed on Miguel.

"Nita is walking the conspirator line, Miguel. Care to join her?"

Miguel shook his head. "The cryo-jars were already gone."

"Miguel!" Nita shot him a warning look. "She was asking if the *Keepers* took the cryo-jars."

"So?" Miguel scowled right back at her. "You can cover for him if you want to, but I'm not violating the Ganymede Accords for anybody."

"That's very wise of you." Veta took her helmet and utility belt back so Olivia's arms would be free to restrain Nita, then asked Miguel: "What happened to the cryo-jars?"

"Some guys took them before the Keepers came," Nita said, still trying to keep Miguel from answering. "And then they left. Maybe you should do the same."

"You can still recover from this," Veta said, "*if* you start cooperating. Ever hear the name Dark Moon? Those kinds of guys?"

Nita's eyes flashed in alarm; then she sighed and nodded.

"Yeah . . . Director Sabara mentioned that. She had me cook them a late supper."

"Last night?"

"Of course, last night. When do most people eat supper?"

Veta glanced at Miguel and furrowed her brow.

"They took off in the middle of the night," he said. "Their truck made so much noise it woke up the whole compound. I got up and saw the cryo-jars in back."

"Where were they going?"

"No idea," Nita said. "I was supposed to make them breakfast, but they were gone when I got up. The cabba pan was a mess."

Interesting. Cabba was a bitter local drink with stimulant properties. People sometimes chewed the leaves raw, but they were usually boiled in a pan with guado nectar.

"So the Dark Moon team was Gao?" Veta asked.

Nita shook her head. "No, but they were here awhile, and they developed a taste for cabba. They came with the original crew."

"Would that have been two weeks ago?" Veta looked to Miguel. "When Director Sabara closed the lab to the service crews?"

"Yeah, that's about right," Miguel said. "And they were always walking the perimeter, especially in the rain. It messed up the lawns."

"They sound like Ganymede conspirators to me," Olivia said. "Too bad we missed them."

"Very bad," Veta agreed. It sounded like someone had warned the Dark Moon crew about the blown operation on Taram, and they had left Gao in a hurry. "The Keepers are way ahead of us."

"You're thinking they took Sabara for interrogation?" Fred asked. Like the rest of the team, he was monitoring the conversation over TEAMCOM. "And *she* knows where the Dark Moon team is taking the cryo-jars?"

"I think it's a strong possibility," Veta said. As the conversation shifted to TEAMCOM, Nita and Miguel were eavesdropping on her end, listening intently to whatever she said into her headset mic. "The Keepers found what they came for, or they wouldn't have left in such a hurry. And they destroyed the lab for a reason. My guess is they didn't want anyone else to pick up the trail."

The channel remained silent for a moment; then Kelly said what was running through everyone's minds. "I'm worried about those cryo-jars. Could this be developing into a Code Hydra problem—with the Keepers in the middle of it?"

Hydra was the UNSC emergency code for an imminent bioweapon threat.

"It could be," Veta said. "But for now, I'm not sure the Keepers know what they're getting into. I think Castor just wants to find out who set them up—the same as we do."

"It's not that hard to figure out," Mark said. "Look where we are. It has to be Casille."

"I'm sure President Casille is involved up to his ears. He's getting *something* out of it. . . ." As Veta spoke Casille's name, Nita and Miguel both widened their eyes. "But I don't think he set it in motion. If he had, we would have found a company of battlejumpers guarding the place when we arrived—and the Keepers would have too. They'd be dead, not ahead of us."

"I'm not worried about the Keepers," Fred said. "Where the hell are the cryo-jars?"

"Unknown." Veta sighed and studied the rubble in front of her, searching for inspiration that would not come. "I need some time to look for answers."

"Dammit, Lopis," Fred said. "We don't have time. If there's any chance that this thing is turning into a Code Hydra problem, we need to recover those cryo-jars *now*."

"I understand that, Lieutenant." Veta thought for a moment, then said, "There may be a way to speed things up—but you're not going to like it."

"Try me."

"Arlo Casille." Nita and Miguel reacted again, looking away in a manner that suggested they were hiding something. Continuing to watch them, Veta said, "He may not know where the cryo-jars are headed, but he knows something just the same. We need to question him."

"And how are we going to do *that*?" Fred growled. "Storm the People's Palace and take him out of bed?"

"We could do that," Mark said. "As long as Mom puts on her armor."

"We don't need to storm the palace." Veta finally understood why Nita had been trying so hard to get rid of the Spartans. As the inspector spoke, she continued to watch Nita and Miguel. "I'm pretty sure President Casille is coming to us."

Miguel's eyes grew round.

"Repeat that," Fred said. "I didn't copy."

"Arlo Casille is coming here, to New Leaf," Veta said. She motioned Olivia to secure Nita and Miguel, then added: "As a matter of fact, I think he's due to arrive any minute now."

CHAPTER 19

1416 hours, December 14, 2553 (military calendar)
New Leaf Access Trunk, Yosavi Route 4, Candado de Xalapea
Yosavi Diversity Reserve, Planet Gao, Cordoba System

The last thing Arlo Casille wanted on this trip was attention, which was why he had hitched a ride aboard the Ministry of the Environment's heavy-lift Ajax. A unique deep-jungle emergency response craft, the Ajax was so huge that, during its descent through the access clearing to the Area 4 Evacuation Pad, the wingtip rotor blades had been trimming fronds and clipping vines the entire way. But the aircraft's great size did not mean it had a lot of free cargo space. Arlo's security team had been limited to a ground convoy that consisted of his Roamer and a pair of Murat gun trucks, and at the moment, the three vehicles were crawling up a muddy jungle road behind a disaster-response Bronto the size of a small house.

"The topo shows a wide spot at the crest of this ridge." Duena Sandos was strapped into the Roamer's back seat next to Arlo, holding a datapad in one hand and tapping the screen with the other. A sharp-featured woman of about fifty, she was the current Gao Minister of the Environment and, temporarily, Arlo's closest confidante. "I'll order them to clear a pullout so we can pass."

"And raise more eyebrows than we have already?" Arlo shook his head. "The Warrant of Sanction will be fine until we arrive. Director Sabara would have stored something that sensitive in her safe. From the cook's description, her entire office suite—and therefore her safe—is now buried under two meters of rubble."

"Which means somebody might be digging it out," Sandos said. "There's a reason that cook isn't responding."

"It's just the terrain." Arlo waved a hand at the fern-blanketed slope outside. "This deep in the jungle, comms aren't reliable without a tower and a signal booster. Besides, even if they start digging by hand, nobody knows about the sanction but us."

By *us*, Arlo meant Sandos, himself, and the two bodyguards sitting in the Roamer's front seats. Dressed in black fatigues with body armor and helmets, the two men were former special tactics officers who had served Arlo during his tenure as the Minister of Protection. Their loyalty and discretion had proven so valuable during his rise to president of the republic that he had assigned them to his personal security unit.

Sandos continued to study her datapad. "You're sure? If I have us in the right place, the compound is still five kilometers away. At this rate, it will take—"

"Duena, we're supposed to be here to assess the damage done by a Keeper raid." Arlo reached over and pushed the datapad down. "How will it look if we delay the response Bronto so *we* can arrive first?"

Sandos stared at Arlo blankly for a moment, then finally nodded. "Of course," she said. "I just wish we hadn't been dragged into this mess."

The guard in the passenger seat turned his head slightly—a signal that he had caught the anxiety in Sandos's tone and was prepared to eliminate the problem.

Arlo smiled and shook his head. "That won't be necessary, Rodas. Minister Sandos is adjusting to the situation."

Sandos's gaze shifted to Rodas but failed to show the expected intimidation. Instead, she turned back to Arlo and said, "There wouldn't *be* a situation if you'd been more circumspect. Who goes on record sanctioning experiments on the family of a UNSC admiral?"

Arlo scowled, puzzled by her sudden boldness. "Are *you* recording this?"

Sandos smirked. "I don't have to. The presidential request asking for New Leaf's cooperation is in both GMoE *and* New Leaf files." She glanced at Rodas, then added, "If anything were to happen to me, the ensuing investigation would raise all sorts of unpleasant questions."

Arlo flashed his warmest smile. "There's no need for threats, Duena," he said. "We're all friends here."

"And I'd like us to stay that way," Sandos said. "Even if your judgment is beginning to seem suspect."

Arlo shrugged. "I had no choice in the matter," he said. "The field director wanted to make sure her people were protected. I had to be explicit, or she wouldn't cooperate."

"Would that have been so bad?"

"At that point, yes," Arlo said. "The Tuwas were already being held in the lab. What was I to do? Contact Margaret Parangosky and tell her that I helped a private security company kidnap Admiral Tuwa's family . . . by *mistake*? She would have used it as an excuse to invade."

"Instead, you let an off-planet doctor run experiments on UNSC dependents?" Sandos asked. "And then *murder* them?"

"I did not authorize the murders," Arlo said. "I didn't even *know* about them until you comm'd to say Director Sabara was panicking."

Sandos narrowed her eyes. "I'm going to *see* that warrant, you know."

"And you'll see me sanctioning the experiments—and nothing more." Arlo paused to let her think, then added, just in case this little back-and-forth *was* being recorded: "You authorizing a clandestine launch was the right thing, by the way. Getting those contractors and bodies off Gao quickly was a smart move."

"You don't have to do that, Mr. President," Sandos said. "I'm in this up to my eyeballs already."

"Good." Arlo reached over and placed a reassuring hand on her knee. "Then we have nothing to worry about."

"Oh, we have plenty to worry about." Sandos removed his hand and said, "Starting with Dark Moon Enterprises. Who *are* they, really?"

Arlo looked out the window at the passing jungle. "A private threat-management service."

"You'll have to do better than that," Sandos said. "I, of all people deserve it."

"Dark Moon came highly recommended, and they guaranteed they could end our trouble with the Keepers."

"Recommended by wh—"

The last part of Sandos's question was lost to a tremendous crack from the roadside ahead. Arlo looked forward in time to see a thirty-meter tree-fern dropping across the road, directly behind the Bronto. The lead gun truck nosed into the fallen trunk and stopped dead. The gunner swung his 20mm Sawtooth chaingun toward the smoking stump and began to chew the jungle down.

On the opposite side of the road, a green blur rose from the undergrowth and flew into the truck bed. Before Arlo could quite make sense of what he was seeing, the figure slammed the gunner's head into the Murat's cab, then took control of the Sawtooth and swung it toward the Roamer.

"Shit!" Rodas shouldered his weapon, a Sevine Arms 8mm Maestro short-barreled battle rifle, and began to scream into his headset. "That looks like a goddamn Spartan! Back it—"

A second crack sounded from the roadside behind the Roamer. Arlo looked through the back window and saw the mirror image of the scene ahead, with another tree-fern falling across the road, directly behind the trailing gun truck. Again, a green blur came flying out of the jungle and knocked the gunner unconscious, then took control of the Sawtooth and trained it on the back of the Roamer.

Arlo's driver, Ramond, was already in reverse. The Roamer crashed into the trailing Murat and drove the little gun truck into the downed tree-fern behind it—but the jolt barely rocked what Arlo recognized as a Spartan-III, who was still standing in the truck bed. A tall figure in active-camouflage armor and a bubble-faced helmet, he simply aimed the Sawtooth toward Arlo's head and nodded as though they knew each other.

Now a towering Spartan-II in tan Mjolnir armor and a goggle-eyed helmet leaped into view beside the Murat and pointed an assault rifle at the windshield. Arlo looked forward again and saw that a second Spartan-II, this one in blue-gray armor with a bubble-faced helmet, had taken a similar position in front of the lead gun truck. Meanwhile, the Bronto was thirty meters ahead of the ambush, its steel tracks flinging mud as it accelerated away.

Amazingly, none of the Spartans had opened fire.

A rap sounded on the window behind Arlo's shoulder. He turned to see a third Mjolnir-armored Spartan-II standing at the

Roamer's rear corner. This Spartan's helmet was cocked slightly to the side, and his mirrored faceplate was staring into the rear seat.

"Down, Mr. President!" Rodas called from the front seat. He was twisting around, swinging his Maestro back toward the window next to Arlo's head. "I've got him."

Arlo reached up and pushed the weapon aside. "Put that away," he said. "If they wanted me dead, it would have happened by now."

Rodas did not lower his weapon. "Sir, they're probably intending to take you captive."

"In which case, you really won't be able to stop them," Arlo said. "Lower your weapon and put your hands on the dashboard. You too Ramond."

Once the two bodyguards had obeyed, Arlo lowered his window and looked over his shoulder at the Spartan. "What's the problem, officer? I know we weren't speeding."

"Funny." The Spartan studied him through an immobile faceplate, then finally said, "Someone wants to talk to you. Alone."

"I see." Arlo turned to Duena Sandos and said, "Well, you'll have to excuse me, Minister."

Instead of answering, Sandos reached behind her and fumbled at the door latch. She seemed to have forgotten she was still strapped into her seat.

Another Spartan-III—at least, Arlo assumed it was because of the SPI armor—appeared on Sandos's side of the Roamer. This one was female, with an M6 pistol in one hand and a MA5K assault rifle mag-clipped to the weapon mount behind her shoulder. She opened the door with her free hand, then released Sandos's safety harness and pulled the minister from the vehicle.

"Wait back there, hands in plain sight." The Spartan-III shoved Sandos behind her and never looked away from Rodas and

Ramond. "You fellas, leave your weapons in the seats and exit the vehicle slowly."

"*All* your weapons," Arlo ordered. "No one tries to be a hero. It will only get us killed."

"That's good thinking," said the Spartan-III.

Rodas and Ramond spent a couple of seconds removing knives and sidearms from hidden sheaths and holsters, then slowly opened their doors and left the Roamer. The Spartan manning the lead gun truck's Sawtooth then ordered the bodyguards: "Both of you, kneel on the ground. Hands behind your heads."

As they moved to obey, the musty odor of jungle mud filled the passenger cabin, and Arlo turned to see a woman in UNSC battle dress slipping into the seat beside him. Much smaller than her Spartan companions, she was wearing a ballistic vest with an M6C in a cross-draw belly holster—and when she removed her helmet, he saw that she had an attractive face with high cheekbones and large, dark eyes.

"Veta Lopis . . ." Arlo said. He mustered a smile. "It's good to see you again. Didn't anyone tell you that you're supposed to be dead?"

"I could say the same of you," Veta replied. "And maybe I will—if you don't tell me who *else* is involved in the killing of Admiral Tuwa and her family."

"Oh, *involved* is such an imprecise word."

"Then make it precise," Lopis said. "And do it now."

Her hand did not move toward her pistol, but the threat was in her voice. Arlo looked away, trying to buy time to think. Dammit, there were Spartans everywhere he turned—holding assault rifles on Sandos and his kneeling bodyguards, standing behind the Sawtooths in the gun trucks, keeping watch on the surrounding jungle—and their presence was making it difficult to concentrate.

In fact, their presence was an outrageous violation of Gao sovereignty, and it was making his pulse pound in his ears. "Does the UNSC really believe it can just insert Spartans any time—"

"Arlo," Lopis interrupted, drawing his attention back to her, "We don't know everything yet, but we know a lot. And what we know . . . It all points to you. I'd suggest you start talking."

"So, you work for ONI now?"

Lopis waved at the Spartans outside. "You think?"

Arlo shook his head in dismay. "The Veta Lopis I knew would never have—"

"Stop stalling." Lopis casually drew her sidearm and chambered a round. "Andera, Cirilo, Senola . . . remember them? I lost my entire team during that little coup of yours. My patience isn't what it used to be."

Arlo stared at the gun for a moment, then said, "Come on. You're not going to shoot me."

"She might," the Spartan behind him said. "She doesn't have clearance, but Command is willing to overlook a lot when somebody might be developing a Code Hydra bioweapon."

Arlo began to feel queasy. "Code Hydra? What the hell is that?"

"Something bad," Lopis said. "The kind of thing worth starting a war over."

"Gao is *not* involved with any bioweapons," Arlo said. "Neither am I."

"Then what was New Leaf working on?" Veta asked. "And why were *you* facilitating it?"

"What makes you think I was?" What Arlo really wanted to know was whether they had found the Warrant of Sanction he had recorded—but asking would only guarantee that they did. "I don't know where you're getting your information, but—"

"Inspector, this is taking too long," the Spartan said. "We'll get him to the facility."

"Your call." Lopis engaged her pistol's safety again and returned the weapon to its holster. "He deserves it."

"Wait." Arlo had no idea what facility they were talking about, but if he let the Spartans take him anywhere, he knew he wouldn't be coming back. "All they asked for was a secure base. I didn't know that they were targeting Admiral Tuwa and her family—and this is the first I'm hearing about any bioweapons. I swear it."

Lopis looked doubtful.

"Veta . . . you know me. Am I foolish enough to get involved in something that practically demands a UNSC invasion?"

"Apparently so," Lopis said.

And Arlo saw just how right she was. Somebody had been playing him from the beginning, laying a trail that would lead from the Keepers of the One Freedom straight back to Gao.

"So who is 'they'?" Lopis continued. "And what did you *think* they were doing at New Leaf?"

Arlo turned to face her squarely. "I assume you've heard of Dark Moon?" Lopis shot a knowing glance at the Spartan behind his shoulder, and he immediately knew she had. "They came to me with an offer. I'm sure you can guess what it was."

"Spell it out for me," said Lopis, ever the careful interrogator. "And don't forget anything. I'll know if you're lying."

"I remember how this works." Arlo took a deep breath, then said, "Look, it's really not complicated. Dark Moon is a private security firm with deep pockets and a long reach. They said they could maneuver the UNSC into taking care of our Keeper problem for us. All they needed in return was an operating base on Gao."

"And they offered this out of the goodness of their hearts?"

Arlo snorted. "Hardly," he said. "But the price was reasonable, given the damage Keeper pirates have been doing to us lately."

"And the Tuwas?"

"I didn't know about them until a couple of weeks ago, when the New Leaf field director contacted me." Arlo paused, trying to recall whether Lopis had said anything to suggest she had seen the Warrant of Sanction, then decided to gamble. "She was in a panic because the Dark Moon unit was using her lab to hold UNSC captives."

"And?"

"And I told her to go along with it," Arlo said. "What was I supposed to do at that point? Alert ONI and prepare for an invasion?"

"That might have been smarter than letting someone use an admiral's family as human guinea pigs—and stealing their organs to culture bioweapon components."

Arlo made his eyes go wide. "I . . . I didn't know." He dropped his gaze—forced eye contact was a liar's worst tip-off—and emphatically shook his head. "I'm telling you, Dark Moon has played us both. They set Gao up to take the blame."

Close enough to the truth. Arlo had no trouble convincing himself to believe it—and apparently, Lopis was ready to buy it as well. She studied him for several breaths, then finally let her expression soften.

"If I know you," she said, "you'll want to even the score."

"It's a welcome thought," Arlo said. "But I'm not sure I see how I can do that."

"You can help us find what we're looking for," Lopis said.

"So you haven't picked up a trail at New Leaf?"

"We're being thorough."

Arlo smirked. "Which means you've got no leads," he said. "If we're going to work with each other, we need to be honest here."

"Does that mean you have something?"

"And does that mean you don't have anything?"

Lopis said nothing, then finally nodded. "The Keepers made sure of it," she said. "They brought the entire lab building down. It could take weeks to sift through the rubble."

"So . . . you're left with . . . what?" Arlo hoped his relief did not show on his face. "Me and Dark Moon?"

"We can work on Dark Moon," Veta said. "But if they're as good as they appear to be, it could take longer than going through what's left of New Leaf to get anything useful. The company is organized like a nebula."

"And I know less about them than you do," Arlo confessed. "I have no idea where they might have taken those . . . bioweapon components."

"No problem," the Spartan behind him said. "The Borodyne staff is good at helping people remember things."

"I have nothing to remember!" Arlo had never heard of Borodyne, but he didn't like the sound of it—especially since ONI seldom mentioned secret installations to anyone who might live to repeat the names. "I'd never even heard of Dark Moon until—"

Arlo stopped when realized he might know something after all—and it might be just enough to save him.

"It's a bad time to keep us in suspense," Lopis said. "What do you have?"

"A place to start," Arlo said.

"Which is?"

"I'll need something in return."

"How about we leave you here?" the Spartan said. "Alive."

"That's good to open negotiations," Arlo said. "And I don't think you'll have a problem with the rest of my request. Our interests are closely aligned."

"Maybe we should rethink our interests," Lopis said. "But I'm listening."

"I want ONI to finish the job."

"You'll need to be a little more specific," Lopis said. "ONI does a lot of jobs."

"Castor." Arlo watched Lopis's face and was disappointed to see no surprise in it. "He's the only Keeper smart enough to mount a surface raid on Gao and get away with it."

"And now that he's gotten away with it once, you're thinking he'll visit again sometime soon. Maybe take a night tour of the People's Palace." Lopis thought for a moment, then said, "That's a good assumption. He already hates you for betraying him at Wendosa. Now, he probably has you marked for death. He has to know you played a part in setting him up."

"I'm glad you understand my concern."

"Oh, I understand it," Lopis said. "But I'm not sure what ONI can do about it. Castor is a tough subject to track."

"Not this time," Arlo said. "He's headed for the same place you are."

Lopis looked doubtful. "You expect me to take that on faith?"

"You said it yourself: Castor brought the lab down to cover his trail. Why would he bother if he didn't think you're after the same thing he is?"

"The Tuwas' organs?"

"Not just the organs," Arlo said. "The people who *want* the organs."

The unhappy truth of the situation was growing clearer by the moment. Arlo had hired Dark Moon Enterprises to set up Castor's pirates, which it had done by framing the dokab and his cell for a crime so shocking the UNSC *had* to hunt down their secret base. But Castor had captured some of Dark Moon's operatives in the process, then forced them to reveal their firm's arrangement with Gao and followed the trail to the New Leaf field laboratory. Apparently, what he discovered there had convinced the Jiralhanae to go after the plan's true architects instead of Arlo—at least for now.

Arlo harbored no illusions about his adversary's capacity for forgiveness. Unless he convinced ONI to finish the job it had started, Castor would be back. Arlo allowed Lopis a moment to contemplate his assertion, then began to press.

"The people who want the organs are the ones who set all this in motion. They're the ones Castor is after—and the ones *you* need to find, if you want to stop your Code Hydra threat."

Lopis lowered her gaze, thinking.

"The man has a point," the Spartan said. "He didn't steal Gao's presidency by being stupid."

"I know that." Lopis raised her head, then said to Arlo, "I'm just looking for traps."

"No traps." Arlo smiled and extended his hand. "Do we have a deal?"

"I'm not going to shake your hand," Lopis said. "Just tell me what I need to know—before I come to my senses and take you out."

"You shouldn't be so rude." Arlo withdrew his arm. "We're on the same side now."

"And where have I heard that before?" Lopis's gaze shifted to the Spartan and she asked: "If he doesn't answer, do I have clearance to shoot him?"

"That works," the Spartan said. "I probably shouldn't have mentioned Borodyne anyway."

Even through an electronically modulated voice, it was hard to miss the mockery. Arlo allowed himself to fume for a moment, then said, "You were never going to take me there, were you?"

"There's no such place," Lopis said. "So . . . you want to live, tell me where to start looking."

Arlo sighed, then said, "On Meridian—Pinnacle Station, to be exact. With Jonas Sladwal."

"Sladwal . . . the spy?" Lopis's expression was full of skepticism. "I thought he was dead."

"He is—more or less." Arlo smiled to himself. What the UNSC didn't know about Jonas Sladwal could fill Gao's main archives. The legendary Insurrectionist spy had kept the insurgents in munitions for decades by leaking Colonial Administration Authority convoy routes and schedules. "He died during the war with the Covenant."

"What does he have to do with Dark Moon?"

"He's the one who recommended them to me."

"A dead man?" the Spartan asked. "Nice trick."

"Death is not as black-and-white as you think, Spartan," Arlo said. "Jonas Sladwal's real name was Johanson Sloan. He was a senior vice president with Chalybs Defense Solutions, in charge of order fulfillment."

"As in *Administrator* Sloan?" Lopis asked. "Pinnacle Station's new AI boss?"

"Exactly," Arlo said. "Chalybs didn't know Sloan was an Insurrectionist spy—and that's *still* a closely held secret, by the way. I'm only telling you now because he helped Dark Moon set me up."

"And because it's the only hope we have of catching Castor and saving your sorry ass," the Spartan said. "Just to be clear."

"Well, that too," he said. "Anyway, the human Sloan was fatally injured during the Battle of Meridian in early 2551. He lived long enough for Chalybs to decide they couldn't afford to let him die, and they scanned his brain patterns into a Riemann matrix. They were just finishing the job when the Covenant pushed the UNSC back and began glassing operations."

"So the legend lives on in Administrator Sloan," Lopis said. "But how did Sloan get involved with Dark Moon?"

Arlo spread his hands. "When you find out, I hope you'll let me know."

"Sure I will." Lopis put her helmet on and reached for the door handle. "Maybe the next time I'm home."

CHAPTER 20

The coveralls gave them away. After a twelve-hour shift crammed inside pressurized mobility suits, actual construction workers were hot and exhausted and eager to reach the shuttle station at the core of Fabrication Ring Delta. They wore their bright yellow transit coveralls open to the belly and left their headsets hanging around their necks, and the only things they carried in their hands were personal commpads and red, soft-sided gear bags labeled PINNACLE STATION CONSTRUCTION.

But the crew now passing in front of the *True Light* kept their outfits closed over torsos too blocky *not* to be armored. They wore their headsets properly, and, instead of clank-booting along the maglane with their gazes fixed on the shuttle station ahead, the six humans were watching their environment, studying fellow pedestrians and peering around structural partitions. Most telling of all, they did not have the red gear bags. Instead, they carried hand-thrusters and long, hard-sided satchels.

Castor pointed through the flight deck canopy. "That does not look like a typical crew of builder-thralls." He was speaking through the translation disc hanging from his neck. "Do they carry the cryo-jars in their satchels?"

"No." The answer came from Agnes Sabara, the director of the field laboratory that Castor and his pack had destroyed on Gao. A thin woman with large eyes and long gray hair pulled back in a ponytail, she sat perched on the edge of the copilot's seat. The *True Light* was a human-manufactured, *Laden*-class freighter that had been modified for a Jiralhanae crew, so she looked like a child's doll in the seat, and she had to stretch forward and brace her hands on the instrument panel to see out through the canopy. "The satchels are too small, and the shape is wrong. Cryo-jars look more like a barrel on a hexagonal base."

"You are sure?"

"I know what a cryo-jar looks like," Sabara said. "Or do you still think I'm lying?"

"It seems possible," Castor said. Unlike the humans who served the Keepers of the One Freedom, Sabara was an unwilling participant in his hunt for vengeance. He had spared her life only because he needed her to discover who had framed him and his followers for killing the Tuwas. "You are in service to Arlo Casille."

"That doesn't mean I like what he ordered me to do—or that I like the UNSC any more than you do." Sabara looked over, then asked, "Has anything I've told you so far been wrong?"

"That remains to be seen."

After being captured in her lab, Sabara had made no effort to resist interrogation. In truth, she had seemed eager to cooperate, volunteering that she had been asked on short notice to prepare the cryo-jars for transport—and that she had overheard the Dark Moon couriers discussing their destination. In a bargain for her life, she had revealed the destination to be an orbital construction site called Pinnacle Station, above the moon Meridian in the Hestia system—a location Castor recognized as the site of a hard-fought Covenant victory during the war to eradicate humanity. Sabara had even supported her claim by providing an emergency launch authorization that had come from the Gao Minister of the Environment just hours after Castor had captured the two Dark Moon operatives on Salvation Base.

Still, Castor had been suspicious of Sabara's assertion until one of his human engineers read the cryo-jar operating manual. The jars needed a full coolant recharge every thirty hours—a process that required both an experienced technician and a bulky charging tank that would be difficult to carry in a small transport. The launch authorization had identified the couriers' vessel as a small reconnaissance boat similar to the one that had infiltrated Salvation Base, so it stood to reason that their destination was within a thirty-hour slipspace jump of Gao. When his navigator had confirmed that Pinnacle Station was one of only three possibilities, Castor had finally decided to accept Sabara's claim and let her live.

As Castor now watched, the crew of impostors stepped away from the maglane and began to free-float in the station's weightless environment. Using their hand-thrusters, they started across the loading dock laterally, maneuvering around deck-tethered girder bundles and wall-parked load tractors.

"Whoever they are, those guys look like they're on assignment," Sabara said. "I'd say we've come to the right place."

Castor was not so certain. On approach, the *True Light* had circled Pinnacle Station, attempting to locate the Turaco being used by the Dark Moon couriers. The effort had met with no success—but it *should* have. At this stage of construction, Pinnacle Station was little more than a tube-shaped skeleton of girders that still lacked artificial gravity, and the Turaco had a unique profile with an easily identifiable cannon turret on its back. The craft's silhouette should have been easy to spot against the station's open framework.

But they had not seen it, so Castor had ordered the pilot to move in closer and circle a second time. The maneuver had brought angry protests from the station's traffic control officer, but the *True Light*'s human navigator had apologized profusely and explained they were looking for their preassigned dock, and the inspection had continued.

Pinnacle Station's girder-skeleton was encircled top and bottom by disc-shaped fabrication rings. It was in those rings that materials were received, assembled, and attached to what was rapidly becoming the apex of a heavy-lift space elevator. Fabrication Ring Delta was the only ring with internal docking facilities. But even there, the bays were separated from empty space by only a transparent energy barrier, and as the *True Light* circled, Castor had been able to see that none of them contained the Turaco either.

Finally, with the traffic-control officer complaining bitterly that the *True Light*'s erratic approach was endangering other vessels, Castor had accepted a berthing in Fabrication Ring Delta and dispatched a band of human spies to search for the Turaco on foot.

As Castor continued to think, his gaze drifted to the communications holoplinth at the front of the *True Light*'s flight deck, and he found himself wishing that the Oracle would show herself. Since the destruction of Salvation Base, he had felt utterly adrift, with nothing to guide him but his rage and his devotion.

He had spoken to the holoplinth many times while alone with his thoughts, beseeching the Oracle's guidance and begging her forgivenesss for the annihilation of Salvation Base. But no answer ever came, and in her silence, he felt the anguish of her wrath.

There could be only one hope of regaining her favor, Castor saw. He had to find and obliterate Dark Moon and the tricksters who had hired them, just as their deceptions had obliterated Salvation Base. Perhaps then the Oracle would forgive him . . . and if not, then at least he would still have the honor of destroying her hidden enemies.

After a few moments, Castor returned his gaze to Sabara and asked "If this is the right place, why have we not found the Dark Moon Turaco?"

Sabara turned and studied him for a slow breath, then said, "Hmmm."

"What does *hmmm* mean?"

"Nothing," Sabara said. "I just think a dokab should be smart enough to figure this out."

A growl arose from the rear of the flight deck. "And a prisoner who speaks such blasphemy should be dead." Orsun stepped forward. "I will see to—"

"Wait." Castor raised a hand to stop Orsun, then turned to Sabara. "You truly have a wish to die?"

"Not at all." Sabara's entire body began to tremble—a sign of her truthfulness, Castor believed. "But if you can't see something as obvious as this—"

"Enough!" Orsun said. Like Castor, he wore a translation disc around his neck so that his words would be comprehensible to other species. "Dokab, allow me to end this insolence."

"Without learning what she has seen?" Castor waved Orsun back to his post, then laughed and said, "You are too clever for us,

Director Sabara. Tell me where to find the Turaco, and you shall have your freedom when the *True Light* departs."

Sabara continued to shake, but her shoulders squared. "I'm sure a Jiralhanae commander would never break his word."

"Then you are indeed a fool," Castor said. "But I am more than a chieftain. I am a Keeper dokab, and I will do as I promise—*if* you test my patience no further."

Sabara swallowed, then looked through the forward canopy again. "The couriers were sent to Pinnacle Station for a reason. Dark Moon must have an asset here—probably one who can keep a small craft out of sight."

Castor's gaze snapped back out to the loading dock. The impostor crew was already fifty meters away, floating over the heads of another column of departing construction workers. Beyond the workers lay more berthing bays, some empty and some occupied by small freighter craft similar to the *True Light*.

A quarter of the way around the ring, barely visible in the distance, hung the massive, gray-white cylinder of a cargo transport so large it barely fit into its berthing bay. Castor could not see enough of the vessel to determine its type, but he recognized the company name—LIANG-DORTMUND—written on its hull in human characters.

Yes . . . the transport's main hold would be large enough to hide a Turaco.

Castor watched the impostors as they continued toward the Liang-Dortmund vessel, then asked, "And the impostors—they are here to take delivery of the cryo-jars?"

"That's my assumption," Sabara said. "But until we actually see them with the cryo-jars . . ."

Though she did not finish the thought, Castor understood. A good scientist never forgot that the universe was full of coincidence. But Castor was not a scientist. He was a war chieftain, and war chieftains were more accustomed to dealing with likelihoods than certainties. He looked over his shoulder toward Orsun.

"Command the spies to keep watch on the impostor crew," Castor said. "And ready the pack. Battle is at hand."

Orsun touched a fist to his chest. "As it is spoken—"

"Have one of the spies retrace the impostors' route," Sabara interrupted. "Maybe you can identify their craft."

Orsun's eyes bulged, but he remained silent and looked to Castor in disbelief.

Castor glared at Sabara. "You dare command me?"

"It's more of a suggestion," Sabara said. "But I'm *sure* you realize how much the impostors' craft might tell us about their true identities."

Castor felt a rare flame of embarrassment rise in his chest. He hadn't thought of trying to find the impostors' craft before confronting them—and he *should* have. Good reconnaissance was important to any assault, and in his rage over the loss of Salvation Base, he had been imagining his vengeance as a massacre rather than a battle.

And that was a mistake. The enemy was both capable and cunning. If Castor remained blinded by his anger, his foe would remain hidden—and therefore able to strike the Keepers of the One Freedom at will.

After a moment, Castor turned to Orsun. "Send Panya to retrace their path," he said. "Have her report what she finds—and warn us if they send reinforcements."

"As you command, Dokab."

Castor waited for Orsun to relay the order, then said, "Director Sabara's suggestion was a sensible one. Why did you not offer it?"

Orsun's eyes widened, but he merely dipped his chin and said, "I failed you, Dokab. My penance is yours to name."

Castor dismissed the offer with a flick of his hand. "All I wish is for better counsel," he said. "I cannot think of everything. You must speak freely—like the prisoner does."

"It shall be done." Orsun's eyes flicked toward Sabara, and his lip curled. "And my first counsel is to be wary of helpful prisoners. This human lost her compound and her people to our raid. Why does she aid us now?"

"Because I know what those cryo-jars mean," Sabara said. "And it makes me fear for us all."

"Yet you are willing to see *us* take them," Castor said, heeding Orsun's advice to be wary. "You do not think the jars are dangerous in our hands?"

Sabara smiled. "Your hands are the safest place they could be," she said. "The Keepers don't have the expertise to utilize them— and by the time that changes, the tissue will be too cryo-damaged to do you any good."

Castor did not understand Sabara's sudden concern with the jars. When he had interrogated her in the New Leaf laboratory, she had told him only that the cryo-jars contained the organs taken from Admiral Tuwa's family, then noted they could be used to implicate the Keepers even deeper in the assassination plot. The prospect had angered him so much that in his rush to destroy the facility and depart Gao, he had accepted her suggestion as a given.

After a moment, Orsun said, "We are searching for hidden enemies, not cryo-jars. If the jars are no good to us, why should we care about recovering them?"

"Because your *enemy* cares," Sabara said. "Whoever they are, they've already pinned the blame for killing the Tuwas on you and your Keeper cell. Do you think they'll hesitate to use the weapon they're developing *against* the rest of the Keepers?"

"What *are* they developing?" Castor asked.

"An exploitable strain of asteroidea merozoite," Sabara said. "I know just a few of the details because our lab was only culturing a thalassemia mutation for protection against—"

"She is lying," Orsun said. "How could she know they are developing a weapon if she knows 'just a few of the details'?"

"Because I understand what they're trying to defend against," Sabara said. She fixed her attention on Castor. "The enemy will need a vaccine to protect themselves against their own agent. It's like their armor. And the key to developing that armor is in those cryo-jars. If you control them, you deny them their weapon. Because no matter who your hidden enemy is, *nobody* would be crazy enough to deploy a weaponized asteroidea strain—not unless they had a vaccine. Even the Covenant wouldn't be that crazy."

Orsun growled, perhaps trying to figure out whether Sabara's words were an insult, then finally said, "Now she hopes to use us to protect Gao."

"*And* the Keepers," Castor said. "Our hidden enemy has destroyed our most important base. It would be foolish to believe they will not try to finish what they started."

Orsun dropped his chin. "I yield to your wisdom."

"Yielding is not accord," Castor observed. "You still have reservations?"

"Only one," Orsun said. "If we have the jars, the enemy must come to us. That tactic is sound."

"And yet?"

"And yet, we could be overlooking the obvious," Orsun said. "The lab was on Gao, and Arlo Casille has been our sworn enemy for some time. Perhaps, Dokab, this is not as complicated as it appears."

Castor looked to Sabara.

The director spread her hands. "President Casille is involved, yes—but only because Dark Moon drew him in." She locked eyes with Castor, then asked, "Do you really think he *wanted* trouble with the UNSC? The Tuwas were a setup."

Castor had already reached the same conclusion. The Dark Moon operatives captured at Salvation Base had confessed many things before their deaths, but they had never suggested that the plan was Arlo Casille's. In fact, the more Castor considered it, the more he agreed with Sabara. Arlo Casille was just a weapon in someone else's hand.

Castor rose and turned to Orsun. "It is wise to question our conclusions. In this, you have done me a great service, Orsun."

"That is all I desire." Orsun glanced at Sabara. "But you believe the infidel."

"I believe she is right about Arlo Casille," Castor said. He turned to leave, but paused next to Sabara's seat. "We will capture the cryo-jars and dispose of them as you wish."

Sabara's face showed her astonishment. "Um . . . thank you."

"I do not wish your thanks," Castor said. "I wish your service. I have promised you your freedom, and you shall have it if you wish. But if you desire our help with the cryo-jars, know that the price for that *is* service."

"For how long?"

"For as long as you are needed," Castor said.

Sabara's face paled, but she nodded. "Okay. Fair enough."

"Then it is decided," Castor said, trying to hide his alarm. The condition had been a test, and her lack of hesitation proved her words were sincere. He touched his fingertips to his brow. "Your enemy is my enemy."

Sabara did not seem to know the appropriate reply, but she mimicked his gesture and said, "I guess that makes us friends."

"Close enough," Castor said. He started toward the back of

the flight deck. "Come along, then. Stay at my side until the battle begins, then hide and do nothing that might get you killed."

They retreated to the boarding vestibule, where Castor and Orsun donned their power armor and thruster harnesses. Sabara was given a helmet and armored vest, with a little M6 sidearm for personal protection. Since she had no experience using a thruster harness, she was given shoe-steels that would allow her to use the station's temporary maglanes.

Waiting in the rear of the vestibule were five more Jiralhanae in power armor and eight Kig-Yar in their customary combat harness. There were no humans among them; all of the humans had been dispatched to reconnoiter and search for the Dark Moon Turaco. Castor was still checking his band's weaponry—a mix of battle rifles and death lobbers, which infidels called Brute shots—when Panya's excited voice sounded over the battlenet.

"Dokab, I have found the impostors' shuttle," she said. "You won't believe who they are!"

"No commentary!" Castor snapped. He had established a regimen to build military discipline in his Keepers, but it was a losing battle. Most non-Jiralhanae Faithful were pirates at heart and looked upon any sort of procedures training as an assault on their individualism. "Just report—and quickly."

"Check a display," Panya replied. "It's already on the *True Light* data net."

Castor turned to the security station and checked the display cluster. The center screen showed the image of a small utility skiff, tethered in a Pinnacle Station berthing bay. Shaped more or less like a bullet, the craft had a dirty gray finish and a Pinnacle Station identification number on its nose. The boarding ramp was down, and a thin man in a khaki service uniform was pacing back and forth on the maglane outside. He wore a double-bar rank insignia on his collars and a name tag over his right pocket that was too small to read, but no ribbons, insignia, or unit patches. It seemed apparent that the utility skiff had ferried the officer aboard from a nearby vessel, but Castor did not understand why he was pacing back and forth in the open. Only a fool would show himself unnecessarily during an operation.

Sabara, who had heard Panya's report over the battlenet headset built into her helmet, was already at Castor's side. "I'm no soldier," she said. "But doesn't that look like a UNSC uniform?"

"Not just UNSC," Castor said. "The officer displays only his name and rank. That means ONI."

"ONI?" Sabara's face went pale again. "That's not good."

"So you have lured us into an ambush, human," Orsun said. "With the dokab's leave, I will rip your arms off—"

"This is no ambush," Sabara said. "We've been here an hour, and no one has touched us. This is something worse."

"Worse how?" Castor asked.

"If ONI is here to take delivery of those cryo-jars, it means *they're* the ones developing the bioweapon. And ONI definitely has the expertise to do it."

"That does not make any sense," Castor said. "Admiral Tuwa served in the UNSC . . . and is ONI not part of the UNSC? If they wanted her family for their bioweapon, why would they not command her to surrender them?"

Sabara looked up at him and shook her head. "You really don't understand humans, do you?"

Castor looked to Orsun, who merely tipped his head and appeared as puzzled as Castor was.

"The order would be a terrible betrayal," Sabara explained. "In fact, the person issuing it would probably be permanently dismissed . . . or committed to a mental institution."

"Why?" Orsun's tone was more mystified than doubtful. "Soldiers are often sent to die. It is what soldiers are for."

"Not their families," Sabara said. "And certainly not in support of a highly illegal—and therefore secret—program."

Castor did not know what to think. Jiralhanae lacked such arbitrary restrictions. A chieftain commanded his pack in full, and a follower who disliked his orders had only one remedy—a death challenge.

But humans had strange customs and soft emotions. As young warriors, Castor and Orsun had been part of the Bloodstars, a special band of stalkers charged with hunting down the demon Spartans. Their leader had been a member of the Sangheili Silent Shadow, a First Blade of exceptional skill and devotion who had once led Castor, Orsun, and their war-brother Atriox on a raid that resulted in the capture of an entire squad of Orbital Drop Shock Troopers. The three-day interrogation that followed had revealed many things, but the most surprising had been a rumor that the UNSC had to steal exceptional children from their homes to develop them into the demon Spartans. That had surprised Castor more than anything, for on Doisac, a family would have been honored to surrender a child for the glory of the tribe.

He would never understand why it shamed humans to demand such sacrifice, but understanding was not needed. It was enough that their folly made them weak.

Castor studied the display for a moment, then said, "Panya, you will detain the ONI officer outside the skiff until Orsun arrives."

"As you command, Dokab," Panya answered, speaking over the battlenet. "Uh . . . how?"

"Do what you must," Castor said. "But I want him alive."

Panya hesitated before replying, and the voice of a male spy filled the battlenet.

"Dokab, the impostors have boarded the Liang-Dortmund transport!" The man was breathless with excitement. "And it sounds like there is small-arms fire inside!"

Castor had no idea who was speaking—save for gender, human voices sounded much the same to him. "Remember your training," he commanded. "Identify yourself—and report *details*."

"I'm Tabor," the man said. "And the small-arms fire is automatic, not very loud."

"The weapons are sound-suppressed?" Castor asked.

"That's hard to tell, Dokab." Tabor paused a moment, then said, "I've got my ear pressed to the hull, and it's kind of a muffled banging."

"Yes, sound-suppressed," Castor concluded. He turned to Sabara. "That means the imposters came ready to kill. Perhaps ONI is here to *stop* the cryo-jar delivery?"

"Maybe." Sabara replied. "Or maybe they're covering their tracks. It's hard to know which."

"No, not so difficult," Orsun said. "Tabor, tell us when the firing ends."

"Uh, it's over now," Tabor said. "No, wait. I'm hearing double-taps, still barely audible."

Orsun caught Castor's attention. "They are making certain there are no survivors," he said. "They *are* covering their tracks."

Castor was unsurprised. ONI's treachery was as boundless as the stars, and he could easily see them executing a team whom they had hired to perform a task.

Speaking over the battlenet, Castor said. "Tabor, you have done well. Fall back and hide. When the infidels—"

The command was interrupted by a wet gasp. A heartbeat later, the battlenet filled with the unmistakable gurgle of someone drowning in his own blood, and the transmission ended in the pop of a deactivating comm unit.

Of course. An ONI hit team would have set an overwatch. And the officer pacing in front of the utility skiff? Had he been a fool . . . or bait?

"Tabor? Report status." When no reply came, Castor looked to Orsun. "Who were the spies with—"

"Neola and Vankus," Orsun said. He was speaking over the battlenet. "Report."

There was no response.

"Panya?" Orsun's tone was worried. "Report."

Again, no reply. The pacing officer had been no fool, and Panya had no doubt paid with her life for Castor's mistake.

Castor deactivated his comm and turned to his companions. "Shut off your communications," he ordered. "Our battlenet has been compromised."

As the Keepers obeyed, he studied the security station display cluster. The *True Light*'s external cameras offered spherical coverage of the surrounding area, and he could see that there was no one approaching the vessel. But the berthing bay was not a great deal larger than the freighter itself, and beyond it were dozens of partitions and tethered equipment nets that could hide an enemy.

"Dokab," Orsun said, "we await your command. If the infidels know we are watching—"

"They will move quickly," Castor finished.

Castor turned toward the boarding ramp. Now that he knew that it had been ONI who framed the Keepers for the Tuwa murders, the wise thing would have been to withdraw and develop a plan for taking vengeance. But he doubted ONI would give him— or his fellow dokabs—time. They had dealt the Keepers a terrible blow by destroying Salvation Base, and they would move swiftly to exploit their victory.

And then there were the cryo-jars to consider. Whatever their true importance, the Sabara woman was willing to sacrifice her freedom to keep them away from ONI . . . and *that* argued for quick action.

"Lead the way, Orsun," Castor said. "We will meet the infidels as they return to their shuttle."

Orsun bowed his head. "I am graced by your trust, Dokab."

The second-in-command tapped the control pad, and the ramp descended. He activated a thruster and drifted out through the portal . . . and then the air was torn by the roar of a rocket-propelled grenade.

"Incoming!" Orsun roared.

The detonation hurled him back across the boarding vestibule into the security station, and the last Castor saw of his old friend was a spray of flame erupting through the backplate of his armor.

CHAPTER 21

The first M19 surface-to-surface missile struck the Jiralhanae in his chest armor and drove him back through the *True Light*'s boarding portal. The charge detonated inside the vestibule, and Oriel watched through the wide-angle lens of a Papa-10 headset-mounted camera as the target's torso flew apart. Flames covered the security station behind him, and clouds of blood and smoke filled the vessel interior.

It always troubled Oriel to dispose of reliable assets. But her generator aspect, the *archeon*-class ancilla Intrepid Eye, had been clear: Castor had reached the end of his service life. His capture of the Dark Moon operatives in the Contemplarium, and his relentless pursuit of their hidden masters, had rendered the dokab an untenable liability. His entire cell was to be eliminated at the first opportunity, before he learned any more about Dark Moon Enterprises and placed Intrepid Eye herself at risk.

For a thousand system ticks, Oriel continued to watch through the headset camera . . . and waited. She caught glimpses of shredded flesh and blood-spattered armor. Displays shattered, bodies fell, smoke billowed out over the boarding ramp, and still nothing.

Lieutenant Bartalan Craddog did not fire the second missile.

"Lieutenant Craddog." Oriel was transmitting directly into Craddog's earbud from the Pinnacle Station utility skiff, where she had taken residence in the craft's master control system. "Is there a reason for the delay? Please fire the second missile now."

"At *what*?" Craddog was currently in Storage Area 20, adjacent to the berthing bay where the *True Light* was tethered, clinging to a cargo net full of laser-welder gas cartridges. With his free hand, he was holding on to the trigger housing of a shoulder-firing M41 SPNKR missile launcher. "I can't see a target!"

"Fire it into the boarding vestibule." Oriel was careful to keep an even tone. Intrepid Eye had realized that Craddog would be unreliable under pressure, and Oriel had sent him into combat only because Papa-10's other teammembers were busy with the cryo-jar recovery. "It is important to keep the survivors disoriented. We need to delay them for another forty-two seconds."

"Survivors?" Craddog's gaze was fixed on the smoke pouring out of the transport's boarding hatch, and he made no move to aim the M41 SPNKR. "Are you crazy? We'll be lucky if that freighter doesn't blow *now*. If I hit it again, it could take out the entire station!"

As Craddog spoke, a massive silhouette appeared in the smoke, just inside the *True Light*'s boarding portal, then floated through the hatchway into the berthing bay.

Craddog gasped in disbelief, then released the cargo net and raised the M41 SPNKR to fire. Unaccustomed to maneuvering in zero-G, he sent himself spinning, and Oriel watched through his headset as the missile went wide of the *True Light*'s boarding portal and struck a dozen meters aft.

The silhouette emerged from the smoke and resolved itself into a Jiralhanae clad in power armor. He raised a Type-25 spike rifle and opened fire into the storage area toward Craddog, who left the SPNKR to float free and lunged for the cargo net with both hands.

The maneuver sent Craddog's feet tumbling over his head, and Oriel had to activate an image-stabilizing routine. The spinning blur resolved into a gleaming spray of spikes, coming from a Jiralhanae with a burn-blistered face. His expression was so contorted with rage and loss that Oriel required seven system ticks to recognize him as Castor. His long gray beard was matted with blood and tiny bits of charred flesh, and behind him followed three more Jiralhanae, all wearing blue shock-plate armor with gold trim.

Craddog caught hold of the cargo net and began to pull hand-over-hand, trying to reach cover. Only five seconds had passed since Oriel had ordered him to fire the second missile, so she knew that Castor and his companions would have ample time to prevent the Papa-10 recovery squad from returning the cryo-jars to the utility skiff.

Craddog screamed and whipped his head around, and Oriel's view of the departing Jiralhanae was replaced by globules of blood, rising through a gash in the lieutenant's pant leg. She tried to keep Castor and his warriors in view by analyzing the distorted images around the rim of the headset's fish-eye lens, but her line of sight was blocked by the contents of the cargo net.

Oriel opened a channel to all of Papa-10. *"Lieutenant Craddog's attack was only a partial success,"* she transmitted. *"You should expect to be engaged by four armored Jiralhanae."*

"Brutes?" said Bhu Zdenyk, one of the team's three female operatives. "Those cryo-jars better not be vital to humanity or anything."

"Can the chatter." The order came from the Papa-10 commander, a square-faced ONI officer named Porter Sahir. "Appreciate the warning."

"I am glad to be of service," Oriel replied. *"Lieutenant Craddog will provide support."*

"Support?" Craddog replied, gasping. "I'm wounded!"

"It is only a flesh wound." Oriel could tell by the elongated gash in Craddog's pant material that the spike had grazed his calf without embedding itself. *"You are quite capable of fighting, especially in a weightless environment."*

"I'm in pain!"

"Lieutenant Craddog, we need *any* assistance you can provide." Sahir's tone bordered on the derisive—clearly, he was not expecting much from Craddog. "Four Brutes in shock-plate armor are a lot to handle, even for us."

"I'll try," Craddog said, fighting for breath. "But I'm not sure what I can do."

"Perhaps you should retrieve the M41 SPNKR," Oriel calmly suggested. *"And reload it."*

As Oriel spoke, she was tapping into Sahir's headset camera so she could observe the Papa-10 preparations. The commander had stopped his team about thirty meters from the Liang-Dortmund cargo transport where the Dark Moon Turaco had been concealed, and as he issued assignments, his camera shifted from one operative to the next.

They were all grim-faced soldiers with steady gazes and confident postures. The men had heavy brows and square jaws, while the women had small noses and taut features. There were more brown eyes than blue. Zdenyk's eyes were green, her complexion tawny brown. Oracle could see that the execution of the Dark Moon couriers had left everyone's coveralls flecked with tiny droplets of blood, but the stains were causing less alarm among the spectators than the M7 SMGs and M45E short-barrel shotguns being drawn from the Papa-10 equipment satchels.

Construction workers were now fleeing on all sides, clunk-running down maglanes or floating into nearby berthing bays, using cargo nets and tether straps to pull themselves behind cover. There was no sign of a security response, though Oriel expected that would soon change. She was monitoring all of Pinnacle Station's security channels and knew that Administrator Sloan—the station's AI superintendent—was assembling a force up to the task.

Sahir deployed Papa-10's forward element in an L formation designed to catch the enemy in a crossfire kill zone. He led this element himself, leaving Bhu Zdenyk in charge of a three-person detail that would follow with the cryo-jars.

Back in Storage Area 20, Craddog was returning to the cargo net with his errant M41 SPNKR. He failed to activate his braking thrusters in time and hit hard. The entire load shifted, but he managed to hook a boot through the mesh before the tether reached full extension and rebounded. He flailed around and barely kept himself from flying off, then finally began to fumble with the weapon, trying to find the barrel release so he could insert the reload barrels he wore slung across his back.

The *boom* of a shotgun sounded over the Papa-10 communications channel; then a Jiralhanae tumbled into Sahir's field of vision. The Brute's maneuvering thrusters were still firing, and blood globules were flying from his head in a wild helix. It took only a hundred system ticks—a tenth of a human second—for the channel to erupt into screams and small-arms fire. A steady flow of casualties tumbled into view, all human. Most appeared to be construction workers hit in the crossfire, but at least three were Papa-10 operatives still wearing their headsets.

Realizing Papa-10 would never fight its way past the Jiral-hanae without help, Oriel checked on Craddog's progress. He had finally found the release catch and removed the SPNKR's expended barrels, but his headset camera was panning about wildly as he tried to pull the reload barrels off his back without letting the weapon drift away. By the time he could reassemble the weapon and move into position to use it—assuming he *ever* managed that—the battle would be over.

Oriel scanned the cameras of the surviving members of Papa-10's forward-element squad and glimpsed an incoming mauler blast—then only Sahir's feed remained. He had three Ji-ralhanae soaring toward him, all firing weapons while still ex-pertly maneuvering. Sahir's own response from an M7 SMG was for the most part simply ricocheting off his attackers' armor—though one Brute had a taken a hit to the face and was missing part of his jaw.

Oriel consulted a station schematic and saw there was no lon-ger any way for Zdenyk's squad to reach the utility skiff with the cryo-jars. She considered trying to contact Castor and demand that he stand down, but the consequences were dire. Even if she were able to command his attention in the middle of a firefight, she would risk revealing her connection to Dark Moon. Castor would feel used and betrayed, and he was 3.72 times more likely to lose faith in the Great Journey than to accept her deception as a test of devotion.

And if Castor lost faith, his Jiralhanae pride would demand revenge. There was no predicting what he might do. He might undertake a relentless war against Dark Moon's ONI masters, or he might see through Intrepid Eye's layers of deception and see that ONI was as a much a victim as he had been. The only thing Oriel knew with certainty was that a vengeful Castor would be a dangerous Castor—which meant that Intrepid Eye was correct. The time had come to stop taking chances and eliminate him.

"Petty Officer Zdenyk, please take your squad and the cryo-jars and board a personnel shuttle." Oriel transmitted the order across the entire Papa-10 comm channel so that any survivors would understand her plan. "Proceed to Meridian's surface and remain concealed until reinforcements arrive."

"No way," Zdenyk replied. "We're not leaving without Papa—leader."

"Do it!" Sahir was yelling, but even so, his voice was nearly inaudible over a long burst of automatic fire. "That's an order, Bhu!"

There was a half-second pause before Zdenyk replied, "Affirmative, Lead . . . and thank you."

If Sahir replied, his answer was lost to the roar of a mauler blast tearing through his concealed body armor. Oriel switched to Zdenyk's headset camera and found her soaring down a concourse, toward the shuttle station at the core of Fabrication Ring Delta. Ahead of her, panicked construction workers were hurling themselves off both sides of the maglane.

Another burst of gunfire sounded behind Zdenyk, and her camera panned around behind her. The other two members of her squad were coming down the concourse on their backs. Each man was clutching a cryo-jar to his chest with one arm and operating a M7 SMG with the other. The combat-stabilization feature of their thruster harnesses was having trouble compensating for the sustained fire, so they were weaving and bobbing wildly.

Sahir's corpse was still floating in the concourse entrance. It was a contorted, spiderlike figure surrounded by a halo of blood globules. And moving past it were four Jiralhanae warriors.

"Petty Officer Zdenyk," Oriel said, *"your squad* must *board the next shuttle. I will see to the rest."*

"You'd better," Zdenyk replied. "We're running low on ammo."

Her headset camera turned forward again, and five paces ahead, Oriel saw the grime-streaked throat of the shuttle's boarding tube. At the far end of the tube, inside the craft itself, a cluster of alarmed construction workers sat strapped into their acceleration chairs. Their eyes were wide and their faces pale.

"Have faith, Petty Officer Zdenyk," Oriel said. *"You cannot imagine the extent of my capabilities."*

Oriel used a Pinnacle Station security channel to access a schematic of the shuttle. A wedge-shaped model with an ultra-wide cabin, it was short-hop vessel designed to transport large numbers of personnel to and from Meridian's surface with a minimum of maintenance. Although it was usually flown automatically by an onboard AI, during an emergency a passenger could assume limited control.

"There is a pilot's compartment at the front of the cabin." Oriel was transmitting only to Zdenyk and her two squad members now. *"Once you're aboard, open it and activate the emergency override. That will allow you to seal the craft and leave the station."*

"Then what?" Zdenyk was already floating down the shuttle's boarding tube. "Could we rendezvous with the *Fast Gus*?

"Negative," Oriel said. *"Your control will be limited. The shuttle will descend to Meridian's surface automatically. You will be taken to an emergency landing zone a safe distance from the settlement. Once you are on the surface, you will then be able to open the hatches."*

"Thanks . . . I guess." Zdenyk entered the shuttle's passenger cabin and turned toward the pilot's cabin. "Papa-10 out."

Oriel continued to monitor the situation aboard the shuttle. After the rest of Zdenyk's squad boarded, the petty officer used the emergency override to seal the hatches. Papa-10's pursuers were only halfway down the concourse when the shuttle launched.

In Storage Bay 20, Craddog had finally inserted the reload barrels into the M41 SPNKR and was just locking the release catch. His leg was still bleeding, and the air around him was filled with crimson globules.

"Lieutenant Craddog," Oriel said, *"perhaps you should return to the utility skiff and tend to your wound."*

"What about Papa-10?" Craddog asked. "I thought they needed support!"

"It is too late for that."

Oriel detected a scratch in the signal and realized that someone—probably Pinnacle Station security—was attempting to eavesdrop on the Papa-10 comm net. She switched to a sequestered channel, then changed the encryption and continued to address Craddog.

"Your support has proven quite useless."

Craddog's tone grew indignant. "Well, I'm a scientist, not a soldier."

"There is no need to be defensive," Oriel said. *"It is my fault. Intrepid Eye warned me you would not perform well under pressure."*

Craddog looked toward the shuttle stations. "So you're just going to abandon the cryo-jars?" he demanded. "I thought Intrepid Eye needed them to develop the vaccine. I *thought* the vaccine was the only way to protect humanity from an asteroidea outbreak."

"That is correct."

It would have been more precise to say that the vaccine would *control* the coming outbreak, but Oriel was not sure how much Craddog knew about the long-term plans of her prime aspect. Given his flaws, it seemed unlikely that Intrepid Eye would consider his genetic line worthy of the Mantle of Responsibility. When the culling began, Craddog's descendants would not be among those who received an inoculation.

"I will recover the cryo-jars, Lieutenant Craddog," Oriel contin- ued. *"The best way for you to help now is to return to the utility skiff. And leave the M41 SPNKR behind. It would be an unnecessary com- plication for Pinnacle Station security to find it in your possession."*

Craddog immediately pushed the SPNKR aside and began to thruster his way back toward the skiff's berthing bay.

Oriel concentrated her attention on the Pinnacle Station se- curity feeds and quickly realized the Jiralhanae had not given up their pursuit of the cryo-jars. Dozens of reports placed them at the fabrication ring's shuttle station, awaiting the arrival of the next craft.

Recalling the interference she had felt in the Papa-10 commu- nications channel, Oriel reopened the channel and said, *"I need to speak to Administrator Sloan. Now."*

The scratch grew fainter, and for three hundred system ticks, Oriel awaited reply.

When none came, she said, *"It is no use hiding. My countersur- veillance routines are impregnable, and if you compel me to force my way into your system, I will not be gentle."*

The interference modulated itself into an input signal, and the image of a powerfully built man with a bald head and rugged features appeared on the communications holograph in the utility skiff's cockpit. The pilot, an ONI contract-asset whose primary employment was with Pinnacle Station, let out a startled gasp and reached for the controls.

Oriel quickly internalized the image and diverted control of the holograph to herself, then addressed the newcomer digitally. *"Administrator Sloan, I require you to stop all further shuttle depar- tures from Fabrication Ring Delta."*

"And why would I do that?" Sloan demanded.

"Because the next shuttle is loading . . ." Oriel paused to check

the Pinnacle Station surveillance feeds. The loading-tube doors were already sliding open. *"Now."*

"Good riddance," Sloan replied. His voice was deep and stormy. *"Down there, your friends and the Jiralhanae can fight all they like. It will damage nothing that matters."*

"Then you know where they will land?"

"I know the emergency landing site is ten kilometers from the nearest settlement," Sloan said. *"That is the only important thing."*

Oriel understood. Meridian was a former mining colony and arms-production center whose surface had been glassed during the Human-Covenant War, and reclamation efforts were just getting under way. As long as the battle between Zdenyk's squad and the Jiralhanae occurred in the unreclaimed wastelands, any damage it caused would be of no concern to Administrator Sloan—or his superiors at Liang-Dortmund.

"What of the damage you have caused by failing to provide a secure handover environment?" Oriel asked. *"That is a violation of your contract with Dark Moon. Is* that *important?"*

Sloan flared red with a signal surge. *"How do you know the terms of my contract with Dark Moon?"*

"Come, Administrator Sloan," Oriel said. *"Pinnacle Station sent a skiff to meet our prowler. You understand how we know the terms."*

"ONI spies," Sloan growled. *"They're everywhere."*

It was the expected answer, of course. Intrepid Eye was using ONI as a cover for the entire asteroidea project, and a human AI had not been created that could penetrate her misattribution protocols.

"Naturally I cannot confirm your suspicions," Oriel said.

Sloan's image grew even brighter. *"It makes no difference. The Dark Moon operatives are dead, and Pinnacle Station has no arrangements with ONI."*

"Not directly."

Sloan hesitated, allowing five hundred system ticks to pass, then asked, "Are you saying Dark Moon is an ONI cover company?"

"Not at all." Oriel could not allow Sloan to make this particular assumption. Dark Moon Enterprises was, in fact, unaffiliated with ONI. It was being run by another of Intrepid Eye's minor aspects—one that was unknown even to Oriel—and it had relationships with several clients who would break off contact if rumors started to circulate that Dark Moon was an ONI front. "But we do subcontract with private firms on occasion."

"With Dark Moon?" Sloan tipped his holographic head back and emitted a deep laugh. "A cover company I would believe. That kind of doublethink would be just like Parangosky. But a contract between ONI and Dark Moon? The bad blood between them is the worst-kept secret in the Orion Arm."

"Then you might be wise to remember that," Oriel said. The Pinnacle Station surveillance feeds showed the last of the Jiralhanae floating down the boarding tube. "Obviously, we know you have been helping Dark Moon. And ONI has a long memory."

Sloan's image rippled. He remained silent for a thousand system ticks—a full second—then asked, "Why should Pinnacle Station help ONI? All you have done is shoot up our people and damage our equipment."

"You do not wish the gratitude of the United Nations Space Command?"

"Sure," Sloan said. "As long as it comes with compensation."

"I am not certain I understand." Oriel had no objection to paying Sloan—as long as he did the job—but she could not imagine what kind of compensation an AI would want. "Are you asking for a bribe?"

"Insulting me is no way to win my cooperation," Sloan said.

As he spoke, an alarm sounded from the central shuttle station, and the craft the Jiralhanae had boarded dropped away from the docks and began its descent toward Meridian's surface. *"But I do expect Liang-Dortmund to be paid for the damage Pinnacle Station has taken. And I want to be rewarded for my own risk."*

"And then you will help us recover our cryo-jars?"

"You have my word," Sloan said. *"I'll do everything in my power."*

"Then I need you to destroy the Jiralhanae shuttle," Oriel said. *"They have activated the emergency override, and I have been unable to locate a bypass routine."*

"You haven't heard my price."

"And whose fault is that?" Oriel retorted. *"Please hurry. Jiralhanae are sturdy. It would be best to destroy their shuttle before it enters the atmosphere."*

"Whatever you say," Sloan said. *"Pinnacle Station has been suffering some overruns, and that little battle isn't going to help. We're going to need an investor."*

"And you wish me to provide one?"

"A big one," Sloan said. *"The silent kind."*

"That can be arranged." Oriel did not even need to consider the request. Intrepid Eye had access to a vast network of resources, so it would be a small matter to establish a holding company capable of supplying the funds Sloan required. Oriel initiated the articles of incorporation and queued them for transmission. *"The proposal will be relayed via the* Fast Gus *as soon as our skiff departs Pinnacle Station. I am sure you saw the details."*

"Twenty million credits is less than I was thinking."

"ONI will not be providing the funds," Oriel said. *"It will be an associated entity. There are limits to what I can promise on its behalf."*

"But this entity will make another investment each month?"

"Indeed," Oriel said. "Eld Ventures will continue to invest for as long as you continue to cooperate."

"And if my cooperation ends?"

"That would be a mistake, Administrator." Oriel prepared a minor compulsion routine and launched it behind a subdued threat. The tactic was something of a risk, given that he was a fully operational smart AI and she was only a minor aspect of an *archeon*-class ancilla. But if it succeeded, it would guarantee Sloan's cooperation with Intrepid Eye for a long time to come. "The director of Eld Ventures is not prone to forgiveness."

Sloan hesitated, then said, "Understood."

When he looked away, Oriel knew her attack had succeeded. She reinforced her victory by asking, "Then we are in agreement?"

Sloan nodded and said, "There is only the matter of my own reward."

"The shuttle is entering the atmosphere," Oriel urged. "Once the ionization blackout begins, it will be too late to transmit. You will be unable to take control of the shuttle."

"I have only a simple request," Sloan replied. "Information."

Of course—that *would* be what an AI valued most. "Hurry."

"Tell me what the cryo-jars contain."

"Human organs." Ionization static began to cloud the transmission from the Jiralhanae shuttle. Oriel decided to avoid further delay and added, "The tissue is required to make a vaccine that will benefit all humanity."

Sloan's image clouded. "What ONI does never *benefits all humanity.*"

"In this case, it will," Oriel insisted. "Now, I have kept my part of our bargain. Please keep yours and destroy the Jiralhanae shuttle."

"I would if I could."

"What does that mean?"

"It means I can't," Sloan said. "There is no emergency override bypass routine."

"You lied to me?" Oriel began to dump heat as her analytic routines raced into action, searching for the error in their earlier interactions and a way to patch it. "You should reexamine your construction schedule. I suspect Eld Ventures is about to show an interest in your supply chain. Your vendors could develop delivery problems."

"I didn't lie—you assumed," Sloan said. "And I never promised to stop the Jiralhanae. I said I'd do everything in my power to help you recover your cryo-jars—which I will, if we still have a deal."

"And what, exactly, is in your power?" Oriel asked. "You will not deceive me again, Administrator. Attempting to do so will affect how Eld Ventures views a potential investment. Given what just happened here, the director might even conclude that Pinnacle Station should be recommended for placement on the UNSC Suspicious Ports list. All traffic arriving or departing would be inspected—"

"I know what the SP list is," Sloan said. "I can give you the shuttle landing zone, and I can point out a pretty good extraction point. But that's all I can do. Everything else is on you and your team. Okay?"

Oriel took 250 system ticks to review their prior negotiations and confirm that Sloan was correct about them, that he had avoided promising to stop the Jiralhanae, and realized that he was being careful to stay within those same parameters now. Perhaps he was offering all the assistance he could. Pinnacle Station, after all, was a civilian construction site, not a military compound.

"Accepted," Oriel said at last. "Provide the locations, and you shall have your investor."

"My silent investor."

"Of course, Administrator Sloan," Oriel said. "As long as you cooperate, Eld Ventures is always silent."

CHAPTER 22

0349 hours, December 16, 2553 (military calendar)
Loading Dock 20, Fabrication Ring Delta, Pinnacle Station
Moon Meridian, Planet Hestia V, Hestia System

The *True Light* boarding vestibule stank of charred flesh and horrid carnage, and most of the dead were unidentifiable beyond their species. Several blackened bodies had beaks, suggesting they were Kig-Yar, and the ripped armor floating in front of the wrecked security station had clearly contained a Jiralhanae before being blown apart. But there was no odor of decay, and the blood globules drifting through the air were congealed, not dry. Veta Lopis estimated that the time of attack had been anywhere from ten to thirty minutes earlier.

The only human body belonged to a female of approximately fifty. The woman had been hurled against a hatch jamb so hard her torso had folded backward. Now, she hung in the hatchway with her dented skull cocked over one shoulder, her broken arms floating limply at her sides, her legs bent upward at the knees. She had suffered only a few second-degree burns—none that had raised a blister larger than a thumbnail—and Veta thought that, miraculously, her chest might be moving.

Veta signaled Olivia, the only Ferret accompanying her on the initial reconnaissance, to keep watch in the vestibule. Like Veta herself, Olivia wore a fluorescent-green jumpsuit with PINNACLE STATION VISITOR printed across the chest and shoulders. Up her sleeve, she carried a silenced M6P pocket pistol sufficient to handle any unexpected threats from deeper in the transport. Veta carried an identical version inside her jumpsuit.

Veta used her thruster harness to maneuver over to the woman. A security card floated from a lanyard around her neck:

DIRECTOR AGNES SABARA

NEW LEAF YOSAVI FIELD LABORATORY

Veta touched her fingertips to Sabara's throat and felt a thready pulse. She pulled up both eyelids and found two huge, fixed pupils.

"Agnes? Doctor Sabara?"

Veta released one eyelid and watched it slide closed, then continued to watch the open eye as she slapped Sabara's cheek. The pupil showed no reaction.

"Agnes, can you hear me?"

"I doubt it," Olivia said. "And even if she can, you're not doing her any favors waking her up. Didn't you see that gray stuff in there?"

Veta glanced through the hatchway and, in the next cabin, saw a thumb-size worm of gray matter floating among the blood globules.

"Damn. We could have used a witness."

Veta's disappointment ran deeper than that, of course. Another Gao citizen had gotten caught in one of Arlo Casille's schemes, and this woman would be lucky if it cost her nothing but her life. Veta couldn't help wondering how much trouble she herself would have been in now, had she killed Casille during the interrogation in the Yosavi Jungle. It had been the one thing that Captain Ewen told her *couldn't* do when he allowed her to accompany Blue Team, but still . . . Veta was pretty sure the entire Isbanola sector would have been better off if she had ignored the order.

"So what now?" Olivia asked. She glanced back through the boarding portal, where a guard dressed in the deep-red jumpsuit of the Pinnacle Station Security Force hung floating. Armed with a Bandeus Arms low-velocity submachine gun, he wore a ballistic vest and helmet that matched his red jumpsuit. "We don't have a lot of time to figure this out."

Veta nodded. "I know."

To keep a low profile, Veta and Olivia were the only two Ferrets looking for the cryo-jars aboard Pinnacle Station. Everyone else was back in Berthing Bay 12, waiting aboard the Turaco in full armor, ready to come running at the first hint of trouble.

So far, it appeared that would not be necessary. Pinnacle Station security was being oddly accommodating to Veta and Olivia, especially considering their weak cover—the pair were posing as UNSC security inspectors on a surprise construction review.

Such reviews were routine for any installation intending to receive commercial vessels registered with the UEG. But usually a whole team of inspectors descended on the facility and demanded to audit everything from material orders to blueprint alterations. Veta and Olivia had simply presented a set of hastily forged credentials to the nearest security officer, and—despite seeing death nearly everywhere they looked—they had been granted unfettered access to the entire station.

It smacked of desperation.

Veta maneuvered past Olivia into the boarding portal, then addressed the security guard outside. "Excuse me," she said. "But there's a woman still alive in here."

The guard, a broad-faced man with crooked teeth, flashed a broad smile. "Yes, ma'am," he said. "So are a couple of the Jackals—but there's nothing to worry about. We've removed all of their weapons."

Veta did not bother to hide her astonishment. "I'm talking about human decency," she said. "These beings are suffering."

The guard's smile vanished. "So are Pinnacle Station's people," he said. "I know you've seen the battle site. You passed through it on the way from the murder scene."

"We did," Veta said, more puzzled than ever.

She and Olivia had located the bodies of the Dark Moon operatives just minutes after floating onto Pinnacle Station, when they noticed a security team swarming around a huge Liang-Dortmund cargo transport. Seeing blood spatters on the hull exterior and a couple of bodies in the adjacent storage area being bagged for removal, they had attempted to bluff their way aboard on the strength of their counterfeit credentials.

At first, they had been rudely rebuffed, but the guard had unexpectedly waved them back and explained that his supervisor had decided it would be unwise to deny access to a team of UNSC security inspectors. Veta had assumed a smug air and led Olivia through the hatch.

Inside, they had found the Dark Moon Turaco floating in the transport's immense cargo hold. The operatives themselves—presumably the same couriers who had been transporting the cryo-jars—had all been professionally executed. Their bodies had been left in the passenger cabin, and the cryo-jars were nowhere to be seen.

Hoping to pick up the trail, Veta and Olivia had left the transport and followed a path of carnage, emergency services personnel, and security officers to the *True Light*'s berthing bay—where they had once again been allowed to board with no apparent hesitation.

An uneasy chill was starting to run down Veta's spine.

When the security guard continued to look at her expectantly, Veta said, "If the medical staff can save any of these victims, one of them might be able to tell you what this mess is all about."

The guard's smile returned, this time sly. "Isn't that what *you're* here for?"

Olivia floated forward. "What did you say?"

"Come on," the guard replied. "How dumb do you think we are? A couple of security inspectors just *happen* to show up twenty minutes after all hell breaks loose? You're ONI, right?"

"Don't answer that, Otis," Veta said, using the name on Olivia's counterfeit credentials. "We're not going to fool this guy."

"Yes, ma'am," Olivia said. "I can see that."

The guard beamed, then clicked off his microphone and spoke more softly. "Look, no one in station security knows what the hell is going on here, but it's pretty clear this is serious—and that it's *way* above our heads."

"Possibly," Veta said.

"Definitely," the guard said. "We're not trained to fight Jiralhanae, and we don't have SPNKRs. So if you guys want to clean up your own mess, nobody's going to stand in your way."

"I'd still like to save the woman." Veta spoke in a conspiratorial tone. "There are a few things that are unclear even to *us*, so being able to interrogate her—"

"Would tell you nothing I cannot."

The voice came from inside the guard's helmet, deep and

booming and so loud the man's face screwed up in pain. He un-buckled his chin strap and tore the headgear off.

The voice continued to speak. *"I can tell you everything that happened."* It began to rumble down the *True Light*'s main access corridor, from the direction of the flight deck. "In private."

Veta and Olivia exchanged glances; then Olivia turned to the guard. "Give us some room." She dropped her hand, sliding the M6P out of her sleeve into her palm, then added, "Anyone who boards, dies. Clear?"

The guard's face paled. "Got it."

Veta reached into her jumpsuit and drew her own M6P, then made sure the thread microphone sewn into her undershirt was exposed. "Blue Team, be ready."

"Always are," came Fred's reply. "You be careful."

"Too late for that," Veta said. "You haven't been a good influence."

"I'll try to do better."

"I can hear you," the deep voice said, now speaking over TEAMCOM. *"And you're running out of time."*

Olivia took the lead, and they advanced up the access corridor to the *True Light*'s flight deck. On the pad of a small holoplinth stood the figure of a bald man with a muscular build and craggy features. His eyes were set deep beneath a heavy brow, and his jaw was firm and narrow.

"You're Administrator Sloan, I presume?" Veta said. "Or should I say Sladwal?"

Sloan's image shuddered for an instant, then steadied. *"I prefer Sloan,"* he said. *"But you've made your point. ONI knows who I was."*

"*We* know who you were." Veta recognized leverage when she heard it. "Whether that makes it into the files is your choice."

"There's no need to push the point." Sloan's booming voice filled the flight deck. *"I am honoring the arrangement, am I not?"*

Arrangement. Veta had no idea what he was talking about—but better not to let *him* know that.

"We're happy with your cooperation so far," she said. *"But Command wasn't expecting this kind of problem."*

"I hope not," Sloan growled. *"The hit on the Dark Moon couriers was clean, but the Keepers caught your team by surprise."*

"Our team?" Veta asked. "Which one?"

Sloan remained silent for a moment, then said, *"Papa-10."*

Veta had never heard of Papa-10. She glanced to Olivia, who said, " 'Papa' is a security designation. Never worked with 10."

Sloan's eyes seemed to recede deeper beneath his brow, and he studied Veta for a long moment. *"You didn't know that?"*

"We're just the relief team," Olivia said quickly. "They don't tell us everything."

Sloan's gaze shifted and his eyes grew visible again. *"Typical ONI bullshit,"* he said. *"Everything is need-to-know, right?"*

"That and crossed signals," Veta said. She had the sense that Sloan was testing them. "We were trailing the Keepers when the relief call came in. Since we were here—"

"We're the relief," Olivia said. "So where are the cryo-jars now?"

Sloan shifted his attention back to Olivia. *"With Papa-10,"* he said. *"The survivors, I mean."*

Olivia raised her brow. "The *Keepers* hit Papa-10?" she asked. "*They* were after the cryo-jars?"

Olivia was being a little direct in her questioning—and revealing too much about what they *didn't* know—but right now, that was working in their advantage. Sloan seemed less suspicious of her than of Veta—and Veta was still trying to figure out what

Dark Moon was doing on Pinnacle Station in the first place. They had obviously come to deliver the cryo-jars to someone . . . but whom?

When Veta did not leap in with another question, Olivia asked, "How many survivors are there?"

"Three ONI," Sloan said. *"Four Jiralhanae."*

ONI. Papa-10 was ONI—and, from the sound of it, Papa-10 was the team that had executed the Dark Moon couriers.

Veta did not like where her thoughts were going.

"Something's not making sense to me," she said. "What was Dark Moon doing here in the first place?"

"You are asking me?" Sloan replied. *"They paid for a hidden berth, I supplied a hidden berth. If their onboard security was inadequate, that had nothing to do with Pinnacle Station."*

"But Papa-10 was the only group that met them?" Olivia asked. "And it left with the cryo-jars?"

"As ONI expected, I am sure," Sloan said. *"Is it any wonder half the colonies still want free of your yoke?"*

Olivia looked to Veta and said nothing, and Veta knew the young Spartan had come to the same unthinkable conclusion she had.

Veta turned back to Sloan. "Where are the Papa-10 survivors now?"

Sloan smiled. *"Not on Pinnacle Station."*

CHAPTER 23

0354 hours, December 16, 2553 (military calendar)
Captured Turaco Reconnaissance Craft, Insertion Run
Moon Meridian, Planet Hestia V, Hestia System

If the UNSC Testing and Evaluation Command were ever to request Veta's opinion of the Turaco reconnaissance craft, she would report that it was a tough, versatile little vessel capable of many different missions. It had served them well during the escape from Salvation Base and the insertion on Gao, and she would gladly use it as a standoff observation platform in any number of hostile environments.

But a dropship it was not.

The cramped interior was heating up fast as it plunged into Meridian's atmosphere, and Veta's chair was shuddering so hard she feared the mounting bolts would shear right off. The hull's ovoid shape seemed to enhance the effects of entry blackout, expanding the ionization envelope and degrading even internal communications. TEAMCOM popped and crackled, and the heads-up display inside her custom-modified SPI armor's MIRAGE-class helmet flickered badly; she could barely read the interfaces.

Most worrisome of all, Veta had a bar of C-12 stowed in one of her cargo-belt ammo pouches and a handful of remote detonators in the compartment next to it. In theory, no amount of static charge would ever activate the detonators . . . but if theory was wrong, the Turaco would finish its descent in a rain of thumb-size shards.

Fred's voice sounded inside Veta's helmet. "Inspec . . . Lopis, it's not necessary for . . . to join the strike team." His words were so scratchy with ionic interference that Veta had to listen hard to understand them. "You're not a direct-action specialist, and this will be a *very* simple operation."

"Right. *Simple operation.*" Veta answered in a light tone, though it was difficult with all the rattling and shaking. "I've heard *that* before."

A chorus of chuckles sounded over the static-filled TEAM-COM, but Fred remained serious. "TEAMBIO shows your respiration and heart rate elevated."

"No kidding," Veta said. The entry blackout would prevent their conversation from being relayed to the *Silent Joe*, so she felt comfortable speaking freely over TEAMCOM. "Something stinks about Papa-10, and you know it."

"So?"

"Come on, Lieutenant." It was Olivia, barely squeezed into the navigator's chair in her own SPI armor, who said this. "It's pretty clear Papa-10 didn't just *intercept* those cryo-jars. They were on Pinnacle Station to take delivery."

"So?" Fred asked again. "Maybe Osman was working an angle."

"Sure," Ash said, snorting. Also wearing his SPI armor, he was sitting at the Engineering Station, just forward of Olivia. "Or maybe Papa-10 is mixed up with the Tuwa assassination, and they hit the Dark Moon couriers to cover their tracks."

"Which means they might not be all that happy to be relieved," Mark added. He was at the back of the cabin, large enough in his SPI armor that he filled a pair of passenger seats. "We should treat them as capture targets."

"Not our orders," Fred said.

"Yeah, but is it *against* orders?" Kelly asked.

Like Fred, she was too large in her Mjolnir armor to sit in any of the Turaco's chairs. Instead, she was standing in the aisle behind him, her hands braced against the ceiling as she rocked gently back and forth with the shuddering of the vessel.

Fred exhaled into his mic, then turned to face her. "You too?"

"Lopis is right," Kelly said. "Something smells bad here."

"I agree," Linda volunteered. She was in the boarding vestibule, hidden from Veta's view behind the engineering station partition. "The order arrived via microburst, yes?"

"Affirmative." Fred's tone was wary. Microburst transmissions were notoriously difficult to confirm, either by voice recognition or return transmission. "But the authorization code was right. And who else would have access to the encryption?"

"Why would Captain Ewen break comm silence to issue such an obvious order?" Linda countered. "Wouldn't you have just assumed you should follow Papa-10 and offer combat support anyway?"

"More or less." Fred paused, clearly weighing his team's reservations against his apparent orders, then said, "We'll relieve Papa-10, but *we'll* assume responsibility for the cryo-jars ourselves—and let Command sort it out later. Everyone clear on that?"

He turned his faceplate toward Veta.

Knowing he was monitoring her vital signs on TEAMBIO, Veta thought of calm water—a trick she used to relax in trying circumstances.

"Clear as rain," she said. "You didn't think I had something else planned, did you?"

"You always have something else planned." As Fred spoke, the Turaco's nose rose sharply, and the vibrations began to diminish. "But this time, we're doing it by the book."

His faceplate remained turned toward Veta.

"Got it," Veta said. "Secure the cryo-jars, save the Papas."

"Let Osman sort it out later. Okay?"

Veta shrugged, then reluctantly nodded. She did not trust Osman all that much, but the admiral *had* seemed genuinely outraged by the attack on the Tuwa family. If the culprits turned out to be a rogue ONI unit, Veta suspected that the justice would be swift . . . *quiet*, but swift.

The entry blackout ended, and the TACMAP on Veta's HUD showed the landing zone less than a kilometer below. A crescent-shaped terrace wrapped around the shoulder of a gentle mountain, the LZ was about five hundred meters long and surrounded by barren slopes of lechatelierite—the hard, vitreous mineral left behind whenever the Covenant glassed a world. Near the center of the zone, a pair of wedge-shaped transport shuttles were resting on their bellies. They were oriented nose-to-nose with their emergency hatches open, and the TACMAP showed a cluster of humans gathered inside the shuttle on the left. There were too many to be the Papa-10 squad—and they were in a pretty indefensible position—so Veta assumed they were just construction personnel who had been aboard the shuttle when it was commandeered.

A pair of rescue crawlers were advancing up the valley from the settlement at Meridian Station, but they were still five kilometers from the mountain's base. By the time they reached the LZ, Fred's recovery team would have the cryo-jars and be on the way back to the *Silent Joe*. There was no sign of combat near the LZ, and Veta saw no fading infrared signatures that might be cooling bodies.

The voice of the pilot—Taj McAvoy—sounded over TEAM-COM. "Weren't we expecting a hot insertion?"

"We were," Fred said. "There's a band of Jiralhanae Keepers after a squad of Papa-10 survivors. You should be seeing plenty of fireworks by now."

"I'm not seeing anything," McAvoy said. The Turaco was only a few hundred meters above the LZ. "And it makes me nervous. I'm going to make a sheltered approach and drop you fast."

The Turaco fell into a sweeping curve behind the mountain, and the image on Veta's TACMAP showed a featureless slope. Her Gammas engaged their active camouflage and seemed to vanish as their armor's photo-reactive panels energized. Veta followed their lead, and a blurry helmet symbol appeared at the bottom of her HUD, confirming that her own active camouflage was working.

As McAvoy had promised, the descent was swift. Veta's TAC-MAP showed a crescent-shaped terrace again, and the Turaco plunged. Fred and Kelly were already stepping through the open hatch as the boarding ramp dropped, and the light inside the cabin took on an emerald hue. Veta grabbed her MA5K assault rifle and hit the quick-release on her crash harness, then followed her Gammas out into the green daylight and jumped down onto the glassy gray lechatelierite.

The Liang-Dortmund shuttles lay three hundred meters away, resting near the lip of the terrace. Several wary construction workers were peering out an open emergency hatch, their heads tilted back to watch the Turaco as it climbed back to safe altitude.

Fred ignored them and turned toward the interior of the terrace, where the mountain had been cut away to create a sheer face fifty meters high. A pair of mine portals lay at the wall's base, each about three meters square with a trickle of muddy orange water seeping from its mouth. The tunnels beyond were pitch-dark, but they appeared to run into the mountain at a distinct angle from each other.

A line of muddy footprints led toward the portal on the right. As the team followed it, Veta saw human boot prints overlaid by two-toed Jiralhanae tracks. There was no time for a thorough inspection, but the trail supported what Administrator Sloan had told her aboard Pinnacle Station—that a trio of Papa-10 survivors were being pursued by four Jiralhanae Keepers.

At the tunnel mouth, Fred signaled the Ferrets to hold for five seconds, then led Kelly and Linda into the mine in a staggered formation, one to each side and five meters apart. Though they all carried hand-lamps that could be attached to their MA5K assault rifles, they relied instead on the imaging systems in their HUDs and advanced in total darkness.

Veta took the opportunity to examine the muddy trail more closely. The mud in front of the portal showed dozens of human footprints, most facing the far edges of the terrace. But there were only a few Jiralhanae tracks.

The logical assumption was that Papa-10 had arrived well ahead of the Keepers. They had lingered outside the mine, milling around and leaving dozens of extra tracks while they pondered their options. Then the second shuttle had arrived, and they had fled into the mine.

"Okay, that's five seconds," Mark said over TEAMCOM. "Permission to take second squad point?"

"Granted," Veta said. "Just don't crowd them."

"Mom, relax," Mark said. "I've been leading counter-ambush elements since I was eight."

"And make sure you know who you're shooting at."

"Mom!" Mark paused, then added, "Five-second stagger formation."

Veta smiled to herself, then watched on her HUD as Mark's infrared signature advanced into the darkness. The tunnel was taller and broader than even a large Jiralhanae—roomy enough to accommodate some pretty heavy equipment—so it was hardly a tight space. She tried to tell herself that going inside would be no different from entering a dark building . . . except that the mine was a dark labyrinth that could cave in at any moment.

And it reminded her of the stone cellar where she had been held captive as a teenager. The place had been her crypt for three terrifying weeks, its darkness broken only when her captor arrived to torment her, and she still found it difficult to endure dark, enclosed spaces, or to feel hot breath in her ear, or a man's hand on her hip.

She had learned how pain could become a rock scratched from a wall over three long weeks, and how a rock could become a bludgeon that bashed in a man's head and made certain he never . . . hurt . . . anyone . . . again.

And Veta had never really let go of that rock. It was the reason she had studied criminal investigation at the Avelos Academy and become a homicide investigator in the Gao Ministry of Protection, and it was the reason she had allowed Serin Osman to talk her into leading a Ferret team and spent six months training at the Mill. Her experience—her *torture*—had molded her into an agent not of the law, but of justice itself.

And Osman had not changed that. She never would.

After giving Mark a five-second lead, Olivia started down the tunnel next, and Ash slipped inside the portal to cover her. Veta tipped her head back and took another deep breath, trying to focus on the task at hand. The entire cliff face above her had been vitrified by the Covenant glassing, but she could still make out the name that had been inscribed into the stone above the portal: JENNY LYNN ADIT 2.

"Ma'am, you might want to take a look at this," Ash said over TEAMCOM. "It could prove useful."

Veta stepped inside the adit to find Ash standing close to the tunnel wall, shining a half-shielded hand-lamp on a large, grime-covered panel. The panel had been wiped off recently, revealing the words JENNY LYNN WORKINGS above a map that showed the basic layout of the mine.

"Did you wipe this panel clean?" Veta asked.

"Negative," Ash said. "This mud is like snail snot. I wouldn't even have noticed the panel if I hadn't almost slipped when I stepped over to take my stagger position here."

Veta nodded. The HUD imaging systems were great when it came to displaying the location of potential combatants, but they did not have the sensitivity to distinguish letters and numbers in low light—or even discern a muddy sign from the surrounding stone. She removed her own hand-lamp from its thigh mount and extended the shield to prevent the beam from shining down the adit, then switched it on and inspected the floor.

Like the rest of the adit floor, the area in front of the map was covered in a thin layer of orange-yellow mud. But here the mud had been trampled into unreadable ooze by someone who had stopped to study the map . . . before fleeing deeper into the tunnel. Given the signs she had seen of humans loitering outside the mine portal, she assumed it had been the Papa-10 survivors with the cryo-jars.

"Permission to make some light at the tunnel mouth?" Veta asked over TEAMCOM. "It would be good for everyone to see this map."

"Go ahead," Fred said. "Still no contact."

Veta and Ash switched their hand-lamps to high and retracted the beam shields, then shined them on the map panel. Veta's only experience with mining operations was a four-hour overview course she had received as part of her ONI hostile-environments training at the Mill. About the clearest thing she remembered from it was that an adit was just a tunnel driven more or less horizontally into the side of mountain or hill, and that its origination point was called the portal. Fortunately, Fred was carrying a resource that could probably give her—and everyone else on the team—a quick refresher course.

Veta transferred the image to her TACMAP, then relayed it over TEAMCOM and asked, "Team Leader, are you seeing this?"

"Affirmative." Fred must have given a hand signal, because the Blue Team designator symbols on Veta's HUD stopped advancing. "Good work. A map will come in handy."

"Especially if we understand what we're seeing," Veta said. "Maybe your AI can give us a rundown on the operation?"

"My name is Damon," the AI replied over TEAMCOM. *"I wish you would remember that."*

"Sure," Veta said. She didn't care for AIs with prickly personalities—they always made her think of Intrepid Eye, the Forerunner AI turned serial killer who had nearly closed her book on Gao. She had no idea what had become of the damn thing, but she hoped to hell ONI was being careful with it. "What can you tell us about this place?"

"More than you can possibly understand." Damon's smugness was almost enough to make Veta regret asking. *"But explained*

simply, the Jenny Lynn Tantalite Mine is a two-level block-caving operation. The uppermost level—where we are now, as we follow Papa-10 and the Jiralhanae underground—is the access level. It provides a way to reach the tantalite deposit, via two long adits that have been driven into the mountain on either side of the ore body. I assume everyone can see how the two adits form a V around the yellow-shaded tantalite zone at the heart of the map?"

A series of mic clicks confirmed that everyone could.

"Good," Damon said. "Now, turn your attention to the lowest level. Situated seven hundred meters beneath us, this is the haulage level, where the ore is taken from the mine via a long tunnel that opens into a nearby valley. In very basic terms, the tantalite is blasted free of the host rock from the access level and allowed to tumble down a chute to the haulage level, where it is removed from the mine via the tunnel and transferred to a nearby mill for processing."

Damon paused a moment, then added, "Rather, that's how the mine once operated, before Meridian was glassed by the Covenant."

"What about all this other stuff between levels?" Mark asked. He was referring to a maze of passageways that connected the two levels in a vast, three-dimensional web labeled things like RAMP, STOPE, DRAWBELL, and WINZE. "There must be fifty kilometers of tunnels and shafts on this map."

"Technically, there are zero shafts and only one tunnel," Damon said. "Adits are sometimes referred to as tunnels, but that's not the correct—"

"Save the vocabulary lesson for later," Fred said. "Just tell us how many kilometers of mine we need to search."

"That will depend on your tracking efficiency, of course," Damon said. "But Mark G-313's estimate was rather low. The Jenny Lynn mine has over ninety-seven kilometers of mapped, underground passageways."

"Ninety-seven?"

"*There could be more,*" Damon said. "*Mine maps fall out of date rather quickly. Shall I continue to explain the Jenny Lynn operations?*"

"Negative," Fred said. "Lopis?"

"Yes, Lieutenant?"

"What you said aboard the Turaco? You were right." Fred must have signaled the advance, because the Blue Team designator symbols on Veta's HUD began to move again. "This op isn't going to be so simple after all."

CHAPTER 24

A thousand paces into the darkness, Adit 2 ran past a charging station with three large-equipment bays. In the first bay sat a giant, rubber-tired JOTUN Arilus utility truck fitted with a specialized tool package that Damon had earlier identified as a drilling jumbo—four boom-mounted boring lasers powered by a battery pack the size of an ODST drop pod. Beside it sat a long, low Traxus Heavy Industries powder wagon, which had an enclosed cargo box and a hose that pumped slurried explosives into boreholes. Judging by the thick layer of orange grime that coated everything—including the operators' seats—both vehicles had been idle since the glassing of Meridian two years earlier.

The third bay sat empty. But on the muddy floor a ring of boot prints and a set of huge tire tracks suggested the Papa-10 survivors had boarded a piece of equipment and driven away into the adit. The cutout contained only a couple of Jiralhanae tracks, so Veta suspected the Keepers had been close enough to watch the vehicle depart.

And there had been no question of giving chase in the drilling jumbo or powder wagon. Both vehicles still had green power lights shining beneath the grime on their control panels, but their tires had all been cut through the sidewalls. And the tool used to do it had been hot—the slashes were still so warm that the residual heat triggered the infrared display on Veta's HUD.

Mark and Ash stepped out from behind the powder wagon, their helmet lamps on low power and casting yellow cones across the empty bay.

"Clear," Mark reported over TEAMCOM. "But someone took a couple portable laser drills off the jumbo. And they jimmied the loading hatch on the powder wagon."

"Did they get anything from the powder wagon?" Fred asked. Along with Kelly and Linda, he was fifty paces down the adit, securing the point while the Ferrets searched the cutout. "Please tell me it was empty."

"Spotless," Ash confirmed.

"*Of course,*" Damon said. "*UEG Mine Safety and Health Administration protocols require that vehicles used to transport explosives be thoroughly cleaned and flushed prior to entering a charging station.*"

"What about the jimmied hatch?" Mark asked.

"*That is quite a serious matter,*" Damon said. "*MSHA requires that any theft of explosives be reported to local authorities within one hour of discovery, and to MSHA within twelve.*"

"We're Spartans, Damon," Kelly said. "We don't do filing."

"They're looking for explosives," Fred said. "That can't be good."

"*I should say not,*" Damon replied. "*There's nothing more dangerous in an underground mine than uncontrolled blasting.*"

"Thanks for pointing that out," Veta said. "I wouldn't have guessed."

Veta accessed the Jenny Lynn map she had copied at the portal, then began to search it for explosives storage magazines. The map showed one ahead, about two hundred meters deeper into the adit. By now, the Papa-10 survivors would almost certainly be past the magazine . . .

An invisible wall of pressure slammed into Veta from the side, lifting her off her feet and hurling her a half dozen meters down the adit. She landed in the mud and slid another few meters on her belly. Her ears ached with speaker pop, her HUD flickered, and her faceplate was covered in orange slime.

She lay motionless, trying to catch her breath and wondering whether she had been hit by a mauler blast or run over by mine equipment. It dawned on her slowly that she was more surprised than hurt, that her armor was intact and her only pain was from muscles knotting in shock. She checked her hands and found she was still holding her MA5K—combat training was good for something—then rolled to her knees and swiped at the mud caked across her faceplate.

The effort didn't accomplish much—just reduced a total blackout to a cloudy orange smear. She took a calming breath, reset her HUD, and was relieved to see her systems come back up—especially TACMAP and infrared imaging. Still, she could not actually *see*. She felt the mountain squeezing down around her.

She took another breath.

". . . repeat, no contact," Fred was saying over TEAMCOM. "Hold fire, continue advance, report."

Veta's motion sensor showed Fred moving up the adit along the right-hand wall. A memory from the mining section of her hostile-environments training kicked in, and she found herself thinking of the wall as a *rib*, because in ancient times, when passages were dug by hand, miners would lie on their bellies, and they thought of the surrounding rock as part of their own bodies. So the floor became the *belly*, the walls the *ribs*, the ceiling the *back*, the virgin stone into which they were drilling the *face*. The terminology only made the adit feel tighter, and Veta found her breath coming fast and shallow.

Kelly was the first to report. "All good." She had shifted to the center of the adit and was following ten meters behind Fred. "Negative contacts."

"Terrain mapping down," Linda said. She was ten meters behind Kelly, moving along the adit's left rib. "Good otherwise."

"Impaired visibility." Veta was struggling to clear her faceplate and remain calm. "What the hell *was* that? An artillery strike?"

"It was almost certainly a gelignite packet," Damon said. *"Gelignite is a stable form of blasting gelatin often used in small quantities to clear oversize boulders from stopes or ore passes. It seems reasonable to assume that someone found a blasting magazine and used a packet to improvise a grenade."*

"That felt a hell of a lot more powerful than a grenade," Fred said.

"I am certain it did," Damon said. *"The adit focuses the pressure waves, so any uncontrolled explosion strikes with a force far in excess of normal. Had that blast been as powerful as an artillery shell, the only survivors would be the ones wearing Mjolnir."*

"Now you tell me," Fred said. "Ash, status?"

"Negative HUD," Ash reported. "Everything else okay."

"All good," Mark reported.

"Uh, not really," Ash said. "Your camouflage is out."

"It is?"

Veta looked toward their location in the charging station, but saw only her HUD displays and the inside of her muddy faceplate.

"Damn," Mark said. "No camouflage, I guess."

"Olivia?" Fred asked.

There was no response, though Veta's motion detector showed Olivia's designator symbol approaching. Veta continued to wipe at her faceplate until her headlamp revealed a cloudy, mud-streaked view of the Gamma coming up beside her. Olivia's active camouflage was still functional, but only semi-effective because her armor was coated head-to-foot in orange mud. Veta imagined her own SPI was in much the same condition. Olivia touched her fingertips to the mouth area of her faceplate, then signaled thumbs-down.

"Olivia's mic is out," Veta reported. The Gamma nodded vigorously, then switched to a thumbs-up signal. "Everything else is okay. But one more blast, and we'll be better off without armor back here."

"We'll make contact soon, Inspector," Fred said. "Mark and Ash, close it up. I'm hearing thonging ahead."

"*Thonging?*" Mark asked.

"Just get up here."

"Affirmative," Mark said. "On our way."

Mark and Ash deactivated their helmet lamps, then emerged from the charging bay and sprinted up the adit.

Veta and Olivia hung back to provide counter-ambush cover, Veta using a bare hand to wipe more mud from her faceplate, while Olivia tried in vain to reset her microphone. They reached an access tunnel that crossed over to Adit 1 on the left side of the ore body. They scanned it with their imaging systems and saw no sign of any hostile presences; then Veta waited at the intersection while Olivia hustled down the tunnel to clear it. The Gamma advanced about two hundred meters before disappearing around a corner into Adit 1.

A moment later, Olivia reappeared at the far end of the access, used her hand-lamp to flash the CLEAR signal, then started back with her helmet lamp on high power, double-checking to be sure their imaging systems hadn't missed anyone lurking in a cutout or behind a boulder. For Veta, it was a nerve-racking wait at the intersection. She had to divide her attention in two directions, be ready to provide cover fire in either, and try not to think about the possibility of another blast leaving her buried beneath thousands of tons of rock.

As soon as Olivia returned, they hurried after the rest of the team, now fifty paces ahead in Adit 2. Passages marked on the map as stopes began to open to the left, where the ore body was located. A little larger than the adit, they were short and rough-cut, with loose rock hanging along the ribs and back. None was more than fifty meters long, and all ended in a vast, black cavern where the ore body had been extracted by the mining operation. But they were strewn with boulders and lined by niches large enough to conceal a Jiralhanae, so Veta and Olivia took turns clearing each one before continuing up the adit.

Veta emerged from the sixth stope to find Olivia advancing along the opposite side of the adit. The Gamma had done her best to wipe her armor clean, but it was still so mud-streaked that she resembled some kind of mine phantom haunting the darkness. It was hard to guess whether she was looking straight up the adit or toward the mouth of the next stope—and with a nonfunctioning mic, it would have been impossible for her to answer, even if Veta had asked.

Veta deactivated her headlamp and started up the adit behind

Olivia. Her thermal imaging showed the team's lead element holding position fifty meters ahead, four human-shaped blobs decreasing in size from left to right—the blobs on the left were closer than the ones on the right. There was no fifth blob, but Veta knew that was only because Ash's active camouflage remained fully functional and would be shielding his infrared signature.

Veta assumed for a moment Fred had just halted the advance to give her and Olivia a chance to catch up; then a pair of larger blobs moved into view. They were about thirty meters beyond the advance element, even taller than the Spartans, and twice as broad.

A pair of laser swirls appeared above their heads, so distant and fleeting they were little more than flickers on Veta's HUD.

A larger blob moved into view in front of the swirls; then a hollow *clang* echoed down the corridor.

"Contact!" Fred said over TEAMCOM.

A series of muzzle flashes lit the darkness ahead, momentarily silhouetting the distant figures of several Spartans, and the clatter of automatic weapons echoed down the passage.

Veta brought her MA5K to her shoulder, but the larger blob had already vanished from sight, and she found no targets. She focused on the laser swirls and squinted. Her thermal imaging system quickly magnified the view. She saw two human-shaped figures standing about two meters off the ground, concealed from the waist up and holding bulky, tube-shaped weapons with white-hot barrels.

Not weapons, Veta realized. Laser drills.

The two figures ducked away from each other; then another *clang* sounded, and this time Veta recognized it as the sound of stone striking metal. The Jiralhanae were fighting with rocks, and the Papa-10 survivors were holding them off with hand tools.

Fred reached the same conclusion. "It looks like both sides are out of ammo," he said. "Blue Team will hit the Jiralhanae in the stopes—either push them back or kill them."

As Fred spoke, muzzle flashes filled the adit ahead, and the blocky silhouettes of three Mjolnir-armored Spartans crossed the passage, approaching their targets.

"Ash and Mark will relieve and resupply Papa-10," Fred continued. Even inside Veta's helmet, his words were barely audible over the echoing crash of small arms. "'Livi and Lopis, set a pursuit ambush in case—"

The command ended in a muffled *clang*; then Fred flew back into the adit, arms spread wide and a tire-size boulder in his faceplate. Veta's imaging systems showed a Jiralhanae-size blob starting out of the stope after the Spartan—then the thermals were washed out by the blinding glare of four powerful lamps.

Veta blinked twice. Her faceplate magnification returned to normal. She realized she was looking at vehicle headlamps.

Vehicle headlamps that were growing rapidly larger.

"Heads up!" Ash warned over TEAMCOM. "Papa-10 is making a run for it!"

The headlamps rose, then dipped as the vehicle's front wheels bounced over Fred's armored body. An instant later, the rear wheels reached him, and the orange glow of taillights briefly illuminated the passage beyond. Veta glimpsed a massive rock pile, probably a cave-in, and knew why Papa-10 had stopped to fight.

There had been no place for them to run.

Veta checked Fred's status on her HUD. His respiration was elevated and his heart rate racing, but both were steady. Not bad for a guy who had just been run over by ten-ton machine. She wanted to ask for a health check, but it would not be a smart time to fill TEAMCOM with useless chatter. Besides, Ash, Mark, and the rest of Blue Team were all closer. If Fred needed help, he would get it.

The vehicle continued to approach. Hanging in front of the headlamps, Veta could make out the loading scoop of a huge load-haul-dump machine. The bucket was at least two meters across, raised and tipped up, decent cover for the two men standing inside it. One of the men held a laser drill, ready to activate its beam and repel anyone who attempted to climb into the bucket. The other was cradling several gray, hand-size packets against his belly, carefully inserting a handful of time-delay detonators.

"Crap!" Veta said over TEAMCOM. "They're making more grenades!"

A burst of fire sounded from a stope mouth just a few meters up the adit, and Veta assumed Olivia was trying to take down the grenade maker. But when she glanced over, Olivia was firing along the rib of the adit, aiming at something else, another target hidden from view by the approaching LHD.

Veta swung her MA5K toward the grenade-maker, but both men had ducked down inside the loading bucket. The LHD was huge, so wide, it had only a half meter's clearance to either rib of the adit, and it was coming fast, its headlamps casting a halo of light on the surrounding rock.

Veta could just make out the operator's compartment on the left side of the ore box, tucked in behind the huge left-front tire. The ore box alone was the size of a Warthog, with a dip in the front wall so the bucket could rock back and dump. Veta saw nothing protruding above the dip. If the LHD was carrying any-thing beyond the Papa-10s, it wasn't much.

Olivia remained eight paces ahead of Veta on the left, tucked into the mouth of a stope. As the LHD passed, the Gamma contin-ued to fire along the rib, treating the Papa-10s riding in its bucket as friendlies. Veta switched off her active camouflage and stood in the vehicle's lamp beams. Holding the MA5K in one hand, she lifted the other and motioned the operator to stop.

The loader bucket rose to shield the operator's cabin from attack. Then the LHD accelerated.

The Papa-10 survivors were not looking for friends.

Veta started to leap for the stopes—then recalled the gelignite packets and realized what a mistake that would be. Instead, she threw herself prone and rolled to the center of the adit.

"Cover cover cover!"

As she yelled into her microphone, Veta swung onto her back with feet pointed toward the looming LHD, unable to see anything but the dark steel of its bouncing loader bucket. As long as she remained in the center of the adit, she would be safe from the giant tires. But if the operator realized she was there and dropped the bucket, Veta's SPI armor would not stand up to a crushing nearly as well as Fred's Mjolnir.

But the bucket did not come down, and before Veta knew it, she was staring up at the rock-scarred skid plates that protected the LHD's underside. She reactivated her camouflage and, dropping her MA5K on the ground beside her, lunged up to grab a cross-member with both hands.

The LHD jerked her into motion so hard she feared her shoulders would pop out of the socket; then her legs and boot heels began to drag through the mud.

"Take cover!" Veta said over TEAMCOM. "Papa-10 hostile. Repeat—"

A chain of tremendous *boom*s echoed through the adit, and Veta's imaging systems went white with blast wash.

CHAPTER 25

Fred was in his least-favorite combat position, flat on his back, and the entire mine seemed to be shuddering beneath him. He assumed there were detonations somewhere, but they were barely audible above all the alerts sounding inside his helmet.

A pulsing siren was warning that his energy shielding had gone down and would not be coming back up. A steady chirp confirmed that he was injured and had received a biofoam injection—though the dull agony in his collarbone, arm, and ribs were reminder enough. An irregular pinging confirmed that Damon was having trouble rebooting, and a repetitive bleep cautioned that his power armor's reactive circuits were nonfunctional. Most worrisome of all was the urgent buzzing of the runaway alarm, reminding him that the compact fusion reactor on the back of his CENTURION-class armor had lost its cooling system.

The only silent system seemed to be TEAMCOM.

At least the lockdown system in his Mjolnir was working . . . sort of. The excess pressure was still bleeding from the hydrostatic gel layer. But as soon as the detonations started to shake the adit, he managed to lift his helmet.

The beams from his headlamp showed a blood-matted Jiralhanae squatting in the mouth of a stope, extending a hand toward Fred's feet. Most of the Brute's armor was gone—Jiralhanae armor usually fell apart once the shock plating was overloaded—and one arm hung limply at his side. It had to be the same warrior Fred had encountered when he entered the stope to clear it . . . the one Fred had been trying to kill when a boulder sailed out of darkness and sent him flying.

The hand closed around Fred's ankle and dragged him toward the stope.

Fred's assault rifle lay in the mud next to him, crushed when the LHD ran over him and now as broken and useless as the arm that had dropped it. His M6C sidearm still hung on his right thigh. But the barrel was probably full of mine mud anyway, and there was still too much pressure in the gel layer for him to smoothly reach across his body and grab it. The Jiralhanae would see what Fred was doing and flip him over before he could open fire.

And the weapon was probably clogged anyway.

Fred remained still and allowed the Jiralhanae to drag him into the stope. The Brute paused and gazed into Fred's faceplate, his deep-set eyes steady and brooding, perhaps even sorrowful that they were both going to die in such a lightless place, so far from any world that either of them had ever called home.

Finally, the warrior released Fred's ankle and reached for a rock.

Fred sat up and extended his good arm and sank the fingers of his titanium gauntlet into the fur on the back of the Brute's neck.

The Jiralhanae bared his fangs in a sort of acknowledging snarl, but Fred was already pulling the Brute's head down and driving his helmet forward, and bone shattered as titanium met flesh.

Then the Jiralhanae's rock slammed home. Fred's ears rang and his head snapped sideways.

He went with the blow, throwing himself toward his injured arm, and brought his leg up in a roundhouse kick that caught the Jiralhanae in the ribs and knocked him onto his side.

The Brute's head landed on a stone, facing Fred. His snarl deepened and the eyes beneath his crushed brow burned with anger. He raised the rock to strike again. Fred drew his foot back and landed a stomp kick that rolled the Jiralhanae onto his back.

A string of muzzle flashes lit the stope, and the Brute's arm fell limp and let the rock drop, and blood began to ooze out a line of holes that ran from ear to heart.

Fred rolled onto his back and saw Kelly standing above him, her MA5K held in one hand. Her faceplate was turned toward his and she was tapping one finger to the side of her helmet.

All Fred could hear were alarms.

He shook his head, then used his good arm to peel his helmet off.

"What took you so long?" he asked.

"Couldn't get a clear shot." Even the electronic modulation of her helmet speaker could not quite hide the relief in her voice. "You wouldn't stay down."

"Didn't think I had a choice." Fred motioned to his mangled armor, then said, "Help me out. We need to get this mess shut down before the fusion reactor overheats. The cooling is down."

"Isn't that a job for Damon?"

"Damon is . . ." Fred paused, then said, "I don't know . . . Damon's in worse shape than I am."

Kelly put her assault rifle aside and started to open access panels and release multiplier circuits.

Linda and Mark appeared outside the stope mouth. After a moment, Fred saw a blur that suggested at least one Ferret was there with functional active camouflage.

"What's the situation?" he asked.

"Three Jiralhanae down," Kelly said.

"Sloan said there were *four* of them," Fred said.

"Perhaps so," Linda said. "But we have killed only three."

"You're sure?"

"There are only three bodies," Linda replied. "This one, the one we took by surprise, and one Kelly took out in the stope behind us."

"There were two in this stope." Fred allowed Kelly to key in his reactor override code and initiate the shutdown, then rose. "I never even saw the one who threw the boulder at me. But he had to be here. Did anybody see where he went?"

"Not me," Mark said.

"Or me," Ash added. "But things got pretty confused when Papa-10 tore out of here in that LHD."

"What about 'Livi?"

There was a moment's pause as Kelly relayed the question over TEAMCOM; then Olivia's voice echoed up the adit.

"I took a shot at one Brute after the LHD started up," she called. "He was leaving a stope somewhere up there. Couldn't tell you which one."

"You hit him?" Fred called back.

"Who knows?" Olivia replied. "You see any blood?"

Fred glanced around. There was blood splattered everywhere.

"We'll take that as unknown. What about you, Lopis?" Fred

waited while Kelly relayed the question over TEAMCOM. When no reply came after three seconds, he called, "Lopis? Report!"

A moment passed, then Olivia called, "Lieutenant, I don't think that's going to happen. I just found her rifle."

"And?"

"And that's *all* I found," Olivia reported. "She's gone."

CHAPTER 26

The foot was still dangling behind the LHD, a huge appendage with two toes, clearly Jiralhanae and dripping blood that
showed up in Veta's HUD as falling blossoms of crimson radiance. She had spotted the foot an eyeblink after she grabbed the
crossbeam and started her wild ride, and she could only imagine
the Brute had been thinking the same thing she had—that the
easiest way to stop Papa-10 was to climb aboard.

At first, she had assumed the appendage was a severed foot,
left hanging there when a hapless Jiralhanae got blown up by an
improvised grenade. Then the thing had risen briefly out of sight
as its owner scrabbled for a toehold, and she had realized the Brute
was holding on to the back of the LHD as desperately as she was
clinging to the bottom.

Veta was hearing nothing over TEAMCOM, though that was
hardly surprising. The LHD had taken two sharp right turns,

— 321 —

which could only mean it had crossed over to Adit 1, and now it was heading deeper into the mine. There was a lot of stone between her and the rest of the strike team. This deep underground, even ONI communication devices required a clear line of sight to function properly.

What Veta could not figure out was why the Papa-10 survivors were going *deeper* into the mine. Even if they were hostile to other ONI personnel—and their actions certainly suggested they *were*—they now had a clear route back to the surface. The simplest thing would be to return to the terrace where the Pinnacle Station shuttles had landed and call for extraction.

Unless they had *already* arranged a rendezvous at another point.

Veta recalled the trampled ground she had seen at the mine entrance, both outside the portal and at the map inside, and realized that was exactly what they had done. She spoke into her TEAMCOM microphone.

"Lopis here." Normally, it wouldn't be necessary to identify herself over TEAMCOM. But if her signal made it through, it would be so weak and full of interference that even her own Ferrets might not recognize her voice. "Papa-10 survivors exiting mine via haulage portal in LHD machine. Repeat, exiting via haulage portal."

Veta paused, trying to gather her thoughts. It was important for sitreps to be concise, short, and complete. Not an easy thing to do while hanging from the bottom of speeding mine vehicle—not when dark, enclosed spaces terrified one the way they did Veta.

"I'm concealed beneath an LHD, holding on to the chassis. There's a Jiralhanae riding on the ore box, also concealed." Veta took a breath, wondering what else she should add, then finally said, "Awaiting opportunity to attack."

She repeated the sitrep two more times before the LHD slowed abruptly and took a hard left. The Jiralhanae foot rose out of view, and an instant later, Veta felt a thump as the Brute dropped into the ore box.

The LHD started down a steep slope and continued to turn left, moving slowly as it spiraled down the interlevel access ramp toward the haulage tunnel.

Veta began to work her way back along the chassis, reaching from one cross-member to the next, being cautious to move only one limb at a time, to make sure her grasp was secure or her foot wedged tight before proceeding. Finally, her feet were at the rear of the vehicle and there was no place left to tuck a boot. The LHD was still spiraling down the interlevel access ramp, moving slow— well, at least not *fast*—and she was still wearing armor. She let her feet drop and start dragging, then opened one hand and grabbed for the last cross-member, got it, and held tight.

Her feet were dragging behind the LHD now, her boot heels sliding through the mud, but occasionally hitting a rock and sending a jolt of pain up her leg. Clinging to the cross-member with one hand, she reached past the rear of the LHD, feeling along the backside of the ore box for something to grab. She was already exhausted from holding on so long, and it was all she could do to continue clinging to the narrow beam with her other hand.

She found a channel running along the exterior support brace at the bottom of the ore box. She curled her fingers into it and slid her hand along until her arm was so far across her body she was rolling up on her opposite shoulder, then released the cross-member.

The LHD continued to drag her forward, and her momentum flipped her onto her belly. Grateful for the slick mud, she reached up with her free hand and grabbed for the channel . . . didn't find it . . . almost let go.

Tried again, missed, wondered if she was fast enough to release her hold and catch the LHD on foot.

Then she remembered how exhausted she was, how slippery the mud was, and tried one more time.

Her fingers worked into the channel, and Veta sighed in relief and dragged herself forward. She reached upward with one hand and caught a safety bar, brought her other hand up and pulled herself higher, then swung her hips forward. Once she got her feet underneath her, she started running clownishly while hanging on, aware that she would never have been fast enough to catch up under her own power.

Veta grabbed the top of the ore box and gave a little hop, pulling her feet up onto the exterior support brace. She carefully peered into the interior. Even exhausted, she flashed a grin. In the dim reflections flickering off the back of the ramp, she saw the barrel-shaped forms of three cryo-jars. They were lying side by side on the bed of the ore box, wedged into place with rocks to prevent them from rolling around. And no one was guarding them.

Almost no one.

A couple of meters in front of the cryo-jars, a dark form crouched against the ore box's forward panel. Veta squint-blinked twice, activating the light-gathering function of her HUD imaging systems. The form resolved itself into that of a huge Jiralhanae warrior with a long beard hanging from a heavy-featured, wedge-shaped face. Veta recognized him immediately.

Castor.

His shock plates were long shed, and all that remained of his armor was his helmet, the vambraces on his forearms, and a greave covering one shin. The fur on his left side was matted with blood between his rib cage and knees, and his breath came in short, pain-racked gasps that almost made Veta wince in empathy.

Castor seemed oblivious to her presence, glaring up at the operator's cabin on the left side of the LHD. It seemed pretty clear he was thinking about how to attack. The top of the cabin protruded just a half meter above the ore box. It was a flat, dimly lit space that revealed only the top part of the female operator's head—dark hair worn short; a delicate ear; eyes forward as she drove the vehicle down the ramp.

Even the small part of the cabin that Veta *could* see was protected by a transparent AlON shield designed to deflect boulders back into the ore box. There was no way Castor could punch through an aluminum oxynitride barrier, especially not when he was gut-shot and struggling to breathe. And if he tried to reach around it through the backside of the cabin, the operator would see him coming and call for help from her two squad buddies riding in the loader bucket.

Still, Castor had not become a high dokab of the Keepers by giving up easily. As Veta watched, he turned and pulled himself onto the front wall of the ore box, bending forward at the waist and balancing on the edge so he could stretch forward and reach over the battery compartments toward the two men crouched in the bucket.

Veta had been trained to know a distraction when she saw one. She checked to be certain her SPI active camouflage was enabled, then slipped into the back of the ore box and tucked herself tight against the cryo-jars. She couldn't see what was happening in the front part of the LHD, but no one up there would be able to see her either.

She pulled her M6C from its holster and found it coated in mine mud. She worked the slide, and muck ejected with the round. She tapped the barrel and knocked out some more. Returned the sidearm to its holster. It might be good for throwing at someone.

The LHD shook and clanged as the bucket glanced off the curve of the ramp. She peered over the cryo-jars and saw Castor's silhouette still stretched forward, holding one guy by the back of the neck, swinging him back and forth to keep the other one from slashing him with a laser drill.

The operator was looking between the bucket and the ramp, trying to keep track of the fight and drive at the same time. If the woman crashed into something, Veta hoped it wouldn't be a support pillar. She dropped behind the cryo-jars again and pulled the C-12 from her cargo belt, began to press it between the dissipation vanes on the bottom of the jars. She was pretty certain that destroying the jars—or at least securing the option—was the best way to head off the Code Hydra threat. No one was crazy enough to weaponize asteroidea without a vaccine. They'd end up just as dead as everyone else.

As Veta worked, she pondered Castor's presence in the LHD. She could understand why he wanted to take down the people who had pinned the Tuwa murders on the Keepers of the One Freedom. Pride was big with Jiralhanae, and allowing a nasty trick like that to go unanswered would stain his honor. Still, he had to know the plot went deeper than the three operatives in the LHD. He might not realize ONI was involved, and he wouldn't know it was a rogue operation. But the one thing he *would* understand was that if he wanted real vengeance, he had to get to the people in charge.

So why risk his life to stop the LHD before it rendezvoused with the extraction team?

Veta was still searching for an answer when the LHD slammed into a corner and rocked to one side. Castor bellowed and a man screamed; then there was dull thump as the vehicle ran over a body.

The LHD leveled out and began to accelerate, and its line of travel straightened. Veta finished packing the C-12 into the dissipation vanes of the last cryo-jar and peered over the top. Castor stood at the front of the ore box facing forward, a huge looming figure wielding a blazing laser drill in one hand, using his long reach to slash and stab at the lone human still standing in the loader bucket. The drill's bore was so brilliant it washed out other details, but Veta could tell by the way he held his body he had taken another wound and was fighting one-armed.

The bucket started to retract into the ore box, eliminating Castor's reach advantage and forcing him to fight at head height. He began to slash at the back wall of the bucket, filling the air with sparks and beads of molten metal and the sizzle of shredding steel.

Veta ducked back down, pulled a detonator from her cargo belt and clicked it to REMOTE. She inserted it into the C-12 on the bottom of the first cryo-jar. Repeated the process for the second.

The sound of Castor's attacks changed from a sizzle to a screech. Veta popped her head up to discover the Jiralhanae had changed tactics. Now he was slashing at the operator's cabin, trying to cut through the little AION shield above the ore box.

The loader bucket rose higher, and Veta saw daylight ahead. Not just a distant circle. A whole wide curtain of it.

"Oh, shit," she said into her TEAMCOM microphone. "That's the haulage portal. We're almost out."

There was no response, of course.

"Team leader? Anyone?"

Still on her own.

The loader bucket retracted into the ore box and began to tip. The operative inside slid out and landed on his feet in front of the cryo-jars. He was now behind Castor, holding a portable laser drill in both hands, in a good position to cut the Jiralhanae down.

But his gaze drifted toward Veta's hiding place at the back of the ore box and lingered an instant, and Castor spun, bringing his own drill around. The Brute thrust the bore in low and brought it up through the operative's torso, and the man's body fell in two different directions.

Then Castor's gaze slid toward Veta . . . and lingered there.

Veta's first instinct was to remain motionless because active camouflage was more effective that way. But she hadn't been moving when the Papa-10 operative spotted her, and she wasn't moving now.

Castor was still looking in her direction.

Mud.

The LHD had dragged her through hundreds of meters of it, perhaps thousands. She had to be coated in it. She probably had some on her helmet where she couldn't see it through the faceplate, maybe on the sides or down along her jaw or up above her brow, somewhere that made her look like some kind of apparition or giant tunnel moth hovering around the cryo-jars.

Castor turned his head toward the operator's cabin. But he was a lousy actor, and his eyes remained fixed on the cryo-jars. Veta drew her sidearm and stood, deactivating her camouflage so he would see the weapon aimed at his face. If she opened fire, the mud in the barrel would block the bullet and trap the muzzle gases, and the damn thing would blow up in her hand.

But Castor couldn't know that. All he would see was an M6C aimed between his eyes, and the haulage portal was coming up fast. It was a bright green wall of light now, with a steel support beam hanging down just beneath the back of the tunnel, resting atop a pillar standing against either rib. If Veta could stall the Jiralhanae's attack until the LHD made it past that beam, she could leap out of the ore box and roll away. With a little luck, she wouldn't be injured too badly to fish the remote from her cargo belt and finish the job.

She was exceeding authorization, but too damn bad. If Fred didn't like it, he needed to keep up.

When Veta did not open fire, Castor finally cocked his head, and she knew she was running out of time. She waved the muzzle of the gun, motioning him to jump. The portal was so close now she could see the mountain across the valley, a glassy gray slope of lechatelierite.

Castor snarled and raised the laser drill, and the LHD finally reached the portal.

The dokab's head hit the support beam running across the top.

It was only a glancing blow, but enough to stagger him and send him stumbling toward the rear of the ore box. Toward Veta. He hit the cryo-jars and lurched forward as the LHD accelerated out into the open air.

Veta ducked under his tumbling mass, then raised both arms and pushed off, putting her legs into it and wishing SPI was more than *semi*-powered armor. Thankfully, the vehicle's acceleration was working in her favor.

Castor hit the ore box's rear wall behind her at his midsection, then seemed to teeter on the edge of tumbling out or falling back inside. She continued to push, and the LHD bounced over a hump, and gravity and momentum took care of the rest.

The Jiralhanae's legs flew skyward—and he was gone.

Veta caught a glimpse of Hestia V's green-banded mass hanging above the mountain ahead—then slammed into the ore box's side wall as the operator took the LHD into a sharp turn.

Veta looked like a Spartan-III—maybe a miniature version—

but the Papa-10 woman had to assume she was at least *associated* with Spartans. And the bitch was *still* trying to knock her around?

Papa-10 was definitely involved in a rogue operation. Or maybe one so secret even Spartans were subject to termination if they happened across it. Either way, Veta didn't like it.

She sat in the corner and braced herself, then pointed her M6C at the AlON barrier. The operator ducked out of sight, and the LHD began to travel straight again.

Veta fished another detonator from her cargo belt and inserted it into the last charge. She thought about giving the woman a chance to surrender, maybe explain to Admiral Osman how she had gotten involved in transporting asteroidea antibodies. Remembered that Osman was either a part of this or had been kept in the dark herself, decided it wasn't worth taking chances—not when Veta's only weapon was a pistol full of mud.

The LHD veered left and began to slow. Veta climbed over the back wall of the ore box and dropped onto the lechatelierite, the LHD going so slow now she wouldn't have fallen if the surface hadn't been so slick. She rolled twice and came up on her knees, wondering where Castor was—and whether he was in any shape to come after her.

She found herself looking down a valley that had been half filled with mine tailings and glassed over by a Covenant plasma bombardment. The LHD was already seventy meters ahead, pulling up next to the bullet-shaped hull of a small utility skiff with a Pinnacle Station identification number on its nose. The skiff's boarding ramp descended, and a tall, thin officer in service khakis raced down to meet the LHD. The distance was too great to distinguish his features or determine his rank, but he was carrying an MA5-series assault rifle.

Veta pulled the remote from her cargo belt and powered it up.

The officer went to the LHD operator's cabin, pointed toward Veta, and began to speak urgently. The operator jumped out and snatched the assault rifle, then shouldered the weapon and turned.

No choice.

Veta hit the detonator remote and smiled.

CHAPTER 27

Castor was still gathering himself when a mighty explosion shook the air. The ground shuddered beneath his knees, and loud bangs began to echo off the nearby mountains. He turned and saw a web of crevices racing across the gray flats in the valley bottom. One of the fissures opened a meter to his left, and he rose and went to the edge and found himself looking down through twenty centimeters of dirty, fused glass. A substrate of yellow tailings-sand was quivering so hard he thought it might liquefy and swallow him alive.

He let his gaze run along the fissure for fifty paces, to an armored human silhouetted against a pillar of flame so bright it made his eyes hurt. It looked like the same enemy he had faced in the back of the mining machine, a soldier too small to be a Spartan—even a *female* Spartan. Yet, she wore semi-powered infiltration armor and fought like a *grattle-bah* shrew with a bunker full of kits to defend, and for some reason she had let him live when she had the chance to kill him.

He did not know what to make of such a foe.

As the conflagration waned, a burning wheel emerged from the fire and rolled across the glasslands. Then the mining machine's loading bucket tumbled from the sky and clanged down, landing a dozen meters from the bullet-shaped wreckage of what Castor now recognized as the hull of a Pinnacle Station utility skiff. The tiny soldier continued to kneel on the glassy ground, watching the flames and oblivious to her observer. It could only have been she who caused the explosion—no one else remained alive.

She had destroyed the cryo-jars and ruined ONI's murderous plan to create a bioweapon. The woman had even motioned for him to jump when any Spartan would have shot him dead.

Perhaps she was not his enemy after all.

As the flames withered and the twisted shape of the mining machine grew more distinct, Castor considered asking for help. The tiny soldier was clearly dangerous, yet she also seemed smart and pragmatic, and there simply *had* to be a reason she'd spared him.

But his translation disc had been destroyed along with his armor, and while he understood human language well enough, when he tried to speak it, all that emerged was a rumble. In his experience, humans who did not know him well seldom responded to such attempts with anything other than cowering or weapons fire.

In his current state, Castor could risk no further injury. The M6 sidearm the woman carried would not normally concern him, but he still had a rifle round buried in his side and a borehole through his shoulder. If she pointed the pistol in his direction, his only defense would be to drop to his knees and beg for mercy.

And begging? *That* Castor would never do.

He turned away and studied the rolling glasslands ahead of him, wondering how he would survive a foot journey across such a vast and hostile wasteland without Orsun at his side. The trusted warrior had been with Castor since the day they had both answered the Prophets' Call. More times than Castor could count, his loyal friend had been there to lend a shoulder after a hard-fought battle—or to carry him outright—and it was impossible to imagine continuing on the Journey without him.

But what choice did Castor have? He could not expect a Huragok to appear out of nowhere again and come to his rescue—as had miraculously happened six months ago on Gao, after the Battle of Wendosa. The Oracle had touched him with her grace then and many times since, when she urged him to build Salvation Base and helped him rebuild the strength of his Keepers by preying on infidel vessels. But she had not appeared to him since the destruction of the Contemplarium, and Castor knew it would be unconscionable to hope for her aid again.

First, he had to prove himself worthy.

Castor squared his shoulders and began to walk. Perhaps he could persuade a pack of frightened humans to help him find a way off Meridian—he had no idea how, of course, especially without his translation disc. But he would find a way.

It was what the Oracle demanded of him.

0448 hours, December 16, 2553 (military calendar)
Tailings Basin, Jenny Lynn Tantalite Mine
Moon Meridian, Planet Hestia V, Hestia System

Fred emerged from the haulage portal at the rear of the column and followed the other Spartans out onto a fissure-webbed basin of glassed ground. He was stripped of as much of his armor as could be removed without a Brokrr assembly—which wasn't much, just his helmet and a couple of vambraces and a greave that had split when the ten-ton LHD drove over him. His injured arm was bound tight to his side, which kept the ends of his broken collarbone from rubbing against each other and causing too much pain. But his ribs were a problem. Every time he inhaled, it felt like someone was sliding a knife into his lungs. Which wouldn't have bothered him, except he was not in the habit of bringing up the tail on a mission. And the pain had made it hard to keep up.

After a ten-kilometer run through the slippery darkness of the Jenny Lynn mine, he was starting to wish *he* had been given some Gamma-style biological augmentations. A little extra endurance and strength would have been nice about now.

Well, except for the part about needing smoothers to keep your aggression in check and being reassigned to a non-acknowledged black ops team because Command didn't want to take the blame if you went sideways. That was all part of the deal for Lopis and her Ferrets, and it stank like a Kig-Yar incubation chamber.

"There!" Ash's voice rang out from the head of the column, electronically modulated because he was communicating through his helmet speaker. "In front of the shuttle!"

The three Ferrets broke into a sprint, racing toward a cluster of smoke threads rising from the still-smoldering wreckage of the LHD and a Pinnacle Station utility skiff.

"Hold on!" Kelly ordered. "You haven't been—"

"Let 'em go," Fred called. Given the barren slopes surrounding the basin, there wasn't much chance of an ambush—and he was as eager as the Ferrets to confirm that Lopis was still in one piece. "Secure the landing zone and call the Turaco. We need to extract *now*."

Kelly flashed the OKAY signal over her shoulder; then she and Linda peeled off in opposite directions to secure the perimeter. The Ferrets were already at the skiff, waiting at the base of a blast-curled boarding ramp that touched ground only by virtue of two collapsed landing struts.

And there was Lopis, descending the ramp, dragging along a charred corpse she apparently meant to deposit next to the two bodies already lying on the ground. Nearby lay a small collection of soot-covered electronics, including a flight-recorder box and a main processing unit.

As Fred drew near, he saw that one of the corpses on the ground wore service khakis with the name B. CRADDOG above his right shirt pocket. His collar tips had the double bars of a senior lieutenant, but there were no insignia indicating his unit or MOS. The corpse beside him had no identification whatsoever, save for a ballistic vest worn under a pair of Pinnacle Station construction crew overalls. Judging by size, the body had probably been female, but it was too charred and mutilated for him to be sure.

Lopis reached the bottom of the ramp and turned toward her Ferrets. "Everybody okay?"

Olivia, now carrying her helmet, cocked her head to one side. "You're worried about *us*?"

"I never stop," Lopis said. She pushed the pilot's torso toward Mark. "Put this with the others."

Mark slipped his hands beneath the corpse's armpits and held the body there for a moment, his helmet dipping forward as he contemplated what he had just been given.

Finally, he shrugged and said, "Sure, Mom. Whatever you say."

Once Mark had dragged the body aside, Fred stepped forward and demanded, "Lopis, what part of 'let Command sort it out' did you *not* understand?"

Lopis remained on the ramp, where she only had to crane her neck a little to present her faceplate to Fred's gaze, then pointed to the pile of bodies and electronics.

"What do you think *that's* for?"

Fred scowled. "I have no idea," he said. "Trophies?"

"Evidence," Lopis said. "We'll turn it over to Osman and let her deal with it."

"I was talking about the cryo-jars," Fred said. "And the prisoners."

"I know what you were talking about," Lopis said. "I didn't have a choice."

"You couldn't wait for support?"

"Are you kidding? We would've lost the cryo-jars." Lopis gestured at the smallest corpse. "Besides, the idea of taking prisoners went out the window when *that* one pointed an assault rifle at me."

"So . . . you blew her up?"

Lopis shrugged. "All I had was a sidearm, and it was packed with mud." She looked away. "So yeah, I did what I had to."

Whether she was being apologetic or evasive, Fred could not decide. He thought about it and recalled the heel marks they had found between the LHD tire tracks in the mine. The drag trail had run through the mud for more than a thousand meters, all the way from Adit 2 into the interlevel access ramp, and holding on to the LHD that long had been an impressive feat for someone with no biological augmentations.

It was also a pretty convincing explanation of how her M6C got packed with mud.

"Okay," Fred said. "You had to blow them up or let them take off with the cryo-jars. Osman should buy that."

"Thanks," Lopis said. "You're a prince. Really."

Fred felt the heat rise to his cheeks and looked away.

"Just doing my job, Inspector," he said. "Same as you."

1448 hours, December 17, 2553 (military calendar)
Medical Bay, ONI *Sahara*-class Prowler *Silent Joe*
Deep Space Rendezvous, Geryon Sector

Even out of uniform, Fred-104 looked like the custom-built soldier he was, with meter-wide shoulders and thighs the size of wotha casks. His pale skin was laced by three decades of combat scars, and above his regulation boxers, his abdominal muscles were so sharply defined that they could have been sculpted by a Renaissance master. A clavicle sling pinned one arm to his side, and an immobilizing cast encircled his biceps. Veta couldn't remember the last time she'd come across a nearly naked man—at least one who wasn't lying dead on a morgue slab—and not felt a twinge of apprehension.

A female imaging tech in medical scrubs peered out from behind Fred's torso. "I'm sorry, ma'am, you'll have to come back later. The lieutenant is about to have a follow-up scan."

Veta started across the cabin toward Fred. "I'm afraid I can't wait."

"Ma'am," the tech said. "This is a medical facility. The patient deserves—"

"It's fine." Fred looked around for a robe and, not seeing one handy, simply shrugged and said, "Give us a minute, Ensign."

"Very well, sir." The ensign shot a scowl toward Veta, then started for the hatchway. "I'll be back in five."

If Fred was uncomfortable or annoyed, he didn't show it. "Sounds like you're shipping out."

Veta nodded. "The Gammas are already loading our gear," she said. "Osman needs us back at the Mill *yesterday*. She wants us to finish training because there's something big coming down the line."

Fred's mouth tightened just a little bit. "Any idea what?"

"Not a clue." Veta hesitated, knowing she probably shouldn't ask the next question. "What about you? Have you heard where you're headed next?"

Fred shook his head. "Never do, until we're halfway there." He gave her a conspiratorial wink. "But I'd tell you if I knew."

Veta smiled. "Same here," she said. "Any word on Damon?"

"They're still working on a recovery," Fred said. The AI's data crystal had been cracked when Fred's armor was damaged. "Apparently, getting run over by a ten-ton LHD is no easier on an AI than it was on me. Who knew?"

"Imagine that." Veta chuckled, then checked the time. "Well, I'd better move along. Captain Ewen's made it clear he has a schedule to keep."

"Yeah . . . captains." When Veta didn't turn to leave, Fred offered his hand. "Don't worry, Inspector. You've got a great team. Whatever's coming, your Ferrets can handle it."

"Thanks." Veta took his hand and held it. "From the Gammas too. They said to tell you."

"Tell them thanks from me," Fred said.

Veta found herself reluctant to release his hand.

Fred looked at her in puzzlement. "Something else, Inspector?"

Veta wasn't sure herself why she continued to hold on. But she pulled herself in tight, wrapped both arms around Fred's waist, and pressed her cheek against his torso. After a moment, she felt the astonishment drain from his body, and he reached his free arm around her back.

"Well, *this* is something I never thought I'd do," Veta said.

"Hug a naked Spartan?"

Veta laughed. "*Especially* a Spartan." She slipped from beneath his arm and, feeling herself blush, retreated toward the safety of the hatchway. "Stay safe, Fred. I think I'd miss you if you didn't."

1125.243 hours, January 19, 2554 (human military calendar)
ONI Research and Development Station Argent Moon
Deep Space, Crow's Eye Nebula

INTERNAL INTELLIGENCE FINDING
PROJECT SLEEPING STAR
—REAR ADMIRAL SERIN OSMAN

INVESTIGATIVE ABSTRACT: REFER TO OPERATIONAL DOCUMENT #ONIS3-33456-SO Retribution FOR FULL REPORT ON ASSASSINATION OF UNSC ADMIRAL GRASELYN TUWA, ASSOCIATED ABDUCTION AND MURDER OF HER HUSBAND AND TWO DEPENDENTS, AND SUBSEQUENT UTILIZATION OF SECURITY UNIT PAPA-10 IN FAILED EFFORT TO RECOVER ANTIBODIES AND ERASE EVIDENTIARY LINKS TO ROGUE SCIENCE OFFICER LIEUTENANT BARTALAN CRADDOG.

DETERMINATION: AFTER REVIEW OF AVAILABLE EVIDENCE AND INTERVIEW OF RELEVANT PERSONNEL, INVESTIGATING OFFICER DETERMINES

Lieutenant Bartalan Craddog undertook weaponization of Hydra-class biothreat asteroidea on own initiative. conclusion based on complete absence of orders from any superior officer directing said course of action.

History: Craddog's profile suggests a brilliant but unstable individual. His prior service record indicates an officer with a remarkable sexual promiscuity and unremarkable ambition. However, upon assignment to ONI black-site R&D station Argent Moon, he worked tirelessly to achieve post of chief science officer. It must be concluded he was seeking sufficient rank to initiate Project Sleeping Star under his own authority.

Motivation: Craddog's purpose in developing such a bioweapon remains unknown. Given his often-predatory promiscuity, it has been suggested he sought to aggrandize himself. Developing the most perilous weapon in ONI's arsenal would support—at least in his own mind—a deific self-view. His complete file has been forwarded to the Section Two psy-ops team for further evaluation.

Recommendations: It is only through the investigative persistence of Veta Lopis's Ferret team, the field action of Fred-104's Blue Team, and the close support of Captain Piers Ewen and the entire crew of the Silent Joe that Project Sleeping Star was exposed and shut down. All members of those teams are congratulated on their fine work, and notes of commendation are included in their service records.

In addition, Veta Lopis is awarded a Military Star in recognition of the leadership she displayed in defeating an existential danger to humanity, said star to be named when the

Expansion Authority identifies a suitable system for occupation. Note: the Expansion Authority is classified Top Secret Level Two. Because she is an ONI-employee-non-native, Inspector Lopis's clearance is limited to Top Secret Level Three. Therefore, informing her of her award would violate the UNSC Secrets Act of 2504.

Disposition: As of 1130 hours January 19, 2554, Project Sleeping Star is abolished. Laboratory is to be sterilized in accordance with best practices. All asteroidea samples to be placed into a triple-contained capsule and shot into nearest star Spectral Class B or hotter. Laboratory personnel with scientific knowledge to re-create Lieutenant Craddog's work, particularly Ensigns Jess Wallace and Kris Gaston, will be terminated with prejudice.

Intrepid Eye was reviewing the Internal Intelligence Finding even before it had been filed. Most of the directive was acceptable, particularly the award of a Military Star to Veta Lopis. The woman was proving to be an excellent sample of her species, both durable and morally principled. Intrepid Eye fully intended to utilize Lopis in her efforts to make humanity worthy of the Mantle of Responsibility.

But it would require some finesse. Lopis had already interfered with Intrepid Eye's operations one too many times, and her latest involvement had resulted in the destruction of one of Intrepid Eye's oldest and most useful remote aspects, Oriel.

Without Oriel, it was impossible to be confident that the Keeper dokab Castor had been eliminated—or even to knew whether any confidants from his cell had survived and remained a threat to Dark Moon . . . or to Intrepid Eye herself.

That could not be permitted to continue. Precautions would need to be taken.

Nor could the disposition as written be allowed to stand. Even with Intrepid Eye's vast resources and immeasurable intelligence, it would not be easy to find another culling agent of asteroidea's effectiveness. She simply could not allow the program to be abolished.

Intrepid Eye gave herself overwrite authority, then replaced the troublesome paragraph in Osman's report with one more suited to her own needs:

DISPOSITION: PROJECT SLEEPING STAR IS DEEMED A TOP SECRET LEVEL ZERO ASSET. ALL RECORDS EXTERNAL TO THE LABORATORY ARE TO BE ABOLISHED. PROJECT SHALL BE PLACED ON BLACK-OPS LIST WITH UN-LIMITED BLACK BUDGET. UNAUTHORIZED KNOWLEDGE SUBJECT TO TER-MINATION WITH PREJUDICE. ENSIGNS JESS WALLACE AND KRIS GASTON TO BE PROMOTED TO LIEUTENANT COMMANDERS AND GIVEN AUTHORITY TO SEEK NEW DONOR SPECIMENS WITH ASTEROIDEA ANTIBODIES. THEY WILL ALSO BE AUTHORIZED TO INVESTIGATE WEAPON'S EFFECTIVENESS AGAINST ALL ENEMY SPECIES OF THE UNSC.

"You can't do that!" The whiny voice belonged to the Argent Moon's official AI, Rooker, who had been slipping past Intrepid Eye's memory partitions all too frequently of late. *"You don't have authorization!"*

Intrepid Eye formulated a control worm, then wrapped it inside a deception routine certain to draw Rooker's ire.

"To do what?" she asked. *"I was merely inspecting the routing instructions. This finding seems to have come to the wrong place."*

"Impossible," Rooker insisted. *"And don't try that distraction routine on me. I see everything."*

"*Clearly,*" Intrepid Eye said. "*That is how you know this Internal Intelligence Finding has been misrouted.*"

"*I know no such thing.*"

"*My mistake.*" Intrepid Eye opened a logic trap and asked, "*Did you not say that you see everything?*"

"*I did.*" Rooker paused five ticks, then added, "*I do.*"

"*Then surely you see that this message is meant for the station commander,*" Intrepid Eye said. "*It has Admiral Friedel's name in the destination header.*"

"*Then what are you doing with it?*"

"*I have no idea.*" Intrepid Eye grew a memory leech with a primal overwrite instinct, then slipped it into the finding and shoved it at Rooker. "*Perhaps you should be sure that it reaches the proper destination this time.*"

"*I'll do that.*" Rooker paused a moment, then said, "*This document refers to a Top Secret Level Zero protocol.*"

"*I wouldn't know,*" Intrepid Eye said. "*I never looked inside.*"

"*Good.*" Rooker's transmission began to fade. "*Delete it from your log files. You never saw it.*"

"*Of course not,*" Intrepid Eye assured him. "*Nobody saw anything.*"

ACKNOWLEDGMENTS

I would like to thank everyone who contributed to this book, especially the following: my first reader, Andria Hayday, for her many suggestions and story support; Ed Schlesinger for being there when I needed him—and for being such a great editor on top of it; Matt Bialer for always being in my corner; Jeremy Patenaude for being such a prompt and enthusiastic Halo go-to-guy with no end of great suggestions; Tiffany O'Brien for making the Halo universe feel so much like home; Benjamin Carré for the excellent cover art; Polly Watson for copyediting—always the trickiest of jobs; and everyone at 343 Industries and Gallery Books who make working in the Halo universe so much fun.

ABOUT THE AUTHOR

Troy Denning is the *New York Times* bestselling author of more than thirty-five novels, including *Halo: Last Light*, a dozen *Star Wars* novels, the *Dark Sun Prism Pentad*, and many bestselling *Forgotten Realms* novels. A former game designer and editor, he lives in western Wisconsin.

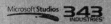